Praise for Marta Perry

"Abundant details turn this Amish romantic thriller into a work of art."

Whe[...]

"Crisp writing and dis[...]ive
Perry's latest novel. *[...]*
entertaining read."

—*RT Book Reviews*

"Perry skillfully continues her chilling, deceptively charming romantic suspense series with a dark, puzzling mystery that features a sweet romance and a nice sprinkling of Amish culture."

—*Library Journal* on *Vanish in Plain Sight*

Praise for Jill Lynn

"Lynn skillfully crafts a story that lingers within the heart while championing second chances, forgiveness, priorities, and love."

—*Hope by the Book* blog on
The Rancher's Unexpected Baby

"A fantastic author who creates a wonderfully penned novel and fills it with tender messages, [a] plot line to hook you all the way throughout, and characters that become your family.... Lynn hits another home run with this cowboy filled, inspirational third installment to the Colorado Groom series."

—*Cover to Cover Cafe* blog on
The Bull Rider's Secret

For Keeps

MARTA PERRY

Previously published as *Twice in a Lifetime*
and *Falling for Texas*

Recycling programs for this product may not exist in your area.

ISBN-13: 978-1-335-40644-6

For Keeps
First published as Twice in a Lifetime in 2009.
This edition published in 2021.
Copyright © 2009 by Martha Johnson

Falling for Texas
First published in 2015. This edition published in 2021.
Copyright © 2015 by Jill Buteyn

This edition published by arrangement with Harlequin Books S.A.

For questions and comments about the quality of this book, please contact us at CustomerService@Harlequin.com.

Harlequin Enterprises ULC
22 Adelaide St. West, 40th Floor
Toronto, Ontario M5H 4E3, Canada
www.Harlequin.com

Printed in U.S.A.

CONTENTS

A lifetime spent in rural Pennsylvania and her Pennsylvania Dutch heritage led **Marta Perry** to write about the Plain People, who add so much richness to her home state. Marta has seen over seventy of her books published, with over seven million books in print. She and her husband live in a beautiful central Pennsylvania valley noted for its farms and orchards. When she's not writing, she's reading, traveling, baking or enjoying her six beautiful grandchildren.

Books by Marta Perry

Brides of Lost Creek

Second Chance Amish Bride
The Wedding Quilt Bride
The Promised Amish Bride
The Amish Widow's Heart
A Secret Amish Crush

An Amish Family Christmas
"Heart of Christmas"
Amish Christmas Blessings
"The Midwife's Christmas Surprise"

Visit the Author Profile page at Harlequin.com for more titles.

TWICE IN A LIFETIME

Marta Perry

When I look at thy heavens,
the work of thy fingers, the moon
and the stars which thou hast established;
what is man, that thou should remember him?
Or mortal man, that thou should care for him?

—*Psalms* 8:3–4

This story is dedicated to my readers,
with the hope they will love the Bodine family.
And, as always, to Brian, with much love.

Chapter 1

Georgia Bodine pulled into the crushed-shell parking space of the aging beach house and got out, the breeze off the ocean lifting her hair and filling her with a wave of courage that was as unexpected as it was welcome. She might be a total failure at standing up for herself, but to protect her beloved grandmother, she could battle anyone.

Couldn't she?

Refusing to let even the hint of a negative thought take hold, Georgia trotted up the worn wooden stairs. The beach house, like most on the Charleston barrier islands, had an elevated first floor to protect against the storms everyone hoped would never come.

The dolphin knocker smiled its usual welcome. The corners of her lips lifted in response, and she rushed through the door, calling for her grandmother as if she were eight instead of twenty-eight.

"Miz Callie! I'm here!"

Her impetuous run took her through the hall and into the large living room that ran the depth of the house. Sunlight pouring through the windows overlooking the Atlantic made her blink.

Someone sat in the shabby old rocker that was her grandmother's favorite chair, but it wasn't Miz Callie.

The man rose, looking as startled by her bursting into the house as she felt finding him here. Aside from the stranger, the room—with its battered, eclectic collection of furniture accumulated over generations and its tall, jammed bookcases—was empty. Where was Miz Callie, and what was this stranger doing here?

The man recovered before she could ask the question. "If you're looking for Mrs. Bodine, she went upstairs to get something. I'm sure she'll be right back."

A warning tingle ran along her skin. The interloper was in his thirties, probably, dressed in a button-down shirt and slacks that were more formal than folks generally wore on Sullivan's Island. He stood as tall as the Bodine men, who tended to height, but tense, as if ready for a fight. Brown hair showed a trace of gold where the sunlight pouring through the window hit it, and his blue eyes were frosty. The few words he'd spoken had a distinctly northern tang.

This was the lawyer, then, the one causing all the trouble. The one who had Uncle Brett muttering about Yankee carpetbaggers and her daddy threatening to call everyone from Charleston's mayor to the South Carolina governor, with a few council members thrown in for good measure. This was—had to be—Matthew Harper.

He took a step toward her, holding out his hand. "I'm Matt Harper. And you are…"

"Georgia Lee Bodine." No matter how rude it was, she would not shake hands with the man. Her fists clenched. "Miz Callie's granddaughter."

Wariness registered in his eyes at the name, and he let his hand drop to his side, his mouth tightening. He knew who she was. Maybe he even knew why the family had called her home from Atlanta in such a rush.

Do something about your grandmother, Georgia Lee. You've always been close. She'll listen to you. You have to talk some sense into her before it's too late.

Who were they kidding? Nobody ever talked Miz Callie out of anything she'd set her mind on. Certainly not Georgia Lee, the least combative of the sprawling Bodine clan.

A flurry of footsteps sounded, and Miz Callie rushed into the room.

"Georgia Lee!"

Georgia barely had time to register a quick impression of her grandmother—five foot nothing, slim and wiry as a girl, white hair that stood out from her head like a halo—before she was wrapped in a warm embrace.

She hugged in return, love rushing through her like a storm tide, and had to blink back tears. Unconditional love, that was what Miz Callie had always offered the shy, uncertain child she'd been, and it was still there for the woman she'd become. Georgia had never been as aware of it as at that moment.

Help me. Her heart murmured a fervent prayer. *Help me keep her safe.*

Over her grandmother's shoulder she stared at Matthew Harper, her determination welling. She had come home because the family said Miz Callie was in trouble—that she was acting irrationally and that this man, this outsider, was trying to con her out of what was hers.

He wouldn't succeed. Not without walking over the prone body of Georgia Lee Bodine, he wouldn't.

Harper's face tightened, as if he could read her mind.

Fine. They knew where they stood, it seemed, without another word being spoken. The battle lines were drawn.

So this was the granddaughter from Atlanta. Matt couldn't help having some preconceived notions about the woman, like it or not, from what he'd seen of Miz Callie and the rest of her family.

He'd already clashed with several members of Miz Callie's large clan over what she planned to do. The two sons he'd spoken to had had the same goal, though they'd gone about it in different ways. Georgia's father, the eldest son, had been all Southern charm and hints of powerful influence, while Brett Bodine, the second of the brothers, intimidating in his Coast Guard uniform, had been blustery and outraged. He hadn't heard from the third brother yet, but no doubt he would.

They hadn't worried him, although he'd been taken aback that Miz Callie's family was so determined to keep her from doing what she wanted with what was hers. Still, he knew, just from the way Miz Callie's face softened when she spoke of Georgia, that this granddaughter had a special place in her heart.

That was undoubtedly why Georgia was here. After failing to influence or intimidate him, the family had sent for her, banking on Miz Callie's affection to sway the decisions she intended to make.

Miz Callie released her granddaughter. "Matthew, I didn't mean to ignore you like that. My manners have gone astray 'cause I'm so excited to see this long-lost granddaughter of mine."

"Miz Callie, you know I was just here at Christmas time." Georgia stood with her arm loosely around her grandmother's waist. Staking out her territory, apparently.

Christmas time? Six months ago, and Atlanta wasn't that far away. If you care so much about your grandmother, Ms. Georgia Lee, why don't you come to see her more often?

"Nice that you could come for a visit, Ms. Bodine." He smiled, sure she'd take that exactly the way he intended. "What brings you back to Charleston—business or pleasure?"

"I'm here to spend a little time with my favorite grandmother."

Miz Callie's cheeks flushed. "Your only grandmother, as you well know. Georgia, this is Matthew Harper. Matthew, my granddaughter, Georgia Bodine."

She hadn't identified him as her attorney, and he wondered if the omission was deliberate. He extended his hand again, his eyebrows lifting. Georgia wouldn't refuse it this time unless she wanted open warfare in front of her grandmother.

Georgia took his hand, holding it as gingerly as if it were a clump of washed-ashore seaweed. He closed his fingers around hers, holding on a bit longer than she'd probably want.

Small, not much taller than her tiny grandmother, Georgia was all softness—soft curves of her body, soft curls in that long, dark brown hair, a soft curve of the smooth cheeks. Until you got to her eyes, that is. A deep, deep brown, he guessed they could look like velvet, but they were hard as stone when they surveyed him.

Those eyes issued a warning, but that wouldn't deter him. Fulfilling his client's wishes was a trust to him.

And on a personal level, he had to succeed at this. He couldn't keep depending on his partner to pull him through. His daughter's face flickered in his mind. For Lindsay's sake, he had to make this work. He was all she had.

"What brought you to Charleston?" Georgia turned his own question back on him. "I can hear from your voice that you're not a native."

"Only of Boston," he said. He doubted she meant the words as a compliment. "I came south to go into partnership with my law-school roommate, Rodney Porter."

Her eyebrows lifted—she obviously recognized the name of an old Charleston family. She couldn't know that Matt was as surprised as anyone at the enduring friendship between the Boston street kid and the Charleston aristocrat, a bond that went back to their first year at Yale.

"I think Rodney was in high school with one of my brothers." Her voice was cool, but he sensed she was giving him a point for that connection.

"I'll have to ask Rod about that."

Her brothers weren't among the family members he'd met, but they were probably all cut from the same cloth—down-home Southern slow-talkers with a touch of innate courtesy, even when they were castigating him as an interfering outsider who should go back where he came from.

Georgia was different, though—moving at a quicker pace, honed to a sharper edge. Her grandmother had called her a big-city businesswoman. That should make her easier to understand than the rest of her family.

"I'm sure Rodney will remember whether it was Adam or Cole." She smiled. "We all tend to know one another around here."

And you don't belong. That was implicit in her tone, although he didn't think her grandmother caught it.

Georgia wouldn't get under his skin that easily. "You work in Atlanta, I understand. What do you do there?"

"I'm a marketing director for a software firm." Something flickered in her eyes as she said the words, so quickly that he couldn't identify it, but it roused his curiosity. Job problems, maybe?

He'd spun this conversation out as long as possible. Clearly he wouldn't make any progress on Miz Callie's problem today.

He shifted his attention to his elderly client. "Why don't we discuss our business later? After all, your granddaughter has just arrived." In the nick of time, she probably thought.

"I don't want to inconvenience you…" she began.

"I'm sure Mr. Harper will be happy to postpone your meeting," Georgia put in.

Until you've had a chance to try and dissuade your grandmother, he thought.

"That's not a problem." Better to take the initiative than have it taken from him. "I'll give you a call."

"At least take this information with you." Miz Callie picked up a folder she'd dropped on the bookcase when she'd rushed into the room. "It contains the notes I've made on what I want."

Georgia's fingers flexed as if she'd like to snatch that folder. "Maybe we could talk about this first—"

"No." Miz Callie cut her off with what was probably unaccustomed sharpness. "Here you are." She thrust it into his hands.

He took the folder, encouraged by the sign that Miz Callie was set on what she wanted. Maybe Georgia wouldn't find this so easy a task.

"Thank you. I'll go through this and give you a call, then." He turned to go.

As he did, the older woman slipped her arm around her granddaughter's waist again, a look of apology on her face.

Miz Callie knew what she wanted, all right. But if there was one person who could talk her out of it, that person was clearly Georgia Bodine.

With Harper gone, Georgia's tension level went down a few degrees. She hadn't been able to prevent him from taking away that folder, but whatever business he'd intended hadn't been accomplished yet.

She had breathing space to find out exactly what was going on with her grandmother, and how much of her family's wild talk was true.

"You must be hungry." Miz Callie spun and started for the kitchen at her usual trot. "I'll fix you a sandwich, some potato salad—"

"I don't need all that." She followed her grandmother to the kitchen, where African violets bloomed on glass shelves across the windows and a pitcher full of fragrant green basil graced the counter next to the sink.

She closed the refrigerator door her grandmother had opened. "Honestly. I stopped for lunch on the way. Maybe just something to drink. Is there any sweet tea?"

Miz Callie's smile blossomed. "It'd be a sad summer day there wasn't sweet tea in this house. You fill up the glasses with ice."

It was like old times, moving around the kitchen with her grandmother. In moments they'd assembled a tray with glasses, the pitcher of tea, a sprig of mint and a plate of Miz Callie's famous pecan tassies.

Georgia's mouth watered at the sight of the rich, sweet tarts. Her favorite. But her grandmother hadn't known she was coming, had she?

She'd ask, but Miz Callie was already heading out to the deck off the living room, picking up the battered sun hat she wore outside. Carrying the tray, Georgia followed.

She stepped through the sliding glass door and inhaled the salty scent of sea air. The breeze from the water caressed her skin as it tossed the sea oats that grew thickly on the dunes.

"I love it here." The words came without thought

as the endless expanse of sea and sky filled her with a sense of well-being.

Miz Callie gave her characteristic short nod. "Then you understand how I feel." She sat down, reaching out to take Georgia's hand and draw her to the chair next to her. "Stay here at the beach house while you're home, won't you? I'd love to have you."

She hadn't really thought about where she'd stay on this rushed visit, but she could combat whatever Matthew Harper was planning better if she were on the spot.

"I'd love to. I'm sure the folks won't mind."

That was a positive step forward. Now if she could get Miz Callie talking about what the family called her odd behavior...

"You want to tell me what happened to your engagement ring?" Her grandmother's soft voice interrupted her thoughts.

Her gaze flew from Miz Callie to her ring finger. "You noticed." Her mother hadn't, when she'd stopped briefly at the house, and that had been a relief.

"Of course I did, the minute I saw you. What happened with you and James, darlin'?"

One part of her wanted to spill the whole sorry mess into her grandmother's sympathetic ear, the way she would have poured out her problems when she was ten. But she was a grown woman now, and maybe she should act like one.

"It was nothing very dramatic." Wasn't it? A shaft of pain went through her. It hadn't been dramatic only because she lacked the courage to make a scene. "We both realized we'd made a mistake."

She could still see James's face—his amazement that she'd object to his stealing her work, jeopardizing her job and lying about it. The irrevocable differences between them had been shown up as if by lightning.

She forced his image from her mind. "Better now than later, right?"

"That's certain." Her grandmother's clear blue eyes said that she knew there was more. "Still, if you want to talk about it…"

"I know where to come." She pressed Miz Callie's hand.

"Does your mamma know?"

Georgia shook her head. "I'm not looking forward to that. The day I told her I was engaged was the first time she felt proud of me since I learned to tie my own shoes."

"Oh, sugar, that's not true." Miz Callie looked concerned. "You and your mother don't always see eye to eye about what your life should be like, but she loves you."

The point wasn't that they didn't love each other. She'd just never managed to be the daughter her mother wanted. "I know. I'll tell her."

Just not right away. It was enough that *she* knew her love life was a disaster. Somebody ought to put up poles and orange tape around her to warn others, the way the turtle ladies did around the loggerhead turtle nests on the beach.

"Enough of my sad story," she said. "Tell me what's happening with you."

Her grandmother's eyebrows lifted. "Don't you already know, Georgia Lee? Didn't the family send for you? Tell you that you had to come talk some sense into your foolish old grandmother?"

It was so near to what the family had said that for a moment she couldn't speak. She took a deep breath and sent up a wordless prayer.

"They love you. They don't understand, and they're worried."

"If they don't understand something, they should ask me instead of jumping to conclusions." Miz Callie's voice was as sharp as she'd ever heard it.

Georgia's heart sank. She was used to her father and uncles overreacting to things. But for Miz Callie to take offense—the chasm between them must be bad.

"I'm asking, Miz Callie. They're saying you're giving away things from the Charleston house. That you brought a derelict home for dinner. That you're talking about living here in the cottage year-round all by yourself. Don't you understand how that worries them? You've never done anything like that before."

"Exactly." Miz Callie leaned back, tipping her battered straw sun hat forward. "I'm seventy-five years old, Georgia Lee, and I've spent my whole life doing exactly what other people think I should. I decided it was high time I tried living the way *I* feel I should."

For a moment Georgia couldn't speak again. Miz Callie was the rock in their lives—the one unchanging point. To think that she'd been dissatisfied all that time… She couldn't get her mind around it.

"But you and Grandfather always seemed so happy together."

"Darlin', of course we were happy. I purely loved Richmond Bodine to distraction." Miz Callie's smile eased the tension that was tying Georgia in knots. "I'm not talking about him. I'm talking about society in general. You can't imagine how often I wanted to do somethin' odd, just to shake everyone up."

That feeling she did get. "I always wanted to walk into dancing class in jeans, just to see what would happen."

Laughing, her grandmother took her hand again. "So we're more alike than you thought."

"I'm honored," she said. "But, Miz Callie, bringing a homeless person back to the house—that could be dangerous."

"That poor old man." Her face crinkled in sorrow. "Georgia Lee, that man fought bravely for his country in World War II, and there he was living on the street. I declare, it made my blood boil. Yes, I brought him home, but I called Lola Wentworth—you remember Lola. Her mother, Alma Sue, was a great friend of mine—and she came over and met us. We gave that poor old soul a good meal, and then Lola was able to get him into a decent living situation."

Georgia untangled the digressions into Lola's heritage and realized that the woman must be in social work of some kind. It sounded as if Miz Callie's actions, if unusual, had at least been sensible.

"Did you tell all this to my daddy?"

"I did not." Miz Callie's lips pressed together in a firm line. "He never asked, just started lecturing me as if I were a child."

Her head began to throb. If she'd been hauled home from Atlanta just because her parents and grandmother couldn't sit down and talk things through…

It couldn't be that simple. They hadn't even touched on Miz Callie's move to the cottage, or the rumors of her plans for the property she owned on remote, un-inhabited Jones Island, just up the coast.

Or, most of all, how Matthew Harper fit into this.

Chapter 2

Before Georgia could open her mouth to get in her next question, she heard quick, light footsteps on the stairs that led up to the deck from the beach.

"Miz Callie, I found a whelk. Wait 'til you see." A young girl reached the top of the stairs, saw Georgia and stopped. Her heart-shaped face, lit with pleasure, closed down in an instant, turning into a polite, self-contained blank.

The girl reminded Georgia of herself as a child, running to Miz Callie with some treasure. But would she have shut down like that at the sight of a stranger? It was oddly disturbing.

"Lindsay, darlin', how nice. Come here and let me see." Miz Callie held out her hand to the child as she would to coax a shy kitten closer.

The little girl—seven or eight, maybe—shook her head, her blond ponytail flying, blue eyes guarded. "I'll come back later."

"No, no, I want you to meet my granddaughter, Georgia Lee. Why, when she was your age, I believe she loved the beach just as much as you do. Georgia, this is Lindsay."

"Hi, Lindsay." Some neighbor child, she supposed. "I'd love to see your shell, too."

"Come on, sugar." Miz Callie's tender words had the desired effect, and the child crossed the deck to put her treasure in Miz Callie's cupped hands. "It is a whelk. What a nice one—there's not a chip on it."

Georgia blinked, as if to clear her vision. For a moment she'd seen herself, her dark head bent close to Miz Callie's white one, both of them enraptured at what her grandmother would have called one of God's small treasures.

Only when the shell had been admired thoroughly did Miz Callie glance at Georgia again. "Georgia Lee, will you bring out a glass of lemonade for Lindsay?"

She started to rise, but the child shook her head. "No, thank you, Miz Callie. I better go."

Miz Callie's arm encircled the girl's waist. "At least you can have a pecan tassie before you go. I know they're your favorite."

So her grandmother hadn't known she was coming after all. The tassies were for Lindsay.

She smiled at the girl. "Do you live near here, Lindsay?"

Lindsay, faced with a direct question from a stranger, turned mute. Face solemn, she pointed toward the next house down the beach, separated from Miz Callie's by a stretch of sea oats and stunted palmettos.

"We've been neighbors for a couple of months now," Miz Callie said. "Didn't I say? Lindsay is Matthew Harper's daughter."

Georgia's assumptions lifted, swirled around as if in a kaleidoscope and settled in a new pattern. Matt Harper wasn't just a strange attorney picked at random from the phone directory. He was a next-door neighbor, and his daughter was welcomed as warmly as if she were a grandchild, with a plate of her favorite cookies. He was far more entrenched than anyone had seen fit to tell her.

Matt welcomed the breeze off the ocean, even when it ruffled the papers he'd been working on at the table on the deck. He leaned back, frowning.

After looking through her notes, he understood what Mrs. Bodine wanted, but it would be more complicated than she probably suspected. He'd have to deal with a tangle of county, federal and state regulations, many no doubt conflicting.

And that wasn't even counting the opposition of her family. How far were they willing to go to stop her?

He put the folder on the glass table top and weighted it down with a piece of driftwood Lindsay had brought from the beach. He'd start work on the project, and he'd fight it through for Miz Callie. But he'd like to be sure she wouldn't call it off after a talk with Georgia.

Standing, he scanned the beach for Lindsay, not seeing her. She was responsible about staying within the boundaries they'd set up together, which meant that if she wasn't on the beach, she'd gone over to the Bodine house.

He trotted down the steps. He should have mentioned to Lindsay that Mrs. Bodine had a guest. Now he'd have to go over there and retrieve her under Georgia's cool gaze.

The woman had gotten under his skin, looking at him as if he were a con man out to steal a little old lady's treasure. Couldn't the Bodine clan understand that this was all Miz Callie's idea? If he didn't do the work for her, she'd find some other attorney who would.

He couldn't afford that. He didn't intend to sponge off Rodney any longer, accepting the clients Rod managed to persuade to use his new colleague. He needed to bring in business of his own, and Miz Callie's project was the first opportunity he'd had since he and Lindsay moved here.

His steps quickened across the hard-packed sand. He'd taken the chance that this move would be good for Lindsay, a fresh start for both of them. Heaven knew they needed that.

The expression caught him off guard. Once he'd have been praying about this. Once he'd thought the faith Jennifer had introduced him to was strong. But when she died, he'd recognized it for what it was. Secondhand. Nowhere near strong enough to handle a blow like that.

He heard the voices as he reached the stairs to Miz Callie's deck. Three of them: two soft with their Southern drawl, and then his daughter's light, quick counterpoint.

She was talking. It was a sign of how desperate he

was about Lindsay's unremitting grief that he didn't care who she was talking to, as long as she talked. At first, after Jennifer's death, the two of them had gone days without saying anything, until he'd realized that he had to rouse himself from the stupor of grief and make an effort for Lindsay's sake.

He went slowly up the steps, hearing the conversation interspersed with gentle female laughter.

"So my brother and I both went under the waves after the shell he'd dropped, but I was the one who came up with it," Georgia said as he reached the top. "Not that I'm suggesting you should do that."

"No, don't, please," he said.

All three of them turned to look at him, but Miz Callie's was the only face that relaxed into a smile. "Matthew, I thought you'd be coming along about now. Come and have some sweet tea."

He shook his head, crossing the deck to them. There was an empty basket in the center of the table, with shells arrayed around it. His daughter was bent over two shells she seemed to be comparing, ignoring him.

"Lindsay and I need to start some dinner."

"At least take a minute to look at our shell collection. Georgia Lee and I were teachin' Lindsay the names of the different shells."

"Not I," Georgia protested, shoving back from the table. "I'm afraid I've forgotten most of what you taught me."

"You'll have to take a refresher course, won't you?" he said, planting his hands on the back of his daughter's chair.

"How are you at naming the shells of the Carolina

coast?" Every time Georgia looked at him, she had a challenge in her eyes.

"Worse than you," he said promptly. "You may have forgotten, but I never knew." He patted Lindsay's shoulder. "Come on, Lindsay. It's time we went home."

"Just a minute. I have to line all the shells up before I go."

He tensed, hating the habit Lindsay had developed, this need to have everything lined up just so. The child psychologist he'd consulted said to go along with it, that when Lindsay's grief didn't require her to seek control in that way, she'd lose interest. But sometimes he wanted to grab her hands and stop her.

A desperation that was too familiar went through him. He'd never known family before Jennifer. Bouncing from one foster home to another hadn't prepared him to be a good father. How could he do this without her?

"How about taking some of these pecan tassies along home for your dessert?" Miz Callie got to her feet, grasping the plate of cookies. "I'll wrap them up for you." She'd headed into the house before he could refuse.

"Don't bother arguing," Georgia said, apparently interpreting his expression. "You can never defeat my grandmother's hospitality. Bodines are noted for being stubborn."

"I've noticed." Something sparked between them on the exchange—maybe an understanding on both their parts that there was a double meaning to everything they said.

She was an interesting woman. If she weren't so

determined to believe that he was some sort of legal ogre, he might enjoy getting to know her.

He realized he was looking at her left hand, pressed against the edge of the table. The white band where a ring used to be stood out like an advertisement.

He hadn't given up wearing his wedding ring. Rodney kept pushing him to get into the dating scene, and putting the ring away was the first step. He wasn't ready to do that. What was the point? There'd never be another Jennifer. A man didn't get that lucky more than once in a lifetime.

The silence had stretched on too long, but surely it was as much Georgia's responsibility as his to break it. He tapped Lindsay's shoulder. "Come on, Lindsay. We'll order in pizza tonight, okay?"

For a moment he thought she'd ignore him, but then Miz Callie came out with the cookies.

"Here you are." She handed the paper plate to Lindsay. "You carry those home and have one for dessert after your supper, y'heah?"

Lindsay got up promptly, good manners surfacing. "I will. Thank you, Miz Callie." She glanced at Georgia, but didn't repeat her thanks. "I'll see you tomorrow."

"That'll be fine, sugar." Miz Callie touched the blond ponytail lightly.

Georgia rose. "I'll walk down with you. I need to get something from my car."

Miz Callie sent her a glance that said she didn't believe a word, but she didn't attempt to deter her. He didn't believe it, either. Georgia had something she wanted to say to him in private.

He followed her down the steps. Lindsay hurried ahead of him along the sand, her gaze fixed on a flight of pelicans overhead. He'd be amazed if those cookies reached home in one piece.

He took a few steps away from the stairs, Georgia moving next to him.

"I didn't realize you lived so close." Georgia's gaze was fixed on his rental. "The Fosters owned that house when I was little. They had five children."

"There are a few kids in the neighborhood now." He watched Lindsay stop and stare at the pelicans as they swooped close to the water. "But Lindsay isn't getting acquainted as easily as I'd hoped. Your grandmother is the only person she's really gotten to know."

"Miz Callie is worth as much as a gaggle of kids any day."

"That sounds like personal experience speaking." Maybe meeting his daughter had softened her attitude toward him.

But she looked at Lindsay, not him. "I was pretty shy as a kid. With my grandmother, there was no pressure. I could play with the other kids if I wanted to, but she never objected to my sitting in the swing with a book, or helping her make cookies in the kitchen."

"Sounds ideal." He spoke lightly, but he thought Georgia had revealed a lot about herself in those few words. Again he had a glimpse of someone he might enjoy getting to know, if not for the fact that she saw him as the enemy.

"I suppose that's how my grandmother came to hire you," Georgia said. "Getting to know you through Lindsay."

"I suppose." He kept it noncommittal. The truce was over already, it seemed.

"Havers and Martin have been the family's attorneys for a couple of generations. It seems a little odd that she came to you instead."

"Does it?" The spark of anger in her eyes amused him.

Her jaw tightened. "I don't believe I heard exactly what it is you're doing for my grandmother."

"You don't really expect me to violate my client's confidence, do you, Ms. Bodine?"

She stopped, her fists clenching, anger out in the open now. "No." She bit off the word. "I don't expect anything from you, Mr. Harper."

She spun and walked quickly back toward the beach house.

Georgia slung her suitcase on the twin bed in the little room under the eaves that had always been hers, the movement edged with the antagonism Matthew Harper had brought out—a quality she hadn't even known she possessed. She'd spent a lifetime unable to confront people, even her own mother. Especially her own mother.

She caught sight of the pale band on her finger in her peripheral vision as she put T-shirts in a drawer. She still had to break that news to Mamma.

Oddly enough, she hadn't had any trouble making her anger clear to Matthew Harper, maybe because she didn't care what he thought of her. Or maybe her love for Miz Callie overrode every other instinct.

Frowning, she shoved the drawer closed. Whatever

Matt had in mind, he wouldn't be easily deterred. She'd
seen that kind of type A personality in action before. In
a way, Matt reminded her of James, although he didn't
have her former fiancé's charm. James's smile could
make you think he cherished you above all others. The
only time it had failed to work on her was when she'd
walked out of the office, knowing things were over.

Anyway, this was about Matt, not James. The only
time she'd seen any softening in Matt was when he
looked at his daughter, and even then his gaze was
more worried than loving.

No, she wouldn't be able to dissuade him. She had
to find out what Miz Callie had him doing for her before she could learn if her family's suspicions were
on target.

She hadn't gotten anywhere with her grandmother
over chicken salad and Miz Callie's featherlight bis-
cuits. Dinner had been an elaborate game, with her
grandmother determined not to talk about her plans
and Georgia equally determined not to talk about her
breakup.

Maybe now they could relax and get things out into
the open. She took a last look around the room, windows open to the evening breeze, and then hurried
down the stairs.

Miz Callie was on the deck, a citronella candle burn-
ing next to her to ward off the bugs. She looked up with
a smile as Georgia came out.

"All done unpacking? Did you speak to your mamma
and daddy?"

She nodded, not eager to get into what her parents
had to say. They'd taken turns talking, Mamma on the

extension, so that it had been like being caught between two soloists, both vying desperately to be heard.

"They're fine," she said, knowing Miz Callie wouldn't believe that. She touched the shells on the glass table, still there from her grandmother's impromptu lesson with Lindsay. "Do you want me to put these away?"

"I want you to relax and enjoy." Miz Callie tilted her head back. "Did you ever see so many stars?"

Obediently she leaned back in the chair, staring heavenward, her mind still scrambling for the right way to bring up the things that concerned her. After a moment or two, the tension began to seep out of her. How could anyone sit here surveying the darkened sea and the starlit sky and fret? The surf murmured softly, accompanying the rustling of the palmetto fronds and the sea oats.

"I don't even notice the stars in Atlanta. Too many city lights."

Miz Callie made a small sound of contentment. "They seem to put us in our places, don't they? 'When I look at the heavens which Thou has created, the moon and the stars, which Thou hast ordained, what is man that Thou are mindful of him, or the son of man, that Thou visiteth him?'"

Her grandmother's gentle voice brought a lump to her throat. "That's always been one of your favorite psalms, hasn't it?"

Miz Callie nodded, and the silence grew comfortably between them. Finally she spoke again, eyes still on the night sky. "I am worried about that child."

The change of subject startled her. "You mean Lindsay?"

"She's so withdrawn. You must have noticed how she was when she saw I had someone here."

"She's probably just shy." She knew how that felt.

"Grief." Miz Callie moved slightly, hand reaching out to the glass of sweet tea beside her. "The child's still grieving her mother's death."

So Matt was a widower. She hadn't been sure, since he still wore a wedding ring, but it had seemed implicit in the interactions with his daughter.

"Maybe he was wrong to take her away from everything that was familiar to her, just for the sake of his career."

Miz Callie turned to look at her in the dim light. "Georgia Lee, you don't know a thing about it, so don't you go judging him."

When Miz Callie spoke in that tone, an apology was in order. "No, ma'am. I'm sorry."

Her grandmother's expression eased. "I suspect he felt it was time for a fresh start. Sometimes that happens."

"Sometimes a fresh start is forced on you." What was she going to do after this interlude? Go back to Atlanta and try to find another job?

"And sometimes you just know it's the right time."

Something in her grandmother's tone caught her attention. "Is that why you want to move to Sullivan's Island permanently? Because you want a fresh start?"

Miz Callie waved her arm. "Who wouldn't want to live here, simply, instead of being enslaved to a lot of *things?*" She said the word with emphasis.

"So that's why you've been giving stuff away at the

Charleston house." A frightening thought struck her. "Miz Callie, you're not dying, are you?"

For a moment her grandmother stared at her. Then her laugh rang out. She chuckled for several moments, shaking her head. "Oh, child, how you do think. We're all of us dying, some of us sooner than later, but no, there's nothing wrong with me."

"Then why…"

Her grandmother sighed, apparently at Georgia's persistence. "Do you remember Mary Lyn Daniels?"

Georgia's mind scrambled among her grandmother's friends and came up with an image. "Yes, I think so. She's the one you always say has been your friend since the cradle, isn't she?"

"Was," Miz Callie said. "She passed away this winter."

"I'm sorry." She clasped her grandmother's hand, aware of the fragility of fine bones covered thinly by soft skin. She should have known about that. She would have, if she'd come back more often. "Did Mary Lyn's death—is that what has you thinking of making so many changes?"

Her grandmother smiled faintly. "This isn't just about grieving my friend, darlin'. At my age, I've learned how to do that. I know I'm going to see them again."

"What then?" She leaned toward her, intent on getting answers. "There must be some reason why you feel such a need to change things."

Miz Callie stared out at the waves. "I'd go and sit with Mary Lyn, most afternoons. Seemed like all she wanted to do was talk about the old days, when we were children here on the island. Her memory of those times was clearer than what happened yesterday."

"I'm sorry you had to go through that." She choked up at the thought of Miz Callie sitting day after day with her dying friend. Small wonder if it made her reflect on her own mortality.

"It was good to sit there with her and remember those years." Miz Callie's tone was soft, far away. "But sometimes she'd start in on things she regretted. Old hurts never mended. Relationships lost." She shook her head slowly. "I don't want to be like that at the end. And I'm thinking maybe God used Mary Lyn to show me it's time to right old wrongs and make my peace with life."

"Miz Callie, I don't believe you ever did anything that needs righting." She hadn't been ready for a conversation about life and death tonight, and she was swimming out of her depth. "If that's why you want to move here to the island full-time, I can understand, but I know there's more. That doesn't explain you hiring an attorney nobody knows to handle business no one knows about."

Miz Callie sighed, suddenly looking her age and more. Then she leaned over to put her hand on Georgia's.

Georgia clung to that grip: the hand she'd always held, the one that had reassured her as a child. Now it felt cool and delicate in hers.

"All right, Georgia Lee. I know you're worrying about me. Tomorrow."

"Tomorrow what?" she asked, confused.

"Matt is comin' tomorrow to meet with me. You can sit in with us. I'll explain everything then."

"But, Miz Callie..." She didn't want to wait. And she certainly didn't want to hear about it—whatever it was—in front of Matt.

"Tomorrow." Her grandmother's voice was tired but firm. "I'm not goin' over it twice, sugar, and that's that. You'll hear all about it then."

Georgia clamped her lips shut on an argument. Tomorrow. She'd have to be content with that.

Chapter 3

Georgia sat in line for the drawbridge leading back onto Sullivan's Island, glancing at her watch as if that would help. She'd be late for the meeting with Matt if she didn't get moving, and she didn't want Miz Callie to say anything to him that she wasn't there to hear.

It was a good thing Miz Callie had reminded her to bring the cooler for the groceries. The closest supermarket was in Mount Pleasant, across the Cooper River from Charleston proper, across the Intracoastal Waterway from Sullivan's Island. Not far, but not just around the corner, either, so islanders tended to stock up when they went.

At least once she got to the house, the secrecy would be over. Miz Callie would come clean with her so that she could resolve this situation, whatever it was, and get back to her own life, whatever was left of it.

A tall sailboat moved serenely past, and the bridge lowered into place. With a sigh of relief, she rumbled across the bridge and back onto the island. Right, then left, then left again, and she pulled up to the house.

She went up the stairs slowly, laden down by the many bags of groceries she was attempting to take in one trip. She fumbled with the door, staggered in and found that Matt was already there.

He rose, coming quickly to help her with the bags, his dress shirt and dark tie reinforcing the fact that this was a business visit and not a neighborly call.

"Where do you want these?" He followed her into the kitchen.

She nodded toward the counter. "Let me put things in the refrigerator, and then I'll join you." She waited for an argument from him, but none came.

"Good. I think you should be in on this."

He sounded sincere enough. Or maybe he was just accepting what he couldn't change. She slid the milk and a bag of perishables onto the shelves and closed the fridge. Then she followed Matt into the living room.

Papers were spread across the round table where she and her girl cousins used to play with their paper dolls. She sat down in the wicker chair opposite Miz Callie.

Now that the moment had come, she wasn't at all sure she wanted to find out what this was all about. She glanced at Matt, but he wore his stolid lawyer's expression that didn't give anything away.

Miz Callie sat very straight in her rocker, hands folded in her lap. "I've made a decision about the Jones

Island property. I'm afraid it won't be popular with the family, but my mind is made up, and there's no point in arguing about it."

"I'm not going to argue, Miz Callie." The piece of property on the uninhabited small barrier island had come down to Miz Callie through her side of the family. It was hers to do what she liked with. Surely she realized nobody would contest that.

"Good." Her grandmother gave a short nod. She sounded very much in control, but Georgia could see her hands were clasped tightly to keep them from trembling. "Matthew is going to turn the Jones Island land into a nature preserve to protect it from ever being developed."

Georgia blinked. Whatever she'd expected, it hadn't been this, not after all the secrecy. "Do you mean you're turning it over to the state?"

"Nothing so simple," Matt said. "Miz Callie wants the land in a private trust, so that she controls what's done there. That makes it considerably more difficult to navigate all the various governmental regulations."

"You're doing fine." Miz Callie waved away the issue. "It'll be exactly the way I want it."

This was a tempest in a teapot, as far as she could tell. "Miz Callie, whatever has all the secrecy been about? You must know that no one in the family will object to turning the land into a nature preserve."

"Yes, child, I know that." Miz Callie's face seemed to tighten, as if the skin were drawing close against the bones. "They won't object to the preserve. They'll object to what I'm going to call it."

"Call it?" Georgia echoed. This was like swimming in a fog.

Her grandmother continued to clasp her hands tightly together. "It's to be named the Edward Austin Bodine Memorial Preserve."

For a moment the name didn't register. Then memories filtered through—of pictures quickly flipped past in the family album, of questions unanswered, of conversations broken off when a child entered the room.

"You mean Great-uncle Ned? Grandfather's older brother? The one who—" She stopped, not sure how much of what she thought she knew was true and how much was a child's imagining.

"They said he was a coward. They said he ran away rather than defend his country in the war." Her grandmother's cheeks flushed. "It wasn't true. It couldn't have been."

Georgia caught the confusion in Matt's eyes. "The Second World War, she means. Supposedly Ned Bodine disappeared instead of enlisting when he was old enough to fight." She tried to think this through, but her instinctive reaction was strong. "Miz Callie, you must know it's not only the family who will be upset about this idea. Other folks have long memories, too. Why don't you dedicate it to Grandfather?"

"To Ned." Her voice was firm. "He's been the family secret for too long."

"Will people really be upset after all this time?" Matt asked. "Would anyone even remember?"

The fact that Matt could ask the question showed how far he had to go in understanding his adopted home.

"They remember. Charleston society is like one big

family with lots of branches. Everyone knows everyone else's heritage nearly as well as they know their own." She ran her fingers through her hair, tugging a little, as if that would clear her thoughts. "And it's not just that. This is a military town, always has been. Bodines have served proudly." Her mind flickered to her brothers. "Miz Callie, please rethink this."

Her grandmother shook her head firmly. Tears shone in her eyes.

Georgia's heart clenched. Miz Callie was the rock of the family. She didn't cry. She didn't show weakness. And she certainly didn't do things that would put half the county in an uproar.

Except…now she did.

She reached across to grasp her grandmother's trembling hands. "It's going to cause a lot of hard feelings, you know."

Miz Callie clutched her hand, her gaze seeking Georgia's face. "Not if it's proved that he didn't run away."

"After all this time? Miz Callie, if people have believed that all these years, surely it must be true. I know you were fond of him, but—"

"I knew him." The words came out firmly. "He wasn't a coward, whatever people say."

"Please, think about what will happen if you do this." Her grandmother was set on a course that would hurt her immeasurably. "Even if you're right, how can you prove it after all these years?"

"Maybe I can't, not alone." Her fingers tightened on Georgia's. "I want you to help me."

"Me?" The word came out in an uncertain squeak.

"I can't die without making this right. I should have done it long ago."

The echo of something lost reverberated in her words, twisting Georgia's heart. So this was the wrong she'd talked about—the one that needed righting.

"Miz Callie, you know I'd do anything for you. But I wouldn't know where to begin."

"Matthew will help you. The two of you can do it. You have to." Her voice didn't waver, but a tear spilled down her cheek.

Georgia's throat tightened as panic swept through her. How? The one thing her grandmother asked of her, and she couldn't even think where to begin.

She turned to Matt and saw the reluctance in his eyes. He was no more eager to take this on than she was, even though he didn't understand the situation the way she did.

As for the family—her stomach clenched at the thought of explaining this to them. It made her want to scurry back to Atlanta until the storm was over.

But she couldn't, because the bottom line was, if she couldn't talk Miz Callie out of this, she also couldn't leave her to face the consequences alone.

"All right." She patted her grandmother's hand. "You win. I'll do my best."

As to whether that would be good enough—well, she seriously doubted it.

Georgia tiptoed out onto the deck when the sun was still low over the ocean, her running shoes in her hands. Miz Callie was sleeping, and she didn't want to disturb her, but an early morning run was just what she needed to clear her mind.

She tugged the laces tight. After a night of trying to think of a good way to explain the situation to her parents, she didn't have an answer. Too bad she wasn't more like her cousin Amanda, the older of Uncle Brett's and Aunt Julia's twins. Amanda never let anyone stand in her way when she was convinced she was right. Of course, that led to the kind of loud arguments that would have Georgia hiding under the bed, but at least Amanda fought for what she wanted.

Well, she wasn't like Amanda and never would be. And their grandmother wasn't turning to Amanda right now. She was turning to Georgia, and it was up to her to do the right thing for Miz Callie.

Once she knew what that was, anyway. She trotted down the stairs and stopped abruptly, halfway down. "Adam!"

Her oldest brother held out his arms when he saw her, and she catapulted into them for a hug that lifted her off her feet.

"Hey, Little Bit, how are you?"

"Don't call me that," she said automatically, though she doubted she'd ever get him to stop, since he'd been teasing her with that since their parents brought her home from the hospital.

"Pardon me, Ms. Georgia Lee." He set her down, grinning. "I just have trouble believing you're all grown up now, and engaged to boot."

She focused on his chest, clad in a Coast Guard Academy T-shirt, instead of his face. She couldn't fool Adam. "That last part's not so true anymore."

"Really?"

She nodded, miserably aware that the news could now be spread to her huge extended family in a matter of minutes. "Listen, Adam, you can't tell anybody the engagement's over. I didn't tell Mamma yet."

He whistled softly. "Okay. Nobody's hearin' it from me, cross my heart. But you probably ought to tell her soon."

"I know. But you know how she'll be, denied the prospect of a wedding. I don't suppose you'd care to get married instead." She peeped up at his face, ready for his grin.

"Not me," he said quickly. "This old boy is not putting his head into a noose, thank you very much."

She shook her head with mock sorrow. "What are you doing over here this early? On your way to or from the station?"

Adam, like his father and many other family members, had gone into the Coast Guard almost automatically. That was what Bodines did. He seemed to thrive on the life. His lean, craggy face lit up whenever anyone gave him a chance to talk about the service.

"I'm on duty in an hour, but I figured I'd catch you jogging and get in a private chat." He glanced toward the cottage. "How's Miz Callie?"

"Fine. Feisty as ever."

"You find out what's going on with her yet?"

She hesitated. The last thing Miz Callie had said to her the previous evening was a plea to keep this quiet, at least for a while, from the family. She'd tell them when she was ready. And maybe, just maybe, Georgia could get her to forget the whole naming thing before anyone exploded.

"Here's the thing." It looked as if she could practice on Adam, who was bound to be more receptive than the older generation. "We talked a little, and honestly, she seems to have logical reasons for most of the things that have the parents so upset."

"Stands to reason Daddy and Uncle Brett and Uncle Harrison would overreact. They always do egg each other on."

Like you and Cole. Their middle sibling piloted a Coast Guard jet in Florida, intercepting drug runners and potential terrorists. It was dangerous, much as Daddy played that down.

"Still." His lean face was troubled. "There's been talk about the property over on Jones Island. You probably don't know, being up to Atlanta so much, but prices on the barrier islands have skyrocketed lately. Jones Island won't be uninhabited much longer."

She shrugged, since there was nothing she could safely say on that subject. "That land does belong to Miz Callie, after all. Came down in her family, not Granddad's, not that it makes much difference."

"Well, sure, I don't care what she does with it. I just don't want to see some shady lawyer cheating her over it, if she's decided to sell."

"We don't know that he's shady." An image of Matt's face formed in her mind. Tough, workaholic, stubborn and inexorable as the tide. But shady? Even on short acquaintance, she found she doubted that.

"We don't know what she's doing." Adam sounded

frustrated. "That's what's driving everyone crazy. Haven't you found out anything yet?"

"I've barely gotten settled in," she reminded him. "And she is talking to me. If everyone would just give us a little time, I'm sure things will settle down." She hoped.

He slung his arm around her shoulders and hugged her, as if he heard the uncertainty that clung to her. "Sorry, Little Bit. I didn't mean to fuss at you. But the folks…"

"Well, since you won't get married to rescue me from their disapproval, could you at least convince them I need a little time? Get them to stop calling me for a progress report every few hours."

"Guess I can do that much for you." He planted a kiss on her cheek. "I'll try to head them off, but sooner or later—"

"I know. But Miz Callie's got her back up. I'd just as soon we not start a family fight over this."

"You've got your work cut out for you, sugar." He tugged at her ponytail. "I'd better get going. It's good to have you here, you know, instead of way up in Atlanta."

"It's good to see you." A wave of love for her big brother swept over her. She threw her arms around him in a hug, then stepped back, feeling better.

He grinned, winking at her. "Later." He went off at an easy lope.

She turned, looking out at the beach. Apparently she wasn't the only person who liked an early morning run. Matt Harper jogged slowly past the house, his gaze fixed on her as if wondering whom she'd been talking to—and why.

* * *

It was late afternoon after a frustrating workday when Matt crossed the sand to where Miz Callie sat. The tide was out, and the beach, glistening and empty, invited him. It had been a relief to change out of office clothes and step outside to this.

"Miz Callie." He nodded to his daughter, who was in the surf with Georgia. "I hope Lindsay's not being a pest."

"Not at all." She tilted the brim of her straw sun hat back to look at him. "Georgia needed someone to play with, and your housekeeper had some laundry to finish up."

"Georgia might not like hearing you refer to her as if she were about eight," he said, and Miz Callie chuckled.

Lindsay was batting a red and white-striped beach ball to Georgia. Knee-deep in the water, she looked more relaxed and open than he'd seen her in months.

"They've been having a good time." Miz Callie was watching them, too, and her face curved with a reminiscent smile. "It's like old times, having Georgia here."

"It must have been a circus when all your grandchildren were young."

"My land, yes." Her smile broadened. "What one of them didn't think of, the others did. Seems like only yesterday they were all children, romping on the beach, and now they're grown up, with lives of their own."

And too busy to spend time with their grandmother? He wondered if that were the case. If so, she probably wouldn't say. It would seem disloyal to her.

"At least you have Georgia back for a while."

Until he and Georgia figured out what to do about the memory of Ned Bodine. He'd hoped to have the chance to start a preliminary search today, but Rod had called him in to help with another client. He and Georgia really needed to sit down and talk through how they were going to approach this, little though she might want to work with him.

"Why don't you get into the game? I'm sure Lindsay would like that."

"Good idea." And maybe he could get a moment or two with Georgia to make some plans. Pulling off his T-shirt, he ran across the wet sand to the water.

Georgia threw the beach ball to Lindsay, but the breeze took it, lifting it out of her reach. He grabbed it.

Lindsay charged toward him, animated. "Me— throw it to me!"

He tossed the beach ball to her, and she threw it to Georgia. Georgia hesitated a moment, clutching the ball. Her damp hair curled around her face, and sunlight glinted off her skin.

"Maybe your dad wants to take over the game now," she suggested.

"No, no!" Lindsay jumped up and down in the water. "Don't quit now, Georgia."

"Don't quit now, Georgia," he echoed. He looked at her with a challenge in his gaze. She surely wouldn't stop playing with his child just because he was there.

"All right." Her smile lit. "We have three, so we can play Monkey in the Middle. My brothers always made me be the monkey first, because I was the smallest. So that's you, Lindsay."

"I can jump high." She bounced, facing Georgia and waving her arms.

"Here goes." Georgia didn't make it easy for Lindsay, tossing it well over her head on the first throw. But a couple of tosses later, she threw the ball a little low, and Lindsay grabbed it.

"You're the monkey," she said, giggling.

For a moment his eyes misted. How long had it been since he'd heard that giggle? How long since he and Lindsay had really played together?

They batted the ball back and forth, keeping it away from Georgia even though she lunged for it as if she were a kid again. When she almost succeeded, he made a dive and grabbed it away just as her fingers touched it.

"No fair." She splashed him. "My brothers always did that, too, because they're taller than I am."

"You're mad because Lindsay and I are so good at this game." He tossed it to his daughter, loving the sound of her laugh, wondering again why he hadn't thought of doing something as simple as this.

Jennifer had always taken the initiative with Lindsay, planning their family time with meticulous care, perhaps because it was so limited. He'd put all of his energy into his career, determined to take good care of them.

But he hadn't been able to protect Jennifer from the cancer that stole her away, and now he had to find a way of doing all the things she'd have done with Lindsay.

Maybe because he was distracted, he tossed the ball

too low, and Georgia grabbed it. She held it aloft tri-
umphantly. "Lindsay and I are going to get you now."

He moved to the middle, and she tossed the ball to
his daughter. Biding his time, he waited until Georgia got a little too confident, then leaped for the ball.

He started to pull it down when Georgia jumped,
batting at the ball. She almost got it, lost her footing
and went splashing down into the water.

He caught her arm and pulled her to her feet. She
surfaced laughing, water streaming down her face, her
head a riot of curls. He took hold of her other arm to
steady her until she got her balance.

Her gaze met his, the brown eyes just as velvety as
he'd imagined they might be. She seemed to glow with
life and vitality. Her gaze grew wider, more vulnerable, and for an instant the world compressed into the
sunlight, the sea and Georgia.

"Who was he?" The question came out before his
brain was in gear. "The man you were hugging the
other morning. Your fiancé?"

"My brother. Adam." She didn't seem to question his
right to know. "How did you know about my fiancé?"

In answer he held up her left hand, water sheeting
off it. The white line was growing fainter after several
days at the shore, but it was still visible.

"Your grandmother mentioned you were engaged
but the ring isn't there now."

She nodded. "I don't expect to be seeing him here.
Or anywhere."

Good. That was what he wanted to say. But why
should it make any difference to him who she hugged?

He fought to focus on business. "We need to get together to make some plans." He said the words quietly, glancing toward Miz Callie. "Soon."

Georgia's face tightened a little, but she nodded. "Right. I can come over this evening if you want. After Lindsay goes to bed."

He almost asked her to come to the office, but that would seem foolish when they were neighbors. He couldn't let his actions be affected by...well, by the attraction that had blindsided him, like a wave crashing into him when he wasn't looking. Attraction to Georgia was a mistake, best ignored.

"Around eight-thirty, then."

Lindsay chose that moment to hurl the ball at them with all her might, cutting off anything else he might have said.

He turned away. Georgia did, too. But he sensed that she, too, was aware that things had shifted between them in some incalculable way.

Chapter 4

Someone who hadn't grown up here might find it scary to be walking on the beach at night. Not Georgia. She used a shielded flashlight through the dunes, but when she reached the flat expanse of sand, she switched it off. The nearly full moon traced a silvery path across the waves, so distinct that when she was a child, she'd imagined that if only she were brave enough, she could walk on it all the way to the horizon and beyond.

She knew better now, but that didn't detract from the beauty. Miz Callie's favorite psalm surfaced in her mind, like a dolphin breaking through the waves.

When I look at the Heavens, which Thou hast created, the moon and the stars, which Thou hast ordained...

She tilted her head back to study the sweep of the

stars. She felt small in the face of that vastness. Insignificant. And wasn't that what the psalm went on to say?

What is man, that Thou art mindful of him, or the son of man, that Thou visiteth him? Yet Thou hast made him a little lower than the angels, and crowned him with glory and honor.

The words created a space of peace in her heart, like the walk on the beach. The distance between Miz Callie's house and Matt's place gave her time to think about what she would say to him. Unfortunately, she couldn't seem to think of much except those moments in the surf earlier.

Where had that instant wave of attraction come from? It was crazy. Neither of them wanted that. What was she supposed to do now—pretend it hadn't happened?

The night, in its stillness, didn't provide an answer, but the murmur of the surf soothed away the edge of her anxiety. She was worrying over nothing. Matt would be as eager to forget it as she was.

Crossing the dunes to Matt's deck, she slipped on the shoes she'd been carrying and walked up the steps to find him waiting for her.

"I saw you coming down the beach." He gestured to a chair, waited until she took it, and sat down next to her.

She perched on the edge of the chair, too aware of his nearness to relax.

Even in the dim light, she could see his eyebrows lift. "You look as if you're ready to take flight. Is something wrong?"

"No, not at all." If she couldn't convince herself, at least she could try convincing him. "Is Lindsay asleep?"

"She conks out pretty quickly. I guess she wears herself out running around on the beach all day."

"I remember that feeling."

He'd spend most of his evenings alone, once Lindsay went to bed. That must be lonely.

"Well, to business." He drained his iced-tea glass and set it on a wide plank of the deck. "We need a plan of action, don't you think?"

"I suppose." Tension grabbed the back of her neck. "The trouble is—well, truthfully, I don't see how this can succeed. I'm afraid Miz Callie will end up being hurt if she can't clear Ned's name. And if she goes ahead with her plans anyway…" She trailed off.

He rubbed the back of his neck, as if he felt the same stress she did. "Will there really be that much bad feeling after all this time?"

She gave him a pitying look. "You don't get it, do you? Charleston—old Charleston, anyway—is a close community for all its size. I don't suppose anyone will start a petition against her plans, although that could happen. But people she's known all her life will disapprove, even be angry about it."

"Maybe she figures that won't bother her."

"Don't kid yourself. She may say that she wants to live to please herself, but I know her. She'll be lost if people turn against her. Lost."

"You know her better than I do." He paused, his face a study in line and shadow in the dim light. "But as her attorney, I have to follow her directions."

She hadn't known him long, but she sensed instinctively that he wouldn't back away from his duty to a client. "Any ideas?"

"Miz Callie must have some reason for her belief in Edward Bodine's innocence. You're in the best position to find out what that is."

"I guess so. I tried to find out what she remembers about his leaving, but it's not much. Just finding Granddad crying because Ned had run away, leaving a note saying he wasn't coming back, but that's all she knows. Maybe it was all Granddad knew. After all, he was just a kid then, too."

"If he left a note saying he was going, there was no question of accident or foul play, apparently."

She blinked. "That hadn't even occurred to me. But no, I suppose not. I can try to get her talking more about her memories. There might be something we can follow up on."

He nodded. "Good. And there have to be records of Edward Bodine somewhere. I'll start there, see what that tells us."

"If there's something else I can do…"

"There is," he said, so promptly that it seemed he was waiting for the offer. He picked something up from the floor next to his chair, and she realized it was a long legal pad. "I just have too little information to search intelligently. That's where you come in."

She should not be annoyed that he was so quick to take charge. She shouldn't, but she was.

She shoved the feeling down. Her grandmother was important now, not her. "What do you need me to find out?"

"Vital statistics, like birth date, parents' names, addresses." He ticked something off on the pad. "And anything you can get from your grandmother about how and when he disappeared. Why did people think he ran away?" His hand tightened into a fist. "It's all just so amorphous. A story that's more than sixty years old and not a single fact to support it."

"It's about more than facts. There's family loyalty and trust involved, too."

"I can't investigate family loyalty." His voice had gone dry, his hand tight on the arm of the chair. "Just get me some facts. Surely your grandmother remembers more than she's told us so far."

Was that just a normal lawyer's reaction, his insistence on sticking to the facts? Or did she sense something deeper in his reaction to her comment about families?

"Miz Callie did say she's started remembering more about that summer. Apparently she'd been talking with a friend from those days, reminiscing."

"Who is the friend?" His question was quick, his pen poised over the legal pad. "Maybe we can interview him."

"Her. And we can't. She died." She sounded as terse as he did.

"I'm sorry. I didn't mean to upset you." He reached across the space between their chairs to touch her hand lightly.

Her skin tingled at his featherlight touch. She shoved her hair back from her face with her other hand, looking up at the stars again. They seemed very far away.

"It's all right. I'm not personally upset about her

death. I mean, I barely remember her. But her passing had a profound effect on my grandmother. That's what convinced her she has to learn the truth about Ned."

"I see." His fingers brushed hers lightly, as if in silent empathy. "One other thing—what about talking to your family about Ned?"

She winced at the thought. "Miz Callie is right to put that off as long as possible."

"I suppose they wouldn't be pleased."

"Pleased?" Her voice rose in spite of herself and she half expected him to pull his hand away, but he didn't. The warmth of his skin began to radiate through her. "You've seen how they reacted already. If they knew this… Trust me, you don't want to see the Bodines in full crisis mode."

"I think I could handle it." He said the words mildly. But then, he wasn't related to them.

"It would only make matters worse, and my dad's generation won't know any more than Miz Callie does."

"All right. If you say so." He seemed to become aware that he was still touching her hand. He grasped the legal pad instead. "We'll work it out, somehow."

"I hope so." It was odd, talking to him this way, relying on him when she barely knew him. More than odd, to feel lonely because he was no longer touching her.

He cleared his throat. "Anyway, you'll try to get a bit more information from your grandmother. Do you think there's anyone else we might talk to about that summer?"

She forced herself to concentrate. "I'll try to find out." She rose, and Matt stood with her.

"Thanks." He looked down at her, his gaze searching her face.

She sucked in a breath. "Good night, Matt." She turned quickly, before he could answer, and hurried down the stairs, her skin still tingling from his touch.

Her mind still occupied with the conversation with Matt as she came back from her run the next morning, Georgia went up the steps to the deck and met her grandmother coming out. The floppy hat, oversized floral shirt and cutoffs were Miz Callie's typical summer outfit. Her red plastic pail represented one of her most prized roles—that of an island turtle lady.

"Miz Callie, you're not going out without breakfast, are you?" She glanced through the glass door, seeing only a coffee mug on the kitchen table.

Her grandmother slid a pair of pink-rimmed sunglasses on her face. "I had coffee. That's all I need now. I'll eat something when I get back from my patrol."

"Why don't you let me fix you some scrambled eggs first?" And talk to me while you're eating. "Surely the turtles can wait that long."

"Georgia Lee, I've been taking care of myself for a good long time, and I don't intend to stop in the foreseeable future." She walked toward the stairs, the red pail swinging. "'Course, you could come along with me to look for nests."

She was just as likely, or unlikely, to get something out of her grandmother on the beach as anywhere else. She followed her toward the beach.

"It's early in the season, isn't it? Have you found any nests so far?"

"Well, it's May already." Miz Callie set off along the dunes. "We haven't found any on Sullivan's Island yet, but they've spotted quite a few over at the national seashore. And two on Isle of Palms."

There was the faintest thread of envy in her grandmother's voice. She, like the rest of the turtle ladies, wanted to be the first one to spot the marks that showed a turtle had nested in the dunes, depositing her eighty or more eggs in the sand.

"Maybe today will be your lucky day," she said. "For finding a nest, I mean."

Miz Callie smiled as her gaze scanned the dunes. "I'd purely love that, to find a turtle nest with you. It's been a long time—maybe since that summer before you went off to college."

Georgia's mind slid automatically away from the memory of that summer. *Don't think about that. Remember other times, happier times.*

She tilted her head back, loving the warmth of the sun on her face, the scent of the sea teasing her nose. "I'd forgotten how much I love this place." The note of surprise in her voice caught her off guard.

"You always did, from the time you were a little bitty child." Her grandmother slowed, as if she didn't have quite enough breath for both walking and talking. "You should come more often. Why did you stop?"

Again her mind shied away from the memory she'd never shared with her grandmother. "I got older. Life got complicated."

"It does. Believe me, I know. Are you so surprised that I want to simplify it now?"

"I guess not." Except that this quest her grandmother

had embarked on was likely to provide plenty of complications. Didn't she realize that? Maybe she did, and she just wanted the other parts of her life settled so she could save her strength for the battle over Ned's name.

Miz Callie stopped, staring at the gentle ruffle of the waves. The tide was going out, leaving long, shallow tidal pools behind—a favorite playground for children. In an hour or two, they'd start appearing on the beach, little family parties of a mother or a set of grandparents laden down with chairs, umbrellas, maybe a cooler, ready for a few hours on the beach with the kids. The air would fill with the excited voices of the young.

"We fall into the rhythm of the ocean when we're born here," Miz Callie said softly, almost as if she were talking to herself. "Maybe that's why Bodines never really thrive away from the sea."

Her grandmother had a point. Her brothers had followed the family tradition and gone into the Coast Guard. They couldn't conceive of a life that didn't involve the sea.

"We all love this place," Georgia said. "But still…"

Miz Callie stiffened. She wasn't reacting to Georgia's words. In fact, it was doubtful that she'd even heard them.

She stared, taking off her sunglasses and shielding her eyes with her hand. Georgia looked, too, scanning sand, sea oats and morning glories for the telltale signs.

"There!" Miz Callie pointed and scurried toward the spot. "It might be a nest!"

She spotted it now—the tracks in the sand leading to the dunes, as if a small tractor had gone through. Georgia hurried after her grandmother, Miz Callie's enthusiasm infectious. She was thirteen or fourteen again, running after her grandmother, sharing the thrill of being first to find a viable nest.

"She's picked a good site." Miz Callie lowered herself to her knees next to a patch of disturbed sand. "Well above the high-tide line, thank goodness."

If it hadn't been, the volunteers would have taken on the risky task of moving the nest farther back. That would be the only chance the babies had of surviving. It was all coming back to her.

Georgia knelt beside her grandmother. "Are there eggs in it?" That was the crucial question. The mother could have been frightened away before she'd finished the job.

"Only one way to find out." Miz Callie took a long, thin stick from the pail. Slowly, her face intent, she inserted it into the sand, probing delicately for the eggs.

Her grandmother's expression touched Georgia's heart. Miz Callie's love for the sea creatures native to this coast went so deep. It was an act of faith for her, a part of her reverence for all that God had created.

Georgia made herself comfortable on the dune. This could take a while, and she knew better than to offer help. Miz Callie had never let any of the grandchildren touch the precious eggs. If the grandkids were lucky, they'd be roused from sleep some night and taken out on the beach. Huddled in blankets, they'd watch the babies struggle from the sand and make their run to the ocean.

Predators waited, ready to pounce on the hatchlings. The outer world could be a cruel place. Her mind flickered to Atlanta. If she'd known about the pain that waited for her there, would she still have gone?

The baby turtles didn't have a choice. They made it to the relative safety of the ocean or they perished. She had choices. So why did she so often seem to make the wrong one?

At last Miz Callie sank down next to her, face brimming with pleasure. "A fine nest, filled with eggs. Let's rest a moment, and then we can put tape up around it to keep the curious from getting too close."

"Your first nest of the season. That's reason to celebrate."

Miz Callie adjusted the brim of her sun hat and linked her hands around her knees, smiling a little. "Reminds me of the very first time Mary Lyn and I found one. We couldn't have been more than six or seven."

This was the opening Georgia had hoped for. Now she had to figure out how to make the most of it. "Did Mary Lyn know Granddad's brother, too?"

"Land, yes, child. We all knew each other. Mary Lyn and Richmond and I were the same age, and we three did everything together." Her gaze softened, as if she looked back through time, seeing three bare-legged children running across the sand. "Ned was Richmond's big brother, you see. Such a kind boy. He always had time for us. Loved teaching us about the tides and the sea creatures, taking us shrimping with him. We purely adored him."

She patted her grandmother's hand. "I know you loved him. But that doesn't mean—"

"Sugar, I know all the arguments. I've had them in my head for months. That I saw him through a child's eyes. That I didn't know everything that happened.

That even if he didn't want to fight, that didn't make him a coward."

"That's true, isn't it?" She said the words gently.

"I can't explain it," Miz Callie said. "All I can say is the more Mary Lyn and I talked about those days, the clearer that last summer came in my mind. I knew Ned, just about as well as Richmond did. He was brave and good. He couldn't suddenly turn around and become a coward. If he'd thought he couldn't fight, he'd have found another way to serve."

"Even so..." Even if her grandmother was right, it would be impossible to prove.

Miz Callie sighed. "I can't just leave it, child. I can't be like Mary Lyn, grieving for things left undone when she was dying." Her hand turned in Georgia's, so that she gripped it tightly. "I believe God led me to those memories for a reason, and it would be wrong to ignore that. You understand, don't you?"

She nodded. She understood that Miz Callie had a fierce need to do what she felt was right. She just hoped she hadn't chosen the wrong grandchild to help her.

Georgia's stomach fluttered as she and Miz Callie approached the Sullivan's Island playground that evening, and not with excitement over the dessert that awaited at the fire company's ice cream and cake social. She'd tried to beg off, but Miz Callie had looked at her as if she were crazy.

Miz Callie didn't understand. It was highly likely that some of her other relatives would show up tonight, casually seizing the opportunity to check in. The last thing she needed was questioning from her folks about her nonexistent progress in changing her grandmother's mind.

Or, for that matter, questions from her grandmother about Georgia's nonexistent progress on her quest.

The playground was filled with people—kids swarming over the swings and the slides, teenagers gathered in groups to self-consciously ignore their elders, grown-ups visiting with neighbors as they lined up for ice cream and cake.

"We may as well get right in line for dessert," Miz Callie said, chugging through the crowd with a firm grip on Georgia's arm. "I wonder if they've cut my cake yet."

Georgia had delivered her grandmother's delectable praline applesauce cake to the waiting refrigerated truck earlier in the afternoon. "It's probably gone already. You know how people love that cake."

Miz Callie flushed at the compliment even while brushing it off with a sweep of her hand. "There'll be plenty fancier than mine, I'm sure. Land, there's Marcy Dawson and her daughter. I haven't seen them in an age."

She veered off. Georgia followed, forcibly preventing herself from rolling her eyes like a disgruntled teenager. If you went anywhere in the greater Charleston area with Miz Callie, she'd be bound to find someone she knew.

The good thing about coming home was remembering how much she loved this place. The bad thing was a tendency to revert to a younger version of herself.

Marcy Dawson proved to be not a contemporary of her grandmother's but someone more her mother's age, with windswept blond hair and perfectly tanned skin that was complemented by her white tennis shorts. Her daughter, with an apologetic smile, dashed off after an exploring toddler.

Ms. Dawson assessed Georgia with the air of someone fitting her into her proper niche. "You're Ashton and Delia's daughter, aren't you? I thought I heard you were working up in Atlanta, got yourself engaged, I believe your mother told me."

"I'm just back to visit for a bit." She slid her left hand behind her. "Helping my grandmother get settled at the cottage."

That distracted the woman, thank goodness, and she turned back to Miz Callie. "Is it true, then, that you're planning to stay on the island year-round?"

"That's right. My, word does get around. But then, you play bridge with my daughter-in-law, I believe." There was an icy edge to her grandmother's voice that Georgia didn't miss, maybe the faintest of suggestions that Georgia's mother had been talking out of turn.

"Well, I…" The woman looked around as if seeking escape. "I guess she might have mentioned something about it."

Miz Callie straightened, and Georgia caught her arm before she could say something Mamma and Daddy wouldn't appreciate.

"Miz Callie, we'd better get in line for our cake or we'll never get a table. Or better yet, why don't you find a table for us and save me a seat?"

Her grandmother sent her a look that said she knew exactly what Georgia was doing, but she allowed herself to be diverted. "I'll go find a seat, then. Mind you get me something chocolate now, y'heah?"

"I will." Miz Callie's passion for chocolate was second only to her love of the turtles. With a murmured good-bye to the Dawson woman, Georgia headed for the ticket booth.

Just her luck, to run into a bosom buddy of her mother's first thing. Not that she could keep her engagement-less status a secret for long, but Mamma had to hear about it from her, not from across the bridge table.

Deal with it, her conscience insisted, and she did her best to ignore that small voice.

Clutching the tickets, she headed for the long tables holding the cakes. A man stood, surveying the array, and an unwelcome tingle of awareness went through her. Matt.

She took a deep breath, pinned a smile to her face and stepped up to him. "What's wrong? Can't decide which one to choose?"

He turned and seemed genuinely pleased to see Georgia standing there. She felt her face flush with heat. "For someone who doesn't normally eat dessert, this is overwhelming. What do you recommend?"

"Well, first you eliminate all the ones you don't like and focus on what you do. Miz Callie has to have chocolate, the gooier the better, so I'm going for a slice of the double chocolate fudge cake for her."

"Decadent," he said, smiling as she put a slice on a paper plate. "What about you? Are you a chocolate addict like your grandmother?"

"I've always wanted to be like her," she admitted.

"Somehow I thought that might be true." His smile didn't slip, but his eyes were grave.

Maybe he understood that their special bond meant she had to protect her grandmother. And how was she going to do that when Miz Callie was headed straight for trouble?

"So, chocolate for you?" He held the server poised over the chocolate fudge.

"Actually, I think tonight I'll go with Miz Callie's praline applesauce cake." She slid the knife into the rich, moist layer. "She always wants to know that folks are eating what she baked."

"That's a sign of a loving heart, I've always heard— the need to feed people."

"She has that, all right." She hesitated, but no one was close enough to overhear them. "I just hope her loving heart won't lead her to a lot of pain."

"I know." His gaze warmed again as it rested on her face, and it was almost as if he touched her. "I don't want to see her hurt over this, either. I hope you can believe that."

"We both want the same thing, then," she said. "I just have to pray we can find some way to avoid disaster."

He stiffened. "If you're still thinking you can talk her out of this…"

"No." Her mind fled back to those moments on the dunes. "We talked about it. I understand why she's determined to go ahead. The only way we can prevent—"

"Georgia."

The voice behind her made her jump. She swung around, to be swept into a hug by her father.

"Mr. Harper," he said, with steel in his voice. "I see you've met my little girl."

Chapter 5

Matt nodded, not sure whether to offer his hand or not. Ashton Bodine hadn't been quite as outspoken as his brother on the subject of Matt's work for Miz Callie, but he'd certainly made his disapproval clear.

"Miz Callie introduced me to Georgia." It was on the tip of his tongue to add "...when she arrived," but he cut himself off. *Don't elaborate on your answers.* That's what he'd tell a client facing a hostile question, so maybe he'd better take his own advice.

Bodine's already erect figure straightened until he was almost standing at attention, his eyes as frosty as the touch of white in his hair. "I see."

Bodine could hardly control who his mother introduced to Matt, although it was clear that he'd like to. The silence stretched on awkwardly until someone moved between them, obviously impatient to reach the cake table.

Taking a step back, an excuse to leave already forming in his mind, he glanced at Georgia. And stopped. Georgia looked even more uncomfortable than he felt.

"You need a piece of cake for Lindsay." She rushed into speech, as if to deny that there was anything odd about this encounter. "What does she like?"

"Chocolate every time," he said, just as glad to turn away from Georgia's father.

Georgia snatched a piece of the double chocolate from the table. "What about you, Daddy? Aren't you having some cake?"

"I'll wait for your mother."

Georgia's tension level went up perceptibly at his words. She probably hated keeping Miz Callie's plans a secret from her parents, and he wasn't sure why she even bothered trying. It would all come out eventually.

Still, he couldn't claim he knew a thing about the complexities of families, since he'd had none to speak of. The series of foster homes he'd been in and out of hardly counted.

Jennifer had been his family, and then Lindsay.

"Well, I should take this to Miz Callie." She sounded relieved to have a reason to move.

"Not yet." Bodine's hand touched her elbow, staying her. "Here's your mamma now."

The woman who approached had Georgia's dark brown hair and brown eyes, but there the resemblance ended. While Georgia's hair dropped to her shoulders in unruly ringlets, her mother's was cut in a sleek, chin-length style. In contrast to her daughter's jeans and T-shirt, Mrs. Bodine wore silky white pants and a blouse, a sweater slung around her shoulders like a cape. She had the smooth elegance so many Southern women seemed born with.

Ignoring him, she touched her daughter's hair with a manicured fingernail. "Really, Georgia Lee." The soft drawl was gently chiding. "Let me make an appointment for you with my stylist while you're here. They must not know how to cut hair up there in Atlanta."

"It's fine, Mamma." Georgia pulled away, as she'd probably been doing since she was a teenager. "I didn't expect to see y'all here."

"We wouldn't miss the ice cream and cake social," her mother said, voice as silky as her blouse. "Come on, now, let's go find Miz Callie."

She turned away without even looking at him. As a cut, it was masterful.

"Mamma, have you met Miz Callie's attorney?" Georgia displayed unexpected steel. "This is Matthew Harper. Matt, my mother, Delia Bodine."

The woman shot Georgia an outraged stare before nodding coolly. "Mr. Harper. Now, what was it you're attending to for my mother-in-law?"

"I'm afraid I can't discuss a client's business," he said, careful to keep his tone pleasant. "Now, if you'll excuse me, I need to find my daughter."

Georgia meant well, he supposed, but there didn't seem to be any value in prolonging a conversation with her parents. Overcoming their antagonism was an impossible task.

He turned to scan the area, expecting to see Lindsay still on the swings. But she was sitting at a picnic table next to Miz Callie.

Suppressing a totally unreasonable surge of annoyance, he headed for them. He'd retrieve Lindsay, move to another table, and try to enjoy the evening without thinking about the inimical gazes directed at him.

As it turned out, Miz Callie had other ideas. She greeted him with a wide smile and a sweep of her hand to the bench.

"Come, sit down. We've been saving a place for you."

"I think Lindsay and I should find a table of our own, since your son and his wife are joining you." He rested his hand on Lindsay's shoulder.

She pulled away, shaking her head. "Miz Callie said we could sit with her."

"That's right." She waved to the Bodines, gesturing to the benches. "Come on, everyone sit down. Lindsay and I picked the best table here in the shade."

Short of being rude, there was nothing he could do. Apparently Georgia's parents felt the same, and in a moment they were all seated around the picnic table.

Spanish moss, drifting in the breeze, made moving shadows on Georgia's face as she leaned over to hand out cups of ice cream. When she slid one to Lindsay, his daughter shoved it away.

"I don't want chocolate."

"Lindsay, that's your favorite." Her comment was impolite, but he didn't want to scold her in front of other people.

Her lips tightened for a moment. Then she took the ice cream. "Thank you," she muttered.

Miz Callie diverted attention with a comment about the turnout, Georgia's father responded and the talk became general.

Matt glanced at his child under cover of the conversation. Lindsay was snuggled close to Miz Callie, almost deliberately ignoring the others.

What was that all about? That too-familiar helpless feeling rolled over him. Jennifer had been the one to handle everything where their daughter was concerned, and he'd been so busy getting his career going that he'd let her. Even then, he'd sometimes felt a little envious of their close bond. Now...now too often he felt adrift, ill-prepared for the role he had to fill.

Georgia sat next to her father, her face relaxing when he said something in a low, relaxing tone. For just an instant he envied their closeness.

"Georgia's always been her daddy's girl," Miz Callie said softly. "She missed him terribly when he had to be away."

"Away?"

"Ashton was in the Coast Guard for thirty years. The boys missed him, too, of course, but it affected Georgia the most."

So the Bodines were a military family. That went a long way toward explaining Miz Callie's reluctance to confide in them about her plans.

"Tell me, Mr. Harper. Where were you raised?" Delia Bodine's question, cutting across the table, startled him.

"Boston," he said. And not raised so much as thrown out to strive or fail on his own. "I lived there all my life until we moved down here."

"Let me think." She gazed at her husband. "Ashton, do we know anybody in Boston?"

"There was that Carlton boy who was in Cole's year at the Citadel. He was from Boston."

"Margo Lawton's daughter married someone from Boston, I believe," Delia said. "Or Cambridge, maybe. Now, what was his name?"

He recognized what was going on. His partner had explained to him the particularly Southern passion that could be encapsulated in one question: *Who are your family?* They wanted to place people.

Well, they wouldn't place him, no matter how they tried.

"Cambridge is near Boston, isn't it?" Delia fixed a cool stare on him. "Was your home anywhere close?"

"More cake, Miz Callie?" Georgia reached for her grandmother's plate.

Delia broke off her questioning to stare at her daughter's hand, gasping a little. "Georgia! Your ring! Don't tell me you've lost it. What on earth will James say?"

Georgia snatched her hand back as if she could hide the evidence. "I didn't lose it, Mamma."

"Well, then, where is it?"

Delia had forgotten about him. The relief he felt was tempered with regret that his reprieve had come at Georgia's expense.

Georgia put down the plate she was holding. "I gave it back to James. The engagement is off."

How much it cost her to say that bluntly in front of all of them, he couldn't imagine.

"What do you mean?" Delia Bodine looked as horrified as if her daughter had announced that she was taking up bank robbery. "How could you—"

"Enough, Delia." Georgia's father didn't raise his voice, but it held a tone of command. "We can talk about this later. I'm sure Georgia had a good reason for her decision."

Georgia's eyes sparkled with unshed tears. "Thank you, Daddy."

He'd like to say something comforting, but it wasn't his place. Maybe the best thing he could do for her was make himself scarce, so the Bodine family could have this out in private.

"About done, Lindsay?" He slid off the bench. "I think we should head for home."

"I don't want to go yet," Lindsay wailed. "It's not late. Why do we have to go?"

He resisted the urge to explain and held out his hand to his daughter. "It's time."

For an instant he thought she'd argue. Then, pouting, she slid off the bench.

"Say good-night to everyone," he prompted.

"Good night," she mumbled, gaze on her feet.

He was conscious of Delia's critical eye on his child, and irritation flared. She had no right to criticize. Currently, she wasn't doing such a great job with her own daughter.

Georgia leaned against her father, and Ashton Bodine put his arm around her.

Matt said good-night, wondering whether he'd ever have that kind of closeness with his child.

Georgia stretched, cracking one eye open to glare at the sunlight streaming through the bedroom window. She always put the shade up when she slept in this bedroom so that she could see the stars when she fell asleep and be awakened by the sunlight on the waves. But today she could have easily pulled the covers back over her head.

Instead, she swung her feet to the floor, toes curling into the rag rug that covered the bare boards. Normally she slept soundly, but last night her dreams had been a confused kaleidoscope of people and images. She couldn't remember specifics, but she'd woken with her throat clogged with unshed tears.

Because of James? Maybe so.

She stretched, trying to shake off the feeling, but it persisted, even while she pulled on shorts and a T-shirt and drew her hair into a ponytail.

James had shown he wasn't the man she'd thought he was—the man she'd fallen in love with. She'd been right to break it off, no matter what anyone said—anyone, in this case, being her mother. She'd tried to explain, hampered by the fact that she didn't want to tell them she'd lost her job as well as her fiancé. There'd be time enough for that revelation when she'd decided what she was going to do with herself.

And in the meantime, there was Miz Callie's problem to focus on. She shoved her feet into sneakers and headed for the stairs.

No sign of Miz Callie until she glanced through the sliding glass doors. Her grandmother was on the deck, red plastic bucket in hand, saying something to Lindsay, who looked up at her with an adoring expression.

Grabbing an apple from the pewter bowl on the table, she hurried out to join them.

"Hi. Wow, it's going to be a hot one."

Miz Callie settled her floppy hat on her head. "That's why Lindsay and I are going on turtle patrol so early."

"You like the turtles, too?" She smiled at Lindsay.

The child nodded, but her gaze slid away from Georgia's.

"Come along," Miz Callie said. "You may as well get some exercise with us, since you slept right through your runnin' time."

"I did, didn't I?" She stretched again, stifling a yawn, and nodded. "Okay, let's go."

Miz Callie handed her the bucket, filled with the paraphernalia they'd need if they found a new nest.

Lindsay's lower lip came out in a pout. "You said I could carry it. That's not fair."

Georgia gave the bucket to the child. "Sure thing, Lindsay."

Lindsay snatched the bucket and spun to hurry down the stairs. A reluctant "thanks" floated back.

Georgia looked at her grandmother as they followed her. Miz Callie shrugged and shook her head in a not-in-front-of-the-child way.

When they reached the packed sand where the walking was easier, Lindsay danced along the lacy ripples of incoming waves.

Miz Callie smiled. "You used to do that very thing."

"All kids do, don't they? Well, maybe the boys didn't. They always had some plan to carry out."

"Mischief, as often as not." Miz Callie was smiling.

Lindsay's small figure looked as light and insubstantial as one of the sandpipers when she spun, her hair swinging in a pale arc.

"She doesn't like me, does she?"

"I wouldn't say that." Miz Callie shook her head, sighing a little. "Truth is, she's probably a bit jealous. You coming along, snagging my attention. And her father's."

"I haven't—" She gulped. "I haven't snagged Matt's attention, as you so elegantly put it. I'm only spending time with him because you got me into this."

"Lindsay doesn't know that." Her grandmother watched the child, frowning. "She's just desperate for folks to make her feel safe in this new place, with her mother gone and all. She's a bit lost."

Georgia winced. She'd felt that way herself.

"I should let her have her walk with you." She stopped. "I could make some excuse…"

Miz Callie linked her arm in Georgia's. "You'll do no such thing. Might be good for that child to see that family can be bigger than just a couple of people."

"She and Matt do seem pretty much on their own. Has he ever mentioned any other family to you?"

"I can't say he has." She sent Georgia a shadowed glance. "Speaking of family, I got together the information Matt asked for. I'll show you when we get back to the house."

Georgia blinked. "What did you do—stay up all night looking for things?"

"Most of it was right there in your grandfather's family Bible. The rest—well, I guess I did sit up a mite late. When you're my age, you don't need as much sleep as you used to."

"Even so—" She stopped, because Miz Callie was clearly not listening.

Instead, her grandmother was staring landward with a look of outrage on her face. Before Georgia could react, Miz Callie went striding toward the dunes, waving her hat.

"What do you think you're doing? Get away from that!"

Georgia ran to catch up as Miz Callie approached the people on the dunes. Tourists, she could see at a glance. A sunburned man with a kid in tow. The boy had crawled under the plastic tape that marked off the turtle's nest and was burrowing in the sand.

"Stop it, you hear me?"

The boy kept right on with what he was doing, and the man shot her an annoyed glance. "The kid's not doing any harm, lady. He just wants to see the turtle eggs."

"Get him out of there." Miz Callie glared at him. "This is a protected area. As the tape clearly shows."

"Hey, we're just trying to see a little nature. Something for him to talk about when he gets home."

Miz Callie, apparently too impatient to argue, shoved past the man and tapped the boy. "Out!"

"Ow! Leave me alone!" The boy, as ill-mannered as his father, swung his shovel at Miz Callie's arm.

Her grandmother winced as it landed with a thwack. Georgia stepped over the tape, grasped the boy's arms and pulled him away from the hole he'd made, avoiding the kick he aimed at her shins.

"It is a federal crime to interfere with the sea turtles," she said loudly, drowning out the kid's yells and the father's protests. "If you're not out of here in two minutes, I'm calling the police."

That silenced them. The man grabbed his son and pulled him away. With a fulminating glance, he stalked off, the boy wailing his desire to dig up the turtle's nest.

Georgia took a deep breath and turned to her grandmother. "Are you all right?"

"I'm fine, darlin'. Just fine." She smoothed her hand along her wrist. "The little monster just landed a hit on my bad wrist, that's all. But you…" She looked at Georgia with the beginnings of a smile in her eyes. "Child, you purely tore a strip off them. I didn't know you had it in you to lose your temper like that."

Georgia gave a shaky laugh. "I didn't, either. I guess when I saw him hit you—"

"He was a bad kid." The small voice came from behind them. They'd forgotten Lindsay in the excitement.

Her grandmother reached for the child and pulled her close in a comforting hug. "Let's just say he's been badly brought up. No one has taught him to observe the rules."

Lindsay put her arm around Miz Callie's waist, as if to assure herself that she was all right. "He didn't understand about the turtles, did he?"

Georgia grinned. "I see you've indoctrinated her already."

"Of course." She hugged Lindsay. "I'm fine, child. He'll think twice before he bothers a nest again."

"Georgia sure told him." Lindsay's solemn gaze rested on her, a little more favorably.

"Well, I tried." She got down on her knees and crawled under the tape. "Want to help me fix the nest?"

Nodding, Lindsay crawled in next to her and imitated Georgia's movements, filling in the hole and smoothing sand over it.

When they'd finished, they crawled back out again and stood to survey their handiwork.

"Good job." She rested her hands on her hips. "Looks just like it should, don't you think?"

Lindsay put her own small hands on her hips. "Yes, I do," she said definitely.

Georgia suppressed a smile. Maybe Lindsay's quarrel with her had been overcome.

That seemed borne out as they started back down the beach. Lindsay skipped along between them.

"Did you used to look for turtle nests with your grandmother when you were little?" she asked, tilting her face up toward Georgia.

"I sure did. Miz Callie taught me and my brothers everything I know about the ocean and the shore."

"How many brothers do you have?"

"Two. Both older than me. And a whole mess of cousins. When we were all here together, we made quite a tribe." She smiled at the memory. They were all close enough in age that they'd played and fought as equals.

"I wish I had cousins. Or brothers." Lindsay's voice sounded very small.

Georgia exchanged a concerned glance with her grandmother over the child's head. "Maybe you'll get some cousins. If your aunt or uncle gets married, then their children would be your cousins."

"I don't have any aunts or uncles. Just Daddy. And my grandparents. They live in Arizona."

It sounded lonely. She tried to imagine what her life would have been like without her big, sprawling, noisy, interfering family. She couldn't.

"Tell you what," she said, putting her hand lightly on Lindsay's shoulder. "Next time we all get together, you can be a part of our tribe. Okay?"

Lindsay stared up at her as if measuring the sincerity of her words. Finally she gave a quick little nod.

"Okay," she said. She sighed, a very grown-up sound. "I have to go. I'm going to Bible school this morning."

"That'll be fun," Miz Callie said. "You come by later and tell us all about it, okay?"

"Okay." Lindsay looked a little brighter. "I'll see you later." She trudged off toward her house.

Georgia stood and watched her until she reached the deck. "I see what you mean. Poor kid. She's lonely."

"Hopefully she'll make some friends at Bible school." Miz Callie put her arm around Georgia's waist as they headed to the house.

"Did you arrange that?"

"I might have suggested it," her grandmother admitted. "Let's get something to eat, and you can go over my notes. And I thought, since you're going to have lunch downtown, you might drop them off at Matt's office so he can get going right away."

"How did you hear about my lunch date?" She lifted an eyebrow at Miz Callie as they walked up the stairs. She didn't think her grandmother had been around when her cousin Amanda had called with an invitation to meet for lunch.

Miz Callie chuckled. "Child, if you want to keep secrets, don't belong to such a nosy family. I just happened to be talking to your brother, and he mentioned that Lucas mentioned it to him."

Lucas was Amanda's big brother and just as inclined to butt into everyone else's business as the rest of them.

Her thoughts drifted to Matt and Lindsay, alone and isolated. All in all, she guessed she'd take the family she had, annoying as they could be.

Chapter 6

"Mr. Harper?" Madie Dillon, the secretary Matt shared with Rodney Porter, tapped and opened his office door a few inches. "You have a visitor. Shall I ask her to make an appointment?"

Visitors were so unusual that for a moment he couldn't think how to answer. "Who is it?"

"Georgia Bodine." Madie seemed surprised, too. Clients hadn't exactly been beating down his door.

"Show her in." He rose, buttoning the top button of his shirt and tightening his tie.

There she was, the door closing behind her. Instead of her usual shorts and T-shirt, she wore a turquoise sundress that swirled around her slim body and emphasized her tan legs.

"I'm so sorry if I'm disturbing you." She sent a

quick, curious glance around the office. "Miz Callie insisted I stop by."

"Not a problem." He rounded the desk and drew one of the comfortable leather chairs around for her. "Please sit down."

She slid onto the chair. "Nice."

"Nothing but the best for Rodney Porter's clients." He took the other chair and sat facing her.

She lifted an eyebrow. "And Matthew Harper's clients, too?"

"I'm a very small cog in the wheel right now," he said. He swung his hand in a gesture that encompassed the whole office. "I feel like a fraud sometimes, sitting in the midst of all this Southern elegance. This was Rod's brother-in-law's office, before he ran off with his secretary."

"I remember. That news traveled all the way to Atlanta. So Rodney brought you in to replace him."

"Not exactly." He felt compelled to be more open with her than he'd been with most people he'd met here. "Rod was being a friend. He knew I wanted to leave Boston for a fresh start after Jennifer's death, and he made it possible."

Georgia's gaze lit on something on his desk. Without turning, he felt quite sure it was the silver-framed photo of Jennifer.

"Is that Jennifer?"

Nodding, he lifted the frame and handed it to her. "That was taken on our honeymoon."

Jennifer sat on a rock in the black-and-white photo, staring out at a foggy sea. The wind whipped her hair around her face, and her hands were clasped around her knees. They'd gone up the Maine coast, dawdling in one small town after another, with no set destination and no timetable to keep.

"She was very beautiful." Georgia stared at the image for a moment longer, as if it would tell her something about him. Then she handed it back. "Thank you for letting me see it. Lindsay's like her, isn't she?"

He nodded, throat tightening. Most of the time he ignored the resemblance, but sometimes a turn of the head or a quick, light movement brought hot tears to his eyes.

He cleared his throat. "What can I do for Miz Callie today?"

Georgia bent to pick up a folder she'd placed on the floor next to her handbag. "These are the notes she came up with last night—names, dates, addresses." She handed him the folder.

He flipped it open, then leaned over so she could see it, too. As she'd said, names and addresses, birth dates, death dates, all in Miz Callie's fine, spidery writing.

"Is this information you'd be familiar with?"

She traced a fingertip down the page. "Pretty much, although I'd never have come up with the dates." She pointed to an address on King Street in Charleston. "That's the house Miz Callie lived in before she got the idea to move out to the island full-time. I guess Granddad inherited it from his parents after Ned…" She paused. "After Ned left. Or died." Her gaze met his. "I mean, he was older than my grandfather by several years, so he's probably dead by now, don't you think?"

"Hard to say. You'd think, if he were alive, he'd

have gotten in touch with the family sometime in all these years."

She shrugged, frowning. "True. But if he died, you'd think the family would have been notified."

"Maybe, maybe not. It depends on the circumstances and how well he'd created a new life."

Her frown deepened. "It's not impossible, is it? To find the answers my grandmother wants?"

"Not impossible." He wouldn't sugarcoat it for her. "But it may be very difficult. And even if we find the answers, they may not make her happy."

Georgia sighed deeply, running a hand through her hair.

He smiled. "I understand the frustration, believe me. It's not the first time a client has insisted on doing something I advised against."

"At least you're not going up against the rest of the family, too."

"I wouldn't count on that. I've already had visits from your father and your uncle."

"I'm sorry about that."

She looked so distressed that he nearly laughed.

"Don't worry, Georgia. Your father was the soul of politeness."

"He would be. Not Uncle Brett, though, I'll bet. It was Brett, wasn't it, and not Harrison?"

"Yes. Do I have another one to look forward to?"

"I hope not." She seemed relieved by his light tone. "They just want to protect Miz Callie, you know."

"I know. It's good that she has so many relatives who care about her. Sometimes elderly people don't."

"There are lots of us, that's for sure." She sounded

as if she thought it a mixed blessing. "Lindsay was tell-ing us about her grandparents this morning. That they live clear out in Arizona, so she doesn't see them very often. Are they your folks?"

"Jennifer's parents. My father-in-law's health isn't great, and he seems to do better out there."

"It's a shame they're so far away. And your par-ents?"

"Dead." At least, he supposed they were. They were certainly dead to him.

"I'm sorry." Sympathy filled her eyes, turning them that deep, velvety brown. "It must be rough, being so alone."

He shrugged. "I'm used to it." If he kept on looking into those eyes, he'd lean so far forward that he'd be in danger of falling off his chair.

He busied himself shuffling through the few papers in the folder. He'd felt the attraction last night, when he'd held her hand so briefly. Felt it again now.

But that was all it was. He'd already had the big love of his life. He wasn't foolish enough to think he could replace that.

"I'll put in some time on the search this afternoon." He closed the folder and put it on his desk. "I'm sorry Miz Callie sent you into town on such a hot day. I'm sure you'd rather be on the beach."

"I was coming anyway. I'm meeting my cousin Amanda for lunch." She glanced at her watch, a slim gold bracelet on her tanned wrist. "And I'm late."

He stood when she did and followed her toward the door. "Thanks again."

She turned so suddenly that he nearly bumped into

her. "I just—I wanted to thank you. I don't suppose Miz Callie realizes it, but I know you're taking valuable time away from your other business in order to do this."

She was so close he could almost count the freckles the sun had spattered on her nose. "Don't worry about it. I'm not exactly overwhelmed with business, believe me."

"I see." She gave him a wry smile. "Not easy for an outsider to break in, is it? Folks around here tend to be a little clannish."

"I've noticed." He was so distracted by Georgia's proximity, he hardly knew what he was saying. "I'll hang in. It's too important to me not to. Just one good case could make all the difference."

She stiffened, taking a step backward.

"I guess Miz Callie is that big case, isn't she?" Her eyes were accusing him of something.

He clamped his lips for a moment before answering. "If Miz Callie is pleased with my services, naturally I hope she'll mention me to people. Word of mouth really is the best advertising."

"Yes, of course." Her voice was cold as she reached behind her for the doorknob. "I hope it works out for you."

Before he could come up with something else to say, she'd slipped out the door.

Georgia parked carefully in the restaurant's minuscule parking lot, holding her breath as she slipped between two oversized SUVs. Parking space in Charleston was at a premium. A city built centuries ago on a peninsula was bound to have that issue.

She walked toward the restaurant that backed onto the water. It was new since the last time she'd been here, occupying a building that had once belonged to the navy.

The breeze off the water cooled her overheated face but not her disposition.

Matt hadn't even realized he'd upset her. She was just part of the job. And Miz Callie was a way of making inroads into the tight mesh that was Charleston society.

What else had she expected? She'd seen enough workaholic males in her time. She just hadn't recognized it quite soon enough in Matt.

A wall of cool air and the scent of frying hush puppies greeted her when she pushed through the door. Before the hostess could speak to her, Georgia spotted her cousin sitting at the far end of the room in front of the windows. With a quick wave, Georgia wove her way between the tables to reach her.

"Georgia Lee, it is mighty good to see you." Amanda surged from the chair to wrap her arms around her. "It's been way too long. Let me look at you." She gave her a critical stare. "Well, I don't see it."

"See what?"

"Your mother told my mother you looked like you'd been dragged through a knothole backwards." She grinned. "But you look pretty good to me."

"You know my mother. She's only pleased if I'm dressed for the cotillion."

She slid into the seat opposite Amanda, looking at her cousin with pleasure. Amanda's sleek brown hair dropped to her shoulders, her green eyes sparkled in a lightly tanned face and she had the polished look down to an art. Come to think of it, Mamma probably wondered why her daughter couldn't be more like Cousin Amanda.

"Mothers." Amanda dismissed them with a wave of a well-manicured hand. "Tell the truth now. Miz Callie's been spoiling you since you got back, now hasn't she?"

"Just like always," she said lightly. She'd love to tell Amanda what was going on with their grandmother and have the benefit of Amanda's shrewd advice. With her nimble brain and deep interest in people, Amanda seemed born for her job on the daily newspaper.

But she couldn't tell. It wasn't her secret to share.

"I got you a sweet tea." Amanda shoved the glass toward her, ice tinkling with the movement. "And I went ahead and ordered our shrimp salads, so we could get on with lunch. Some of us aren't on vacation, you know."

"I'm sure your boss will have you drawn and quartered if you're not back in time." She took a sip of the tea.

"He might." Amanda scowled at the table. She'd been complaining about her boss the last time they'd talked, and apparently things were no better.

"How is work going? You getting to cover anything bigger than the latest oyster roast?"

"I'll have you know I graduated to the dog show last week." Amanda grinned, affection flowing easily between them.

Cousins were special, Miz Callie had always reminded them when they fought, and she'd been right.

The bonds she'd formed early with her cousins were nearly as strong as those with her brothers. And at least some of the cousins were girls.

"How's Annabel?" Amanda's twin sister looked like her, but the resemblance was strictly on the surface. In every other way, they were polar opposites.

Amanda made a face. "Still running that horse farm over on James Island. Go see her—she'd love it. But don't wear your good shoes."

"That sounds like the voice of experience talking."

"Believe me, it is." Amanda's eyes grew solemn suddenly, and she reached out to grasp Georgia's hand. "Enough chitchat. What's this about your engagement being over, sugar? You catch him with another girl?"

"Not quite. I take it the news is all over the family already." Not that she'd expected anything else.

"Honey, it's probably all over Charleston. You know how the family is."

"I know, believe me, I know."

"So what's the scoop? Now, don't tell me if you don't want to, but you know I'm dying to hear."

She hesitated, but the cat was already out of the bag. Amanda might sound acerbic, but underneath was a strong vein of empathy, and the urge to spill the story was strong. "Take my advice and never get engaged to someone you work with. It makes for messy loyalties. I thought we were partners, you know? Then I found out he was taking my work and presenting it as his own. He even had the nerve to think I should be pleased about that."

Amanda squeezed her hand. "He was a jerk. A

charming jerk. You take my advice and never get involved with a charmer. You're well rid of him."

She managed a smile. "Unfortunately I'm rid of a job, as well. He managed to blame his mistakes on me, and I got the axe."

Amanda's eyes sparked with outrage. "Didn't you fight back? Go to his boss?"

"I just wanted to get away and forget the whole thing."

"Honey..."

The waitress appeared with their salads, and Georgia leaned back while she put them on the table along with a basket of hush puppies. Beyond the window, boats moved busily in and out of Charleston harbor—pleasure boats, container ships from who-knew-where, a tour boat on its way to Fort Sumter. The gulls wheeled and shrieked, a background so familiar that she almost didn't hear it any longer.

When the woman moved away, she shook her head at Amanda. "Don't bother to give me the pep talk. You'd fight back. But I'm not like you. Listen, just forget about it, okay? I'm moving on."

"If you say so. Anyway, you know I'm on your side, every time." Amanda speared her fork into a mound of shrimp salad. "If we're not going to talk about your engagement, I guess we'd better fall back on Miz Callie. Sorry you got landed with trying to change her mind, but that's what happens when you're the favorite granddaughter."

"Get out. You know very well Miz Callie doesn't play favorites."

"Maybe not." Amanda tapped her pink nail on her

glass. "But I'm glad I'm not the one trying to convince her."

"You know, and I know, that trying to convince Miz Callie to stop doing something she wants to do is...is..."

"...like trying to stop the tide," Amanda finished for her. "Why do you s'pose our folks don't see that?"

"I can't imagine." Her life would be so much easier if they did.

Amanda glanced at her wristwatch. "You talk. I've got to eat so I can get back to the newspaper."

The newspaper. In her job, Amanda would have ready access to the papers from the time they were interested in.

Did she really want to bring Amanda in on this? She hesitated, eying her cousin.

"Whatever it is, you might as well just spit it out." Amanda's eyebrows lifted. "Come on, Georgia Lee. I know when you're chewing on something."

"What elegant phrasing. You use that in the paper?"

"Out with it. You want something. I can tell."

She hesitated, studying her cousin's face. "Could you look up something in the newspaper files for me without asking questions or mentioning it to anyone else?"

Amanda tilted her head slightly. "Even family?"

"Especially family."

Her smile curved. "I promise. Cousins' honor." She made a quick gesture, crossing her heart.

Georgia took a breath and prayed she was doing the right thing. "Will you check the papers for the summer of 1942 and see if you can find anything about Edward Bodine?"

For a moment Amanda's green eyes simply looked puzzled. Then Georgia saw recognition dawn.

"Edward Bodine. Granddad's brother? The one who…" She didn't finish the sentence.

"Uncle Ned. Right." She grasped Amanda's hand. "Say no if you want to. Just don't tell anyone."

Amanda studied her for a long moment. Then she grinned. "When did I ever say no to trouble? I'll do my best. But I wish I knew what you're up to."

Relief swept through her. She could count on Amanda. "You're better off not knowing."

"Okay. I'll buy that." Amanda stared at her for a long moment. "But just remember one thing, Georgia Lee. People who play with fire are likely to get burned."

Chapter 7

Georgia had hoped to get her grandmother reminiscing about Uncle Ned that evening, but once they'd finished the dishes, she found that Lindsay was joining them. Something in her expression must have alerted Miz Callie that she wasn't thrilled at the thought.

"I enjoy having Lindsay here," Miz Callie said, emphasizing the words with the clatter of a pot lid into the sink. "Is that a problem for you?"

Her disenchantment with Matt couldn't be allowed to affect her attitude toward the little girl. "I'm glad to see Lindsay. I was looking forward to having a nice talk with my favorite grandmother, that's all."

Miz Callie waved the words away with a flip of her dish towel, smiling. "She won't stay long, so we can talk all you want later. Matt has to finish up some work at the office after supper."

It was probably the work he'd neglected while he was searching through tedious computer records for Ned Bodine. She ought to feel grateful. She would, if she didn't understand his motives so clearly.

"Here she comes now." Miz Callie peered out the kitchen window. "We're goin' on the beach. You coming?"

"I'll be along in a minute. I want to get something."

When she descended the stairs a few minutes later, Miz Callie was ensconced in her favorite beach chair, with Lindsay digging in the sand at her feet.

Grabbing a chair, Georgia slung the cloth bag containing her sketching materials over her shoulder. She walked down the short path through the dunes.

"Hey." She flipped the beach chair open and sat down. "You diggin' your way to China, Lindsay?"

"I'm making a lake for Julie and Janie to play in." Julie and Janie were apparently the two tiny plastic dolls that lay on the sand.

"They'll like that." She opened the sketch pad and sat back, taking in the scene.

The tide ebbed, leaving an expanse of shining sand traced with an intricate pattern of ghost crab trails and sandpiper prints. She began to draw.

Lindsay appeared at her elbow. "What are you drawing?"

"What I see." That probably sounded a little short, though she didn't mean it that way. "I have an extra pad with me. Would you like to draw?"

Lindsay clasped her hands behind her back. "I'm not very good."

It was the sort of thing she said about herself. She

didn't like hearing it from Lindsay. "Drawing is one of those things you can do just for fun." She held the pad and a few colored pencils out to Lindsay.

"What should I draw?" She sat on the sand.

"What do you see?"

Lindsay craned her neck as she looked around. "I see a sea gull sitting in the sand. But that'd be hard to draw."

"For fun, remember?"

Lindsay nodded. Then she bent over the pad.

Georgia tried to concentrate on her own drawing, but she couldn't help watching Lindsay. The child was certainly tied up in knots. Was that part of the aftermath of losing her mother? She couldn't even guess.

She'd never thought herself particularly maternal. Annabel, Amanda's twin, had all the maternal instincts. Even when they were children, it was always Annabel who comforted people and critters when they hurt. She'd collected more strays than the animal shelter.

She didn't have those instincts, but she felt the softening of her heart when she watched Lindsay. Despite a large, loving family, she knew what it was to feel lonely.

Lindsay held the pad back a little, frowning at her picture. "It doesn't look right. See?"

True, the picture didn't look much like the sea gull, but at least it was identifiable as a bird.

"I like it," she said. "I don't believe I drew birds that well when I was seven." She handed it to her grandmother.

"I do like it, too. I'll bet you'd enjoy coloring it, wouldn't you?"

"Yes, ma'am."

That was the first time she'd heard Lindsay add the familiar Southern grace note of calling Miz Callie "ma'am," and it made both of them smile.

"You're turning into a real island girl," Miz Callie said. "Even sounding like a native."

Lindsay frowned. "What's a native?"

"Somebody who was born here, sugar." Georgia tugged the blond ponytail lightly. "But we take outlanders, too, long as they learn as fast as you do."

Lindsay bent over her picture, but Georgia didn't miss the smile that tugged at the corner of her mouth.

Lindsay shot a sideways glance at Georgia. "You said I was seven. But I'm almost eight."

"It's a good picture, even for an eight-year-old," Georgia said promptly.

"Almost eight." Miz Callie echoed the child's words. "When is your birthday?"

"Tuesday." A cloud crossed Lindsay's face. "Last year I had a party at the jump palace with all my friends. My mommy got me a cake with a princess on it."

They were silent for a moment.

"I'll bet your daddy is planning to do something special." *He'd better be.*

She shrugged. "He said maybe I could have a party. But I don't know enough kids to invite to a party."

"You know me," Miz Callie said briskly. "And you know Georgia, and I'll bet you're meeting some friends at Bible school."

"That's right." At this point, she'd say just about anything to wipe that woebegone look from Lindsay's face. "You'll have a real island celebration for your birthday."

"What's this about a birthday?" Matt's voice sounded behind them.

Georgia jerked around. She'd expected to see him walking down the beach, at which point she could have disappeared into the house. He'd evidently parked in front of Miz Callie's and come back on the path instead.

"We were talking about Lindsay's birthday," Miz Callie said, getting up and stretching. "We can't believe she's going to be eight already."

"Next week." Matt leaned over Lindsay's chair. "What a great picture. Did Georgia help you?"

"She did it all herself," Georgia said quickly.

"Georgia let me use her paper and pencils," Lindsay said. "I want to give it to Miz Callie."

"Why, thank you so much." Miz Callie held out her arm, and Lindsay went to lean against her. "We'll hang it up in the kitchen so I can see it every day."

Miz Callie's refrigerator had always been host to a rotating display of grandkids' art. Now Lindsay's picture would take its place there.

Lindsay glanced at her father. "Can I help hang it up before we go home?"

"Sure enough." Miz Callie started to pick up her chair, but Matt took it from her.

"You go ahead. I'll help Georgia take the chairs up."

Obviously he had something to say to her. Miz Callie held out her hand to Lindsay. "We'll see if there are any cookies in the jar, long as we're going to the kitchen."

Georgia watched them head for the cottage, her throat tightening. Her grandmother had become a little stooped, moving more slowly than she once did. But she still focused her total attention on the child by her side.

She bent to pick up a chair, but Matt stopped her.

"Wait. Please." The *please* sounded like an afterthought. "We need to talk."

"I have to go in." She didn't want to hear anything he had to say, not right at the moment. Maybe they had to work together, but she wouldn't let herself be drawn into believing this was anything more than business to him.

"It's important."

Her gaze rose to his face. "Did you find out something?"

"No, I didn't. Why are you angry with me?"

The blunt question shook her. She looked away, refusing to meet his eyes. "Why would I be angry?" Her voice sounded calm and detached, and she was proud of that.

"That's what I'd like to know." His fingers closed on her hand, as if to keep her there, and his palm was warm against her skin. "One minute we were talking about your grandmother's case, and the next you shot out of my office as if a monster were after you."

"I didn't... I mean, I was late." Why didn't she just tell him? Amanda would. Amanda would square up to him and tell him just what she thought.

But she wasn't Amanda.

"That's not it, and you know it." His voice was edged with frustration, and his fingers pressed against her skin. "Tell me what's wrong."

Her heart began to thud. "You! You're what's wrong."

He stared at her blankly. "What are you talking about?" His eyes grew icy. "I'm an outsider, is that it?"

"No, that's not it. I don't care where you're from. I do care that you're using my grandmother to further your career."

He stiffened. "Is that really what you think of me?"

"That's what you said. You need a big case involving someone who'll give you the opening you need to break in here. My grandmother was perfect for you, wasn't she? Everybody knows the Bodine name. You took advantage of living next door to her. You talked her into—"

"Stop right there." The words were so heavy with anger that they silenced her.

But he didn't continue. Instead he took a breath, looked down at his hand gripping hers and loosened his hold so that his fingers encircled her wrist lightly.

"Let's back up. All right, yes, I did say that I needed a client of my own." His eyes darkened with pain. "I'm not going to apologize for wanting to succeed here. I have Lindsay to consider."

His voice roughened, twisting her heart against her will.

"My daughter doesn't have anybody else. I took a chance, moving here. I have to make it work."

She didn't want to sympathize. Didn't want to understand. "My grandmother—"

"Miz Callie came to me." He said the words evenly, as if to give equal weight to each of them. "Georgia, I did not try to convince her to do this. She had already decided exactly what she wanted. She laid it all out for me." His lips twisted in a wry smile. "Do you really think I could talk her into anything she didn't want to do?"

"No." Her voice was small when she admitted it. "I guess not. But I thought you were doing this because you wanted to help her. Because you liked her. Not because you thought her influence would establish you here."

"I do like her. How could I help it? Her kindness to Lindsay is enough to put me in her debt."

The passion in his voice moved her. "Even so…"

"Even so, I hope doing this job for her will bring me new clients. But from what you've said, it might have exactly the opposite effect."

She hadn't thought of that. She'd jumped to conclusions about his motives without thinking it through, maybe because she'd had enough of men who'd sacrifice anything or anyone for the sake of success. Shame colored her cheeks.

"I hope that won't happen. For all of our sakes. I'm sorry, Matt. I reacted without thinking." Her cheeks were hot, and she had to force herself to meet his eyes.

He didn't speak for a minute, though he looked as if words hovered on his tongue. With his hand closed around her wrist, he must feel the way her pulse was racing.

"It's okay," he said finally, and she had the feeling that wasn't what he'd intended to say. "I hope that, too, but either way, I'm in this to the finish. No matter what happens."

She nodded, her throat too tight to speak.

He held her hand for a moment longer. Then he let it go slowly, maybe reluctantly. He picked up the chairs. "We'd better go in."

As she followed him toward the house, she knew that something had changed between them again, like the sand shifting under her feet when she stood in the waves on the ebbing tide. She knew how to keep her balance in the surf. But this change—she didn't know whether to be excited or afraid or both.

Window panes rattled as the wind whipped around the beach house. Georgia leaned against the sliding glass door, shielding her eyes with her hand as she peered out into the dark.

"It sounds as if there's rain coming." She couldn't see much, but she recognized the signs.

"A line of thunderstorms is coming through, according to the weather." Miz Callie looked up from the newspaper she was reading. "I already drew some water and got the candles out, just in case it gets bad."

Miz Callie believed in being prepared, like most of the old-timers. The island had seen its share of bad weather over the years.

Thunder boomed overhead, and her grandmother put the paper aside. "I'll get the candles..."

"I'll do it."

Georgia waved her back to her padded rocking chair and hurried into the kitchen. The candles, stuck into a motley assortment of holders, sat on the counter, along with a pack of matches. Georgia carried three into the living room, setting one on the table next to Miz Callie and the others on the mantel.

As she did so, lightning cracked in a spectacular display over the water, lighting up the beach for a split second. Then the power went off.

"That was fast." Georgia groped her way back to her grandmother, fumbled with the matches and lit the candle. She made quick work of lighting the other two, welcoming their soft yellow glow.

"Thank you, sugar." Miz Callie patted the over-stuffed hassock next to her, and Georgia sat down. "There now, all safe and cozy."

A roll of thunder sounded, so loud it seemed to rattle the dishes in the cupboard. Georgia moved a little closer to her grandmother. "This is just like old times. How many summer thunderstorms have we waited out in here?"

Her grandmother chuckled softly. "Remember when Amanda hid under the bed?"

"I sure do. But it's probably not safe to remind her of that anymore." The polished, efficient Amanda she'd lunched with bore little resemblance to the terrified child who'd refused to come out from under the bed in a storm.

"This house stood through Hugo. I don't reckon anything short of that will bother it."

Sorrow touched her grandmother's face for a moment, and Georgia knew she was thinking about her own family home. Before Hurricane Hugo, it had been on the lot beyond where Matt's rental house stood.

"I'm sorry. You lost so much in Hugo."

"Plenty of people did." Miz Callie patted her hand. "I just hope Lindsay's not frightened. Maybe I should have warned Matt to have some candles ready."

"I'm sure he's capable of handling the situation." The mention of his name brought back those moments on the beach. She wrapped her fingers around her wrist. She could feel his grasp, see the play of emotion in his eyes.

Miz Callie leaned back in the rocker, her gaze on Georgia's face. "I s'pose it's too soon, but I can't help but wonder…"

"Nothing new to report yet. Matt is searching the military records as a starting point." She needed to do her part—to get Miz Callie talking in hopes that more would emerge. "If there's anything else you can remember about that time, it might help."

"I've been thinking about that." She took something from the bookcase behind her. "I had a look around today, and I found this."

Georgia took the book she held out—an old leather album, its cover watermarked. She opened it carefully. The brittle pages cracked at a touch, and some of the photos had washed out so much that they were indecipherable, especially by candlelight.

"They're in a bad way, I'm afraid." Miz Callie touched a faded picture. "That's my mamma and my little sister, your Great-aunt Lizbet. Mamma and Daddy bought me that little Brownie camera for my birthday, and I was so proud of it. Never stopped taking pictures that whole summer."

"The summer Ned left?" A little shiver of excitement went through her.

Her grandmother looked surprised. "That's right, it must have been, because that's the year I got the camera, 1942. We had a crab boil on the beach, I remember, but we had to have it before sunset because of the blackout."

"Blackout?"

"Georgia Lee, don't tell me you didn't know there were blackout regulations during the war." Miz Callie shook her head at such ignorance.

Georgia flushed. "I knew. I just didn't think about it affecting your having a fire on the beach, I guess." It seemed incredibly long ago to her, but obviously not to her grandmother.

"Goodness, child, that was crucial, because of the U-boats. German submarines," she added, as if doubting Georgia would know the term.

"You mean you were actually in danger here?"

Her grandmother's gaze misted. "They sank ships along the coast from here up to Cape Cod, so I've heard. Grown-ups would stop talking about it when we came into the room. But we knew. We talked about what we'd do if the Germans landed. Your granddad was going to fight them off with his slingshot, as I recall."

Miz Callie's words made it all too real. Her skin prickled, and she rubbed her arm. "I can't imagine living through that."

"You mustn't think we were frightened all the time. Land, no. We played on the beach just like we always did—a whole crew of us kids. We just weren't allowed to roam as far as we wanted—there was a gunnery range from Station 28 all the way up to Breech's Inlet, and of course they expanded Fort Moultrie down at the other end."

She tried to picture it. "You were living right in the middle of a military installation, it sounds like. I'm surprised your folks stayed on the island."

"Pride, I guess. My daddy used to say that Hitler wasn't going to chase him out of his house." Miz Callie smiled, as if she could still hear her daddy's voice. "Folks took it personally, you know. I guess that's why the family was so upset with Ned."

"Did you know that at the time?"

Her grandmother turned a page in the album, frowning down at it. "I think maybe us kids knew something was going on, even if we didn't know what it was. We were in and out of each other's houses, and we'd hear things. I remember Ned's daddy being in an awful mood, it seemed." She pointed to a faded photo. "There we are—the whole bunch of us."

The photo was a five by seven, so it was a little easier to see than the others. Kids in swimsuits, the front row kneeling in the sand. She picked out Miz Callie and Granddad without any trouble. She put her finger on a tall figure in the second row. "Is that Ned?"

Miz Callie nodded. "Fine-looking boy, wasn't he? And there's my cousin Jessie, and the Whitcomb boys—my, I haven't thought of them in years."

This might be exactly what she needed, and there seemed no way to ask the question except to blurt it out. "Are any of them still around?"

"My sister Lizbet, down in Beaufort, you know that." She touched the young faces with her finger. "I don't know about the Whitcomb boys. They were good friends of your granddad and Ned, but they moved away to Atlanta, I think. Tommy Barton—he was Ned's pal. He got into the army that next winter, died somewhere in the South Pacific."

All those young faces, their lives encapsulated in a few brief sentences. Georgia glanced at her grandmother, another question on her lips. But she stifled it. Miz Callie had tears in her eyes, and the finger that touched the photo was trembling.

Georgia clasped her hand. "Will you let me borrow the album for a few days? Adam has a scanner, and I know he'd be glad to scan the pictures into his photo program on the computer. He can probably restore them, at least a bit. Okay?"

Miz Callie nodded, leaning back in the chair. "You do that, sugar. We'll look at them again. Maybe I'll remember somethin' useful."

"You've already helped." She rose, bending to kiss her grandmother's cheek. "We'll work it out. I promise."

Chapter 8

Matt hesitated on the dock at the Isle of Palms Marina, watching as Georgia stepped lightly onto the deck of a small boat. When he didn't immediately follow her, she looked at him, eyebrows lifting.

"Is something wrong?"

"You're sure you know how to drive this thing?" He grabbed a convenient piling, using it to steady himself as he negotiated the transfer to the boat. Falling into the water wouldn't do a thing for his confidence level.

"Positive." Her face relaxed in a grin. "Trust me, Adam wouldn't let me take his boat if he weren't sure I knew how to handle it. He taught me himself, and he was a tough taskmaster. He had me in tears more than once, but I learned."

"Adam is the brother that's in the Coast Guard, isn't

he?" He slid onto the seat, hoping he could get through this day without making a fool of himself.

"They both are." She bent over a locker and came up with two life vests, tossing him one. "But sometimes I think Adam has saltwater in his veins. It's not enough for him that his work is on the water—his play has to be, too."

She moved to the seat behind the controls, tugging her ball cap down over her forehead. With white shorts showing off her tanned legs and that well-worn Cooper River Run T-shirt, she didn't look much like the Atlanta businesswoman he'd originally thought her to be.

"Do you want me to do anything?" Assuming there was anything here he could do.

"Just sit still." Moving with easy grace, she cast off the lines. In a moment the boat pulled away from the dock.

Georgia concentrated on steering them through the maze of boats in the marina, and he concentrated on her, impressed by her competence. He just liked watching competence. This wasn't about Georgia.

Lying to yourself doesn't help, he thought. When Miz Callie had suggested he have a look at the island property, he'd quickly agreed. Then he'd discovered that her plans included having Georgia take him there by boat.

If he could have found a way out, he'd have taken it. Georgia Bodine was too disturbing to his peace of mind. Every time he thought he had a grip on who she was and how to deal with her, she showed him another aspect of herself.

And he was beginning to like all aspects of Georgia Lee Bodine.

This trip was business, he reminded himself. All he had to do was keep it on that plane, and he'd be fine.

Georgia didn't speak again until they were clear of the marina and out into the channel. Then she gave him a questioning glance. "You don't seem very comfortable on the water. I always thought there was a lot of boating in the Boston area."

Not in his neighborhood, where an open fire hydrant provided the most water he'd seen. "I never got into it, unless you count the swan boats on the Common."

"I've seen pictures of them. They look like fun."

"Not like this." He lifted his face to the breeze. "I didn't realize we had to go by boat to see your grandmother's property."

"Consider it a bonus," Georgia suggested. She pointed off to the side ahead of them. "Look. Bottlenose dolphins."

He leaned forward, watching as two sleek gray dolphins arced through the water, wearing their perpetual smiles as if they were enjoying themselves.

"It looks as if they're keeping pace with us."

"They probably are." Georgia's face glowed with pleasure. "They're very social."

Her expression moved him. She was in her element here. "You love this."

"Who wouldn't?" She gave a sigh of pure pleasure. "I never miss a chance to get out on the water."

"Then why did you leave?"

She shrugged, turning so that the bill of her cap

hid her face from him. "I went where the job was, that's all."

He had a feeling that wasn't all. But he didn't want to know, remember? He didn't need to get any closer to Georgia than he already was.

The boat slowed slightly, and she pointed again, as if showing him the sights would keep him off the subject of her personal life. "That's an osprey's nest on that post. They don't seem bothered by all the boat traffic."

"Wish I'd brought a camera. Your grandmother has Lindsay fascinated with the coastal wildlife. She's always asking questions I can't answer."

"I could take her out sometime. Or you could take her on an organized tour to Capers Island. Kids love that."

"Capers Island?" Once again, he was sounding ignorant of his new surroundings.

"It's a state heritage preserve, one of the few untouched barrier islands. What my grandmother has planned for her property is going to be similar, except that she owns just part of an island." She swung the boat in a wide semicircle. "Which we're coming up on now."

The island emerged from the water as they drew closer—a stretch of sandy beach littered with driftwood, dunes covered by wavy sea grass, then the trees: live oaks, palmettos and pines.

Georgia headed straight for it, with no dock in sight. He found he was gripping the side rail.

"Where do we dock?"

"We don't." She eased back on the throttle, so that they rocked gently toward the beach. "Actually there is a dock up one of the tidal creeks, but we usually just pull right in to the beach."

Sure enough, in a moment or two they were on the beach, shoes in hand. Georgia groped in her backpack and pulled out a bottle of insect repellent. "Better douse yourself pretty well. The bugs can be fierce out here."

Following orders, he rubbed the repellent on every inch of exposed skin and pulled his hat down on his forehead. She did the same, then put the bottle away and slung the backpack on her shoulder.

"Okay, let's go. Miz Callie says I should show you everything, so we'd best do as she says."

He fell into step beside her. "Sand, water, dunes... What else do I have to remember?"

Georgia waded into the water, bent, and came up with something in her hand. "Tell her you felt a star-fish wiggle." She put the creature onto his hand, where it tickled gently.

He couldn't help but grin.

"I remember the first time Miz Callie put one on my hand." Her smile was soft. "I wasn't much more than three. First I was scared. Then I wanted to keep it for a pet. She explained that we can enjoy all the wonderful creatures God created, but that He has put them where they should be."

The words were simple, but they touched something deep inside him. "She still follows that," he murmured, thinking of the turtles.

Georgia nodded. Taking the starfish, she stooped to put it gently back where it belonged. "Miz Callie would think this a wasted trip if all you came back with was facts about the case."

"Well, the case is important. So is my job."

He'd told himself that concentrating on work would keep him from making a foolish mistake where Georgia was concerned, but with every second, making a foolish mistake seemed more likely.

"I understand." She tilted her head back as she said the words, looking up at him.

His heart lurched, and he took an instinctive step back. He hadn't felt like that since Jennifer. He didn't want to—didn't expect to, ever feel that way again.

"Do you—does your family often come here?"

If Georgia was disappointed in his reaction, she didn't show it. She washed her hand off in the surf.

"We did all the time when we were kids. We'd come out for the day, look for turtle nests, fish and kayak. The boys would bring along lines and chicken necks to catch crabs, and we'd end with a crab boil on the beach. I always thought—" She stopped, shook her head. "I guess I thought that would go on forever. But we all grew up, got too busy with lives and careers."

He couldn't imagine a childhood that would provide memories like that. "I ought to be doing things like that with Lindsay."

"You can."

"She's shut away from me." The words came out before he could censor them. "I didn't get close enough to her before Jennifer died, and now I can't break through."

He shouldn't have said it. He didn't—couldn't—open his heart to anyone.

"You can't give up." Georgia leaned toward him, her voice passionate. "She's still adjusting to life without her mother. She'll grow to depend on you more and more. You have to believe that."

Georgia's brown eyes had filled with such caring that he was drowning in it, sinking into warmth and comfort that he hadn't known in longer than he could remember. The ice that had encapsulated his heart for so long seemed to shiver and splinter.

She reached out, and her hand touched his arm. Her touch reverberated through him, echoing in his body.

He couldn't look away from her. The water washed over their feet, warm and caressing, and the sun beat down on them, bringing out the faint freckles that dusted her cheeks.

He touched her shoulder, feeling her skin smooth and warm under his hand, and drew her closer. His heart was pounding in his ears so loudly that surely she must be able to hear it.

He shouldn't. But he was going to. His lips found hers.

For a moment she didn't respond. Then she leaned into the kiss, her hands on his arms, her face tilted to his. She tasted like salt and sunshine and the mysterious ocean, and he didn't want to let her go.

Georgia couldn't be sure who drew back first. Was it her, or was it Matt? Given the fact that she still leaned toward him, her heart thudding, she suspected she hadn't done it.

She forced herself to look into his face, half-afraid of what she might read there. He was gazing down at her, his hands still warm on her arms, an expression that mingled surprise and concern in his eyes. He must be as startled by what had happened between them as she was.

The moment stretched out, the silence growing, weighted with meaning. One of them should speak, but she felt intuitively that whatever was said now could affect their relationship for a long time to come.

"I..." She stopped, clearing her suddenly parched throat. "I didn't expect that."

Didn't she? Certainly she had been aware of the strong current between them, like the tide running high.

Had she ever felt anything like that with James? Even the thought seemed disloyal to James. She'd loved him, hadn't she? But she couldn't ignore this.

Matt raised one hand to brush a wisp of hair back from her face, his touch as gentle as the breeze. His fingers lingered for a moment against her skin.

Then his hand dropped to his side, and he took a step back, his expression suddenly guarded.

"I didn't, either." He shook his head. "I shouldn't have done that." His smile flickered faintly. "Not that I didn't enjoy it. But Lindsay——"

"It's too soon," she said quickly. "For me, too."

She tried to picture James's face, but the image was fading. He'd never been part of her life here——that was why. He represented Atlanta and the pressure cooker that had been their business routine. He had no place in island life, attuned to the rhythm of the sea.

"Right." He took a breath, running his hand through his sun-streaked hair as if trying to clear his mind. "We're agreed, then."

She nodded, trying to ignore a spasm of hurt that

he could dismiss it so readily. "We should get on with the tour."

He fell into step with her as she started down the beach. Despite what he'd said, he reached for her hand, surprising her. His fingers entwined with hers so that they were palm to palm, and every fiber of her body seemed to react to the strength of his hand.

She forced herself to concentrate. "This could be similar to Capers Island, if that's Miz Callie's idea."

"She's told me she wants it preserved in as natural a state as possible." He frowned a little. "But she wants some sort of marker as a dedication to your great-uncle."

Georgia tried not to wince. "Just ahead you can see the highest part of the island. That seems the logical site for something like that."

Matt looked where she pointed, at the gentle rise of land beyond the dunes, where the trees began. Then his gaze shifted, and he stared at the beach ahead with an awed expression. "What on earth is that?"

The disbelief in his voice made her smile. She'd forgotten how strange the sight was the first time someone came upon it.

"The boneyard—that's what the locals call it."

"I can see why." Matt approached the closest downed tree, its massive trunk bleached white and rubbed as smooth as a bone by the water and the sun. "It looks like a dinosaur graveyard."

"It does, doesn't it?" Pleased at the comparison, she grasped a branch and pulled herself up to sit on it. "I remember having dreams—nightmares, really—after the first time I came here. Cole told me some wild story about how it really was a graveyard, and naturally I believed him."

Matt seemed to be counting the numbers of downed trees that covered the stretch of beach. "But what caused this? Why did all these trees end up here? A storm?"

She shrugged. "Not necessarily. The coast is constantly changing—washing away in one place, building up in another. You just notice it more on the outermost barrier islands." She ran her hand along smooth, sun-warmed wood. "Something about the way the tide flows makes downed trees wash up here. Eerie, isn't it?"

"I'll say." He hoisted himself up next to her. "I'm beginning to see why this piece of land is such a treasure to Miz Callie."

"It's been in her family for quite a few generations." She hesitated. "You have to understand, nobody has designs on it. They'd all be happy to see her donate it to the state or turn it into a nature preserve."

"The name is the problem."

"Yes. I wish I could see a happy ending with all of this, but I can't. Just a major family row." She shivered a little, in spite of the heat of the sun.

His hand, planted on the trunk, brushed hers lightly. "That really upsets you." It was a statement, not a question.

She tried to smile. "I hate battles. I've never been good at confronting people. The thought makes me want to hide under the bed."

He was silent for a moment.

"Is that what went wrong with your engagement?" he finally asked.

She couldn't possibly take offense at the question, not when his voice was filled with such caring.

"Maybe that was part of it." Would it have made a difference if she had been angry instead of hurt, if she'd lashed out at James instead of running away?

She hesitated, Matt's question echoing in her heart. She'd thought she didn't want to talk about it, but the urge to tell him was strong.

"If I'm out of line…"

She shook her head. "It's all right." She tried to smile. "I'm afraid it's a pretty clichéd story, though."

"Another woman?"

"James wasn't tempted by other women. What drove him was being successful." Even as she said it, she knew how true that was. Why hadn't she seen it sooner—before she was engaged, for instance?

"Plenty of people want to be successful." Matt said the words mildly enough, but she could hear an edge under them, as if she'd criticized him.

She stared down at her feet, bare and sandy, dangling from the branch. "That's true. I just don't think that excuses claiming someone else's work as your own."

His fingers brushed the back of her hand. "Yours?"

She nodded, not wanting to look at him. "Maybe it wasn't as big a deal as I thought. Maybe I made too much of it. But when I realized what he'd done—well, I just couldn't look at him the same way again. And then, when something went wrong with his project, he laid the blame on me. Which accounts for my current jobless state."

"I didn't realize. What did he say when you confronted him?"

She swallowed. "I didn't. I couldn't." She shot a sideways glance at him. "I told you I wasn't any good at confrontation."

The corner of his mouth twitched. "You didn't seem to have any trouble confronting me."

Georgia laughed. "That was different. I thought you were trying to cheat my grandmother."

"And you'd do anything for her."

"Of course." She might doubt herself in other ways, but she never doubted her commitment to Miz Callie.

His arm came around her shoulders, holding her close, warm and strong. Comforting.

The words came out on an impulse. "You aren't the person I thought you were."

His smile reached his eyes, lighting them. "Neither are you, Georgia Lee. Neither are you."

Chapter 9

She was like one of the ghost crabs, Georgia decided several days later. Running to duck into a hole in the sand at the slightest sign of any disturbance in her world.

She stood at the sliding glass door, looking out at waves foaming gently on the shore. Miz Callie sat in her beach chair, her battered straw hat perched on her head. As a concession to the growing heat, her striped beach umbrella was tilted at an angle to block the sun. Lindsay, a few yards away, was intent on her sand castle.

Georgia shoved the door open and stepped outside. Her own thoughts weren't particularly good company. She'd join them and talk about something—anything—else.

She trotted down the steps, grabbed a beach chair from underneath the deck and walked down to them.

Miz Callie looked up with a welcoming smile. "Glad you decided to come out."

Georgia sank into the chair, tilting her face toward the breeze. "I feel as if I ought to be doing something more useful than sitting here."

"Nonsense. You need a little rest." Miz Callie shot her a shrewd glance. "Any chance you're ready now to tell me what happened when you and Matt went to the island?"

"I... I don't know what you mean." She'd always thought her grandmother could read her thoughts, and this just proved it. "I told you what we did."

"Sugar, taking a tour of the property isn't enough to make you as distracted as you've been ever since you got back. If you don't want to tell me, you can always say I should mind my own business."

"I would never say that." And she didn't want to. She valued her grandmother's solid wisdom too much for that. "I told Matt about what happened with James."

"I thought you might."

"Well, I didn't. I didn't expect to tell him. I hardly know him."

But she had, and his reaction had surprised her. She could still feel the warm, comforting weight of his arm around her shoulders.

"At a guess, I'd say he understood."

"Yes." He'd understood—or at least he hadn't blamed her for feeling she couldn't go on with James once she realized his true character.

"He's a good man," Miz Callie said. "In spite of being from up north. A little too private, but he has integrity."

The way Miz Callie said it left no doubt that she valued that quality highly.

Georgia stared at a shrimp boat making its way slowly parallel to the shore, its nets down. "I thought maybe he'd feel I should have been glad to further James's career. That's what Mamma said. It's James's career that's important. He was trying to get ahead for my sake. Wasn't I willing to sacrifice for him?"

The words came out in a rush, and she hadn't realized until this moment how much they'd rankled, like a splinter she couldn't get out.

"Maybe she's right. Maybe I didn't love him enough to sacrifice for him."

"Don't be foolish, child." Miz Callie's voice was as tart as it ever got. "If he'd come to you, asked you to help him, of course you'd have done it, wouldn't you?"

She nodded. Of course she would. "That wasn't James's way. He didn't ask. He took."

"Not a good quality in a husband, I'd say. And if your mamma had thought it through, she'd say the same. Goodness, she wouldn't want someone like that in the family."

Wouldn't she? Georgia wasn't so sure of that, but she felt stronger knowing that Miz Callie understood.

Lindsay came running up to them and flopped down on a towel at Miz Callie's feet. "Hot." She pushed damp hair back from her forehead.

"You need to spend a little time in the shade, sugar." Miz Callie handed her a water bottle. "Goodness, what was I thinkin', letting you stay out in the heat this long?"

Lindsay leaned against her knee. "Tell me a story, please? About when you were a little girl on the island."

Georgia's attention sharpened. That was what she wanted to hear, too, but they had different reasons.

Miz Callie smiled, her eyes seeming to focus on the past. "When I was a little girl, the island was so different, you couldn't imagine." The smile faded a little. "That was a long time ago, back in the 1940s. We were at war then." She touched Lindsay's hair lightly. "I pray you never have to experience that."

"I know about that. I have a doll that my Grammy gave me, with a book about living then."

"It was hard all over. Here, the military took over a lot of the island. Why, there were folks in uniform everywhere you looked, and big guns along the shore in places."

Lindsay's eyes grew wide. "What were the guns for?"

"Folks said the enemy might bring their submarines in real close." Miz Callie caught herself, probably thinking that might not be a suitable story for a child. "Anyway, it was exciting for us kids. We played just like we always had, except for our parents being more particular about us getting in early."

"I don't like to go in while it's still light out," Lindsay observed. "Except Daddy lets me watch television."

"We didn't have television then, you know. We had the radio, and sometimes we'd listen to that." She shook her head. "Funny. I s'pose the parents listened to the news, but all I remember hearing is the music. 'Tangerine,' played by the Jimmy Dorsey band. That was one we listened to over and over."

Miz Callie's memory of those days seemed to be getting clearer and clearer.

"Did you go swimming in the ocean?" Lindsay prompted, apparently not interested in long-ago radio programs.

"We went swimming, sure thing. And crabbing. We loved to go crabbing. One of the older boys would take us." A faint shadow crossed her face, and Georgia knew she was thinking of Ned. "We'd bring back a mess of crabs and then have a crab boil, right here on the beach."

"That sounds so fun." Lindsay's tone was wistful. "I wish I could do that."

"Maybe you will." Miz Callie leaned back in the chair, her eyes closing.

For an instant she looked her age, and Georgia's heart hurt. Did Miz Callie want to share her memories because she feared one day soon she wouldn't be able to?

"Maybe you ought to go in and take a rest." Georgia made the suggestion tentatively, knowing how little Miz Callie liked being told what to do. "It is awful hot today."

Her grandmother planted her hands on the arms of her chair. "I haven't checked the nest yet. I have to make sure those visitors haven't been back, fooling with it again."

"I'll do that." She rose as her grandmother did, touching her arm. "Lindsay and I will do that for you, won't we, Lindsay?"

The child scrambled to her feet. "Sure we will, Miz Callie. We'll take care of it."

Miz Callie split a smile between the two of them. "Well, then, I guess I can't say no. Y'all come in and have some nice cold lemonade when you get back, y'heah?"

She'd suggest Miz Callie lie down for a while, but that wouldn't be well received. "Yes, ma'am. And I'll bring the chairs and umbrella when I come, so just leave them."

To her surprise, that didn't lead to an argument. Her grandmother nodded and walked slowly toward the house.

Lindsay watched her as intently as Georgia. "Is Miz Callie sick?" Anxiety filled her voice.

The poor child—she'd had enough losses.

"I'm sure she'll be fine once she gets inside where it's cool. Ready to check the nest?"

Lindsay slipped her feet into the sandals she'd discarded while building her castle. "I'm ready."

They walked down the beach together. It was easy enough to spare Miz Callie by checking the nest. Not so easy to resolve the bigger burden that weighed on her. So far they'd come up with exactly nothing to explain why Ned had left or what had happened to him afterward.

"A lot of people Miz Callie knows died, didn't they?"

The child's voice was so solemn that for an instant Georgia wondered if she was talking about Ned. But no, they hadn't discussed that in front of her.

"I guess so." Since she didn't know what prompted the question, she'd better be cautious in her answer. "Miz Callie's lived a long time. She'd say that it's natural that some folks she loved would go ahead of her to Heaven."

"But it makes her sad. And mad sometimes, too."

Lindsay's face wore an expression of utmost concentration. They were no longer talking about Miz Callie. They were talking about Lindsay and her losses.

"I'm sure it makes her feel sad and angry sometimes," she said carefully. "But she knows they're safe with Jesus, and she knows she'll see them again someday."

"That's what my grammy says about my mommy." Lindsay's lips pressed together, as if to hold something back.

"Does that make you angry?" She ventured a question, knowing she was out of her depth.

"No." Lindsay snapped the word, her face assuming a stoic facade.

Like the one Matthew wore at times. Somehow she didn't think stoicism was working well for either of them.

Dear Lord, show me what to say to this child. She's hurting more than I imagined, and I haven't the faintest idea how to help her.

And she didn't have the right to help her, either— it felt like she was interfering. But did that matter, if Lindsay turned to her?

"Lindsay…"

Before she could find any words, Lindsay darted across the sand. "There's the nest," she cried.

Georgia followed, half relieved, half sorry that Lindsay wasn't going to open up to her after all.

"Everything looks okay." Georgia tightened the tape

on one of the sticks. "I don't think anybody has bothered it."

"Have to make sure." Lindsay made a circle around
the nest, touching each stick with her fingers.

Georgia's heart clenched. It reminded her of that
first day, when she'd watched the child lining up the
seashells just so.

Her circuit done, Lindsay sat down where Miz Callie always sat when she visited the nest. With another
silent prayer for guidance, Georgia sat down next to
her.

Lindsay stared at the nest. "We have to take care of
the baby turtles." Her face was solemn. "They don't
have anyone else."

Please, Lord, her heart murmured. "The mamma
turtle put the eggs in a safe place. Unless someone
comes along and bothers it—"

"She went away!" The words burst out of Lindsay.
"Their mother just went away and left them."

Her heart seemed to be lodged in her throat. "That's
in the nature of sea turtles," she said slowly, carefully.
"The mamma turtles travel a very long way to lay their
eggs on the same beach every year. That's what their
instinct tells them to do."

She dared a look at Lindsay, praying she was taking
the right tack with her. The child sat with her knees
pulled up, arms wrapped around them. Her head was
bent, her hair falling forward to expose the nape of
her neck.

The sight of that pale, fragile column did funny
things to Georgia. The urge to protect stormed through
her, taking her breath away with its strength.

She's not my responsibility. Instinct, compelling as the instinct that drove the turtles, countered that feeble claim. Lindsay had come to her—why, she didn't know. She had to find a way to help her.

"People aren't turtles." Lindsay whispered the words. "They're not s'posed to leave their children."

She touched the curve of the child's back. "No, people aren't meant to be like that. Mammas want to protect and help their children grow." She took a deep breath. "But sometimes they can't, no matter how much they might want to."

"I didn't want my mom to die." There was still that trace of anger in the words.

"Of course you didn't, sugar." The touch turned into a caress. To her surprise, Lindsay didn't pull away. "You know, it's natural to feel angry with your mamma for dying, even though you know it wasn't her fault."

Silence for a moment. "That's what Dr. Annie said."

"Dr. Annie sounds like a wise woman." Obviously Matt had tried to get professional help for his daughter.

"I guess." Her mouth clamped shut on the words. The shield came down over her expression again. It was as if the tide were carrying her away, and Georgia couldn't reach her now, no matter how she tried.

"Lindsay…"

This time the child did pull away from her touch, but she had to keep trying, even if it did no good.

"Lindsay, you should talk to your daddy about how you're feeling. He'd understand, really he would."

She shook her head, her face stoic. "I can't. He'd get upset. I can't." She jumped to her feet. "I have to go."

"Wait." But it was too late. Lindsay was already running down the beach.

Running to find a hole to hide in. She understood the feeling. It was what she did, all too often. She couldn't, not now. If she were going to help Lindsay, to say nothing of Miz Callie, she'd have to stop hiding and start speaking her mind.

Georgia hadn't imagined, when she'd mentioned going to see Miz Callie's sister in Beaufort, that Matt would have the slightest interest in joining her. She'd been wrong.

At the moment he was frowning as he negotiated the heavy traffic along the strip development on the other side of the Ashley River.

"You really didn't have to come today. I could have talked to my great-aunt on my own."

He shot her a glance, his eyes unreadable behind his sunglasses. "Didn't want me butting in on it?"

"It's not that." He smiled, and she realized he'd been teasing her. She was unaccountably flustered today.

Well, maybe not unaccountably.

She ought to be honest with herself, at least. She'd been aware of Matt's magnetism since the moment they met, when she'd still considered him the enemy. Then, that day they'd played with Lindsay in the surf, she'd felt the pull of attraction between them, strong as the ebb tide.

She'd been able to handle that. But once they'd kissed...

She could still handle it, she assured herself hurriedly. Neither of them was ready for anything serious now, and both of them realized it. That should be protection enough.

"It wasn't a problem to come with you. Lindsay is happy with the sitter your grandmother recommended. I just feel I haven't done enough for Miz Callie," Matt said. "Not nearly enough."

There was an undercurrent in his voice that she didn't entirely understand.

"You've set the wheels in motion for turning the land into a preserve, just as she wants."

He shrugged, hands moving a little restlessly on the steering wheel. "That, sure. Any lawyer could do that for her. What she really wants is to find out what happened to Ned. That's where I've let her down."

His concern touched her. He really did care about her grandmother as more than just a client.

"I can't say I've done any better. It's felt fairly hopeless from the beginning."

He nodded. They'd passed the last of the development now, and the road stretched ahead, bordered only by tall pines and live oaks with their swags of Spanish moss.

"You know..." He hesitated. "We haven't really talked about how to handle it if Miz Callie is wrong. If everyone else believes that Ned was a coward who ran away rather than fight..." He shrugged. "There has to be some basis for that belief."

"Miz Callie believes in Ned."

"And you?"

"Let's say I'm trying to have faith that she's right."

He gave her a half smile that did funny things to her

heart. "I've heard it said that faith is believing when common sense tells you not to."

"'The substance of things hoped for,'" she quoted softly. "I guess I'm praying that, as well."

The silence stretched between them for a moment. It would have been natural for him to reply in kind, but he hadn't. Because he didn't believe?

Surely it wasn't that. He sent Lindsay to Bible school, and Miz Callie said he'd come to church with her several times.

"Those war years seem far away to me," he said in what Georgia thought was a deliberate attempt to change the subject. "I've done some reading since Miz Callie got me involved. None of my school history courses ever got as far as World War II."

"I know what you mean." If he needed to shy away from the subject of faith, she had to respect that. "We'd make it to the Roaring Twenties if we were lucky, and then school would be out and the next year we'd start with Columbus again. Most of my ideas about the war come from old movies."

He nodded, frowning at a motorcyclist who had just swung widely around them. For an instant she saw him as one of those gallant heroes off to fight. A hint of something tough and ready for battle under Matt's civilized exterior made him fit the part.

Who was he, really, under that facade he wore so well? She'd had glimpses from time to time, but all they served to do was whet her curiosity.

He'd come through adversity—she could see that in the lines around his eyes and the wary expression he wore so often.

At first she'd thought that was the effect of his wife's death, but she'd begun to believe it ran deeper. She'd never know, unless he let her. The massive control he exerted kept his feelings well hidden.

His daughter was trying to emulate his control, and it wasn't working for her.

Georgia's heart twisted. Poor child. Had anything she'd said to Lindsay helped at all? She doubted it.

Matt was the only one who could help. Someone had to talk to him about it.

Not me. Please, Father. I wouldn't be any good at it.

That selfish prayer got just the answer it deserved. She knew what she had to do. Had known since those moments with Lindsay at the turtle nest.

She fought to quell the nervous tremor that came from deep inside her. If she had to be the one to bring it up, she would, but after they'd talked to her great-aunt, not before. One difficult conversation at a time was plenty.

When the landmarks began to appear, she leaned forward. "Have you been to Beaufort yet?"

"Afraid not. I've been too busy with work to take any side trips."

"You're in for a treat, then. Great-aunt Lizbet claims it's the most beautiful town on the coast, and there are plenty who'd agree with her. Not a Charlestonian, of course."

"Of course," he said with mock seriousness and a hint of a smile. "I've already noticed how humble Charlestonians are about their city."

"It's yours, too, now."

He didn't say anything for a moment, then shrugged. "I guess adoption may take a few generations."

The busy outskirts of Beaufort gave way suddenly to the gracious old town with its antebellum houses and hundred-year-old live oaks.

"We turn left at the next light." Maybe a warning was in order. "Miz Callie and her sister aren't much alike. And Lizbet is a couple of years younger, so I'm not sure we can expect her to remember much. She might not have known the same people."

He negotiated the turn. "At this point, any lead is a good one."

She tried to hang on to that thought as they pulled to the side of the road in front of her great-aunt's house. Graceful old trees arched over the street adding an air of serenity.

Matt walked around the car to join her at the gate. "I feel as if we've stepped back a couple of centuries."

"Me, too. Progress passed Beaufort by, and I think the town is the better for it."

She started to open the gate, but Matt reached around her to do it, his arm brushing hers. A wave of warmth swept over her skin at the simple touch. He smiled down at her.

She took a breath. She'd better put on a little armor—Aunt Lizbet had an unquenchable urge to spot romance in the most unlikely duos. Georgia preceded Matt up the walk, trying not to notice his protective hand on her elbow as she negotiated the uneven flag-stone walk.

"Aunt Lizbet better get those stones fixed before one of her cronies takes a tumble on them." Trying to ignore the slightly breathless sound of her voice, she went up the four steps to the wide, gracious porch. She had to be careful, very careful. And not just because of the uneven walk.

Chapter 10

The door was flung open, and Aunt Lizbet threw her arms around Georgia in an exuberant hug. "Here you are at last, Georgia Lee! Goodness, it's about time you're coming to see me. I'd begun to think I'd have to trek way up to the island if I wanted a glimpse of you."

"You ought to come, even if not to see me. I know Miz Callie would love that."

She looked affectionately at her great-aunt. Callie and her sister had a strong family resemblance, but they couldn't be more different in personality. Callie was most at home in cut-offs, sandals and a floppy beach hat, while Lizbet made seasonal trips to Atlanta to replenish an already extensive wardrobe. And while Callie was walking on the beach looking for her beloved turtles, her sister spent her days in a round of social activities that would exhaust a woman half her age.

"You're looking wonderful, Aunt Lizbet." The compliment was true. She was perfection from the delicate blush on her cheeks to the soles of her Italian leather pumps. "You didn't need to dress up for us."

"Oh, darlin', not that I wouldn't have, but you know, my garden club is coming for a meeting in an hour." She turned toward Matt. "And who's this? Have you replaced that fiancé of yours already?"

Her own cheeks were suddenly pinker than anything Aunt Lizbet's blush could achieve. "This is Matthew Harper. He's taking care of some legal work for Miz Callie. Matt, this is my great-aunt, Elizabeth Dayton."

Aunt Lizbet extended her hand as if she expected it to be kissed. Matt shook hands with a faint twinkle of amusement in his eyes.

"Mrs. Dayton, it's a pleasure. Thank you for inviting us to your home."

"Well, now, the pleasure is all mine, especially when Georgia brings such a handsome young man." She batted her eyelashes in her most extravagant manner, knowing perfectly well she was being outrageous. If Matt hadn't figured out by now that her family tree was filled with eccentrics, he was a lot slower than she'd given him credit for being.

"Behave yourself, Auntie." Georgia put her arm around her great-aunt's waist. "If your garden club is coming in an hour, we don't have time to waste on flirting."

"Flirting is never a waste, darlin'." Aunt Lizbet patted her cheek and swept another glance over Matt. "Next you'll be telling me that I'm too old for him."

"I'm afraid I might be too old for you, Miz Dayton,"

Matt said smoothly. Georgia was enjoying this gallant Matt—he was full of surprises.

Clearly flattered, her great-aunt led the way into her parlor. "Georgia, sugar, you need to snap this one up right away."

If she got any redder, she might just go up in flames. "I just broke my engagement. I'm not—"

"Oh, poof, what's a little broken engagement? Why, a girl has to have a few discarded sweethearts in her wake, or how's she going to know she's got the right one?"

"You stop playing Scarlett O'Hara for a minute and sit down." She tried her best to frown at her great-aunt, but it was impossible. It would be like frowning at the frilly, unlikely angel on top of the Christmas tree. "We've got to get our business taken care of before your ladies descend upon us."

Matt took the seat her great-aunt indicated, looking slightly appalled at the thought of a whole garden club full of Scarlett O'Haras, and Georgia sat next to her on the rose velvet loveseat. It was hard to concentrate seriously on anything in Aunt Lizbet's parlor, decorated as it was in the very height of Victorian whimsy by some earlier generation of Daytons, and accented by her great-aunt with Dresden shepherdesses and lacy pillows.

"Miz Callie has asked Matt to try and find out what happened to Uncle Ned—my granddad's brother, that is…"

"I know who your uncle Ned was, child, even though he's not related to me, exactly." She tipped her head to one side. "Let's see, he'd be my sister's brother-in-law, so that would make him—"

"We hoped you might remember him," Matt interrupted.

Good, Georgia thought. Let her embark on family connections, and they'd never get anywhere. "We'd like to find out what happened to him after he left Sullivan's Island in 1942."

Aunt Lizbet turned to him with a flattering smile. "Oh, goodness, so long ago. You might not realize it, but I'm quite a bit younger than Callie. Why, I was hardly more than a baby at the time."

Georgia bit her lip to keep herself from pointing out that, according to the family tree, there were only eighteen months between them.

"Of course I understand that," Matt said, his tone soothing. "But sometimes very young children do remember the oddest things. We're especially interested in anything that happened that summer involving Ned."

Her aunt's gaze strayed to the drop-leaf table, already arrayed with a silver bowl of roses and her heavy silver tea service. "I just don't believe I can help."

"That's all right," Georgia said briskly. "I told Matt that you wouldn't have nearly the memory that Miz Callie does, but he insisted we come and see you anyway."

If Matt was surprised, he managed to hide it.

"Callie, indeed!" Aunt Lizbet's indignation peaked. "I remember things twice as well as she does. Anybody who knows us will tell you that I always had the better memory. I won the county spelling bee three years in a row."

"That's a wonderful accomplishment." Matt leaned forward, capturing one of Aunt Lizbet's hands in his own. "I can see we should have come to you right off. Won't you tell us about Ned?"

"Well…" For a moment, she seemed to be at a loss, but then her eyes brightened. "I can tell you something nobody else knows, not even Callie. It was a secret, and I kept it all these years."

Georgia's pulse quickened. A secret? Were they really going to learn something helpful? She opened her mouth and closed it again at a commanding glance from Matt.

Well, all right, if he thought he could get more out of her great-aunt than she could, let him try. Although come to think of it, Aunt Lizbet was far more likely to respond to a handsome man any day of the week.

"It was a rainy evenin', I remember." Aunt Lizbet's hand rested in Matt's. "The others were all inside, listening to the radio, but I went out on the beach."

"By yourself?" Matt prompted.

She nodded. "Mamma wouldn't have let me if I'd asked, so I didn't ask. It wasn't curfew yet, just dark because of the rain. I'd left my pail full of shells where we'd been playing, and I wanted to get it before the tide came in."

There was something soothing and timeless about that, something in common between those children who'd played on the beach in the midst of a war and the ones who played on it today.

"I got the bucket and then stopped there on the dunes for a minute, just looking at the water. Then

I saw her." She stopped, as if the image was one she didn't want to see.

"Who was it?" Matt asked softly.

She shook her head. "I don't know. One of the summer people. She'd waded way out in the water with her clothes on. Imagine. She even had a hat on her head, and there she was. All of a sudden a wave knocked her down." Her face puckered in imitation of long-ago distress. "Before I could think what to do, Ned Bodine came running past me. Straight into the water, with his clothes on, too, and swimming out toward her." She smiled, seeming to recall herself to the present. "Funny how that picture is still so fresh in my mind. Ned was always the best swimmer of all the kids."

"He pulled her out?"

"Land, yes. It didn't take him any time at all. Then he brought her up the path, and he saw me and stopped. He patted my cheek, and he said I should go home. And not to tell anyone, because the lady would be embarrassed. It was our secret."

"And you kept it."

She fluttered a little. "Well, truth to tell, I probably forgot about it pretty quick, but there it was, stored in my mind, ready to fall out the minute you asked."

"I'm glad you remembered."

"That's fine, darlin'. I don't suppose it helps you know what happened to Ned, but it's good you know that story." She rose with one of her sudden movements. "Look at the time. I'll get y'all some sweet tea, and then I'm going to have to shoo you out before my ladies get here."

"You don't have to—" Matt began, but she was already gone. He turned to Georgia. "What did you think of that?"

"I think she was telling the exact truth, the way a child would remember something," she said, feeling a little deflated. "But I'm afraid it doesn't get us anywhere."

"I don't agree."

Matt leaned toward her, much as he had leaned toward Aunt Lizbet, and took her hand in his. She hoped her great-aunt hadn't had the breathless reaction that she was having.

"What do you think we found out?" She kept her voice even with an effort.

"We learned something valuable about Ned Bodine," he said. "Whatever he did, and whatever else he was, he certainly wasn't a coward."

"You were right about the restaurant." Matt scrawled his signature on the credit-card receipt and glanced across the table at Georgia, enjoying the sight of her more than he wanted to. "The shrimp burger was amazing."

"I'm glad you liked it. Sorry it was so crowded."

The crowd had kept him from pursuing the topic on both their minds, but maybe that was just as well.

When he'd suggested lunch before they headed back to Charleston, Georgia had directed him to Bay Street, lined with shops, restaurants and elegant old buildings. He'd followed her down a walkway between two buildings and into one of the smallest restaurants he'd ever seen. It offered windows looking out onto the water and food that was well worth the crush.

He touched Georgia's elbow as she rose and nodded toward the back door that opened onto the waterfront park. "Let's stretch our legs before we get back in the car."

For a moment he thought she'd refuse. Then she nodded.

Warm, moist air settled on them the instant they stepped outside, mitigated a little by the breeze off the water. He stole a glance at Georgia's face as they started down the walk toward the low wall that bordered the sound.

She'd seemed tense underneath the surface conversation over lunch. He couldn't think of anything to account for that. The story from her great-aunt, and the conclusion he'd drawn from it, surely hadn't upset her.

They reached the path that ran along the water and turned wordlessly to walk along it. Ahead of them, a father with two young children was attempting to get a kite in the air. Several women, perhaps workers from the shops along the street, sat with sack lunches on park benches, talking, and a pair of intent joggers passed them, earphones blocking out the world.

Did Georgia realize how quiet she was being? Had she been upset by her great-aunt's obvious matchmaking? It was so good-humored, so much a part of the Southern-belle persona she'd put on, that no one could take it seriously.

From the street above them, he could hear the voice of a tour guide perched on the high seat of a horse-drawn carriage. She must have said something amusing, because her carriage of tourists laughed.

He glanced again at Georgia's intent face. They

understood each other, didn't they? Understood the attraction they both felt, but recognized that it couldn't go any deeper for either of them?

Still, that didn't mean he couldn't enjoy being with her, watching the way her hair curled rebelliously against her neck, listening to the soft cadences of her voice.

Except that at the moment, she wasn't talking.

"I can understand why your great-aunt loves this place. It really is beautiful," he ventured.

Roused from her abstraction, she smiled. "If she hadn't been so busy playing the Southern belle today, she'd have given you the history of Beaufort in one intensive lecture. Including how many films have been shot here."

"Really?" He wouldn't have pictured the sleepy place as a southern Hollywood.

"Oh, yes." Her smile widened. "Cole and I ditched school one day when they were making a movie, and he drove us down here. We were sure we were going to have a personal encounter with a star."

"Did you?"

"The closest we came was a glimpse of a motor home that might have belonged to the film company. And a three-week grounding for Cole when we got home."

"Not you?" He liked the affection on her face when she talked about her brothers.

"I only got two, because Cole was older. He was supposed to be more responsible." She paused, watching a sparkling white sailboat move soundlessly past them.

"Cole—that's the brother next to you in age, isn't it?"

She nodded. "He's a jet pilot." Something, some faint shadow, crossed her eyes.

"Dangerous work," he guessed.

"Not as bad as when he was a rescue swimmer, dropping from the chopper into the water. Mamma spent so much time worrying about him that she said she was going to need a face-lift by the time he decided to make the change."

"I take it Cole's a bit of a daredevil."

"Always trying to keep up with Adam."

"And you tried to keep up with both of them, I suppose." A bench swing was mounted facing the water, and he touched her arm to lead her to it, adding the feel of her skin to the list of things he enjoyed about being with her.

She leaned back, tilting her face to the sun. "If my mamma didn't want a tomboy, she shouldn't have had the two boys first." As if she realized she'd betrayed something, she pointed out across the water. "That's Lady's Island. Beyond it is St. Helena's. You ought to drive out there one day. At the very end is Hunting Island State Park. You can stand at the lighthouse and look out at the ocean where streets and houses used to be."

"Another moving barrier island?"

She nodded. "I'm probably telling you things you already know, since you grew up in Boston."

"Not much maritime lore in my part of the city," he said shortly.

"No?" Her eyes widened a little.

He was about to turn the subject away, as he always

did. He'd had plenty of practice in avoiding the subject of his childhood.

But somehow, despite his best efforts, he and Georgia had become close. And he couldn't put her off with something that wasn't a lie but wasn't quite the truth, either.

"I don't know what you're imagining," he said slowly. "But just because I went to law school with Rod doesn't mean I grew up in a home like his."

She half turned toward him, her arm brushing his. "I don't know that I was imagining anything. You've learned a good bit about my people since we met, but I don't know anything about yours."

"I don't have people, not in the sense you mean."

Her eyes grew troubled. "But you had parents…"

"My father disappeared before I was born." Better to get it out bluntly if he was going to tell her. "My mother was an alcoholic who gave up trying to get her life together before I was out of diapers."

"I'm sorry." Her face held compassion, not the shock he was expecting. "How hard that must have been for you."

He shrugged. "If you haven't experienced anything else, you don't know what you're missing."

She rested her hand on his arm, and her empathy flowed through the contact. "You must have known, or you wouldn't have had the drive to become what you are."

"Maybe."

He didn't like to look back at who he'd been then—liked it even less since he'd become a parent himself. It was painful to imagine Lindsay living the way he had—always afraid, always yearning for something he couldn't even imagine.

"Someone helped you." She said it as if she knew. "Someone gave you a goal to strive for."

He nodded. "Several someones, I guess. The pastor at a shelter we stayed in. A teacher who cared. A businessman who thought he should pay back what he'd received by helping someone else."

"God sent them into your life." Her voice was so soft, so gentle, that it flowed over him in a wave of comfort.

"I guess. I mean, yes." For just an instant his mind clouded. He believed that, didn't he? Since Jennifer died, he'd lost sight of what he believed.

"But you became who you are by your own efforts, too. That shows a lot of character."

He shrugged, not eager to prolong the subject. "I was lucky."

It was too hard to believe that he'd inherited any degree of character from either of his parents.

"Attribute it to luck if you want to, but that's not going to stop me from admiring what you've accomplished." Her voice was firm. "I'm glad you told me."

He still remembered how he'd felt when he'd told Jennifer—he'd been so sure she'd back politely away from their relationship. She hadn't, and her love had made him feel as if he could conquer anything that stood in the way of their happiness.

He'd been wrong.

Seeming to recognize that he'd said all he intended to, Georgia leaned back on the swing.

"Maybe this isn't the right time, but there's something I've been wanting to talk to you about."

He tried to clear his mind of the lingering cobwebs of the past. "Now's as good a time as any. What is it? Something about your grandmother?"

She took a breath, and he realized she was trying to compose herself. This was what had caused her abstraction, then.

His hand brushed hers. "Just tell me, whatever it is."

She looked down so that her hair fell forward, brushing her cheek. "The other day Lindsay and I went to check out the turtle nest together."

At the sound of his daughter's name, everything inside him tensed. "What happened?"

"Nothing happened, exactly." She looked up at him, velvet-brown eyes earnest. "Please understand, I wouldn't ordinarily repeat a conversation with a child. But I think—"

"If it has to do with my daughter, I need to hear it." He chopped off the words, willing her to come out with it.

"She expressed a lot of angry feelings about the mother turtles leaving their babies to fend for themselves. It seemed to me she was talking about her mother's death."

"Did she say that?" She was right. He knew she was right, but he didn't want to admit it, because that meant admitting he hadn't solved this for his child.

Pity filled Georgia's face. "She did. I think she understands that her mamma didn't choose what happened to her, but still—"

"What did you say to her?"

Georgia stiffened, pulling away from him a little. "I didn't pry into her feelings, if that's what you're imagining. It just came out."

He didn't have the right to be mad at Georgia because his daughter had gone to her, not to him. He forced down the anger that threatened to overpower him.

"Sorry. I didn't mean it that way." He shook his head, as if he could clear it. "She saw a counselor before we moved here. I hoped things were getting better."

"I'm sure they are." Her face warmed, and she leaned toward him, eagerness to help evident in every movement. "I said she should talk to you, but she didn't seem to feel she could. Maybe if you were to share your feelings, she'd think—"

"No." He shot off the seat, leaving it swinging. "Just leave it alone, Georgia. You don't understand."

"Of course." She said the words quietly, but he knew they hid a world of pain. "You have to decide what's best for your daughter." She rose, not looking at him.

He wanted to say something that would wipe the hurt from her eyes. But he couldn't.

He couldn't, because what she suggested was impossible. He'd do anything for his daughter's happiness, anything but open up and expose his own pain, because if he did, the ferocity of it might shatter them both forever.

Chapter 11

Matt was right—Georgia didn't understand. She watched the countryside roll past as they drove back toward the island. One moment they were closer than they'd ever been, and the next the doors had slammed shut with a resounding crash.

She'd ventured her opinion on Lindsay. Matt considered his daughter's emotional health out of bounds.

A faint annoyance hovered. Did he really think that she and Miz Callie could spend as much time as they did with Lindsay and not grow to care for her? Maybe she didn't have much experience with children, but she did know what it was like to feel desperate for someone to understand her. That was what Lindsay needed right now, and that someone should be her father.

And if he couldn't or wouldn't? She ventured a

glance at Matt. She knew him well enough now to recognize what a stranger wouldn't—that extra tension in his jaw, the shutters drawn over his expression. He was blocking her out, and her heart ached.

She could try to be the friend that Lindsay needed, but she'd have to tread carefully. Matt could probably be ruthless where protecting his child was concerned, even if he was wrong about what she needed.

They made the turn at Gardens Corners, and he cleared his throat slightly. "How do you think your grandmother will react to her sister's story?"

Apparently they were talking again, now that he'd warned her off.

"She'll probably feel as you do—that it proves Ned wasn't a coward."

"And you don't agree?" He shot her a glance, frowning.

"It proves he had courage, but diving into the waves to rescue someone in trouble would be almost second nature to a person who'd spent his life on the water."

"He'd know the dangers better than anyone."

"True." She spread her hands, palms up. "Okay, he was brave. That doesn't cover all the reasons why he might have run away. Maybe he was opposed to the war."

"I'd expect we'd have heard about that from someone. Your grandmother didn't imply anything like that."

"Miz Callie was a child. She might not have known."

Matt drummed his fingers on the steering wheel. "What we really need is someone who was Ned's contemporary."

She nodded. Absorbed in discussing the problem, she was almost able to forget how Matt had shut her out. Almost. Still, she could set it aside to deal with the immediate issue.

If one could call something that happened more than sixty years ago "immediate."

"I took some of Miz Callie's old photographs to Adam. They'd faded so much that they were practically invisible, but he thought he could bring them up with his photo program. If so, it might prompt her memories about who was around that summer."

"Good idea." He passed a slow-moving truck with concentrated care. "Give me names, and I'll find out what happened to them. They can't all have vanished."

Frustration filled his voice. Matt was a man who set goals and met them, and he didn't tolerate failure readily, in himself and probably not in others.

"It's not your fault. You can't find what's not there."

"He certainly seemed determined to vanish. You'd think he'd have cared about the people he left behind."

"I've been thinking about that, too. Miz Callie describes someone who was kind, attentive to the younger kids in a way that a teenager often isn't."

He darted a glance at her, his mouth quirking in a faint smile. "Speaking from personal experience?"

"Well…" She considered. "My brothers were protective of me, I guess. They wouldn't let anybody else pick on me, but that didn't prevent them from doing it. And there were plenty of times when having me around was the last thing they wanted. You know how siblings are."

The moment the words were out, she wanted them

back. The childhood Matt had described hadn't included siblings.

"No, I don't," he said, voice dry.

"I'm sorry. I didn't think."

He shrugged. "It doesn't matter. Anyway, let's see what Miz Callie thinks."

Biting her tongue wasn't going to help. "I'll try to get her talking about that, but again, it's the memory of a young child."

He nodded, frowning as the thickening traffic brought him to halt. "Let's hope your brother comes up with something from the photographs, then. That seems to be our best hope at the moment." He glanced across at her, something questioning in his gaze. "Do you want to keep quiet about the story your Aunt Lizbet told us?"

"No, I didn't mean that. Goodness, we'd never be able to, not when she knows where we went today." She pressed her palms on her knees. "I just hate to see her getting buoyed up about it, and then being even more disappointed if we can't come up with anything."

"You want to protect her." The tender note in his voice seemed to reach right into her heart.

"Of course I do." She hesitated, not sure how much she wanted to say to him. "She's always done that for me. It's time I did my part."

"Your grandmother has probably dealt with disappointment. I think she knows how to handle it."

Miz Callie was strong. Georgia didn't doubt that. "This is the only thing she's ever asked of me." Her throat thickened. "I don't want to let her down. I won't."

"We can't always protect the people we love from pain."

Was he talking about her grandmother? Or about his daughter? She wasn't sure, and he wouldn't tell her.

Miz Callie had reacted just about the way Georgia had feared when they'd told her about Aunt Lizbet's story. In fact, she'd kept coming back to it all evening. The theme was always the same. Ned wasn't a coward. He couldn't have done what they said.

Georgia hadn't had the heart to try and burst her grandmother's optimism, which was why she was crossing the bridge at Breech's Inlet the next day, on her way to Isle of Palms to pick up the enhanced photos from Adam.

She headed down Palm Boulevard, glancing at the new houses that lined the road. Much of Isle of Palms had been rebuilt after Hurricane Hugo, giving it a newer look than Sullivan's Island.

She'd called Amanda before she left, hoping that she'd come up with something, but the news had all been negative. Whatever Ned had done back in 1942, it hadn't made the local papers.

She turned onto the side street where Adam rented a house with three of his Coast Guard buddies. Running perpendicular to the coastline, the short street ended at the beach. When Adam wasn't out on the water, he still wanted to be near it.

Her heart sank as she pulled up in front of the tan bungalow. Her mother's car was in the driveway.

She should not feel this way. Mamma meant well. But after the disappointment she'd shown at the news of Georgia's broken engagement, Georgia had been just as glad to avoid further conversation on that topic.

She couldn't hide forever. She slid out of the car and marched to the door.

Giving a cursory knock, she opened it and stepped inside, meeting the gazes of the two people in the room.

"Georgia Lee, at last." Mamma enveloped her in a Chanel-scented hug, kissing the air near her cheek. "I was beginnin' to think you'd forgotten you have other family besides Miz Callie."

Georgia sent an accusing look toward Adam, but he shrugged helplessly, as if denying he'd set this up.

"Mamma, you did bring me home to help Miz Callie, remember?"

"To help us reason with Miz Callie," her mother corrected. "How are you coming with that?"

Georgia took a step back, thinking fast. "I'm making a little progress, I guess." Mamma didn't need to know exactly what she was making progress on, did she?

"Good, good." Her mother glanced from her to Adam. "What are the two of you up to?"

"Nothing," she said quickly, reminded of answering that question in exactly the same way a few hundred times while growing up.

"Miz Callie had some old photographs she wanted me to work on," Adam said easily. "Georgia dropped by to bug me about it." Adam could sound relaxed. After all, he wasn't hiding anything. "Hey, how about some sweet tea?"

"None for me, thanks," Mamma said. "I have a dozen errands to run, and I'd best get on with it."

"Georgia?"

"Yes, thanks." At least the subject of her broken engagement hadn't come up, and if her mother was rushing out, she was safe.

Adam headed for the kitchen, and her mother turned to her, touching her cheek with a quick, light gesture.

"I've been wantin' to talk to you, sugar." The faintest frown showed briefly between her brows. "I wanted to say I'm sorry."

The apology was so unexpected that Georgia could only stare for a moment. "Sorry?" She found her voice. "For what?"

"I reacted badly when you told us about your engagement." She shook her head. "Why you didn't call me to begin with... Well, that doesn't matter," she said hurriedly. "You know I want you to be happy, don't you?"

Her throat was tight. "Yes, Mamma. I know."

Her mother blinked rapidly for an instant. "That's all right, then. I'm sure it will work out for the best." She glanced at the gold bracelet watch on her wrist that was a duplicate of the one Georgia wore—Christmas gifts from Dad. "Goodness, I must be going. You be good now, y'heah?"

With a quick wave, she hurried out the door, her mind already on to the next thing on her list.

"There, that wasn't so bad, was it?" Adam leaned against the door frame, grinning.

"Did you set that up?" she demanded.

"Not me." He tossed her a manila envelope. "That's the best I could do with the photos. I'll get your tea."

She sank down on the leather couch, opened the envelope and let the photos slide out onto her lap. When

Adam returned, a glass in each hand, she looked up at him in amazement.

"These are wonderful. I had no idea you could do so much with your photo software."

"Black and whites are a lot easier than color." He leaned over her, looking at the pictures. "You think Miz Callie will be happy?"

"She'll be delighted. You just might move into the favorite grandchild spot."

"That'll be the day." The laughter in his eyes became muted. "Hey, it's better between you and Mamma, isn't it? She's trying."

"I know. Mamma will support me because she loves me." She managed a smile. "I just can't help wishing she'd support me because I'm right."

He shrugged. "I don't guess we can change the folks at this point. Mamma was raised to believe daughters got married." He eyed her. "'Course, you could still satisfy her on that."

She felt a betraying flush come up in her cheeks. "I don't know what you mean."

"Seems like you've been spending a lot of time with Matthew Harper." His eyes twinkled. "Can't be all business, can it?" He threw his arm over her shoulder in a hug. "Come on. Tell your big brother."

She leaned against him. "It's complicated."

"It always is."

She shoved him gently. "You should talk. You've never been serious about a woman for more than six weeks."

"You're the serious type, Little Bit." The humor left

his eyes, replaced by concern. "Don't talk about it if you don't want to. Just don't get hurt."

"I'll try not to." But that might be out of her control.

Matt had been a little uncomfortable when Miz Callie called with an invitation to come for dessert and to discuss what she'd gleaned from the photographs. But now that he and Lindsay were sitting at the round table in Miz Callie's kitchen, finishing up slices of pecan pie topped with vanilla ice cream, he felt reassured.

Things were back to normal between him and Georgia. He'd been thrown off-balance earlier, but that wouldn't happen again. No more tête-à-têtes, no more exchanging confidences. Georgia was a client's granddaughter, helping him to fulfill a client's wishes.

And even as he thought these things, he knew he was kidding himself. Georgia could never be put into such a restrictive box, and what happened between them had been as inevitable as it was upsetting.

He glanced across the table as she rose and started to collect the dishes. Her hair was fastened at the nape of her neck with a silver clasp, and she wore a white sundress which looked...beautiful on her.

Enough, he ordered himself. "Wonderful pie, Miz Callie. Thanks for inviting us."

"It's our pleasure." Miz Callie glanced toward the living room, where he could see a sheaf of photos spread out on the coffee table. Her bright eyes betrayed her eagerness to get to the main reason for his visit.

Georgia cast a knowing eye at her grandmother and then turned to Lindsay. "I picked up a sketchbook and some drawing pencils for you today. Why don't we go on the deck and try them out?"

His daughter's eyes lit with almost as much enthusiasm as Miz Callie's. "Can we?" She jumped off her chair and then paused, as if caught in flight. "Thank you, Miz Callie. Daddy, may I be excused, please?"

He nodded. Georgia and Miz Callie had planned this to give them privacy to discuss the photos, but it was still a thoughtful act on Georgia's part.

Maybe thoughtful wasn't the right word. He watched her and Lindsay go out on the deck together, talking as easily as if they were the same age. That implied that she'd deliberately figured out what would please his daughter. Rather, she seemed to act instinctively.

He followed Miz Callie into the living room and took the seat she indicated next to her. She turned on the brass floor lamp, casting a pool of light on the table and the black-and-white photographs.

"I can't tell you how excited I am at the way these pictures turned out." Her fingers shook a little as she picked one up and handed it to him. "I had no idea Adam could do anything like this with that computer of his."

"Photo software is pretty sophisticated." He looked down at the picture. Young faces stared back at him, and he picked one out without any difficulty. "This is you, isn't it?"

She nodded. "I was about Lindsay's age then, I guess."

Like Lindsay, she'd been all arms and legs. Her hair was pulled back in a braid, and she wore that intent, impatient expression he sometimes caught on Lindsay's face, as if she'd been interrupted while doing something important.

He glanced through the sliding glass door at his daughter. She and Georgia sat side by side, both bending over their drawing pads.

"Lindsay has warmed up to Georgia now, hasn't she?"

"I guess so." He wasn't sure he wanted to discuss Georgia's relationship with his daughter.

Miz Callie, usually so perceptive, didn't seem to catch the reluctance in his voice. "They're good for each other. They have a lot in common. Georgia was feeling a bit lost when she came home."

He decided to ignore the implication that Lindsay was feeling lost. "I appreciate Georgia taking an interest in her."

"How formal." Miz Callie's eyes twinkled.

Embarrassed, he shook his head. "I didn't mean it that way." He hesitated, but the memory of Georgia's well-meant advice still rankled. "I don't suppose she knows a lot about young children."

"Georgia has a kind heart." Miz Callie's gaze rested fondly on her granddaughter. "I'll take that over book knowledge and degrees any day of the week."

He stiffened, but the last thing he wanted was to disagree with Miz Callie. "Maybe you're right," he said, his tone noncommittal.

Miz Callie was still watching Georgia. "I'm praying she'll decide to stay here, you know. She belongs here. I just hope she'll realize that."

What could he say? That he hoped she'd stay, too? He didn't have the right to hope anything of the kind, because it implied an interest he was determined not to have.

"About these pictures," he said.

"Yes, of course." Miz Callie turned back to the task at hand. "Just looking at them brings back so many memories. All these faces." She touched the picture he held, sighing a little. "We were all so young then."

Untouched by life. They'd had a privileged childhood that was as different as could be from his.

But for all the innocence in the faces, they couldn't have had an easy time of it. The older boys, Ned's contemporaries, were laughing and horsing around in one picture, but not long afterward, most of them were off to war. Even the younger children would have been affected, some with fathers gone for the duration. Or forever.

"There, now." Miz Callie put one photo down in front of him. "Those are Ned's particular friends."

Four boys in their late teens posed on a sailboat pulled up on the beach. Ned Bodine's face was familiar by now. He stood, hand resting against the mast, his air of unconscious pride telling clearly whose boat it was.

"This is Timothy Allen." She pointed to a suntanned blond boy who grinned up at Ned. "He died somewhere in Italy, I know." Her voice trembled.

"What about the other two? Do you remember their names?"

She nodded. "Phil Yancey and Bennett Adams."

"Did they survive the war?" That was the crucial question, if he was going to find someone who'd know what Ned Bodine was up to that summer.

"Yes, they did. I remember seeing them off and on

over the years, but their families weren't really close to us. Just people who rented on the island that summer. I don't know where they are now."

He jotted down the names. "I'll find them." Assuming they were still alive to be found. "Anyone else?"

"Not anyone I think can help." Her hands, thin and deeply veined, moved over the photos. "Even so, I'm glad to have these to enjoy." She shook her head slightly, as if in wonderment. "Strange, but I just remember how happy we were. In spite of all the bad news from the war, and the shortages, and the worry on all the grown-ups' faces, we were still children, playing on the beach."

He was unaccountably touched. He wanted to say something that would let her know he understood, but before he could find the words, the door slid open.

"We finished our pictures," Georgia said as she and Lindsay came inside. "We decided to show them off."

"Look, Daddy. Look at my picture. Georgia showed me how to make the shell look round."

He took the sheet of drawing paper she thrust into his hands. "That's beautiful, Lindsay. I really like what you did with the colors, too."

She beamed, then snatched it from him to show Miz Callie. Georgia bent over them, the three heads close together as they talked about the drawing. Lindsay leaned unselfconsciously against Georgia.

As Miz Callie said, Lindsay was warming up to her. He should be happy to see that.

But what if Miz Callie was wrong about Georgia? What if Lindsay grew to count on her, and then Georgia flitted back to her life in Atlanta?

He stood, shoving his notebook into his pocket. "We have to go."

A questioning glance from Georgia told him that the words had come out too harshly.

"Daddy..." It was almost a wail from Lindsay.

"Sorry, Lindsay, but remember that your big Vacation Bible School program is tomorrow. You still have to practice your lines."

"Oh, right." She came to tug on his hand. "I want to make sure my costume is ready, too."

"Good night, sweet child." Miz Callie blew her a kiss.

"I'll walk out with you," Georgia said, sliding the door open again. A breeze flowed in, bringing with it the steady murmur of the ocean.

They'd reached the steps of the deck when Lindsay stopped.

"Daddy, I want to give my picture to Miz Callie. Can I?"

"Okay, run and do it."

She darted back inside, leaving him alone with Georgia for a moment.

"Any progress with Miz Callie?" she asked in a soft undertone.

"She gave me a couple of names that seem like good possibilities." He grasped the railing, turning back toward her. She was closer than he thought, and he caught a faint whiff of the fragrance she wore. "If she thinks of any other names, let me know."

"I will." She tilted her face to look up at him. The breeze lifted her hair and fluttered the hem of her dress. "Is something wrong? You seem in a hurry to leave."

"No, nothing." Nothing except that the longer he stood here, the less will he had to move away. The breeze seemed to be pressing him toward her. It tossed her hair capriciously, and a strand brushed his face, drawing him in closer. Closer.

Her eyes widened, and her lips parted on a breath. His fingers closed on her arms and he—

"I'm ready." Lindsay came clattering back onto the deck. "Miz Callie is going to hang my picture on the wall."

Georgia took a step back, turning to grasp the rail and stare out at the water.

Somehow he managed to find his breath. "That's great, Lindsay. Tell Georgia good-night, now."

"'Night, Georgia." Lindsay's voice trailed over her shoulder as she started down the steps.

He headed after her, taking them so fast it almost felt like flight. Almost? Who was he kidding? It was flight.

Chapter 12

Georgia took a load of clothes from the dryer and began folding, the chore a silent reminder that she must decide soon what she intended to do with her life.

Back in Atlanta she had an apartment, clothes and personal belongings, some good friends, no job and no fiancé. Here she had family, a set of friends from whom her life had been separate for too many years, no job, no apartment and a tentative relationship with Matthew that he'd backed away from so quickly it was a wonder he hadn't tripped. How did she make a pros-and-cons list out of that?

To be honest, she couldn't say she had no place to live. The peaceful silence of the beach house comforted her. Her grandmother would be delighted to have her stay as long as she wanted. Or she could move in with one of her cousins for a while.

Not home. She and her mother had made a positive step in their relationship yesterday, but she wouldn't kid herself. If she moved home, they'd fall right back into their old way of relating to each other.

As for Matt… That was a story that went nowhere.

The telephone rang, breaking off the futile line of thought. She hurried to answer it, since Miz Callie was off to spend the day with an old friend.

It was Matt, and he sounded a bit disconcerted when he realized she'd picked up. "Hi, Georgia…um, is Miz Callie there?"

"I'm sorry, but she's visiting a friend. Is there a message?" If Matt wanted to keep things strictly business between them, she'd show him that she could do that. Never mind that the sound of his deep voice in her ear did such funny things to her.

"No, no message." He sounded harried. "I wanted to ask a favor, but I'll find some other way to deal with it."

She paused for the briefest of seconds. "If there's something you need, just tell me." It was what her grandmother would say, what neighborliness demanded.

Now it was his turn to hesitate, and the phone line hummed with his unspoken thoughts.

"If you could help, I'd appreciate it. I'm stuck at the office. I can't possibly get away for another half hour, and the Bible school program will be starting soon. I promised Lindsay I'd be there."

She heard the frustration in his tone. He didn't want to let down his child. But he couldn't afford to walk out on a client.

"I'll go right over," she said. "Shall I tell Lindsay that you'll be coming as soon as you can?"

"Yes, please." Relief, so palpable she could almost touch it. "I don't want her to feel she doesn't have anyone to clap for her."

"No problem." She looked down in dismay at her faded T-shirt and oldest shorts. A quick change was in order. "I'm on my way."

A shower would be nice, but that was out of the question. She hit the stairs at a run. Luckily the church was only a few blocks away.

She reached the church with minutes to spare. Parents and grandparents were gathering in the fellowship hall, but the classes hadn't come in yet.

Following the signs, she made her way downstairs and hurried along the corridor. She couldn't let Lindsay walk into that big room and look in vain for her daddy.

She found the classroom, tapped on the door and opened it. The teacher was busily engaged in pinning what seemed to be butterfly wings onto the back of a little boy whose wiggling made it highly likely he'd end up on the pointed end of a pin.

"Georgia Bodine!" Grasping a chair, the woman levered herself to her feet and advanced on Georgia, arms spread wide. "It's great to see you."

"Candy, how are you?" Candy Morris had been in her grade all through school. She hugged her, then held her back. "You look wonderful."

"I look pregnant." Candy grinned and patted her belly. "Due in August, and I feel like a whale."

Georgia felt a pang of envy. "On you, it's beautiful."

A pair of arms clasped her around the waist. "Georgia, did you come to see me in the program?" Lindsay's eyes lit with pleasure.

"I sure did, sugar." She glanced at Candy. "Okay if I talk to Lindsay for a minute?"

"Of course. Then you can help me turn these young ones into birds and butterflies. If I'd known you were around, I'd have recruited you to help with more than that."

Candy turned back to her butterflies, and Georgia drew Lindsay aside, out of the turmoil.

"Is something the matter?" Lindsay's eyes filled with sudden fear. "Did my daddy have an accident?"

"No, no, certainly not." That must be the fear that lingered under the surface in the child's mind—that she would lose her father, too. How uncertain Lindsay's world must feel. "He wants me to tell you that he's on his way. He was delayed at the office for a bit, but he's coming." She brushed a strand of fine hair back from Lindsay's forehead. "Honest."

The child's eyes were wary, seeking confidence. "Okay," she said finally.

"His meeting went longer than it was supposed to." She'd probably already stressed too much that Matt would be here. If Lindsay were disappointed...well, she didn't want to think about that.

"Will you help me with my wings?" Lindsay slid her hand into Georgia's.

"I'd love to." Her heart expanded at the sign of trust. "Show me where they are."

She soon mastered the trick of pinning wings onto overexcited little bodies—just make sure that if the pin slips, you stab yourself.

Over a sea of jumping children, she raised an eyebrow at Candy. "Birds and butterflies?"

"We're doing the Creation story." Candy grinned. "Just be glad we didn't get the sun, moon and stars. Those costumes are tough."

Somewhere a bell rang, and she grabbed Georgia's hand. "Georgia, honey, my aide didn't show up today. Help me keep them in order while they wait to go on. Please?"

What did she know about managing groups of kids? Nothing. But she could hardly say no, so she nodded.

To her surprise, Candy had little difficulty in getting them lined up quietly, now that the time had arrived. Holding hands, the children walked in a line down the hall and up the stairs to the large room that had been turned into a temporary theater for the occasion.

A wave of nostalgia swept over Georgia. She remembered this. Vacation Bible School was a rite of childhood, and she'd always been thrilled when it rolled around. Thanks to her grandmother, she'd come to the one at this church as well as the one at her home church in Mount Pleasant.

Parents and grandparents sat in rows of metal folding chairs, cameras in evidence. At the end of the room nearest the kitchen, helpers buzzed around a table laden with refreshments for after the show. Fruit punch, she'd guess, and more kinds of cookies than anyone should possibly eat, although some of the kids would try. Some things didn't change.

Apparently awed by the audience, Candy's class stood quietly enough along the wall, watching as the youngest children sang songs. Georgia scanned the room. A number of people she knew were here, and she caught several looking at her. Wondering, maybe.

*What's Miz Callie's granddaughter doing here? I
thought she was working up in Atlanta.*

What was she doing here? Plenty of her classmates,
like Candy, had settled down to marriage and family
by now—their lives set in a familiar track. Not adrift
like hers.

"We're next," Candy whispered. "You can sit and
watch if you want. Thanks a million."

"My pleasure." She waved at Lindsay, and then
skirted around the back of the audience to find a seat
at the rear.

And there was Matt, slipping in the door just in
time. She waved. He caught the motion, nodded and
came to join her just as the birds and butterflies were
introduced.

The program went on, as such things always did,
with mistakes here and there that were easily forgiven
by the audience. Each class performed to thunderous
applause, and the finale led to a standing ovation.

She stood with the rest, clapping, feeling a surge
of pride. She couldn't take credit for much, but she'd
been there.

Lindsay raced through the crowd to hurl herself at
her father. "Daddy, you got here!"

"I did." He bent, hugging her. "You were so good,
sweetheart. I loved your song, and the motions were
great."

"We were good, weren't we?" Lindsay did a little
pirouette, beaming.

This was the most animated and outgoing Georgia
had ever seen the child. Miz Callie had known what

she was doing when she'd arranged for Lindsay to attend Vacation Bible School.

Matt straightened a butterfly wing. "It looks like a crush around the refreshments. Suppose I get drinks for all of us, so you don't get your wings ruined." His glance included Georgia.

"Red punch for me," Lindsay said.

"Anything but red punch for me."

"Right." Matt's face relaxed in a smile. "Thank you, Georgia. I owe you."

"It was a pleasure," she said, and meant it.

He began to work his way to the table. Lindsay, clinging to Georgia's hand, chattered away a mile a minute about the performance. "Someday I want to be thunder and lightning, like the big kids."

One of the older classes had produced some very effective weather effects with a metal sheet and some foam lightning bolts.

"You'll get to, when you're older." That was one of the pleasures of coming back year after year—working your way through the classes to play every part in the production.

"Next week I won't have anything to do." Lindsay drooped for a moment. "I wish Bible school wasn't over."

"There are lots of other fun things to do in the summer."

A woman with a daughter about Lindsay's age touched Georgia's arm. "Hi. I wanted to meet you. My Katie will be in the same grade as Lindsay when school starts. Maybe we can get our daughters together over the summer."

Georgia opened her mouth to correct the misconception, but she didn't get a chance. Lindsay did it for her.

"Don't say that!" The words rang out loudly in a sudden silence. "She's not my mother!"

Georgia tried for an apologetic smile and a light explanation, but as she sought the words, she saw Matt a few feet away, hands filled with paper cups, his face far more thunderous than anything the fifth and sixth graders had managed to produce.

He might as well have been hit in the stomach with a two-by-four. Matt stood, the drinks he held dripping on his fingers, fighting to regain control.

It wasn't just the assumption the woman had made. That was tough enough to deal with.

It was Lindsay's reaction that lent power to the punch. She hadn't said anything about her mother in so long that he'd begun to believe she'd moved past her grief.

Obviously she hadn't. How stupid could he get?

Georgia, smiling easily, set the woman straight. "I'm Lindsay's neighbor and friend, Georgia Bodine." She held out her hand.

The woman took it, flushing a little. "I'm so sorry. I didn't realize..." She stopped, started again. "I'm Linda Mulvaney. This is my daughter, Katie." Her flush deepened. "We're new on Sullivan's Island, you see. I was so pleased that Katie had made a friend her age."

Georgia, one hand resting lightly on Lindsay's shoulder, smiled at the other child. "It's nice to meet you, Katie. You're going to love Sullivan's Island Elementary School. It's really a fun place."

"Mommy says we'll go and visit soon." Katie tugged at her hand. "Do you think Lindsay could come to my house for a playdate?"

"I'll bet your mom could arrange that with Lindsay's dad." She nodded toward him, then came and took the cups from his hands. "Linda Mulvaney, this is Matthew Harper."

With half his mind caught up in worrying about his daughter, he fought to speak coherently to the woman. "I'm sure Lindsay would love to get together with Katie. Why don't I give you my number?" He pulled out his card.

"That's great." She tucked it into her bag. "Again, I'm sorry about the misunderstanding."

"Don't be, please. How could you know?" Even as he reassured the woman, he eyed his daughter, nerves jangling.

Georgia bent over Lindsay, talking to her earnestly. Whatever she was saying seemed to wipe the strain from his daughter's face.

Mrs. Mulvaney's attention was distracted by another mother, and she moved off. Georgia gestured toward a pair of folding chairs, and Katie and Lindsay sat down, their legs swinging in unison, heads together.

"It's great that Lindsay made a friend," Georgia said cautiously to Matt.

"She seems okay now. What did you say to her?"

"I just explained that Katie's mother didn't know us. That it was a mistake, easily fixed." She gazed at him, concern plain in her eyes. "I'm sorry if her comment upset you."

"It didn't." He wasn't being honest, and he suspected

Georgia knew that. The incident had bothered him, upsetting his precarious view of how things were. "Katie's mother is going to call me so we can set a time to get the girls together."

"Life was simpler when I was a kid. Our neighborhood in Mount Pleasant had kids in every house. All you had to do to make a friend was go out the front door. Now the parents have to get involved."

"Jennifer used to do that. Even before Lindsay started school, she'd organized a playgroup for her." Jennifer had been so intent on doing everything right when it came to raising their daughter. "I should have picked up on that."

"It's tough in a new place." Georgia's voice was warm with sympathy. "Now that Lindsay has one friend, she'll meet others. By the time school starts, she'll have a group of girls to hang around with."

That would have been what Georgia's life was like at eight. A nice house in a nice neighborhood, lots of friends. He had no basis for comparison. But his daughter would. He'd make sure of it.

"I should have seen it sooner." His gaze fixed on his daughter. "I should have realized that she needed help making friends."

She patted his arm lightly, sympathy flowing through her very touch. "You've had plenty to deal with. If you'd stayed in Boston..." She let that trail off, as if she didn't want to go there.

"If we'd stayed in Boston, we'd have had friends to support us." He took a breath, remembering what it had been like. "But Lindsay couldn't deal with that.

Neither could I. Maybe the two of us are more alike than I thought."

"It bothered you, being with friends whose families were still intact." She seemed to understand without questions.

"It did." He glanced around, but no one was close enough to hear. "We were rattling around in that house together, looking for Jennifer around every corner." His voice thickened. "The grief was everywhere. I felt as if we were both drowning in it."

"So you decided to make a fresh start here."

"Yes." His throat was tight. "I guess I thought we could outrun our grief, but I was wrong. We can't."

And now he'd complicated everything by showing Georgia the depth of his emotional failings. He hated not being in control of his feelings. He'd thought he could get over his grief, help Lindsay get over her grief, by starting fresh.

Guilt flooded him. He'd been disloyal, trying to escape the fact of Jennifer's death. Then doubly disloyal for having feelings for Georgia.

Wouldn't Jennifer want him to love again? The thought, coming out of nowhere, was like a punch in the heart. For an instant he was numb. The anger rushed in. It wasn't fair. None of this was fair.

Chapter 13

After yesterday's revelation, Georgia hadn't been sure how Matt would react to her today. But he'd picked her up right on time, and a glance had assured her that he had his game face on.

"Are you sure that this man understood why we want to talk with him?" Matt had already located one of the two men Miz Callie had identified, living just a few minutes' drive away in North Charleston. "He must be getting up in years."

"In his eighties, but very much all there, from what I could tell." Matt smiled. "We had to come this morning, because he has a bocce-ball tournament this afternoon."

Georgia glanced down at the Ashley River far below as they drove across the bridge. "That does sound pretty lively."

"He may not know anything, but it's worth the effort."

He was right. So far they had absolutely nothing. Even Miz Callie's hope had begun to dim a little, she thought. She was losing her faith that they'd ever find evidence to exonerate Ned.

She glanced at Matt, but his face didn't give anything away. She longed to speak to him again about Lindsay. Even an amateur like her could see that the child needed help with her grief.

Steeling herself for his reaction, she took a breath. "I want to talk to you again about Lindsay."

He shot her a look that threatened to pin her back against the car door. "I don't—"

"About her birthday," she said quickly, her courage failing. "Miz Callie would like to have a little party for her. They were talking about a crab boil on the beach, and Lindsay was intrigued. So Miz Callie thought we could do that, unless you have other plans."

His face relaxed. "That's very kind of her, but isn't it too much trouble? I don't want her wearing herself out for Lindsay."

"I don't think she's ever gotten tired from planning a party. It's one of her favorite things. When we were little, she loved having our parties on the island. She put on a treasure hunt for my ninth birthday that I still remember."

"Only if she'll let me buy the supplies and help with the work."

She grinned. "You can try arguing with her over that, but I wouldn't make a bet on your winning."

"It's only fair—" he began.

"She loves Lindsay. She wants to do something nice for her. Besides, it'll distract her from the information we don't have."

"You have a point there." His brows drew down. "The paperwork is moving along a lot faster than I expected. You know, the further this goes, the more likely it is that Miz Callie's plans will get out."

She nodded, not liking the sense that time was working against them. "Can't you slow it down a bit?"

"I'd have to reckon with your grandmother if I did that." Matt's navigation system beeped, and he turned onto the street they wanted. "Let's just hope Bennett Adams has something to say."

She leaned forward, watching the house numbers. "If he did, you'd think he'd have come out with it before this."

The navigation system announced their arrival just as Georgia pointed to the house, and Matt pulled to the curb. "There could be a lot of reasons why he'd keep quiet," he said. "We'll just have to play it by ear."

They got out of the car. As they started up the flagstone walk toward the small cottage, Matt's hand was at her back. She felt its warmth right through her.

The front door swung open at their approach. "Hey, there. Welcome. Y'all come in now."

Bennett Adams was tiny, barely taller than Georgia. Bald and a bit frail-looking, he had snapping brown eyes that were full of life.

"Mr. Adams, I'm Matt Harper." Matt extended his hand. "And this is Georgia Bodine."

"Call me Benny. So you're Georgia." He took her

hand, holding it for a long moment. "Little Callie's granddaughter. You have the look of her, you know."

"I hope so." She warmed to him at once. Like Miz Callie, Adams seemed to be the kind of person who didn't let age keep him from enjoying life.

"Come and sit down." He waved his hand toward a sofa in front of the window of the crowded, minuscule living room. He sat in a threadbare recliner and leaned forward, elbows on his knees. "So what's this all about, then?"

"Miz Callie is living out at the Sullivan's Island house now, the one that belonged to the Bodines. Do you remember it?"

"'Course I do. The Bodines pretty much held open house for their kids' friends during the summer, even during the war years."

"My grandmother has been thinking a lot about that time, especially the summer of 1942." She took a breath and plunged ahead. "She wants to find out what happened to her husband's older brother, Ned Bodine."

His eyes grew guarded at the name. "Seems way too late for that, don't it?"

Georgia leaned forward, hands clasped. "She's desperate to do this. She believes Ned has been treated unjustly all these years—that he'd never have run away rather than join up. Please, if you know anything, tell us."

"I don't know what happened to him when he went away, if that's what you mean." He shook his head. "I'm right sorry to let little Callie down, but I don't know."

Her heart sank. That was it, then.

"You were on the island when he disappeared," Matt

said. "Anything you can remember about Ned might help."

"I don't see how." He leaned back, as if retreating from them.

"Please." She extended a hand, palm up, asking.

He shrugged. Shook his head. "I do remember he fought with his father all that summer about enlisting," Benny said slowly. "Funny, that was. All any of us boys could talk about was how we were going to enlist, minute we were old enough."

"Ned didn't feel that way?" Matt put the question quietly.

"At first he did. Beginning of the summer, we made a pact that we'd go enlist together. Our birthdays were only a couple days apart, you see."

"But that changed?"

He nodded. "That was what all the fighting with his daddy was about. Seemed like Ned was changing his mind, delaying in a way. Old Mr. Bodine was a real fire-eater. He'd have gone off to fight himself if they'd have taken him."

"Do you know why Ned changed his mind?"

"Not because he was scared, if that's what you're thinking." Brown eyes locked on to them. "Mind, Ned wasn't foolish daring, like some of us were, but he never backed away from anything or anybody."

"Then why did he change his mind about enlisting?"

Benny's gaze slid away, and he picked at a loose thread on the arm of the recliner. "Don't know as I know. I wouldn't want to guess."

She exchanged a look with Matt. The man knew something. Whether they could get it out of him…

Matt nodded, as if telling her to pursue it, probably thinking the man was more likely to tell her. He had good insight into what made people tick—no doubt an asset to an attorney.

"Mr. Adams—Benny, please. If you know something, even guess something, please tell us. My grandmother is so set on finding out the truth. It will hurt her terribly to never know. And hurt me, too, if I can't do this thing for her."

"Well, now, young lady, you know how to make it hard on a person. If I had a granddaughter like you..." He shook his head. "Suppose I told you something about Ned that...well, some folks might think was a slur on his character. Don't you think your grandmother would rather remember him the way she does?"

She straightened. "If you still knew Callie Bodine, you wouldn't ask that. She'd rather have the truth, every time."

He studied her face for a long moment, as if assessing her determination. Finally he nodded.

"All right then. I'll tell you what I thought, but mind, Ned never confided in me about it. I'm just saying what I thought."

Her fingers twined tightly. Were they finally going to get some insight? She could sense Matt's tension, his yearning to find answers at last.

Benny frowned, gazing back into the past. "There was a couple from Charleston rented a place out on the island that summer. Can't say anybody really took to him—big, blustery kind of guy, wore flashy clothes and talked loud all the time. Gossip said he was into the black market, but I don't know if that was true."

He surely wasn't going to imply that Ned was involved in anything like that—was he?

"Now, his wife was something different altogether. A lady. Pretty, too. Why she wanted to take up with a fella like that, nobody could figure." He shook his head. "It wasn't a very happy marriage, by all accounts." He stopped, as if reluctant to go on.

"Please…"

"You're thinking Ned was involved with the wife," Matt said, quicker than she was to reach the conclusion.

"I'm not saying that." He held up his hands in denial. "But she was an awful pretty woman. She'd be out on the beach lots of times when us kids were out, and seemed like she enjoyed our company."

"How did Ned react?" Matt asked.

Benny shrugged. "Didn't talk about it much. I remember one time when the husband had been drinking too much and making a fool of himself, Ned said that it was a pity with all the good men getting killed, a skunk like that was still walking around."

"Do you remember what their name was?" She held her breath, hoping they weren't going to have to track down every summer visitor to the island in 1942.

He frowned. "Malloy, that was it. Don't recall first names, but the last name was Malloy."

"Do you know which house they rented?" Some of the rental agents could have records.

"It's not there anymore, is it?" He shook his head, as if regretting all that was gone. "Tore it down like they did a lot of places, but it was the second place down island from the Bodine house. That's how we come to see her on the beach so often, you see."

He shook his head, some of the spirit seeming to go out of him. "Ah, it's a long time ago now. We were all close as could be that summer, but come Labor Day, folks started to leave. I enlisted—infantry. Got over to Europe in time to do my share. Most of those folks I lost track of by the time I finally come home again. You know how it is."

She didn't, but she could imagine. The world had been turned upside down, and they'd all been part of it.

"Thank you." She took his hand, clasping it firmly in hers. "I can't tell you how much it means to me to hear your story."

He put his other hand over hers. "Mind, I can't say anything for sure. It's just my idea of what was going on."

"I know." She rose, bending to kiss his cheek.

He flushed. "I hope it does some good."

Matt shook his hand. "Thanks for letting us impose on you this morning."

"Impose nothing." He rose to walk with them to the door. "It's rare enough when I get company, and even rarer when somebody wants to talk about the old days. Now, you give my respects to your grandmother, y'heah?"

"I will. I'm sure she'll be grateful, too."

But doubt assailed her as they stepped off the narrow porch. She glanced up at Matt. "At least, she will if we tell her."

He lifted an eyebrow. "Afraid Miz Callie wouldn't like having her hero's image clouded?"

"I don't know. Maybe."

He opened the gate, holding it for her. "Miz Callie

always struck me as being wise in the ways of the heart. I doubt she's going to be shocked by this."

She thought of her grandmother's calm comfort over her broken engagement. "Maybe you're right."

Matt squeezed her hand. "Don't worry so much. Miz Callie wants the truth, no matter where it takes us."

She managed a nod, despite the fact that she felt as if he'd squeezed her heart instead of her hand. A wave of panic swept through her. She was getting in way over her head with Matt. What would Miz Callie have to say about that?

"Exactly how many people have you invited to this party?" Georgia paused while cutting up cantaloupe for the fruit salad, assessing the size of the bowl—Miz Callie's largest, she felt sure.

Her grandmother evaded her gaze. "Oh, I don't know exactly. Folks just hear about it. You know how it is."

She did indeed know how it was. Miz Callie's beach parties always started out small. They never ended up that way. An unpleasant sensation crawled across her skin at the memory of how one particular crab boil had ended up.

"Does it still bother you?" Miz Callie, exhibiting her uncanny ability to read one's thoughts through the smallest reaction, stopped stirring a pitcher of lemonade to cast a look of concern at Georgia. "What happened with Cole's roommate, I mean."

"No, of course not." She forced a smile she didn't feel. "I didn't even think you knew. How silly would that be, to brood about something that happened ages ago?"

She didn't think Miz Callie bought that, but she didn't push, either, thank goodness.

Georgia didn't want to remember that incident. She'd been young for her years, inexperienced, and she'd acted like an idiot. End of story.

"If you think the crowd is going to be bigger than expected, maybe I ought to pick up more crabs and shrimp." She looked down at her fruit-stained T-shirt. "But I'd have to change clothes first."

"No need," she said. "Adam's taking care of it."

"Adam. As in my brother Adam? But he doesn't even know Lindsay."

"Well, now he will." Miz Callie shut the refrigerator door firmly on the lemonade.

A sinking feeling gripped her stomach. "Just how many Bodines are going to show up tonight?"

"Anybody who wants to. Now, Georgia, you stop worrying. Things are going to turn out fine. Look how much progress you and Matt have made already."

She wasn't sure she'd define what they found out as progress. On Sunday, sitting in the simple, airy sanctuary of the church Ned must have attended, she'd found herself wondering what it would have been like for him. Had he looked up at the plain wooden cross and wrestled with God over his feelings for a married woman? Had he begged for forgiveness and then run away with her?

"Matt's trying to trace the woman, but I don't know how easy it will be." She hesitated, not sure she should bring up the thing that bothered her most. But someone had to. "Suppose we do find her. Suppose we find that Ned left everything behind—his family, his duty—and ran off with her. Can you forgive that?"

The sorrow in Miz Callie's eyes told Georgia that she had already considered that. "Forgiveness wouldn't be up to me. That would be between Ned and God."

"I know. But…" She frowned down at the bowl of fruit and tried to find the words to express what she felt. "When you let somebody love you, it seems to me you become responsible. You can't turn your back on them without hurting them and losing a little bit of yourself."

That was as good an explanation as any for what had been wrong between her and James. He'd turned his back on her, and it hadn't, as far as she could tell, cost him anything. His heart had remained perfectly intact, which must mean that it hadn't been engaged at all.

"You have something there." Her grandmother's voice was soft. "Love costs. How did you get so smart?"

She smiled, despite the tears that stung her eyes. "From watching my grandmother."

Miz Callie shook her head. "Took me a lot longer to figure out how people work, it seems to me. But I know that forgiveness isn't up to us. We've all done things—" She stopped suddenly, hands tightening around a dish towel, staring out the window at the dunes.

"What's wrong?" Georgia peered through the window, seeing nothing unusual.

Miz Callie planted her hands on the table. "We were talkin', and all of a sudden it was like a door opened in my mind and a memory fell out."

"A memory of what?" For a moment she'd been

alarmed, but Miz Callie seemed all right. It was what Aunt Lizbet had said, too, when a memory from the distant past emerged.

"Your granddad and I, out way later than we should have been, I'm sure, 'cause it was already getting dark. Enough moonlight to see where we were going, though, and Richmond—well, he could have found his way home blindfolded from anywhere on the island. We were coming by one of the cottages, and we could hear somebody inside." She shivered, as if she were that child again, standing out in the dunes on a summer night. "Not that we never heard folks yelling— our folks yelled at us when we needed it. But this was different—a man's voice, mean. We stood there, holding hands, scared and not knowing what to do. And then there was the sound of a slap, and a woman crying."

Georgia didn't need to ask whose house it had been. It fit only too clearly with what Benny had said.

Miz Callie's hand was extended, as if she still clasped the hand of her Richmond. "Then we saw we weren't alone. Ned stood there in the dunes, stiff as a statue, staring at that house. Only thing that moved was his hands, working like he wanted to tear something. I'd never seen him like that—never even dreamed he could look that way."

Miz Callie stopped, seeming stuck at that image.

"Did he see you?"

"He did, and then he was himself again. Told us to cut along home. Richmond wanted him to come with us, but he said he wasn't ready to go in yet." She rubbed her hands on her apron. "Funny. I thought we'd ask him about what happened. Ned was good at explaining things grown-ups might not want to talk about. But Richmond said better not, so we never did. Guess it doesn't mean much."

Georgia wouldn't soon get that image out of her mind of a young Ned, standing out in the dunes, unable to help the woman he loved.

Love costs, Miz Callie had said. What had it cost Ned?

"Miz Callie! Georgia! I'm here. Can I help?"

Lindsay slid the glass door back and burst into the kitchen, shattering the silence.

"If it isn't the birthday girl." Miz Callie grabbed her and kissed her. "You best get used to being kissed, child, 'cause we give lots of kisses on your birthday."

"I'm eight. That's getting pretty grown-up, isn't it?" She came to Georgia, lifting her face for a kiss.

Georgia kissed her and held her close for a moment. "Almost old enough to vote," she said. "Happy birthday, sugar. Where's your daddy?"

"He's on the beach, helping the men. What can I do?"

On the beach, helping the men. What men? Georgia stepped out to the deck and looked down. She spotted Matt instantly among the group stacking driftwood for a fire. Matt was being exposed to way too many Bodine males at once—her father, Adam, a couple of cousins—and there wasn't a thing she could do to help him.

She turned back to Lindsay. Maybe she and Lindsay should go out and dilute all that testosterone.

"How about if you help me carry things out, okay?"

"Okay." Lindsay danced in place while Georgia loaded a basket for her with paper plates, napkins and cups. "Did you know that a bunch of my friends from Bible school are going to be here? And Miz Candy, my teacher, too."

"That'll be great." Georgia grabbed a roll of plastic tablecover, scissors and tape, and a thermos of sweet tea. "Okay, let's go."

Lindsay hurried out ahead of her, but her steps slowed as she started down toward the dunes. Georgia caught up with her, and they went side by side.

"Last year I had a party at the bouncy place," she said. "And the year before at the gym."

"I'll bet those were fun," Georgia said, noticing the sudden frown on Lindsay's face.

"They were." She emphasized the words. "My mommy did them, and she invited all my friends and decorated and had my favorite kind of cake and pizza and everything."

Georgia's heart twisted. Poor child. She felt disloyal enjoying a party that was so different from what her mother would have done.

She fought to keep emotion out of her voice. "Your mommy gave you really special parties."

Lindsay nodded.

"This year Daddy and Miz Callie are giving you an island-girl party, because you're an island girl now. That's different, but it's okay to like different things."

Lindsay didn't say anything for a moment.

Had she said the right thing? *Don't let me make a*

mistake when it comes to this child, Lord. She's had too many hurts already.

She'd been praying for Lindsay since the day they'd met, but a little extra prayer for help never went amiss.

They reached the beach, and Lindsay ran ahead to Matt. "I'm having an island-girl party this year," she said. "It's okay to like different kinds of parties."

Matt's gaze caught hers and held warmly for a moment. Then he turned back to his daughter.

"That's exactly right, Lindsay. It's just fine."

"What's not to like about any kind of party?" Georgia's cousin Win threw an arm around her waist and lifted her off her feet in a hug. "Hey, G, how come you haven't been out here helping with the work?"

"Put me down, you idiot." Georgia swatted at him. "Matt, Lindsay, this is my cousin Win Bodine. Win's a rescue swimmer, so he has to show off how strong he is."

Lindsay looked up at him solemnly. "Is your name really Win?"

He bent to shake her hand. "It's really Winthrop Richmond Bodine, but that's too big a mouthful, sugar, so you just call me Win."

Lindsay responded to the honey in Win's voice like women of every age seemed to, the corners of her lips curling up. "What's a rescue swimmer?"

Win, bless him, showed no sign of impatience with her questions. "That's just my job, darlin'."

"He jumps out of helicopters instead of piloting a cutter like any self-respecting Bodine ought to," Adam put in. He gave Win a cousinly shove. "Go say hi to Matt and let me talk to the birthday girl for a minute."

Georgia kept a watchful eye on Win as he approached Matt, but he seemed to be on his best behavior. Adam led Lindsay off to help him find some driftwood. Daddy, on his way toward her, paused to wave at folks coming down the path from the cottage. The beach party had begun—for better or worse.

Chapter 14

Matt leaned back on his elbows, watching the fire as it burned lower. The party was slowly winding down. The sun had slid from sight, painting the fair-weather clouds on the horizon in shades that began as iridescent pink and faded to pale lilac and deep purple.

Across from him, Win Bodine reached forward to throw another piece of driftwood on the fire, sending sparks showering upward. Maybe he, too, hated to see this perfect evening come to an end.

The families with young children had been the first to go, trudging toward the road or down the beach with protesting youngsters in tow. But by then, he'd had the satisfying sense that Lindsay now had friends and acceptance here.

Thanks to the Bodines. Whether intentional or not,

he and Lindsay were now associated with the Bodine family in people's minds.

A faint unease touched him. That could blow up in his face, depending on how things worked out with Miz Callie's plan.

Another shower of sparks flew up, casting light on those who surrounded the fire. Lindsay was curled on a blanket next to Miz Callie, and it looked as if the older woman was telling her a story. Across from him, Georgia's father was deep in conversation with her uncle Brett, while Adam and Win threw in an occasional comment. He didn't have the Bodine family tree worked out yet, but he thought Win was the son of Harrison, the brother he had yet to meet.

Amanda was telling some anecdote, complete with extravagant gestures, to her mother, her aunt and another young woman who'd been introduced as Amanda's twin. Georgia worked her way around the fire, offering coffee.

He probably should make a move toward home, but no one seemed in any hurry. Lindsay was content, so he lingered, enjoying watching the Bodines in their natural habitat.

From what he'd observed, Bodines, especially the males, came in a couple of distinct types. Georgia's father, for instance, was deliberate, calm, slow to speak and probably slow to anger as well. Adam was like him in temperament, listening with a wry smile to something his impassioned cousin was telling him.

Win was another kettle of fish altogether. Volatile, quick, probably daring or even reckless—the type who'd flare up in an instant. Georgia's uncle had shown him that side as well in their private encounter.

"Coffee?" Georgia leaned over him, coffee pot poised.

"I couldn't put another thing in my stomach." He patted the blanket beside him. "Can't you sit down and relax?"

"I can." She sank bonelessly into a cross-legged seat, her gaze moving from face to face. "I love this part of the evening. I used to be curled up on the blanket next to Miz Callie like Lindsay is." She smiled. "The voices were like sweet music, lulling me to sleep."

He could almost imagine a childhood like that. "I don't know how to thank you for doing this—"

She cut him off with a wave of her hand. "Miz Callie loved every minute of it. As for the rest of them— well, they love any excuse for a beach party, and giving Lindsay a happy birthday was a good one."

A soft outburst of laughter came from the women across the fire, and Win leaned forward, saying something that brought another ripple of laughter.

Georgia leaned closer to him. "What are you thinking about? You've been watching my kinfolk the way Miz Callie watches the turtles. Learning about a different species?"

"Something like that. I'm intrigued by how the Bodines seem to fall into two distinct personality types. Makes you believe in the power of genetics."

Georgia laughed. "You've exposed the Bodine family secret, though I wonder sometimes if it's not a case of living up to expectations. Adam—"

"Calm, fair, evenhanded," he put in.

"Like my daddy, and his daddy before him. And Win is just like Uncle Brett."

"Quick-tempered?"

She nodded. "But good-hearted and generous to a fault."

"What about your brother Cole? Is he the quick-tempered one of your family?"

She glanced away from him. "You could say that," she said, her voice barely audible.

"Georgia?" He touched her hand, smoothing his fingers over hers. "Did I say something wrong?"

She shook her head, managing a low laugh that didn't sound very amused. "Sorry. It's silly. Your comment about Cole just reminded me of something."

He shouldn't pry, but instinct stronger than common sense drove him. "Tell me." They were very close, their voices so soft they were in a small world of their own.

Her breath came out in a sigh. "It was stupid. Not my proudest moment, believe me."

Where was this leading? Whatever it was, it obviously hurt more than she wanted to show.

"I can't believe you did anything that stupid." It was something to do with her brother, obviously. "Cole lost his temper with you?"

"Not with me," she said quickly. She shook her head. "I'm making this sound worse than it is. It's just—nothing really."

He waited. She wanted, or needed, to say this tonight. He could feel the pressure inside her.

"Cole was at the Citadel then. I was a senior in high school. He brought his roommate home for the weekend, and we entertained him with a crab boil on the beach."

Her hand twisted a little in his—the only outward sign of her inward perturbation. "He acted—well, interested in me. I was flattered. None of Cole's friends had ever seen me as anything other than a little sister."

Now he thought he saw where this was going.

"Anyway, to make a long story short, he got carried away, and I didn't know how to handle it. That was the stupid part. Any other girl my age probably could have cut the thing short before it escalated...."

She stopped, her breath catching. He felt a totally irrational urge to find that unknown jerk and show him what you learned growing up on the streets of Boston.

"I take it Cole flew to your defense." He made an effort to keep his voice calm. It wouldn't do her any good if he overreacted to a ten-year-old trauma.

She nodded. "They had to pull him off the boy. He got into trouble at school as well, since that's not the kind of behavior the Citadel expects from its cadets." She tried to smile and failed. "All because I didn't know how to handle—"

"Don't." He couldn't help it—he had to touch her lips to stop her. Aware of her parents across the fire, he took his hand away quickly. "It wasn't your fault. And if Cole was here, I'd shake his hand right now."

That earned a shaky smile from her. "The last thing he needs is encouragement. Daddy rarely gets angry, but that time was the exception. And Mamma pointed out that if I'd shown a bit of maturity, it never would have happened."

The depth of empathy he felt for her shocked him.

It probably wasn't a good idea to say what he thought of her mother's response.

"Georgia—"

"Daddy!" Lindsay's voice was almost a wail. "I can't find my new stuffed turtle that Georgia gave me."

"It's right here, sugar." Georgia was on her feet even faster than he was. "I put it in this shopping bag so it'd be easier to carry home."

Lindsay nuzzled the toy sleepily. "I want him to go to bed with me tonight."

"Sure you do. And we should be heading in that direction already." He stood and went to her.

"But I don't want to go home. I don't want my beautiful party to be over." Her voice hinted at tears not far away.

He heard a murmur of empathy and a soft "Bless her heart" from someone.

"Nobody ever wants a beautiful day to end," Miz Callie said quietly but with a firm note in her voice that he suspected most eight-year-olds would heed. "But the stars are in their places, and all the little beach creatures are in their sandy beds. It's time you were as well."

"I want Georgia to walk us home." Lindsay grabbed Georgia's hand. "Please."

"Sure thing." She picked up one of the gift bags. "I'll help you carry all your loot home, birthday girl."

He bent over Miz Callie. "Thank you isn't enough." He kissed her cheek.

"It's more than enough," she said. "Bless you, dear."

He'd better go before he showed how much that meant to him. He picked up the rest of their belong-

ings, and they started off down the beach to a chorus
of good-nights.

Georgia, holding Lindsay's hand, was jollying her
along, averting a meltdown better than he would have.
That gave him a few minutes to digest what Georgia had told him. The incident had hurt her, and she'd
been made to feel it was her fault. Oh, probably no
one had intended that. He was even willing to give
her mother the benefit of the doubt now that his temper had cooled a bit.

But they had handled it wrong, and Georgia had
been the loser. The fact that the story had bubbled to
the surface after all this time showed that she hadn't
really resolved it.

His hands clenched again at the thought of that
testosterone-laden teenager. Hopefully Cole had landed
a few good punches before they'd pulled him off.

That did no good, he reminded himself. He should
have said—well, he didn't know what he should have
said, but he knew he couldn't leave it alone yet.

They'd reached the house, and he pulled out the key
to unlock the door.

"I'll help you get things inside, and then I'll be off,"
Georgia said.

"Wait a minute, please." He touched Lindsay's
shoulder. "You go on and slip into your pajamas, Lindsay. I need to tell Georgia something."

Lindsay was too sleepy to argue. Clutching the
stuffed turtle, she headed for her room.

His hand on the curve of Georgia's back, he led her
to the deck. Her face was a smooth, ivory oval in the
moonlight.

"What is it?"

"Just something I didn't have the wit to say earlier. You were putting yourself down for not being able to handle a guy who was older, bigger, stronger and probably very determined. That's nonsense."

"If it had been Amanda, she'd have let him know—"

He put his fingers on her lips to stop her. This time her parents weren't sitting across from them. This time he didn't take them away.

"Don't. Don't compare yourself to your cousin. I'm sure she's a very admirable person—"

Her lips curved in a smile against his fingers. "She is."

"But she's not you." His fingers moved from her lips, caressing her cheek. "Don't you know how valuable you are? You're warmhearted, loving, filled with integrity. That's Georgia, no one else."

Her eyes sparkled in the moonlight, as if with tears. "That's the kind of thing Miz Callie would say. She always says that God created each one of us unique."

"Your grandmother is a wise woman." His heart seemed to be yearning toward the faith he'd once felt was so strong. "I can't pretend to be as wise as she is, but I try to believe that God has a purpose for who we are and a role we're meant to fill."

His own words startled him. How often had he stopped to ask if he was filling the role God had for him?

"So God needs an Amanda for one destiny, and he gives her the gifts she needs to fulfill that." She seemed to be turning it over in her mind.

"And He's created you for a role only you can fill."

"I just have to find it." She was taking his words seriously, and that moved him.

"Yes." He wanted to say more, but his feelings were too near the surface.

"Thank you, Matt." She spoke softly, her voice a murmur on the breeze. "I'm glad we talked."

"I am, too."

She'd told him something he suspected she'd told very few other people. He was honored—and scared. They were dangerously close in the moonlight, and his hand cradled the smooth, soft line of her cheek.

"Daddy," Lindsay called from upstairs. "I'm ready."

"I should go." But she didn't move.

Neither did he. And then his lips found hers in a kiss that seemed irrevocable. His fingers raked back through her curls so that he held the back of her head, her hair twining around his hand as if to hold him fast.

Every cell in his body was aware of her. A wave of tenderness swept through him, mixed with longing. He should end this, but he couldn't.

She did it for him. She moved, taking a step back. Her fingers touched her lips and her breath was uneven.

"Lindsay wants you." Her smile trembled. "Good night, Matt."

He should go to Lindsay. He would, but he stood watching first as Georgia went swiftly down the steps.

When Matt pulled up at the cottage the next day, Georgia hurried down the stairs, holding an umbrella to ward off the rain that had started during the night.

She was trying to ignore the fluttering in the pit of her stomach, trying to tell herself she felt that way because Matt had tracked down the woman Ned might have gone off with.

She couldn't quite convince herself of that, not with the memory of last night's kiss so fresh in her mind that she could still feel his lips on hers.

He reached across to open the door as she approached, and she slid in, tossing the umbrella into the backseat.

"Good morning." His gaze lingered on her face for a moment, so warm that it brought a flush to her cheeks.

"Good morning to you, too." She smoothed back unruly curls, hoping he didn't see just how affected she was by his presence. "This is amazing news. I can't believe you found her so quickly."

"Once we had a name, it wasn't that hard." He pulled out onto the road. "There's an investigator the firm sometimes uses, so I put him onto it. Don't worry—he doesn't know why I was looking for her."

Worry was too constant a companion on this subject. She knew the truth was bound to come out, but she couldn't help wanting to delay that moment as long as possible.

"But if she ran away with Ned, he'd know—"

"She didn't," he said quickly.

She didn't know whether to be relieved or disappointed. "He's sure of that?"

He nodded, turning toward the drawbridge. "There's no mystery about it at all. Mr. and Mrs. Malloy went back to their home in Summerville after that summer on the island. They lived there until his death in the seventies. She moved to Charleston then, living first in a retirement community and now in a nursing home.

They had one child, a daughter, who also lives in the city." He glanced at her. "If there had been any gap in the story, our investigator would have found it."

"So that was a dead end."

"Not necessarily." His eyes were focused on the traffic, giving her the freedom to study his strong, capable hands on the wheel, the firm line of his jaw, the tiny wrinkles at the corners of his eyes.

"What do you mean? If he didn't go away with her, we still don't know what happened to him."

"She might know. If Benny was right about the relationship, she might be the one person who did know."

"Did?"

He shrugged. "Did. Does. As I told you, she's in a nursing home, apparently not expected to live long. Whether she's able to talk..."

"That's why you said we had to go right away." She'd wondered at the urgency in his voice when he'd called this morning. Now she knew.

He nodded, glancing at the screen of his GPS. "I just wish I knew how we were going to get in to see her."

"That part won't be too difficult. I've visited more nursing homes than I can count. It's part of growing up Southern, like visits to the cemetery. We'll need to make a stop to pick up some flowers, that's all." She smiled at his expression. "Trust me on this one."

The nursing home proved to be the one on the outskirts of Mount Pleasant, making things even easier than she'd predicted. Her mother had visited here regularly, bringing flowers and seasonal treats to elderly church members. A few minutes' chat with the nurse on duty at the desk, and they were soon pushing open the door to Mrs. Malloy's room.

The woman sleeping in the railed bed didn't bear much resemblance to the picture that had formed in Georgia's mind of the heroine of that wartime romance. But then, Ned, if he were still alive, would be eighty-four, and the woman he'd supposedly loved would be even older.

A faded wedding picture stood on the bedside table, and she moved closer to have a look. The woman had been a delicate beauty, with masses of fair hair and a fragile grace that had probably appealed to Ned's chivalrous instincts. The man had a square, red, bulldog face. He gripped his young bride with a possessive air.

She glanced from the photo to the woman in the bed. There were still traces of that fragile beauty in the worn face, like an echo of the vanished past.

Matt stood back from the bed, clearly uncomfortable. This was up to her, it seemed.

"Grace." She said the name softly, touching a thin, veined hand. "We've come to visit you. We brought you some flowers."

Eyelids flickered, then opened, and faded blue eyes attempted to focus. "Flowers," she murmured.

Georgia held the mixed bouquet closer, so that she could see and smell them. "Daisies and roses, with a little baby's breath. Shall I put them in a vase for you?"

A faint nod, which she took for yes. This part of the visit was familiar. She'd always found a vase and arranged the flowers while her mother made cheerful small talk, never acting bothered if there was no response.

Emulating her, Georgia chattered about the flowers, about the weather, about the room while she fixed the flowers at the small sink and carried them to the bedside.

Grace smiled faintly, as if the aroma of the flowers touched some memory hidden deep in the recesses of her mind. "Who?" she whispered.

"I'm Georgia." She took the woman's hand again, her heart beating a little faster. "Georgia Bodine. I think you once knew my family, that summer you spent on Sullivan's Island, a long time ago."

She frowned, as if chasing an elusive memory.

"You'd better ask her directly," Matt said.

Georgia held the wasted hand in both of hers. "Ned Bodine," she said. "Do you remember him, Grace?"

For a moment there was nothing. Then the faintest trace of animation lit the woman's features. "Ned," she murmured. "Ned."

Georgia leaned closer. "Yes, Ned Bodine. Do you remember Ned? He loved you, I think."

For a moment a smile lingered on her lips. Then her brow furrowed, and she closed her eyes.

She was slipping off into whatever world she inhabited now. Georgia's heart wrenched.

Bless her, dear Lord. Ease her passage into Your presence.

"Grace?" She tried again. "Do you remember Ned?"

The only answer came from behind her as the door swung open.

"Who are you people? What are you doing in my mother's room?"

The woman who swept in moved protectively to

ward the bed, forcing Georgia to retreat. She didn't have her mother's beauty, but there was a faint resemblance between the faded creature on the bed and the erect, assertive sixty-something woman who stood next to her.

"I'm sorry to intrude, ma'am...." She hesitated, not sure of the daughter's name.

"Ms. Wilson," Matt said quietly. "I assume you're Beatrice Wilson. My name is Matthew Harper. I'm an attorney with Porter and Harper. This is Georgia Bodine."

"That doesn't explain what you're doing here," the woman said tartly.

Georgia exchanged glances with Matt. "I believe that your mother was acquainted with my great-uncle. We were hoping she might remember something about him. His name was Ned Bodine."

The woman knew his name. Georgia could see it in the sudden tensing of her body, in the quick, dismissing movement of one hand, as if she'd brush them away.

"My mother never knew anyone by the name. You'll have to leave. She's in no condition to have company."

"Please, Ms. Wilson." She held her hand out in appeal. "It's very important to my grandmother to find out what happened to Ned. If your mother remembers anything—"

"She doesn't." She clipped off the words, her gaze sliding away from Georgia's as she took her mother's hand in a protective grasp. "Please leave."

"But I just want—"

Matt touched her arm gently, and she could feel his sympathy through the light caress. He held out his card to Ms. Wilson. "Anything your mother knows or might have told you could be of great value. If you think of something, please believe we'd treat it with discretion."

She made no response, so he put the card down on the bedside table.

"If you're willing to talk to us later, I hope you'll call me."

She pressed her lips together for a moment, then shook her head.

"If only you'd let me—"

Matt grasped her elbow, piloting her out of the room before she could finish the sentence. The door swung shut behind them.

Georgia tried to shake him off, but he didn't loosen his grip. "I'm sure she knows something."

"And I'm just as sure that she's not going to tell you." He hustled her down the hallway. "You can't badger a dying woman, Georgia. Or her grieving daughter."

"But she knew…" She let that trail off. He was right, of course. She couldn't let her need to help Miz Callie override common kindness. Miz Callie was the last person to want that.

She glanced at Matt. His face was set, and lines of tension radiated from his eyes. He moved so quickly that she could barely keep up with him.

"I don't think we need to run," she said mildly.

"I don't like nursing homes." He clipped off the words. "Let's get out of here."

His shuttered expression warned her. Her heart twisted. His wife—had she been in a nursing home, making this visit a painful reminder?

She didn't know, because Matt wouldn't, or couldn't

talk about that. All she knew was what everyone knew—that his wife had died, and that it had nearly destroyed him.

He'd kissed her. He seemed to care about her. But he wouldn't let her into what was really important to him, and judging by the look on his face, she didn't think he ever would.

Chapter 15

Georgia jogged slowly from the beach to the stairs that led up to Miz Callie's deck the next morning, stopping at the bottom to stretch. As the heat intensified, she'd had to get her run in earlier and earlier.

She'd had some vague hope that jogging along the beach in the morning light might clear her mind, but she was no nearer any decisions than she had been. Her own future was still a tangle that she couldn't seem to unravel. As for her grandmother's problem, the more they learned, the less they knew.

She'd looked up Ms. Wilson's phone number and address the night before, and a half-dozen times she'd reached for the phone. Each time, something held her back. She couldn't badger the woman when her mother was dying. But with the woman's death might go their last chance of learning the truth.

Matt clearly didn't want to pursue that angle any further. But was his opinion based on logic or emotion? She wasn't sure.

She glanced down the beach, shielding her eyes with her hand. There was Miz Callie, back from her turtle patrol, but where was Lindsay? The two of them had set off together when she'd left for her run.

Impelled by something that seemed amiss in the solitary figure, she trotted down to meet her grandmother.

"Hey, Miz Callie. What happened to Lindsay? I thought she was with you."

"She's down there at the turtle nest. She didn't want to come back yet." Her grandmother's eyes showed concern. "Somethin's ailing that child, but she wouldn't say what. You go, Georgia. Maybe she'll talk to you."

She put her arm around her grandmother's waist in a quick hug. "If she wouldn't tell you what's troubling her, she surely won't tell me."

Miz Callie patted her cheek, but her gaze was stern. "Don't you belittle yourself, Georgia Lee. Goodness, you're the one everyone wants to tell their troubles to. You go and try your luck with Lindsay. She needs you."

Still doubtful, she nodded. She certainly couldn't leave Lindsay there all alone. "I'll try."

She began to jog again, her legs protesting a little. Was her grandmother serious about people wanting to confide in her? She'd always considered that Miz Callie's role in the family, not hers.

Matt certainly didn't want to do any confiding in her.

The turtle nest came into view. Lindsay was a small, lonely figure, sitting with her arms wrapped around her

knees next to the orange tape. She looked so desolate
that for a moment Georgia's heart failed her.

*Lord, that child is hurting so much. I don't feel qual-
ified to help her, but there doesn't seem to be anyone
else. Please, if this is Your will, guide my words. Let
me bring her some comfort.*

Lindsay didn't acknowledge her presence as Georgia
jogged up and dropped to the sand next to her.

"Hey, Lindsay. Are you visiting with the baby turtles this mornin'?"

Lindsay turned her face away, as if looking at the
nest, but not before Georgia had seen the traces of tears
on her cheeks. Her heart clenched.

"It…it takes them a long time to hatch, doesn't it?"

"Quite a while." She searched her memory for the
turtle lore her grandmother had planted there over the
years. "I don't think they'll hatch out until later in the
summer. Miz Callie will know. She'll watch for the
signs."

Lindsay sat still, face averted. This was obviously
not about turtles, but if she prodded, Lindsay would
retreat further into her shell, protecting herself as one
of the loggerheads would.

"That'll be their birthday," Lindsay said softly. "When
they hatch."

"I guess so." She waited for more.

"Where will their mother be on their birthday?"

Georgia was ill-prepared to talk to the child about
her mother. She'd done her best when it had come
up the day of Lindsay's party, but obviously her best
hadn't been good enough.

Please, Lord.

"She'll be out in the ocean. That's where her nature tells her to be, and that's where the baby turtles will go when they hatch. And then, when they're grown up and ready to lay their eggs, they'll come back to this same beach to make their nests, right back where they were born."

Those that survive, she added silently. Now was not the time for a lesson on how endangered the logger-head turtles were.

"My mommy used to tell me the story about when I was born. How my daddy drove her to the hospital, and how they were so happy when they had a little girl." Lindsay rubbed her eyes with the heels of her hands. "When Mommy got sick, I prayed that Jesus would make her well. But He didn't."

It wasn't the time for a theology lesson, either; she knew that instinctively. She had to say something that would comfort, but all she could feel was fear that she'd say the wrong thing.

Please, Father. Please give me the words.

"I know your mommy and daddy were the happi-est people in the world when you were born." Now came the hard part, and she tested each word before she spoke. "I don't think anybody understands why some-times people don't get well when we pray for them. But we know that Jesus loves us and will always be with us, no matter how sad or lonely we feel."

Lindsay swung to face her. "I miss her. Georgia, I miss Mommy so much."

Her heart seemed to crack as she put her arm around Lindsay's shoulders and drew her close. "Oh, honey, of course you miss her."

Lindsay burrowed her face into Georgia's chest. "I wanted to talk to Daddy about her, but I couldn't." Her voice was muffled.

Georgia held her tighter. "Why not, sugar?"

But she already knew. Matt held his grief so close that he couldn't let anyone in, not even his child.

"It might make him mad," she whispered.

"Not mad, Lindsay. Just sad, that's all. Sometimes it's hard to tell what someone else is feeling, but I know your daddy would never get mad at you for that."

Oh, Matt. Don't you see what you're doing? You're closing her out.

She smoothed her hand down the curve of Lindsay's back, feeling the fragility of tiny bones, the small shoulder blades like a bird's wings.

"How would it be if I went with you to tell your daddy that you want to talk about your mommy? Is he home this morning?"

Lindsay nodded. The movement seemed to bruise her heart. "I'm afraid," she whispered. "I don't want Daddy to be mad. Or sad. Maybe I shouldn't."

"I think you should." Conviction grew in her. Silence brought barriers between people. She knew. She and her mother were a great example of that.

Lindsay was motionless for a moment. Then she drew back. "Okay. If you promise you'll go with me."

Georgia stood, holding out her hand to Lindsay. "I promise."

Lindsay scrambled to her feet and took Georgia's hand. Together they started down the beach.

As they approached the house, Georgia's breath hitched. Was she doing the right thing?

She was doing the only thing. Someone had to help Matt see what his silence was doing to his daughter, and God had plopped the issue right in her lap.

Are You sure You've picked the right person for this job, Lord? You know how I am about confronting people. Hopeless, that's how. I quake inside. I run away.

If she'd longed for a sense that she could pass this off to someone else, she didn't get it. Come what may, she had to do this. And what was most likely to come was that Matt would be so furious that whatever existed between them would be extinguished in an instant.

She glanced at Lindsay as they started up the stairs together. One ponytail was slipping to the side, and the part in her hair was slightly crooked. The sight choked Georgia's throat with unshed tears. This vulnerable child deserved to have someone speak for her. This time there'd be no running away.

Lindsay tugged at the sliding glass door, and Georgia helped her push it back. Cool air floated out in greeting as they stepped inside.

Matt sat at the desk in the living room, a laptop open in front of him. At the sight of her, his eyebrows lifted in a question.

"Hi, Lindsay. I thought you were out checking turtle nests with Miz Callie."

Lindsay hesitated, and Georgia could feel the tension that gripped her. "I was. I... I..." She pressed her fingers against her shorts, seeming unable to go on.

Georgia placed a gentle hand on the child's shoulder. "Lindsay didn't want to leave the turtle nest, so my grandmother asked me to talk with her."

Concern darkened the steel blue of Matt's eyes. He

shoved his chair back and reached out a hand toward his daughter. "Lindsay? What's wrong?"

"I..." Lindsay tilted her face to Georgia, her gaze pleading. "I can't," she whispered.

"It's all right." She took a deep breath, hoping it would release the stranglehold around her throat, and uttered a wordless prayer. "Lindsay told me she wanted to talk to you about something, but she was afraid it might upset you."

"My daughter can talk to me about anything." But even as he said the words, he drew away from them, his body language saying exactly the opposite.

For Lindsay's sake, she had to go on. "She misses her mommy, and she needs to talk about her. To you."

Understand, Matt. Please understand.

Lindsay clung to her hand. Without it, she'd probably run from the room. That was exactly how Georgia felt, too.

As for Matt—she could sense the battle that raged within him, even if she didn't entirely understand it. Surely he could put his child's welfare ahead of his own feelings.

"Lindsay, honey." He reached for her then, took her hand, drew her close. "We can talk about Mommy if that's what you want." His voice was taut with strain, but it was gentle.

Cautiously, Lindsay reached up to pat his cheek. "Don't be sad, Daddy."

He managed a smile, dropped a kiss on her small palm. "I'll try not to be. Were you feeling sad about Mommy today?"

She nodded. "Sometimes I'm afraid I'm going to

forget about her," she whispered. "I don't want to." She sounded panicked. "I don't want to forget."

"No, no, of course you don't." He put his arms around her, holding her close. "You won't forget. It's okay."

Georgia's throat closed with tears. This hurt him— she could feel it. But he was doing it. Maybe he needed this as much as Lindsay did.

"Remember how Mommy always told the story about how I was born? Every birthday she told me that story."

He smoothed his hand over her hair. "I remember," he said, his voice rough. "Do you want me to tell you?"

She nodded. "Can I get my baby book out to look at while you tell the story, just like me and Mommy did?"

"Sure you can." He released her, giving her a gentle push toward the stairs. "You run up and get it while I walk Georgia out."

"Okay." The smile that dawned on Lindsay's face was a delight to see. "Thank you, Georgia."

"You're welcome, sugar." She managed to hold her smile until the child turned away. Then all she wanted to do was run.

Matt was furious with her. Maybe he had a right to be. She turned and preceded him out to the deck and down the stairs.

But she'd done the right thing. No matter what it cost her, she'd done the right thing.

His tread was heavy on the steps. She could sense the weight of his emotion—the power of will that held it back until they were out of earshot of his daughter.

At the bottom of the steps, he stopped. "I suppose you think you had to do that."

It took all the courage she possessed to meet the grief and anger that clouded his eyes. "I'm sorry if that hurt you, but—"

"If?" The word exploded out of him.

Her cheeks burned. "All right. I knew it would be painful. But Lindsay was hurting, too. She confided in me." She shook her head, longing to reach him, not sure she knew how. "Don't you see, Matt? She is desperate to talk about her mother to someone, and there's no one here who knew her. No one but you."

His jaw clenched at the words, so tightly that it seemed it might break from the pressure. She quailed inside, waiting for an explosion.

It didn't come. Matt took one careful breath. Then another.

"I know you're trying to help. I appreciate that."

Encouraged, she longed to reach out and touch him but didn't quite dare. "She needs you, Matt. She needs you to talk about her mother. If only you could share your grief—"

"No!" Matt grabbed the railing, the tendons of his forearms standing out. "That I can't do. Don't you understand?" He threw the words at her angrily.

Only her love for the little girl kept her from backing away. "No, I don't. Tell me. Or tell someone, if not me. You can't…"

The words trailed off. Who was she to give advice to someone about grieving? She couldn't even imagine the magnitude of his loss. But Lindsay—Lindsay she did understand. And Lindsay needed help.

"You know everything there is to know about my family, I think. And I don't even know how your wife died."

"Cancer." He spit the word out. "Jennifer died of cancer." He paused, but maybe having said that much made it easier for him to go on. "She was so strong, so brave. Her faith never wavered, right to the very end."

She didn't know what to say, and couldn't have said it if she had known.

He shrugged, his shoulders moving stiffly. "I thought my faith was strong, too, until I was finally alone after the funeral." He turned to her then. "You know what I did? I fell apart—acted like a total madman. Screamed, broke things, threw things, raged at God."

"Lindsay…" She whispered the name.

"Lindsay was with her grandparents."

Of course. Certainty built in her. "You wouldn't have done it if she had been there."

"You can't know that." Fury sparked from his eyes. "Don't you see? The only way I can be sure of keeping control is to shut it away." The anger faded, just a little, and he suddenly looked exhausted. "I'll do what I can to satisfy Lindsay, but I can't let go of my control."

"I'm sorry." She whispered the words, sorrow weighing heavily on her. "But I think you're wrong. I'd better go."

As she turned, he grabbed her hand, holding it tightly.

"Don't, Georgia." His voice was ragged. "I don't want to drive you away. I don't want to lose you. But just don't ask me to open my heart, because that's the one thing I can't do."

He was offering her something. It was there under the words. A relationship, but one that had strings attached.

Longing filled her heart. If only she could agree, keep silent, anything to preserve what they had.

But she couldn't. She wasn't the same person she'd been when she came back to the island. Somehow, through knowing him, through struggling to help Lindsay, through dealing with Miz Callie's problem, she'd become stronger.

Maybe God had led her through this for that purpose. She couldn't turn back now, no matter what it cost.

Love costs, Miz Callie had said. She was right.

"I'm sorry." She managed to keep her voice even, but it took an effort. "I can't settle for that. Not for myself, and not for you."

He didn't move. He let go of her hand, and his silence said more than words.

It was over. Feeling her heart splinter in her chest, she turned and walked away.

Chapter 16

Georgia drew her car to a stop in front of Beatrice Wilson's house and hesitated, her hands trembling on the steering wheel. She hadn't called before coming, sure the woman would hang up at the sound of her voice.

Probably Ms. Wilson would slam the door instead, but she had to try. They were out of options. Beatrice Wilson's mother was the only person who might know what happened to Ned when he left Charleston all those years ago.

She'd failed with Matt, and she had a gaping hole in her heart as a souvenir of that encounter. Funny that it had taken this very real pain to show her that what she'd felt about the breakup with James had been nothing but damaged pride.

She took a breath, pressing her palms together to still their quivering. She couldn't do anything about Matt, but maybe she could still salvage something from the wreckage for her grandmother. Georgia slid from the car and headed for the wrought-iron gate in the low brick wall that surrounded the house.

The gate pushed open at a touch, and she walked into a tiny courtyard. The two-story house, set endways to the street, its veranda facing the courtyard, was classic Charleston in style. A brick path led to the veranda, where the front door's frosted glass hid the interior. Breathing a silent prayer, Georgia reached for the shell-shaped knocker and let it fall.

A click of heels resounded faintly from inside, and then the door opened. Beatrice Wilson stared at her for a moment and then swung the door toward her.

Georgia caught it with her hand. She hadn't rehearsed what she'd say, but the words seemed to spring to her lips.

"Please, Ms. Wilson. I know you're trying to protect your mother. I don't mean her any harm or embarrassment, I promise. Just give me five minutes. Then if you're not willing to talk to me, I'll never bother you or her again."

For a moment the woman stood frozen, her face strained, her eyelids red. Then she swung the door open. "You can come in, but it won't do you any good. My mother died early this morning."

A cold hand squeezed Georgia's heart as sorrow swept over her—for Ms. Wilson, for her mother and for Miz Callie, who would never know the truth.

"I'm sorry." She reached out impulsively to clasp

the woman's hand as she stepped into the cool, tiled hallway. "I'm so sorry for your loss."

Ms. Wilson nodded, closing the door. The muscles in her neck worked. "It was expected, but it's still hard. Harder than I thought."

"I'm sorry," she said again. There didn't seem anything else to say. "I should go. I'm sure you have a great deal to do."

"Tell me first." Ms. Wilson's lips trembled, and she pressed them together. "What did you want from my mother?"

She knew something. Georgia was sure of it. She'd reacted to Ned's name before she threw them out of the room at the nursing home.

"Ned Bodine was my grandfather's older brother. He disappeared in 1942—left without telling anyone where he was going." She hesitated, but what point was there in evasion? "People believed he ran away rather than enlist. They called him a coward."

"Why are you interested in it now? What difference could it make to anyone?" The woman's gaze slid away from Georgia's and focused on an arrangement of pink roses on a marble-topped hall stand.

"My grandmother cares. She's starting to see her friends pass away, and that's made her think of things she regrets—like never trying to prove that Ned wasn't the coward people thought him."

"Is she so sure of that?"

"Yes," she said instantly. "She is, and she's desperate to clear his name."

Still the woman didn't look at her. "What does that have to do with my mother?"

She hesitated, wondering whether she dared say what she knew, what she suspected, about Ned and Beatrice's mother. But again, what good would it do to hold it back?

"Your parents rented a house on Sullivan's Island that summer. People remember that Ned and your mother were...friends."

She flared up at that. "My mother was a kind person. People loved her."

"I'm sure they did," Georgia said gently. "My grandmother remembers a night when she found Ned standing in the dunes outside your parents' cottage. She remembers hearing your father shouting and the sound of a slap."

Beatrice Wilson stood perfectly still, but her hands twisted together as if they fought for control.

"We have no intention of making any of that public," Georgia said softly, pity filling her heart. "I just hoped that your mother might have remembered. Might have known why Ned went away the way he did. But I guess it's too late. Thank you for your time. And again, I'm sorry." She turned toward the door.

"Wait." For another instant the woman stood motionless, as if she'd surprised herself by the word. Then she spun and hurried through the archway into the parlor. In a moment she was back, holding something in her hand.

"When Mamma went into the nursing home, I sorted her things. I found these." She hesitated a moment. "I was going to burn them." She took a choking breath, and her eyes welled. "You were right about my father.

Maybe this…" She thrust the papers toward Georgia. "Here. Take them."

They crackled in her fingers. Three envelopes: old, yellowed, the writing faded.

"Please go." The woman looked at the end of her rope. "I hope—I hope they have the answers you're looking for."

Georgia stepped outside and hurried to the car, forcing herself to wait until she was safely inside. She opened the first envelope, her fingers fumbling, breath hitching.

A few minutes later she sat back in her seat, wiping tears from her eyes. She understood now why Ned had left, but whether that would be enough to clear his name, she couldn't guess.

Matt resisted the temptation to put his hands over his ears. It wouldn't help. Nothing would block out the sound of the Bodine clan in full crisis mode.

Georgia had said something once about her family's penchant for noisy interference in each other's business. He saw what she meant. No wonder she was so reluctant to confront them.

Miz Callie sat in her rocking chair while agitated voices swirled, her face set. She wasn't even attempting to explain.

Maybe she had it right. Maybe it was necessary to let them run out of steam, and then they'd be ready to listen.

But he doubted it.

All three of Miz Callie's sons and their wives were here, along with Georgia's brother Adam and her cousin Amanda. He wasn't quite sure why they'd been dragged along—maybe because the older generation blamed them for helping.

Amanda, sitting between her father and Georgia's father, was trying to play peacemaker, but judging by the spark in her eyes, she'd rather just yell at them. Adam stood behind his grandmother, immovable as a boulder, letting the torrent of voices roll around him.

"Don't you have anything to say for yourself?" Ashton Bodine demanded.

Matt realized that was directed at him. Somewhat to his surprise, the talk died down for his answer.

Not that they'd like it.

"Miz Callie is my client," he said. "I'm carrying out her wishes, and I'll continue to do that."

The clamor fell on his ears again. He'd warned Georgia that the further the paperwork went, the more likely someone would leak the plan. That was exactly what had happened.

Georgia should be here, but he was just as glad she wasn't. She would hate this.

Pain wrapped around his heart at the thought of her. He'd hurt her. He hadn't intended to, but he had.

He longed to see her again, to try and make amends, but how could he? She asked the impossible of him.

The front door opened. Georgia stood there, staring at the scene in front of her. For an instant he saw panic in her eyes, and then her fight to control it.

"Georgia!"

Ignoring her mother's exclamation, Georgia crossed the room to her grandmother and bent to kiss her cheek.

"Are you all right?" she asked, as if there were no one else in the room.

"I am." Miz Callie patted her cheek. "But better for having you here, sugar."

"Georgia Lee, I think you'd better explain your part in this." Her father's voice held a note of command.

Other voices lifted as her aunts and uncles chimed in, demanding answers.

Matt saw Georgia exchange glances with her brother and her cousin. But not with him, and the omission nicked his heart. She straightened, holding her grandmother's hand.

"As soon as y'all can get quiet, I do have something to say."

The sudden silence was as weighty as a breaker crashing. Her father blinked. "All right, Georgia Lee. We're listening."

"First of all, Miz Callie asked me to do something for her. She asked me to find out what really happened to Ned Bodine."

There was a strangled noise from one of the uncles, and she shot him a look so stern that he shut up probably from sheer amazement.

"The truth, not just what everyone says. The truth that Miz Callie believes—that Ned Bodine wasn't a coward."

Her father cleared his throat. "Mamma…" His voice gentled. "I'm touched you believe that, but after all this time, no one can possibly find out—"

"But they can," Georgia said, her voice firmer than he'd ever heard it. "I did."

Now he was gaping like the rest of them.

Georgia looked down at her grandmother, patting her hand. "It was just as you thought. Ned was in love with the woman who rented the next cottage that summer. He wanted desperately to protect her from her abusive husband."

"If they ran away," Miz Callie began, voice trembling.

Georgia stroked her hand. "It wasn't that. When Ned realized that she wouldn't let him help her, he decided he had to go away. To join up, as his friends did."

"We didn't find any records," Matt reminded her.

"No." Her gaze finally met his, cautious, guarded, as if just looking at him might hurt her. "Because he didn't enlist under his own name."

Her father was shaking his head. "Georgia, I appreciate your trying to help your grandmother, but you can't know this."

She held up several yellowed sheets of paper. "I have proof—the letters Ned wrote to her that summer. The last one says it all." Carefully, she unfolded the brittle paper. "He tells her that he's leaving, and why. And he says that since his father has spent so much time telling him that he's a disgrace to the Bodine name, he won't be using it." A single tear dropped on the paper, and she carefully blotted it away. "As far as we know, no one ever heard of Ned Bodine again."

"Georgia..." Miz Callie breathed her name, eyes sparkling with tears.

Georgia pressed the letters into her hand. "For you."

She'd done it. She'd obviously gone to the Wilson woman again, and she'd pulled off something he'd thought impossible. Not only that, but she'd stood up to her entire family. His heart swelled with pride. Pride, and regret that in the end, he hadn't helped her.

Her parents and aunts and uncles stared at her in amazement. Her brother reached over to envelop her in a huge congratulatory hug, and she turned her face into his shirt.

A pang shot through Matt, headed straight for his heart. He wanted it to be him comforting her, celebrating with her. But he'd forfeited any possibility of that.

"Astonishing," murmured Brett, Amanda's father. "But y'all know people are still going to talk. We can't very well put his letter in the newspaper as proof."

There was a murmur, maybe of agreement. Georgia turned toward them again. "There's nothing to be ashamed of."

Silence for a moment, and then Georgia's mother rose.

"Let them talk." She held out her hand to her daughter. "We're Bodines. If people talk, we'll hold our heads a little higher, won't we, honey?" The smile she gave Georgia held love and pride.

Georgia took her hand, stepped into her embrace. The others, following Delia's lead, clustered around. The Bodines were a single unit again, surrounding Georgia.

Excluding him. That was the way it should be. Georgia deserved the best. She deserved a man who could offer her a whole heart. He couldn't.

He turned and slipped quietly out.

Chapter 17

Finally the family had gone. Georgia was alone on the beach. The sun slipped toward the horizon, and the last of the day's beachgoers had left. She really was alone.

She should feel lost. Whatever might have been with Matt was gone. She'd finished the job Miz Callie had set for her. But instead of feeling lost, she felt a sense of release. Of freedom. She no longer had to make decisions based on her sense of failure.

She could stay here. The idea took hold, strong as the incoming tide. She didn't have to worry about putting space between herself and her family's expectations. She could stay where her roots ran deep. Even though the love she'd hoped for with Matt could never be, she could build a satisfying life. Surely someone in Charleston needed an employee with her experience.

Her steps grew lighter, quicker, and her mind raced with the decision made. She'd go back to Atlanta and give up the apartment—that was the first thing. She'd spend a couple of days winding up things there, then come back and launch into a serious job hunt. Maybe Amanda would know of something.

She should tell Miz Callie. But first—her steps had taken her as far as Matt's house. Standing on the beach, the incoming tide sending ripples chasing her feet, she looked at the house.

Lights were on, glowing behind the drapes. He was there. Maybe, before she moved on, there was something still to be said between them, no matter how much it might hurt to be with him again.

By the time she'd disentangled herself from her family earlier, he'd gone. She hadn't thanked him yet. If he hadn't tracked down Grace Malloy, she'd never have gotten her hands on the letters, and Miz Callie would still be wondering. She owed him for that, at least.

Her feet felt rooted in the sand. Giving herself a shake, she started walking toward the house. *No more hiding, Georgia Lee. You're finished with that. God has set you free.*

She reached the steps and went steadily up them, then knocked on the glass door. In a moment Matt pushed it back, looking surprised to see her and a bit guarded as well.

"Georgia. I wasn't expecting you." He stepped back, gesturing her inside.

She nodded. A quick glance showed her Lindsay was nowhere in sight. They were alone.

She sucked in a breath. Her heart was beating faster

than a hummingbird's wings, and something seemed
to grip her throat.

Matt stood waiting, the newspaper he'd apparently
been reading dangling from his hand. When he realized he still held it, he tossed it onto the coffee table.

Another breath might help. Breathing was always
a good idea.

"I came over to thank you." She stumbled a little on
the words, but she got them out. "If it weren't for you,
I'd never have found the truth about Ned."

He nodded. "You're welcome, but you're the one
who did it. And your uncle was right. It's not the sort
of thing you'll be able to tell the public."

"My grandmother's happy. That's the only thing
that really matters. And Amanda and Adam are bubbling with ideas for figuring out where he enlisted and
what name he used."

His eyes grew remote. "It'll be easier on you now
that the family is on board with this. You'll be heading
back to Atlanta any day now, I suppose."

"I'm driving up tomorrow, but—"

"No!" A wail was followed by the thud of bare feet
on the stairs. Lindsay, pajama-clad, rushed down the
steps, across the room and threw herself at Georgia.

Georgia knelt to catch the child in her arms. "Hey,
what's this? It's all right. I—"

"You can't go! You can't." Lindsay got the words out
between sobs that were nearly hysterical. "I love you,
Georgia. If you go, I won't have anybody to talk to."

Georgia cradled her in her arms, afraid to look at
Matt for fear of the condemnation she'd see there. She
petted the child, murmuring softly. "You have Miz
Callie, and you have Daddy. Besides—"

"Daddy doesn't want to talk about Mommy." She shook her head so wildly that her braids snapped to and fro. "He doesn't. He doesn't love her any more!"

"Lindsay—"

Before she could say more, Matt dropped to his knees next to her. Instead of the anger she expected, his eyes were filled with tears.

"Lindsay, no. That's not true." He tried to take her from Georgia, but she clung like a barnacle. "Honey, listen to me. I love you. And I love Mommy. Didn't we talk about her when we looked at your baby book?"

"You didn't want to." She threw the words at him. "I know you didn't want to. You just did it cause Georgia told you to."

Georgia winced. What could she do or say that would mend this? *Please, Lord.*

But it wasn't her Lindsay needed to hear from now. It was Matt.

"Lindsay, listen." He took her face between his hands, turning it so that she had to look at him, had to see the tears that were running down his face. "When your mommy died, that was the worst thing that ever happened to me. I've been afraid to let you see how much it hurts me. I was afraid it would scare you."

That caught Lindsay's attention. She looked at him closely. Then she reached out one small hand and wiped at his tears.

"It's all right, Daddy. I'm not scared. You can cry if you want to."

For an instant Georgia thought Matt would shatter into a million pieces. Then he pulled his daughter into his arms. He held her close, his shoulders shaking, and their tears mingled.

Georgia struggled to her feet, trying to control her emotions. They were going to be all right. This time, Matt wasn't holding anything back.

Thank You, Father. Thank You for this.

Struggling to see the way through her own tears, she left them alone.

Georgia kissed her grandmother's cheek the next morning. Juggling a suitcase and the lunch Miz Callie had insisted on packing her, she started down the front steps to her car.

And stopped. Matt stood next to the car, obviously waiting for her.

"Hi." She went the rest of the way, busying herself with putting the bag and lunch in the back so she didn't have to look at him. "Is everything okay?"

"Fine." His smile broke through, erasing the lines of tension in his face. "Lindsay and I are both much better. I think I have you to thank for that."

She shook her head, looking anywhere but at him, because if she did, she might start to cry. "It wasn't my doing. Lindsay's the one who broke through."

"That's exactly what it was. Breaking through." He stood very close, so that she was caught between the car and his body. "I thought if I opened my heart, the grief would shatter me. Instead…" He stopped, and she heard the hitch in his breath. "Instead I found that opening it was the only thing that could heal me."

"I'm glad," she murmured. Inadequate. Words were inadequate.

"Georgia, don't go." He spoke in a sudden rush

of feeling, grabbing her hand and gripping it tight. "Please, don't go away."

"I—"

"Wait, let me explain." He touched her lips gently with his finger, and she felt his touch run straight to her heart. "I'm sorry. So sorry for the way I acted. You were right all along, and I kept trying to shut you out." His fingers fanned against her cheek. "I think God sent you here for that reason—because I wouldn't listen to anyone or anything else, including Him."

Thank You, Lord, she said silently. *Thank You.*

"I want to give life another chance," he said, his voice soft and low. "If you'll help me, I think I can make it."

She dared to look at him then. Love filled his eyes— love and hope that seemed to grow as he read what was in her face.

"You'll stay?" he breathed.

"I'll come back," she said. "I wasn't going to Atlanta to stay, just to close things up. My life is here."

With you. She wouldn't say the words, not yet. But when his lips claimed hers in a kiss, they both knew the truth.

It would take time—time to finish grieving, time for Lindsay to think of her as a parent. She slid her arms around Matt, feeling the strong, solid worth of him as he held her close.

She'd wait as long as she had to. But it would be worth it, because she knew they'd be a family in the end.

Epilogue

Georgia leaned against Matt's shoulder as they sat in the dunes. The sun had slid below the horizon, and the reds and oranges that had painted the sky faded slowly to deep purple. The waves murmured gently as night drew in.

"Hey, wake up, you two." Miz Callie stood a few feet away, next to an excited Lindsay. "This is the real thing. The babies are hatching."

Georgia scrambled to her feet and knelt by the nest. "You're sure?"

Matt squatted next to her, grasping her hand. "I think she knows."

The shallow, concave depression in the sand seemed to deepen as they watched.

"They're coming, they're coming!" Lindsay danced

up and down with excitement. "They're really hatching after we waited forever!"

"Only a couple of months," Matt reminded her.

So much had changed in that time that Georgia could hardly get her mind around it. She glanced down at the diamond winking on her finger.

"This one's for real," Matt had whispered when he put it there. "I'm not James. You won't find it easy to get rid of me."

"I won't ever want to," she'd replied, heart so full of love that it seemed to expand in her chest.

Now she looked across the moving sand at the child who would be her daughter. The love she had for Lindsay was so strong that it continually astonished her.

"Georgia, look, look! The sand is bubbling!"

Lindsay leaned so far over the nest that she nearly fell in. Miz Callie grabbed her.

"That's what we call a boil, remember? They'll all pop out in a big bunch."

"Will they know which way to go?" Lindsay held on to Miz Callie, looking at her with worried eyes.

"'Course they will. All the house lights are off along the beach, and look at the way the moon is shining on the water. They'll head straight for the ocean, mark my words. And if any of them get lost, we'll be right here to help them."

Georgia glanced up, finding Matt's face very close. "You know, I think she might be more excited about getting Miz Callie as a grandmother than getting me as a mother."

He dropped a kiss on the tip of her nose. "We're both

very lucky to get you, and we know it," he murmured. "God has been very good to us."

"Yes. He has." She glanced out at the water moving darkly under the shimmering path of the moon. Sea oats rustled in the breeze. A few faint stars had begun to shine.

Miz Callie's favorite verse drifted through her mind.

When I think of the heavens that Thou hast established, the moon and the stars, which Thou hast ordained...

"His love is overwhelming." Matt's hand tightened on hers. "Look. Here comes one."

A tiny snout broke through the sand. Then, like a pot boiling over, the hatchlings burst out into the cool night air, scrambling over one another in their hurry. They began their rush to the sea, following the instinct God had given them.

"Quick, quick!" Lindsay shrieked. "We have to keep them safe while Miz Callie counts them coming out of the nest."

They fanned out on either side of the moving wave of tiny turtles that scrambled over every obstacle in their fierce need to reach the sea. The moon made a silvery path for them, and Lindsay dashed alongside, face intent as she guarded them.

My place, Georgia thought as she shepherded a tiny turtle toward the waves. My place, my people, my destiny. She looked at Matt, helping his daughter chase off a ghost crab with designs on a hatchling. My love.

Thank You, Father. Thank You.

The first of the babies reached the waves, others

following, their swimming reflexes kicking in. They would soon be safe in the ocean, where they belonged.

In thirty years or so, God willing, the females would return to lay their eggs on this beach again. She glanced at her grandmother. Miz Callie would be gone by then, but she had already passed the torch. A new generation of turtle ladies would take her place, safeguarding God's creation as she had taught them.

* * * * *

Jill Lynn pens stories filled with humor, faith and happily-ever-afters. She's an ACFW Carol Award–winning author and has a bachelor's degree in communications from Bethel University. An avid fan of thrift stores, summer and coffee, she lives in Colorado with her husband and two children, who make her laugh on a daily basis. Connect with her at jill-lynn.com.

Books by Jill Lynn

Love Inspired

Colorado Grooms

The Rancher's Surprise Daughter
The Rancher's Unexpected Baby
The Bull Rider's Secret
Her Hidden Hope
Raising Honor
Choosing His Family

Falling for Texas
Her Texas Family
Her Texas Cowboy

Visit the Author Profile page at Harlequin.com for more titles.

FALLING
FOR TEXAS

Jill Lynn

"For I know the plans I have for you,"
declares the Lord, "plans to prosper you and not to
harm you, plans to give you hope and a future."

—*Jeremiah* 29:11

To my mom—thank you for always being my biggest supporter, a wise counselor and a tenacious prayer warrior.

Chapter 1

His sister's skill for getting into trouble would be impressive if it weren't so discouraging.

Cash Maddox's abused leather cowboy boots echoed down the empty school hallway, the smells of industrial cleaner and mildew transporting him back a decade to his own high school days. At least the scents were better than manure, the cologne he most likely boasted after taking off in the middle of ranch work and not leaving enough time for a shower.

Usually he didn't get called into school until a few weeks into the fall semester. But this year? School hadn't even started. Rachel had only been on school property for one day of preseason volleyball practice yesterday, yet Cash had come in last night to find a note scrawled in his housekeeper's handwriting about meeting the new coach after practice today.

He didn't know what Coach Grayson wanted to meet with him about, but if he had to guess, his sister wasn't going to be winning any awards. Unless there was a gold medal for eye rolling or hair tossing. She'd win those faster than an amateur could get bucked off a bull.

But despite the tension that had invaded their house lately and the way Rachel wanted nothing to do with him, Cash loved his little sister. He'd do just about anything to give her the same great upbringing he'd had. He owed her at least that much.

Catching his reflection in the glass trophy case, Cash paused to pick out a much younger version of himself in the old football team photos. He and his best friend, Jack Smith, had that stoic look in the picture, as if smiling meant they weren't tough.

He shook his head and started walking again, remembering parading down these same hallways. Man, he'd been full of himself back then. Not more than any other football player in this town, but still. At least he and Jack had finally grown up. Cash's maturing had come a bit quicker than most, but then, parenting would do that to anyone.

He paused in the doorway to the French room, where his message said to meet.

"You must be Rachel's father. Please come in." Coach Grayson waved, not looking up from working at her desk. "I'm just finishing up some class notes."

Cash opened his mouth to correct her assumption, then clamped his jaw shut at her look of concentration. Warm cocoa hair scooped into a ponytail hung down over one shoulder as Coach Grayson nibbled on her lip.

Jack. Cash wanted to grab an old-fashioned branding iron and lay one on his friend. Jack and Janie Smith were neighbors with the new woman in town, and they'd had her over for dinner on Sunday night. But while Jack had mentioned that his wife and two-year-old son had seemed equally smitten with the new coach, he'd failed to mention that she looked nothing like Coach Pleater—the woman in her sixties who'd retired last year after two decades with the school.

Coach Grayson wore a fitted pink T-shirt and had tiny stud earrings in her earlobes. Athletic and yet still…professional. Right. That was the word he was going for.

Cash settled his long frame into the high school desk across from her and released a pent-up breath. Didn't matter if the woman was the Gillespie County Fair queen. She was off-limits for him.

He removed his hat, scraping a hand through his hair and causing a cloud of dust to settle on his shoulders. Yep. Definitely should have showered.

"Sorry about that. I didn't want to lose that thought for the first week's lesson plan." Coach Grayson set her pen down and looked up, gracing Cash with breath-stealing blue eyes framed by dark lashes and plenty of reasons to escape from the room right now. Like a heart-shaped face, with a chin that jutted out just enough to emphasize the smooth curve of her cheeks and the line of her lips.

Mercy. What was wrong with him? Had he never seen a woman before?

"No problem." At his raspy voice, he cleared his

throat and tried again. "You wanted to see me about Rachel?"

Coach Grayson's eyebrows pulled together and she looked down at the front of her shirt—searching for words or embarrassed about her clothing, Cash wasn't sure. He only knew the coach didn't look anywhere near as messy in her volleyball gear as he did in grubby ranch clothes. In fact, she looked pretty cute.

Not that he should be looking.

Cash forced his concentration back to his sister instead of the surprising distraction in front of him. After all, he had a promise to keep and a girl who needed him to keep it.

The rest would have to wait.

So far, Olivia Grayson considered her escape from Colorado a success. In one weekend, she'd managed to move across the country, unpack her apartment, become friends with her new neighbors and fall in love.

If that last one happened to be with Jack and Janie Smith's two-year-old son? All the better. Olivia had no intention of meeting a guy in the sleepy little town of Fredericksburg, Texas.

Which was why she absolutely *did not care* that a head-turning cowboy sat across from her while she wore a coffee-stained T-shirt boasting the lovely smell of a productive day in the gym.

Olivia hadn't thought much of it when she'd pictured meeting Rachel Maddox's father. But if the man in front of her was a parent to the seventeen-year-old blonde on her volleyball team, Olivia would swallow her tongue.

She kind of already had.

"You're Warren Maddox?"

"Actually, I'm Cash." He ran a hand through dark hazelnut hair speckled with a few sun-kissed golden highlights. "Warren's my father's name. Technically I'm Warren C. Maddox, but everyone's called me Cash since I was a kid. Warren is probably listed as my legal name on the parent list. Sorry about that."

Olivia waited for some further explanation, but it didn't come. Huh. Maybe he'd had Rachel at a very young age. Or something.

Was it really her business?

"So, what's my sister done this time?"

"Your sister?"

He nodded. "Suppose you wouldn't know the story, being new and all. Rachel is my younger sister by ten years. Our parents died in a car crash a few years ago and I was old enough to take legal guardianship of her."

That made a lot more sense. Except…what a horrible story. "I'm so sorry." Olivia straightened the stack of papers on her desk, floundering for more appropriate words to express her sympathies. She quickly discarded everything that popped into her mind.

Cash raised a hand. "You don't have to stop talking to me now or analyze everything you say before you say it."

She smiled as his mesmerizing hazel eyes turned playful, the color reminding her of leaves changing in the fall.

"I can't believe you thought I was old enough to be Rachel's father, Coach Grayson. Now that's just offensive."

"I didn't think that."

Her gaze traveled from his T-shirt that sported evidence of a hard day's work, down to his dusty jeans and brown leather boots. The way his legs covered the distance between his chair and her desk, he must be over six foot. Which meant he was taller than her... not that that mattered in the least.

He skimmed a hand over strong cheekbones. "I apologize for my appearance, but I had to come in the middle of ranch work to meet with you."

Had he noticed her perusal? Heat rushed to her cheeks. Dust might permeate the man's appearance, but he definitely didn't need to apologize. He looked far too attractive for his disheveled state.

"I'm sorry for pulling you away from work." She glanced down at her clothes. "And I just came from practice, so I completely understand." Olivia swiped her mouth to check for the presence of any chocolate left from her after-practice snack. With the way she was acting, she'd probably find a bit of drool, too.

"It's not a problem, Coach Grayson. Rachel always comes first."

"Call me Olivia, please." If Rachel came first...did that mean Cash wasn't married? He had to be around her age. "Was that your wife that I spoke to on the phone to schedule our meeting?"

An amused grin slid across his face, making Olivia's stomach bounce like one of the volleyballs she'd put away after practice.

"I ask Laura Lee to marry me all the time, but she always says no. Probably because she's already married to my foreman, Frank." His eyes danced. "Laura Lee helps out at the house. She's really more of an aunt or a mother than a housekeeper. She works a few hours a week cleaning and making meals. Freezes a bunch at a time so we have something to eat. If Rachel or I were in charge of meals, it would only be fast food or frozen pizzas."

Olivia let out a breath she didn't realize she'd been holding. Of relief? Did it really matter if he was married or not? She didn't have plans to go anywhere near another man. Not after the mess she'd left behind in Colorado.

She glanced down, the papers on her desk bringing the reason for their meeting back into focus. "Now that I've figured out who you are, I guess we should talk about Rachel." That came out sounding so professional she almost cheered.

Cash leaned back, linking fingers behind his neck and crossing one leg over the other. "I am curious what Rachel did to warrant a meeting this time. Usually it's a few weeks into school before I get the first phone call."

The girl sounded like a bit of trouble. Good thing Olivia had a soft spot for struggling teenage girls. Hoping Cash wouldn't get too upset about what she had to say next, she leaned forward and softened her voice. "She didn't do anything wrong. Yet."

When Cash mirrored her smile, Olivia ignored the way her disobedient legs swam under the desk.

"I've been going over last year's grades, and I'm concerned that if Rachel doesn't make some changes this year she won't be eligible to play due to her GPA. I don't know if you realize this, but your sister's very good."

She paused, wondering how much to share with him. The man probably needed some encouragement if he had to deal with a teenage girl all on his own. "In two days of practice I can tell she's the best player I've ever coached. And if you think I look too young for that to matter, you're wrong. I have enough experience to know what I'm saying. She definitely has the potential to play in college and could easily earn a scholarship. I'd hate to see her lose out on that because of her GPA."

A line cut through Cash's forehead, and Olivia pressed her lips together. Had she pushed too far?

"I'm not sure what to do with that girl. Ever since our parents died she's had trouble, but never to this degree. I try to talk to her, but she won't open up to me. It seems her grades and behavior keep getting worse instead of better."

"What about a tutor or someone to help her complete her class assignments during the school year? I looked up her test scores and I'm pretty sure from what I saw that she's just not applying herself. The scores show she's smart, which makes me think she doesn't care enough to do the work her classes require."

Cash let out an exhale that turned into a laugh as he shook his head. "That sounds like my sister." His arms slid around the cowboy hat on the desk as he shifted forward.

Sensing openness, Olivia's tense muscles relaxed. If only all parents were so receptive.

"Have any free time on your hands, Coach Grayson? Any chance you'd be interested in tutoring one of your new players?"

That was not what Olivia had expected to hear. A

small part of her found the idea intriguing. In practice, she could see the hurt hiding behind Rachel's eye rolls and teenage attitude. But Olivia didn't need to get involved with this family. Not when the man across from her had a melt-her-resolve grin that could get her into serious trouble. Again.

"I…might be able to work something out." She wanted to jump out of her chair, grab the words and stuff them back into her mouth. Why would she offer to help Rachel? She absolutely did not have the time. And she needed to stay far, far away from the magnetic Cash Maddox.

"I'd be happy to pay you for your time."

Did he sense her reluctance? "I can't accept payment for tutoring one of the students. It's against the rules and I wouldn't take it anyway."

Olivia frowned. *Quit making it sound like you're still considering it. Open your mouth right now and tell him you can't do it.*

"Volleyball has games on Wednesday nights, right?" Cash barely waited for her nod before continuing. "How about Thursdays after practice you come out to the ranch and help Rachel? We'll pay you by feeding you dinner. Don't worry, I won't make it myself. I'll warm up whatever Laura Lee has in the freezer."

Take back your semioffer and say no.

But…

What if digging up twenty-six years of roots in Colorado and roaring into this Texas town with a trail of dirt behind her wasn't just about running away from her past? What if God had brought her here to help a young girl?

For such a time as this... The verse she'd read in Esther last night pounded through her head and Olivia sighed, resisting the urge to close her eyes or crawl under the desk to escape. "Guess I could swing that."

"Great." Cash's eyebrows shot up as if her answer surprised him. Kind of like it had her. He extracted himself from the desk and she found out the truth to her theory. Definitely taller than her.

"I'll see you the first week of school, then. I hope you know how much we appreciate this." Cash returned the cowboy hat to his head, tipped the brim in her direction and exited the room, leaving Olivia wondering about the state of her decision-making skills.

What had she been thinking agreeing to help? Better yet, what was God thinking?

If anything, God should want to keep her far away from Cash Maddox. Five minutes with the man and Olivia already felt a tug of attraction—to Cash's personality, not just his looks. But she would just have to bury any thoughts of him under her spinning tires. Moving to Texas was all about starting over and leaving the past behind...which meant no dating, no more mistakes.

She might have arrived in Fredericksburg with memories clinging to the trunk of her car and an empty ring finger stripped of all hope, but she refused to repeat the past here.

No looking back. It could be her Texas motto.

The open-air Jeep Wrangler jerked and dipped as Cash drove toward the new pasture site, hands rumbling on the steering wheel. His meeting with Coach Grayson—Olivia—had eaten enough time out of the afternoon that the guys most likely had the portable electric fences in place.

He shoved the stick shift into first gear, pulled on the parking brake and turned off the engine. Leaving the keys dangling in the ignition, he jumped out.

"How we doing?" Cash approached Frank, adjusting the brim of his hat to better shade against the sizzling mid-August sun.

"Just about ready to move them over." Frank studied the grazing cattle, his face weathered from a lifetime of outdoor work. He'd been the foreman at the Circle M for as long as Cash could remember. Frank didn't say much, but when he did, that usually meant it needed to be said. He had a wise, level head on his shoulders and had helped Cash keep the ranch running after Dad died. Frank knew more about ranching than twenty experienced ranch hands roped together.

A wet snout nosed his hand and Cash looked down into Cocoa's happy face. "Ready to move some cattle, girl?" The Australian cattle dog gave a happy bark, head nodding in agreement. She was as much of an institution around the Circle M as Frank. Mouth painted in a permanent smile, Cocoa looked up at him as if to say, *What are we waiting for?* Cash laughed at the dog's silly grin and leaned down to rub her head. Her eyes squinted shut as if she was enjoying a fancy massage, tongue lolling out the side of her mouth. "Hang on a minute. We're almost there." At Cash's words, Cocoa settled into the grass, laying her black head and contrasting white snout on her tan paws with a pout.

Cash headed for the water trough connected to wells by pipelines that spanned the ranch. While he waited for the trough to fill, he took off his hat and swiped his brow with the back of his arm. Frustration over Rachel's grades boiled up as quickly as the afternoon heat. He knew she wasn't applying herself—knew she had it in her to do better. But he didn't know how to make her. Losing their parents had shaken her to the core. She'd struggled in the four years since their deaths, but lately her attitude and grades seemed even worse.

Blake Renner probably had something to do with that, though Cash had yet to convince his sister that the boy did not have her best interests at heart.

Frank took a wide stance next to Cash, the sun squinting off his larger-than-life belt buckle as Rants and Noble hopped in the ranch truck with a wave, heading back to the barn. The ancient vehicle boasted an impressive oil leak, but it still managed to function for any work that needed to be done on the ranch.

"Sorry I had to take off before we were done."

"No problem. Rachel comes first." Frank's brow crinkled with concern. "Everything okay?"

"Yeah." If he didn't count his sister's failing grades or the volleyball coach he should be avoiding who would be spending Thursday nights at the ranch. "Rach needs to get her grades up to stay on the team."

A slow nod proved Frank had heard. "She'll be all right. Reckon she's had a tough time of it the last few years."

That was an understatement that made Cash's inadequacies as a guardian rear up.

"You're doing the best you can." Frank whacked

Cash on the back. "Enough of that now. Let's get the horses and move these cattle."

Hours later, Cash strode from the barn in time to see Rachel's Wrangler bumping into the yard with typical teenage flair, somehow landing in her parking spot. The vehicle abuse made him wince, though he'd be more concerned about her relaxed habits if he hadn't taught her to drive himself.

Dinner would have to be sandwiches tonight. They'd worked too late for him to defrost anything. But at least his little sister had decided to show up. He had to look for the silver lining with her.

The sun touched the trees to the west, setting the green leaves aflame with gold and orange. Cash tipped his head back, stealing a moment of peace before the storm.

After a deep breath, he headed for Rachel, knowing he needed to tell her about Coach Grayson offering to tutor her. He almost laughed out loud. *Offering* might not be the right word. He'd sensed that Olivia had planned to say no. But then he'd pushed a little harder, hoping she'd give in. Was it for his sister's benefit or his own? He didn't want to think about the answer to that question.

What would his parents have done in this situation? As usual, the thought left Cash feeling ill equipped. In the moment, asking Olivia to help had seemed like the best option. But now the thought of spending time around the coach gave him a bit of panic.

He squared his shoulders. He'd just have to keep any attraction he felt tucked away where no one could see it. Surely he could handle Thursday nights without going back on his promise.

Rachel hopped down from the Wrangler and reached back in to grab her bag. She turned, greeting him with a defiant toss of her ponytail, and he cringed. Like taming a wild mustang.

Somehow, he needed to get through to her. Make her understand that she'd get kicked off the team if her grades didn't improve.

No matter the reason, he knew one thing for sure. She was *not* going to like it.

Chapter 2

"**Y**ou agreed to *what*?" Janie Smith's voice came out as a high-pitched squeak, reminding Olivia of the few months in junior high she'd attempted the clarinet.

So much for the relaxation of a pedicure.

"I'm a little shocked myself." Olivia shifted her feet in the hot, bubbling water, took a sip of her blended mocha and tried to get back to a place of calm. Saturday morning girl time with Janie was *supposed* to be the perfect ending to her first week of all-day practices. And after the stress of yesterday's final team cuts— never an easy decision—she desperately needed some relaxation. Olivia was still praying for the girls she'd had to move to the JV team.

Janie rubbed her hands together, copper eyes sparkling. "I think someone has a little crush on you and wants you around." The massage elements rotated up and down behind her as she did a dance in the over-sized chair, sandy-brown hair swinging around her chin.

"Ha. He offered to pay me. I don't think that constitutes a crush." Olivia turned to better face the woman who already felt like an old friend even though they'd only met eight days ago. "I can see the wheels turning in your head, and you need to let that idea go. He finagled me into helping a struggling high school girl get her grades up—one of my best players, too. No harm in that."

Janie's face perked with interest. "Did you know he's Jack's best friend? You two would be perfect for each other!"

The smell of high-voltage perm wafted over Olivia as the woman on her right leaned closer, tight curls covering her head like bright red caterpillars. She pursed coral-colored lips as she pretended to read a magazine.

"Did you hear anything I just said?" Olivia lowered her voice, leaning closer to Janie. "This is exactly why I should have said no in the first place. Not only are you jumping to conclusions, pretty soon the whole town will be talking about it." She scooted back, letting the *thump-thump-thump* of the massage chair chisel into the tension radiating through her shoulders.

"Okay, okay. I'll let it go." Janie raised an unmanicured hand in defeat. Being a nurse, Janie had agreed with Olivia and opted out of getting her nails done. Both used their hands too much in their jobs for the polish to stay on longer than a day or two without chipping.

"For now." Janie added the last part under her breath as she picked up a magazine, smirk in place.

Olivia went back to perusing the latest fashions in hers. The smell of sample perfumes leaked from the pages, fighting off the chemical smell from the fake nails being done across the room.

She toyed with the tips of her mocha hair, wondering if she should add a new cut or color to her new life. After the shattering of her heart a year ago, she'd done a makeover and ended up with longer layers. She'd kept the style because she liked it and felt as if it softened her face—not because she still had something to prove.

"Just so you know, he hasn't dated anyone in years."

Olivia glanced at the black-and-white clock on the wall with amusement. For three and a half glorious minutes, Janie had managed to stay quiet on the subject of Cash.

"And it's not from a lack of women trying, either. Good-looking. Owns a ranch. Took custody of his little sister. What's not to want?" Janie peeked out from behind her magazine shield.

"He only asked me to tutor his sister. He did not ask me out." Olivia ignored the disappointment that crawled up her spine. She could not, would not, have any interest in Cash. And now she sounded like a Dr. Seuss book. But she felt certain that writing a new beginning in Texas meant that one of these days, her hurt would ebb away and she'd be able to move forward. One of these days, she'd forgive herself for making the biggest mistake of her life.

Unfortunately, those new feelings didn't rush in with the pedicure water bubbling around her feet.

Janie leaned closer and Olivia felt Perm Lady do the same.

"I'm just saying that it's been a long time since he's shown interest in someone. You can think the tutoring is only for Rachel, but I wouldn't be surprised if he has ulterior motives."

Olivia shifted quickly to the right, giggling with Janie when Perm Lady readjusted her position so fast she almost fell out of her pedicure chair.

"Fine." The only way to end the conversation would be to give in—a little. "Here's my compromise. At this point it's strictly business. If anything changes you'll be the first to know." *And nothing is going to change.*

Janie flashed a smile laced with victory—as if she could read Olivia's mind and accepted the challenge. She tapped her plastic coffee cup against Olivia's. "I'll toast to that."

The young girl behind the coffee counter yawned as she took Olivia's money the next morning. *Tell me about it.* Olivia glanced at her watch. Seven a.m. on a Sunday—a day she could sleep in—and yet she'd found herself up at six. Haunted. Just like she'd been in Colorado.

She hadn't had the dream since a week before she moved. She'd hoped and prayed it wouldn't follow her to Texas, but it had. Brown curls. A little girl running. Always out of reach.

Olivia shuddered and moved to the end of the counter as the barista steamed the milk for her mocha. She was supposed to ride to church later this morning with the Smiths, but after waking early from the jarring images, she'd had to get out of her apartment.

The barista handed her a bright yellow mug and matching plate with a blueberry muffin perched on a paper doily. Olivia migrated toward the back of the coffeehouse, snatching a rumpled copy of the *Fredericksburg Standard* from an abandoned table along the way.

She settled into a comfy armchair and took a sip of her mocha, eyes closing in relief as the combination of sugar and caffeine rolled across her tongue. Olivia propped open the paper and ate her muffin, reading about the local pool being fixed, the proposal to plan an alternate truck route around Fredericksburg and the race for city council. Advertisements for the quaint bed-and-breakfasts that permeated Texas Hill Country filled the pages, along with an announcement for an upcoming German festival.

She stopped to text Janie that she'd meet them at church and then moved on to the sports section.

It already held talk about the approaching football season. Olivia perused the opinions, wondering how Jack handled all the pressure as the high school football coach. Made her thankful that Texas football would be at the forefront of everyone's minds, leaving her to manage her team with much less scrutiny.

"Excuse me."

Olivia looked up into the face of a man she didn't recognize. "Yes?"

"I'm sorry to bother you, but are you the new French teacher and volleyball coach?"

Back in Denver, no stranger would ever walk up to her like this, let alone actually know her. Olivia took a deep breath. She was still reeling from the dream. No need to take her frustrations out on the poor guy in front of her.

She said yes and introduced herself, shaking his outstretched hand.

"Gil Schmidt. I'm the counselor over at the high school."

Dressed in khaki shorts and a short-sleeved, button-down shirt, he was just the preppy type her younger—and much shorter—sister would consider attractive. But guys who towered over Lucy only came to Olivia's chin. Not that it bothered her anymore. She'd long ago accepted that she would never own a closet full of fashionable heels.

Unless she met a man like Cash—as tall as Cash, she corrected, stopping that train of thought before it got way off track.

Olivia glanced around the shop, surprised to find it had filled. "Would you like to join me?" She regretted the words the instant they came out of her mouth.

Gil checked his watch. "Thanks, but I've been here for a bit and now I'm headed over to church. Just thought I'd stop and introduce myself. I'm sure I'll be seeing more of you once school starts."

She said goodbye and waved as he walked away, kicking herself for being so judgmental. Gil seemed like a nice guy. She'd have to get used to living in a small town.

Shocked at the time, Olivia grabbed her purse, depositing her mug and plate in the bin for dirty dishes on the way up front.

Gil stood looking out the glass door at the front of

the shop, watching the rain that now covered the sidewalks and street. When had it started raining? Guess she'd been lost in her own world, tucked in the back of the shop.

Cars whooshed by, splashing through puddles with a sizzling noise that made Olivia think about bacon. She probably should have had more than a muffin with her coffee.

She glanced at Gil. "Everything okay?"

He motioned outside with a wry grin. "I hadn't been expecting this. I rode my bike this morning."

"Do you need a ride? I'm going to Cedar Hills Church." They stepped to the side as a couple entered, shaking the water from their clothes.

"That's where I go, too."

"Can you put your bike in my trunk?"

When she pointed out her car, Gil laughed. "I don't think it will fit. It's not a problem, though. I'll wait it out."

"Why don't I give you a ride back after? Surely it will be done raining by then. Can you leave your bike here?"

He nodded slowly. "I don't think they'd mind. Are you sure?"

Olivia studied Gil's brown eyes, smiling in relief when she didn't see a spark of interest. "Absolutely. Let's go."

They chatted about school on the short ride to church and Olivia relaxed. She could use more friends in this town. But during the service, Gil turned attentive—holding open the Bible for them to read together, sitting just a little closer than she'd like.

Had she led him on by offering him a ride? Her no-dating rule applied to everyone in this town, not just the entirely too-attractive man sitting one row behind her with his sister.

Maybe Gil didn't mean anything by his actions. Olivia's instincts could be way off. They had been in the past.

Olivia stood for the closing song, Gil's arm pressing against hers, and the pastor closed with her favorite benediction: "The Lord bless you and keep you. The Lord make His face shine on you and be gracious to you. The Lord turn His face toward you and give you peace."

Amen.

Olivia followed Gil into the aisle, then waited for Janie. She and Jack had sat farther down in the same row.

"I'll meet you in the narthex. I need to find someone." Gil squeezed Olivia's arm, then made his way down the aisle.

She resisted the urge to rub away his touch as Janie came out of the row and latched onto her. "Gil Schmidt?"

The church emptied as Olivia explained her morning—minus the dream.

"Hmm." Janie's brow furrowed. "Guess Cash better get his behind in gear." Her face brightened. "Might light a fire under him, knowing he's not the only admirer you have in town."

"I thought we agreed yesterday to leave things alone in that department."

"You agreed to that. Not me." Grinning like a puppy

who'd demolished a shoe, Janie linked arms with Olivia and directed them to Jack and Cash, standing together in the narthex.

"Jack, we need to get Tucker." Janie slid away from Olivia and tugged on her husband's arm.

Matchmaking woman. Olivia resisted the urge to roll her eyes like she'd seen the girls on her team do more times than she could count.

Jack didn't budge. "Can you run and get him? I need to talk to Cash."

Janie's copper eyes flashed as she braced a hand on her slender hip. "Fine. I'll go myself."

"I'll go with you."

Janie greeted Olivia's offer with a wave of her hand, turning sweet as cherry pie. "No, Liv, don't worry about it. I'll be right back."

Jack watched his wife walk away until she disappeared. When a gorgeous redhead approached Cash, Jack pulled Olivia to the side. "I need to ask a favor. Our anniversary is coming up and I want to surprise Janie and take her to San Antonio for dinner. It's a drive, so it would be a late evening. Usually my parents or Janie's would be available, but they're all attending a church function that night. It's the first Saturday in September."

"And you want me to chauffeur?" Olivia laughed at the scowl on Jack's face. "I'd love to hang out with my favorite little man." *Even if it breaks my heart a little every time.*

"Thanks, I appreciate it. We owe you a dinner."

She waved off Jack's thanks. "You don't owe me a thing."

"Guess I'd better go find my wife." Jack grinned. "She's going to kill me for not leaving you here alone with Cash."

Olivia's chin dropped. So the man only pretended innocence. She shoved him on the arm, then spotted Gil across the way talking to an older gentleman.

After only a few steps in his direction, Olivia felt a warm hand wrap around her arm. Goose bumps spread in waves across her skin, leaving no doubt whom she'd turn to find. Her mind might have made a decision not to have any interest in Cash, but her body didn't seem to accept the verdict as easily.

"Coach Grayson, wait up."

She steeled herself before facing Cash. The supermodel, thankfully, was no longer attached to him. He sported a much cleaner version of the outfit he'd worn Tuesday: nice jeans, newer-looking boots—though they still had that worn, casual look—and an untucked button-down instead of a T-shirt.

"I didn't give you directions to the ranch for tutoring next week. That is, if you're still planning to start the first week of school."

Olivia snapped her attention back to his face. "I am."

Cash didn't answer right away. In fact, he didn't seem to realize she'd answered him. The man was completely distracted. Probably still thinking about the beauty he'd just been talking to.

Frustration coursed through Olivia. Could he not listen to her for two seconds? Why had he even chased her down? *Because he cares about his sister, that's why.*

Janie couldn't be more wrong in her assessment. And the sooner Olivia got her head straight, the better. Thursday nights would be about tutoring Rachel and nothing more.

How many times would she have to remind herself that's exactly what she wanted?

Cash let his gaze travel down from Olivia's flushed face, enjoying the view more than he should. He'd seen her in volleyball gear, but this was the first time he'd seen her together and styled. He wasn't sure which of the looks he liked best. Each had its own particular appeal.

Today she wore a skirt, showcasing legs as long as Texas that tapered into strappy sandals. Her toes were painted the color of pink cotton candy and her arms— what a strange thing to be attracted to—were somehow toned and feminine at the same time.

Seeing Olivia in church this morning only made her more appealing. But watching her with Gil Schmidt? That he could do without. Gil had even held the Bible out for Olivia, as though the two of them were a couple. Who knew, maybe they were. Cash didn't have any right to get involved. Any right to care. But that didn't make it any easier to watch.

Her foot tapped while she studied him with an expectant look. Had she said something to him?

"I'm sorry, what was that you said?"

She crossed her arms. "I'm still planning on it."

"Great." That was a good thing, right? Then why did she look as though someone had broken into her apartment? Spitting mad, eyes flashing. She even tossed her hair. It fell in layers past her shoulders today instead of being up in a ponytail. Her shampoo wafted over.

Something mint. She probably wouldn't appreciate it if he leaned in for closer examination.

What exactly had he done to make her so mad? Or maybe it wasn't him that had her all fired up. Maybe she didn't appreciate Gil's advances. That thought made a slow smile spread across his face.

A breath whooshed out from Olivia, filled with enough frustration to spark the room into a raging inferno.

"Where's your phone?"

He slid it from his pocket and she snatched it, her fingers flying across the keys.

"There's my number." She snapped it back into his palm and he resisted the urge to grab her hand and keep her there. "Text me directions later."

Olivia took off, leaving Cash in a strange wake of confusion. After talking to Gil for a minute, the two of them walked out the doors together. Cash rubbed his chest, wondering why it felt as if one of his longhorns had speared him. He only had enough room in his life to deal with one girl at a time. Olivia being mad at him or even dating Gil should be a good thing.

Too bad it didn't feel that way.

Chapter 3

Cash shook the thoughts of Olivia from his mind, scanning the narthex for his sister. Tera Lawton's eyes gleamed from across the room, reminding him of a jungle cat about to strike its prey. He'd already dealt with her once this morning and he didn't care to do it again.

Why couldn't the woman get the fact that he was taken? At least in one sense of the word. And even if he could date, it wouldn't be her again.

Not after what she'd done.

When Jack reappeared, Cash met his friend by the doors.

"Janie and Tucker must have already gone outside." Jack pushed out into the bright sunlight and glanced at Cash. "Trying to escape the Tera-dactyl?"

He laughed. "You know it. What is that girl thinking? As if I'd ever entertain that idea."

Jack shrugged. "She probably just wants you for your money."

Cash snorted. "You mean she's attracted to the hundred bucks in my bank account? And here I thought she couldn't resist my stunning good looks."

Jack slapped him on the back. Hard. "Must be thinking of someone else there. You never had any of those." Jack's slow drawl brought out the Texan in him, flashing Cash's mind back to their younger days. Both had grown up here, and both had returned after college. Living in Fredericksburg without Jack would be like a football game without a pigskin.

"How's the football team looking?"

"I've got a few boys hoping for scholarships, which usually means I can mold them into the kind of players I need. When they want to get out of here bad enough, they work pretty hard."

"True. But I'm not sure why anyone would want to leave this place." Cash glanced at the Texas sky, now a mixture of clouds and a striking blue color that reminded him an awful lot of a certain volleyball coach's eyes, which had just been flashing at him inside the church.

"I know what you mean."

It took Cash a minute to remember what they'd been talking about. He scanned the still-damp parking lot until he saw Janie and Tucker near Jack's car. He must have searched too long, because Jack's laugh sounded next to him.

"She already left with Gil. Didn't you see?"

Annoying that Jack could read his mind like that.

And yeah, he'd seen. Cash's hand itched to adjust the brim of a hat. Any hat that would shade a bit of his face.

"I was in church this morning, *if* you recall." Jack's amusement increased. "Probably wasn't the only one who witnessed the way you tracked her every move."

Cash winced. He had thought he'd done a better job than that of hiding his attraction to the new volleyball coach and French teacher. *French.* A sophisticated woman, who not only spoke but taught French, would surely never stay in a little town like this. Probably just passing through. Maybe he could tamp down his interest by thinking of her as a hoity-toity French teacher. Although on Tuesday she hadn't seemed too high-and-mighty. She'd seemed sweet. And this morning? Feisty. Unfortunately both of those things appealed to him.

Time for a subject change. "While you're at it, why don't you get a scholarship going for Renner? Hopefully he's got plans that don't involve this town." *Or my sister.* The star running back had a reputation for raising a ruckus, and Jack had just as little patience for him as Cash.

"Couldn't agree more. Are you coming over to watch the Rangers game this afternoon?"

They approached the car and Cash went down in time to receive the direct hit from Tucker, his little body creating a surprisingly strong tackle. "Planning on it," Cash answered Jack and then spoke to Tucker. "Has your daddy been teaching you to tackle?"

Tucker grinned, head bobbing.

"Do you want to go way up?"

At Tucker's nod, Cash hoisted the boy onto his

shoulders. Tucker clapped, then settled in by squealing and gripping Cash's hair like a handlebar.

He ignored the blood rushing to his scalp as Janie looked up to greet him. The tiny woman looked like a wind might blow her over, but she handled Jack—and the whole football team—with ease. Jack hadn't figured out how amazing Janie was until college, but then he'd asked her out and never looked back.

Cash smiled at the best thing that had ever happened to his best friend. "How's my favorite girl?" He only said the phrase to annoy Jack, who promptly elbowed him in the gut.

He grunted and laughed, and Janie shook her head, the sun dancing off her cute little bob of a haircut as she ignored them both.

"Speaking of favorite girls, is Rachel coming over today, too?"

Cash shook his head, forgetting Tucker's grip and quickly regretting it. "Don't think she's planning on it." Annoyance rose up. Rachel had been spending as little time as possible in his presence. He didn't know if it was typical girl stuff or something more. Not that he knew what typical girl stuff was. He wished she'd go over to the Smiths' with him today. Janie would be good for the girl.

They said goodbyes and Cash deposited Tucker in his car seat, leaving the confusion of buckles for Jack to sort through. He headed for his dark blue extended cab truck a few spots away, got in and pressed the horn to make Tucker laugh.

That boy had stolen his heart from the first time Cash saw him in the hospital. He knew he'd done the same to Jack. Watching his friend be a father was pretty touching, but Jack and Cash didn't usually get into sappy conversations like that. The two of them didn't need to say much to know what the other was thinking. For instance, right now, Jack was probably thinking about getting in a quick nap before the Rangers game. Too bad Cash couldn't do the same.

Cash drove up to the church entrance and texted his sister. Minutes later, Rachel came out and hopped into the truck. She messed around on her phone during the fifteen-minute drive home, leaving Cash to process his day and week.

It was his turn to handle the barn today, but that shouldn't take too long. A few chores and he could grab a sandwich and head over to Jack's. But of the list of things that came to mind that he needed to accomplish during the rest of the week, only one thing really mattered. And that was keeping his concentration on his sister instead of the completely distracting volleyball coach who happened to be a Christian.

Olivia stood in the middle of the H-E-B grocery store parking lot on Saturday morning, her team spread around her. The girls had really jelled during the second week of preseason practice—a good thing, since school started on Monday and their first game was on Wednesday. But first, they had to deal with the all-important business of raising money for fall sports, starting with today's car wash.

"There's one rule. No dumping water on the coach. If you think I've already made cuts, think again."

Laughter threaded through the team.

"Come on, Coach! Mom said she'd get doused if we earn enough." Valerie Nettles's silver-braces smile widened when the rest of the team cheered in agreement with her.

Olivia turned to her assistant coach. Trish Nettles hadn't been able to take the two preseason practice weeks off from her job, so she planned to start working with the team once they began after-school practice. Bless the woman for being willing to work the Saturday morning fund-raiser, too.

At first Olivia had been concerned about having a parent as assistant coach, but Trish had assured her she'd be there to help—not control. Including her daughter's playing time. That had given Olivia peace. Truthfully, she was thankful for the help. Trish had a relationship with the girls from years past and twenty-five years' playing experience. From the conversations they'd already had about the team—and life—Olivia thought they'd get along well.

"It's true." Trish shrugged, her eyes dancing with mischief. "It's tradition. But they do need to earn a lot of money."

Olivia's lips curved up. "How much money?"

"A thousand?" At Trish's answer, the team screeched and complained, causing Trish and Olivia to share an amused look.

"A thousand it is."

Dispersing in grumbles, the girls started filling buckets with water and soap. With the sun already baking them, Olivia made sure everyone had sunscreen on, then stationed herself with a hose for rinsing. She welcomed the mist that drifted across her sizzling skin as she sprayed each car down.

Soon a line of cars snaked around the back of the parking lot. The town of Fredericksburg made supporting high school sports an art form.

Janie and Tucker rolled through, then parked after their wash and walked over. Olivia handed her job off to one of the girls and headed over to meet them near the water bottles.

"Hey, little man." Olivia's heart hiccuped when Tucker barreled into her legs. A hug or a tackle, she wasn't sure. Either way, she'd take it. She scooped Tucker up and pushed aside all of the remorse that rushed in with his sweet baby smell.

"Girl, it is hot out here. Are you dying?"

"A little." Olivia took a long swig of her water and wiped the back of her hand across her forehead. She must look a mess. "Where's Jack?"

Janie motioned to the line. "Right behind me. He drove his own car so he could get it washed too. Oh, there's Cash in his truck."

Olivia shaded her eyes, waving at Cash along with Janie. She imagined her friend's pulse didn't race as if she'd just run lines in the gym.

And you're planning to spend time with that man? Not your best move, Liv.

She hadn't seen Cash since last Sunday at church, when she'd let her initial attraction grow into a moment of jealousy. Thankfully she'd had a week to collect herself since then. Olivia had come to the realization that she couldn't avoid the man. She not only coached his sister but she also planned to tutor the girl. And Cash was friends with Jack and Janie. So Olivia had decided that she could hang out with Cash in those various settings, but she wouldn't let her heart get involved. That barely beating organ had been trampled, so keeping it tucked away until it healed only made sense.

Olivia would think of Cash as Rachel's older brother or Jack and Janie's friend and nothing more. How hard could that be?

When Jack parked and joined them, Tucker squealed. Olivia deposited him on the ground, and he toddled over to his dad. Jack snapped him up, making him giggle.

"I've noticed almost the whole football team seems to be in line." Olivia nudged Jack. "School spirit?"

He snorted. "More like girl spirit."

At the sound of screams, Olivia glanced over. One of the football players had jumped out of the passenger seat of a car and stolen a bucket of water. Girls and suds went everywhere as he doused the nearest members of her team. Two more football players emerged from their cars and Olivia groaned.

"Jack." Janie took Tucker and pushed her husband toward the chaos. "Stop them."

Before Jack could take a step, more car doors than Olivia could count opened and shut. One football player climbed out of a sunroof while the rest looked like ants swarming a lemonade spill.

Olivia ran for the hose, securing that. Jack tried yelling for them to stop, but only got himself doused with a bucketful of suds by his players. White bubbles clung to his eyebrows and nose, his look deadly.

"That's it." Jack growled and sprinted for the hose

located across the car from Olivia. He opened fire and the boys ran for cover, trying to find protection from the water spray.

Janie screeched and Olivia looked behind her to see her friend's cute capris and tank top dripping with water, her formerly swaying brown bob now plastered to her head. She pointed at her husband. "Jack Edward Smith. You are a dead man."

From next to Janie's legs, Tucker clapped his hands and chanted, "Wa-wa, wa-wa."

Trish swooped in, claiming Tucker and allowing Janie to run for cover.

Using the hood for protection, Olivia ducked down. Nobody messed with her friends. She closed one eye and aimed the nozzle, then waited for the right moment. Jack's grin evaporated when the cold spray reached his stomach. He caught sight of her and she ducked, but not before a line of water shot across the top of her head.

She wasn't going down without a fight. Bracing for cold water impact, Olivia stood, aiming for Jack. But when Cash bounded around the hood of the car, she quickly switched her aim to him, hand poised on the trigger.

He stopped a foot in front of her, his grin making her stomach do crazy things. "The way I see it, Coach Grayson, you can give up now." Cash glanced around at the chaos, shoulders lifting. "Or I can't do anything to help you."

"You boys really are oversized teenagers, aren't you?"

Eyes narrowing under the brim of his white University of Texas baseball hat, Cash lunged for the sprayer at the same time she squeezed. Water bounced off his rust-orange Longhorns T-shirt, spraying everywhere. He switched tactics, wrapping boa constrictor arms around her from behind. Her grip on the sprayer weakened. Though she prided herself on being in shape, she was no match for him.

"Ready to give up yet?" The proximity of Cash's voice sent tingles down her neck.

Olivia risked a glance over her shoulder. Laugh lines rimmed Cash's eyes, and unlike Sunday, all of his attention was on her. She was enjoying it way too much. Though the phrase *Rachel's brother* sounded like a referee's whistle in her mind, Olivia just shook her head in answer to Cash's question, letting her legs go out from under her. The self-defense move allowed her to drop down and out of Cash's hold.

Janie yelled for Olivia to get out of the way, then threw a bucket of water at Cash. Olivia popped up laughing. Janie only came up to Cash's chest, so most of the water landed on his previously dry cargo shorts.

"Jack, get your woman," Cash yelled to his friend as he resumed the tug-of-war over the hose with Olivia.

Feeling the sprayer slip once more, Olivia shouted for Janie to run as Cash gained control of the hose. Instead of escaping, her friend lurched onto Cash's back, not accomplishing much in the way of help but totally getting points for effort.

Cash let loose, spraying Olivia point-blank. Water ran from her face and neck, soaking her red tank top and athletic shorts. She sputtered, coherent enough to see Jack peel Janie off Cash's back and throw her over his shoulder.

Not above using a ploy when the need called for it, Olivia sank to the ground and cradled her foot. She didn't whine—no need to overdo it. The water stopped and Cash dropped to one knee beside her.

"Are you okay?"

Ugh. Did he have to look so irresistible? Water dripped across his cheeks, wet eyelashes accentuating one of his best features. His neck and shoulders tensed, ready for the water that might come at them from any direction.

It sounded as though a war raged around them, but Olivia didn't see anything but him.

His hand paused inches from her face, as if he intended to wipe the water from her cheeks. Her breath stalled in her chest, then came out in a whoosh of disappointment when his hand lowered.

"Did you hurt your foot?" Cash slid callused hands along her bare skin, her flip-flops doing little to interrupt the current that flowed between them.

His touch was too much. Olivia lunged forward, tackling Cash while screaming for her team at the same time. Though he could easily throw her over his shoulder like Jack had done to Janie, she managed to catch him off balance. Cash fell back onto the asphalt, taking her down with him.

With a war cry, her team descended, Rachel in the lead. Though they aimed for Cash, they managed to get Olivia just as bad. By the time the onslaught ceased, Olivia found herself cradled on Cash's left side, water running into her ears, hair plastered to her head and neck, clothes soaked through again.

Cash's hand tightened around her arm, holding her

captive as his head dropped to the ground. "Shh." He whispered against her hair. "If we're quiet, they won't know we're down here. Play dead."

Shaking with laughter, Olivia left her head in the crook between Cash's arm and chest.

"Well, Coach Grayson." His casual drawl made her grin. "I think that one backfired on you."

She peeked up from his chest, and he returned her smile with one of his own. Olivia hadn't had that much fun in…she didn't know how long.

"I wouldn't say it was a total loss." Olivia laughed as Cash ran a hand through his hair and water flew out in every direction. Sometime during the scuffle, he had lost his baseball hat.

Janie and Jack approached as she and Cash moved to a sitting position. The Smiths sat beside them, and the four of them caught their breath while the students finally called a truce.

Jack shook the water from his hair like an overgrown puppy. "What are you guys up to tonight? Do you want to come over for dinner?"

Hadn't she just talked to herself about this very scenario?

Cash stiffened beside her and found his soaked cap on the ground behind them. He snapped it on his head, then stood. "Thanks, but I can't. I've got to run."

The three of them stood, too, the confusion Olivia felt mirrored on Jack's and Janie's faces.

"But you didn't get your truck washed." Olivia squeezed a hand down her ponytail, releasing a barrage of water.

He dug out his wallet and pressed a somehow still-dry twenty into her damp hand. "For the team." Then he jogged to his truck and pulled out of line.

Olivia stared after him, not quite sure what to do with the feelings coursing through her. The hurt from Colorado flashed back, memories of Josh walking away almost suffocating her. She could still see the positive pregnancy test and the two that followed with the same little plus signs. And then...the stress, the shame, the miscarriage.

Olivia had strayed from God's waiting-for-marriage plan. She'd walked away from God. And her decisions had ended in heartache and regret.

Watching Cash drive away—experiencing that tinge of hurt at his quick disappearance—for the first time in her life, Olivia actually felt momentarily thankful for her jaded past and all those regrets. They kept her from letting her heart get involved with a man who didn't even know it existed.

Just like the last time.

Chapter 4

Cash stirred the chili bubbling in the pot, then checked his watch again. The first day of after-school practice had been over for hours and still no sign of Rachel. And of course she hadn't responded to his call or texts. He sighed, laid the wooden spoon on the holder and headed for the cordless phone. He dialed Trish Nettles's number, hoping the girls had lost track of time and were holed up in Valerie's room doing homework.

Yeah, right.

"Hello?" Trish sounded hurried. And why wouldn't she? It *was* dinnertime. For normal families.

"Hey, Trish, any chance Rachel's at your house?"

"I haven't seen her since practice." And now she sounded sympathetic. "I'll walk down to Val's room to see if she knows anything."

A seed of worry planted itself in Cash's gut. Trish's voice mixed with Val's as a stench filled the kitchen. Cash hurried back to the stove and clicked off the burner for the now-scorched chili, turning on the fan over the stove to help remove the awful smell.

"Val doesn't know where she is." Trish paused and he slid open the window behind the sink. "Last I saw Rachel, she was talking to Blake Renner after practice."

The seed in Cash's stomach twisted into a full-grown ash tree.

Before they hung up, Trish made him promise to call if he needed any more help finding Rachel. The Nettles family joked that Rachel was their second daughter because of all the time she and Val spent joined at the hip. Maybe they should keep her full-time. Trish would be a much better parent than Cash.

He set the chili pot into the sink, flipped on the water and gripped the edge of the counter.

Renner. What did Rachel see in the cocky boy? He only wished her whereabouts were more of a surprise.

Cash scrounged up some leftovers and tried to distract himself with the Monday-night Rangers game, but nothing held his attention. Each tick of the clock increased his anxiety, and the food sat like a rock in his stomach.

He and Rachel had one steadfast rule between them—always let me know where you are and where you're going. The stipulation wasn't that hard to follow. He'd had a similar rule with their parents, but he'd never pushed the way Rachel did. Mom and Dad hadn't known how good they'd had it.

When the Rangers game finished, Cash checked the time again. Almost ten o'clock. His phone showed three reception bars, but still nothing from Rach. He texted her again. He'd give her another ten minutes before he got in the truck and started looking. Cash's fingers slid down his contact list, landing on Coach Grayson's number.

The out-of-town area code flashed on the screen and then disappeared as he contemplated making the call. She was Rachel's coach. Maybe she knew something he didn't.

Though Olivia probably wasn't very happy with the way he'd acted at the car wash on Saturday. He'd had to run, had to get away from how simple it would be to let her in. Jack and Janie loved her. Being with her was too easy. So he'd scrambled out of there, needing some distance.

She'd been in church again yesterday—without Gil—but Cash hadn't talked to her. Somehow, he needed to figure out a way to be friends with her and nothing more. When his parents passed away, he'd promised himself that he'd give Rachel his undivided attention until she graduated from high school and went to college. No dating. No distractions. He owed Rachel the same great upbringing he'd had, the same love and support he'd received from their parents. After all, if Cash hadn't believed Tera the day of his parents' deaths, Rachel's life would have had a different outcome.

The familiar mixture of responsibility and determination weighed down his shoulders, and Cash let out a slow breath. He'd managed not to date for the past four years. Surely he could handle one more.

Cash pressed the send button for Olivia's number. He wasn't going to throw away all of those years of effort in one phone call.

"Hello?" A door closed in the background as she answered. Had he interrupted her evening? What was he thinking? Of course he had.

"Hey, this is Cash. I—"

"Oh, hi." Her voice held curiosity, and surprisingly after how he'd acted on Saturday, a hint of warmth that stopped his train of thought for a few seconds. "Is there anything I can help you with?" She filled in the silence, but she didn't have to fill in the rest of the sentence. Cash could hear the words as if she'd said them: *at ten o'clock at night...on my cell phone.*

"Rachel hasn't come home yet tonight. Any chance you might know where she is?" A commercial flashed on the TV at a high volume and Cash grabbed the remote to mute it.

"Sorry." Sympathy laced the word. "I haven't seen her since the end of practice."

Disappointment clogged his throat. "Sorry to bother you on your cell."

"It's not a problem."

"How was the first day of school?"

At Olivia's silence, Cash checked the cell to make sure they hadn't gotten disconnected. He pressed the phone back to his ear. "I'm giving Rachel a few more minutes to show up. Distract me. Tell me about your day."

"Oh." Olivia paused and Cash envisioned her shrug.

"It was the typical craziness of the first day. The kids were hyper and excited, and I got very little done besides handing out a list of assignments for the quarter. I did tell my advanced class that we'd be speaking only French in the classroom this year."

"How'd that go?"

"They all complained." A smile echoed in her words. "So, tell me about your day."

He ignored the way his heart hitched. "I did a bunch of work in the office. I needed to get the website updated with what cuts we currently have available."

"No roping and riding today?"

He laughed. "Nope. Just office work. Have you ever even been to a ranch?"

"I've driven past one. There's a bunch of them in Colorado."

Cash waited.

"But no, I can't say I've ever visited one on a field trip or anything."

Sassy thing. "I'll give you a tour when you come on Thursday night, city girl." Cash checked the clock. "I better go. Rachel still hasn't shown up. I'm going to call Jack and Janie and see if they've seen her."

"Wait. I was just over there for dinner and they were both home." Her voice lowered. "So...I don't think they've seen Rachel either."

He hated the relief that flooded through him when he realized she'd been at the Smiths'. Instead of what? Out on a date with Gil? Did it matter? He certainly couldn't ask her out himself. Obviously his attention needed to remain on his sister.

Cash grabbed his red Circle M baseball cap perched

on the back of the couch and tugged it on his head. "Guess I'll hop in the truck and start looking." After clicking off the TV, he went in search of his keys.

"I'll help."

He stopped midstride, suspended in a strange time warp as Olivia's words hugged him. "You don't need to do that. I don't want to keep you out late and—" *Rachel's my responsibility.*

"I won't take no for an answer. She's my player." Her words halted for a moment. "And your sister."

Maybe it wasn't all about Rachel. Maybe it had something to do with him. Cash moved again, collecting his keys from the kitchen counter and a flashlight he hoped he wouldn't need from the drawer.

Since his parents' deaths, he'd only focused on Rachel and the ranch. It felt like basking in warm sunlight to think Olivia might possibly be interested in *him*.

Cash tamped down his rampant thoughts. One offer to help and he went crazy with ideas he should not be entertaining.

Time to head back to Friend Land, Maddox.

On that note, he should say no to Olivia's help, but he couldn't resist the idea of someone keeping him from thinking worst-case-scenario thoughts while he looked for Rachel.

"I'll swing by and pick you up."

"Um, how do you know where I live?"

Cash laughed. "I'm not a stalker. You're three houses down from Jack and Janie in Mrs. Faust's above-garage apartment. If you wanted anonymity, this isn't the town for it."

At Olivia's silence, Cash checked the connection

again. He put the phone back to his ear in time to hear her quiet, forced-sounding laugh.

"Right. Wasn't thinking about the size of this town. I'll head down when I see your lights."

Cash stepped onto the porch, locking the door behind him. "Make sure it's me. I don't need to go searching for two girls tonight."

She laughed for real this time, the sound bringing a smile to his lips despite his rising level of stress.

"Are there even criminals in this town?"

"Yes, city girl."

Another laugh set his heart racing, but he ignored it as her words brought comfort of a different level. She was right about there being very little crime in Fredericksburg.

Cash strode across the yard to the garage, pausing when he saw round Wrangler-style headlights about a half mile down the road.

"Cash?"

"Hold on. I see some lights coming."

"Oh, good."

The Wrangler downshifted as it eased into the yard, and Cash's shoulders dropped a mile at the flash of sunshine-blond hair behind the steering wheel.

"It's her. Thanks for keeping me sane."

"No problem."

Cash couldn't resist checking. "I'll see you Thursday?"

"I'll see you Thursday." Olivia hung up and Cash disconnected.

If only his gut didn't roll with anticipation. Because

despite the interest Olivia Grayson stirred in him, Cash wouldn't let his feelings progress beyond friendship.

He might be a poor substitute parent, but he would do everything he could to make up for that…including giving up any thoughts of a relationship with Olivia.

Tonight only proved his promise to keep his attention on Rachel and not on his own love life was right on the mark.

Maybe in a year he could ask Olivia out.

Right. As if she'd still be single by then. Someone as attractive as Olivia moving into this little town was front-page news. He wasn't the first man to notice her and, unfortunately, he wouldn't be the last.

On Thursday, Olivia turned when she saw the sign for the Circle M, taking a long dirt drive that led to a toffee-painted house with white trim. Off to the left, a line of trees bordered the house and to the right, a barn and garage were painted to match.

After parking to the side next to Rachel's Jeep, Olivia walked up the stairs, flip-flops echoing across the wide, wooden-planked porch that ran the length of the front of the house. Since the Texas heat and humidity didn't have an off button, she'd pretty much adopted a different version of the same outfit every day—shorts, T-shirt or tank, flip-flops or tennis shoes.

Guardrail spindles cast shadows onto two rocking chairs that moved in the breeze as she knocked.

"Hey, come on in." Cash greeted her at the door dressed in jeans and a black T-shirt, hair wet. He smelled like some kind of men's soap. Who knew such a simple thing could be so attractive?

Hands off, Liv. After their phone conversation the other night, Olivia felt as if she and Cash had moved into new territory—one where their focus centered on Rachel. Exactly where Olivia needed it to be. And she didn't plan to mess up this newfound harmony with any remnants of buried attraction to Cash.

"I'm warming up one of Laura Lee's lasagnas." Cash motioned to the table where Rachel had her homework spread out. "Have a seat and I'll grab you a glass of lemonade."

An expansive living room with high ceilings connected with the kitchen and dining space that held a round oak table. Summer evening sun came in through large front windows, playing upon the dark burgundy sofas that flanked a stone fireplace stretching all the way up to the second-story ceiling.

Olivia sat at the table next to the girl she'd seen at practice a half hour before. The one who had dominated in their first match last night with five kills and helped them win in only four games.

Rachel tossed her hair. "I can't believe Cash conned you into helping me."

Girl, I've dealt with plenty of teenagers like you in the past. You won't get rid of me that easy.

"It's all selfish." Olivia pretended nonchalance—though she couldn't stop a smile. "I just want you to keep playing volleyball."

A hint of a curve touched Rachel's lips, but she quickly quelled the movement. After rearranging her pencils and notebooks, she huffed and rolled her eyes. "I need help with algebra the most."

Perfect. Olivia's worst subject. "Then let's get started."

While Rachel pulled out her book, Olivia glanced up and shared a small victory grin with Cash.

An hour flew by as Rachel and Olivia switched from algebra to English and then got in a bit of world history before Cash put a stack of plates on the table next to Rachel's papers.

"Ready in a few." He added silverware and napkins.

"I'm almost done." Rachel quickly scribbled in two more answers to her history homework before stacking up her books and papers and dumping the pile onto the floor near her chair.

When Cash put the lasagna on the table and took a seat, laying his palm up next to Olivia's plate, she stared at the callused hand. Rachel accepted the other hand Cash offered her without an eye roll—shocking—and Olivia made herself do the same, trying not to think about how small her hand felt wrapped up in Cash's during the prayer.

They dug into the delicious meal, and after finishing off two full plates of food, Rachel disappeared from the table, cell phone in hand.

Cash leaned back and stretched his arms over his head, plate cleaned a few times over. "So, are you ready for that tour?"

"Sure." Olivia loaded the dishwasher while Cash put away the leftovers.

Cash slid on his boots, and they walked out the front door and over to the barn, the first signs of dusk seeping into the evening.

"Did you always plan to ranch?"

"Pretty much. Dad would have been fine with me doing something else, and I went to college open-minded, but I missed it. I moved back right after to work with him. Of course, I didn't know at the time that I'd end up doing it all myself. Except for Frank. Every day I thank God for Frank."

"How can you talk about your parents so openly? Doesn't it…"

"Hurt?" Cash filled in the word as his gaze swung in her direction. "Yep. But it gets a bit easier with time." He slid open the massive barn door and flipped on the lights. The fluorescents flickered before kicking on with a buzz. An organized wall of tools lined one side of the barn and the other housed a long row of horse stalls. By the names etched into wooden signs on the gated doors, it looked as though only a few of those were occupied.

A whine sounded from another area of the barn and Olivia paused, waiting to see Cash's reaction. Maybe it was nothing…or normal. She didn't have a clue.

His eyebrows pulled together, and he walked in that direction. Olivia followed, thinking everything Cash did had a calculated calm to it. The way his legs covered the distance communicated his concern, but he didn't rush, even waiting for her to catch up. Once she did, he turned and stepped through a small doorway and flipped on the lights. A desk pushed against one wall and rows of cabinets filled the squared space that Olivia could walk off in a few long strides.

"This is Frank's space."

When the whimper sounded again, Cash strode to the desk and dropped to his knees. "Hey, girl." His quiet soothing continued as he reached into the foot space of the desk and gently maneuvered a beautiful black-and-brown dog out into the light.

The dog's breathing seemed labored, and scratches marred her nose and face, including one eye that looked almost swollen shut.

"What's wrong?"

"I'm not sure." Cash ran his hands over the animal. "What happened, Cocoa?"

She answered with a high-pitched whine.

Olivia sank to the cement floor next to Cash, stomach churning when he swiped over the dog's shoulder and his hands came away covered in bright red blood.

"She must have gotten into a tussle with something. She'll be all right. I just need to clean her up and then wrap up that spot on her shoulder."

"You're going to do it yourself?"

When Cash grabbed a rag from one of the cupboards above them and wiped his bloodstained hands on it, Olivia pressed her lips together and looked away.

"Yep." He looked at her, amused. "But that doesn't mean you have to stay."

Cocoa whimpered and scooted over, depositing her head in Olivia's lap. Any reservations Olivia had about staying were forgotten. She took over for Cash's soothing, running her fingers over the soft fur behind Cocoa's ears and along her back—anyplace she didn't seem injured. "If you're staying, I'm staying."

Cash disappeared into the other part of the barn, coming back with a handful of supplies. He cleaned the wound on the dog's shoulder first.

"See? It's not very big. I think I can wrap it up tight instead of doing stitches."

Olivia slammed her eyelids shut when Cash attempted to show her what he was doing.

He chuckled. "Not much for blood?"

"You could say that." Again. Olivia continued to soothe Cocoa as Cash applied topical anesthetic and then ointment to each of the scratches across the dog's face. Cocoa didn't flinch or move at Cash's gentle and efficient movements. But when he moved to the open wound, she whimpered and looked up at Olivia with one good eye, pain evident.

"It's okay, sweet girl. In no time at all you'll be running around again. He's almost done." Olivia glanced at Cash. "Aren't you?"

Cash continued his ministrations. "Yep, but if you keep up all that sweet talk, Cocoa's going to milk this thing some more and find a few more injuries to complain about."

Olivia ignored the warmth cascading through her at Cash's words and his close proximity, instead focusing on the beautiful animal in her lap.

After wrapping a bandage around Cocoa's shoulder, Cash secured it with medical tape. "There. All done. Now we just have to make sure she keeps the thing on." Cash rubbed Cocoa behind the ears. "Do you hear me, girl? No chewing."

The world tilted. Olivia threw a hand out to the cool cement floor, hoping to steady herself. Surely she wouldn't faint now.

Cocoa moved her head to the floor as if she could sense Olivia's unease.

"Olivia?" Cash knelt in front of her, studying her much like he had Cocoa only minutes before. "Are you okay?"

"I'm fine." She forced a smile to her voice and her face. "You have two heads, but other than that, I'm good."

She needed to get out of this barn and find some fresh air. Olivia popped up and the walls swirled and spun. She imagined shoving her feet down through the cement floor in order to steady her swaying body, but instead, two warm arms wrapped around her. She let her face rest against Cash's soft T-shirt and rock-hard shoulder as the scent of that soap surrounded her.

How many times could she end up in this man's arms by accident?

She was afraid the answer to that question was not nearly enough.

Cash should let go. Olivia seemed better, but his own pulse raced as though he'd just run across miles of ranch land. What was it about this woman that messed with him? He'd been attracted before, but not like this. It unnerved him the way she seemed all soft and sweet one second and then toed up to his sister in attitude the next.

Wanting to comfort, Cash allowed himself to slide a hand down her satin hair one time, releasing the scent of her mint shampoo.

"Doing better?" He ducked to look into her face.

She nodded, not meeting his gaze, then stepped away. He clenched his fists to keep from reaching for her again.

"I need to go." Olivia walked outside and Cash followed, turning off the lights and sliding the barn doors shut behind them.

Under the newly darkened sky sprinkled with stars, Olivia paused and took a few deep breaths. The vastness of the charcoal backdrop and the quiet night left Cash feeling as though they were the only two people in the world.

Not exactly what he needed right now.

"Thanks for dinner." Olivia's quiet voice interrupted his off-limits thoughts.

"Thanks for helping my sister."

"You're welcome."

Cash decided she looked a little less green. "Do I need to drive you home? Or follow you?"

She laughed. "I can drive myself home and no, you don't need to follow."

"Are you sure? Because I don't want—"

"I'm fine." Olivia ran a hand through her hair, sending the tips dancing across her light blue V-neck T-shirt. "It usually only takes me a few minutes to recover. I can drive. I promise."

They walked to the house and Olivia retrieved her purse. Cash stood on the front porch and watched as she drove away, thinking the new volleyball coach had revealed something to him tonight that he'd never realized in all the years he'd lived on the ranch.

He could be jealous of his dog.

Chapter 5

Olivia knocked on the Maddoxes' screen door the next Thursday, the sounds and smells of dinner wafting into the evening. An afternoon thunderstorm had provided a break from the stifling heat, and she welcomed the slightly cooler air whispering across her skin. Olivia had seen Cash a few times this week—at a fund-raising event, church and last night's game. Amazingly, she'd managed to avoid falling into the man's arms for the past seven days. The two of them had also kept any conversations at parent-teacher level and mostly centered on Rachel. Now, if Olivia could just keep up the same track record tonight.

"Come in," Cash called from the kitchen and Olivia let herself in, finding him taking a pan out of the oven. And no sign of Rachel. Hopefully the girl was just upstairs…though now that Olivia thought about it, she hadn't seen her Jeep outside.

Cash set the pan on the stove and threw her an apologetic look. "It seems my sister has decided she doesn't need any help tonight. She never showed up after practice. I'm sorry. I would have called you, but I hoped she was just late."

Olivia took a step backward. If Rachel wasn't here, then she had no reason to stay. "No problem, I'll just head—"

"To the table." Cash strode across the kitchen, placed his hands on her shoulders and propelled her into a chair. "You drove out here. The least I can do is feed you."

When Cash went back to the stove, Olivia resisted popping up from her chair. She shouldn't stay. Not if Rachel didn't need her help. But…what if the girl showed up and Olivia had already left? She should probably give her a few minutes.

Cash tossed a blue-and-white crocheted hot pad on the table and then moved back toward the counter. "Tell me about your day."

Olivia shoved down the swell of sweetness that phrase caused her to feel.

"After last night's win, I thought practice would go great. Instead, the girls were distracted messes. I'm not sure why. I made them run lines for the last fifteen minutes. Guess I should call my dad and get some advice."

"Is he a coach?"

"Yes. At a college in Colorado Springs."

Cash whistled. "Now it all makes sense. Were you born with a volleyball in your hand?"

"Not quite. I didn't start until fifth grade. At that point, I was already inches taller than the boys in my class. I decided to take advantage of it."

He set the steaming glass pan on the table along with a container of sour cream and bowl of guacamole. "You're in for a treat. Laura Lee makes the best enchiladas."

"If the smell is any indication, I believe you." Yum. Cooking for herself, Olivia hardly ever took the time to make anything that looked or smelled like this.

"But I'll have you know, I prepared the guacamole myself."

Olivia grinned and nodded toward an empty plastic container on the counter. "Really? Looks like Wholly Guacamole made the guac to me."

Cash filled two glasses with water and ice from the fridge door. "I didn't say I *made* it. Just *prepared* it." He approached the table, expression suddenly serious. "Lying is not something you'll ever catch me doing. I am not a fan." His voice took on an edge that Olivia had never heard before.

Interesting. Olivia wasn't a fan of lying either, but she didn't feel the need to say it out loud.

Cash placed the water glasses in front of their plates, his mischievous smile returning. "I took the guacamole out of the freezer, where Laura Lee put it, defrosted it and put it into a bowl."

Olivia laughed. "Since that's more than one step, I'll give you two points."

"Accepted." Cash sat to her left and reached for Olivia's hand. She startled, having forgotten this habit of his, then tried to catch up when he bowed his head to pray. He acted as if this hand-holding thing were no big deal, as if it shouldn't make her heart crawl into her throat and miss the prayer completely. When he finished, Olivia picked up her fork and said a silent prayer of her own before digging into the food.

Their conversation during dinner didn't require any effort. It just felt…easy. And wasn't that the problem with this man? But she was here to help Rachel, not fall further into friendship with Cash. Although Rachel taking herself out of the equation made that hard to accomplish.

After eating, they cleared the table together and Olivia prepared to leave. Since Rachel hadn't shown up, Olivia didn't have any reason to stay.

She grabbed her purse while Cash put the leftovers in the fridge. He turned. "You ready? Wait, where are you going?"

"Home."

Cash walked over and tugged the purse from her arm, setting it on the table. "I still owe you a tour, city girl. Remember? We didn't get to finish it last time. Instead, we got to witness all of the reasons you never became a nurse."

She laughed and narrowed her eyes. "We can't all be Janie."

He grabbed his boots from next to the front door, pulling them on while Olivia wavered with indecision. She really should go home to her empty apartment.

"Jeep or horse?"

"What?"

"A real tour requires some sort of transportation. And since my lovely sister has decided not to grace us with her presence, we have plenty of daylight left. So which chariot do you prefer? Jeep or horse?"

"I'd say horse, but I wore flip-flops." Huh. Guess she'd made that decision rather quickly. So much for sticking to all-Rachel business.

Cash studied her feet, making her skin flush with heat. Who knew feet could blush?

"I'll be right back." He disappeared into the back of the house and reappeared with a pair of camel-colored cowboy boots that had to be Rachel's.

Olivia sat on a chair and tried them on. Amazingly, they fit. Bless Rachel for having big-girl feet.

"Are you sure Rachel won't care if I wear these?" She stood and chuckled at her outfit, consisting of a light yellow tank top, cutoff jean shorts and boots. Thankfully she hadn't worn capris today. That would be an unusual combination. "This looks hilarious."

"She hasn't worn them in ages. And they actually look…good on you." Cash glanced to the side as red climbed his stubbled cheeks. "Before you know it, I'll be changing your nickname." He moved to open the screen door, holding it for her.

They stepped onto the front porch, the gorgeous evening greeting them. Olivia inhaled the fresh, after-rain scent.

"Have you ever been horseback riding before?"

"A couple of times."

"I mean other than one of those ride-in-line-behind-each-other, follow-the-leader sort of things."

The corners of her mouth lifted. "That's the kind I've been on."

"And there went your chance for a new nickname." Cash gave a dramatic sigh as they walked to the barn. "Such a city girl. At least tell me you know how to bait a fishing hook."

There was a way to do it? "Nope."

"Horseback riding, fishing." He tsked. "What else am I going to have to teach you?"

"I'm guessing not anything about being humble."

He threw his head back and laughed.

They entered the barn and Cash saddled two horses. He ran a hand down the nose of the gray one. "This is Rachel's horse, Freckles. She's sweet." Freckles nuzzled Cash's neck at the compliment. "And should be easy for you to ride."

Cash helped Olivia up and then mounted his own rust-colored horse. They rode at a slow pace toward the hills. Cash brought her up to a fenced area where it looked like hundreds of longhorns grazed.

"This is our herd. We're all grass fed from start to finish, which means we rotate the grazing often so that they get new grass. No corn, no grain. We don't use antibiotics or hormones. The care of the animals is more expensive, but then our meat also brings in a higher price. And it's healthier."

"Where do you sell it?"

"On the website and locally. We supply a few restaurants in town. Some families have been buying from us for thirty years. Right now I'm working on a deal with a natural grocery store down in Austin. If it comes through, we'd need to increase our herd."

Cash started off again, and the two horses walked alongside each other.

"So, what did you do back in Colorado? Besides win volleyball games like a boss and teach French?"

Olivia smiled. "I hung out with friends and my sister, Lucy. She still lived in Colorado Springs for college the last few years while I lived in Denver, but we saw each other a lot. And I used to mentor a group of high school girls. Some of my team went to my church, so they were in my Bible study." And what a stellar leader she'd turned out to be. Tension coiled down her spine. Last school year she'd quit being a mentor and kept to herself. Leaders were supposed to be an example of what to do instead of what not to do.

"You mentored teenage girls." Cash said it more as a statement than question, and Olivia managed a nod, though she didn't know what the fuss was about.

"You have to help me with Rachel."

She'd already agreed to tutor Rachel. What more did the man need?

"I don't have a clue how to help her, how to deal with a teenage girl, and you have all of this experience. You'd be perfect."

Perfect was not the word that came to Olivia's mind.

"It would be so great if you could give me advice. I'm desperate to figure out how to help Rachel out of this rebellious stage she's in."

"You don't ask for much, do you?"

Cash flashed a charming smile in answer, and Olivia's resolve weakened.

"I'm not sure what kind of help I would be. It's not like I have a counseling degree or anything."

"It doesn't matter. You are a chick."

"Thank you for that observation."

At her dry tone, Cash laughed. "Trust me, I've noticed." He cleared his throat, looking at the trail in front of them before glancing back to her. "And you obviously have a desire to help teenage girls. I get the feeling you can't resist the thought of saving one from trouble."

Now that part was true.

"I think it's the least you can do with me letting you tutor Rachel for free."

Olivia laughed. She needed to say no. She didn't need to add another thing that forced her into spending time with Cash. Plus, the thought of helping Cash with Rachel only reminded Olivia of her own mistakes. She wanted to start fresh, not act like a CD stuck on repeat.

"If tonight's any indication, I obviously need help with her." Cash punctuated the quiet statement with a shake of his head, then grew silent, leaving Olivia to her own thoughts.

Could God be showing her, once again, that her purpose in moving to Texas wasn't just to run from the memories? Despite how unqualified she felt, she could offer Cash some insight into the mind of a teenage girl. Olivia might not be able to erase her story, but the possibility that she could help write a young girl's into a better path of some sort…how could she say no?

Freckles dropped back as the path narrowed, following behind Cash's horse as they wound past a patch of scrub oak and started a slight climb.

"Hey." Olivia called ahead to him. "This looks and

feels a lot like those other horseback riding tours I've been on."

His low chuckle floated back to her. "We'll save the racing and jumping fences for another day."

After about fifteen minutes, they reached a clearing. Cash dismounted and helped Olivia down. They walked to the edge of the hill. The path they'd taken wound through the trees below, the setting sun casting yellow, orange and pink streaks across the sky. Although there were no mountains to greet her, the green land and trees had a peaceful beauty all their own.

"It's so quiet. It's like another world."

"Yep." Cash stood beside her, looking out at the land with pride.

"Would you ever want to go anywhere else? Move anywhere else but here?"

"No. If you had all of this, would you?" His gaze never strayed from the view.

Her eyes stayed on the man next to her. "No." She sighed. "I wouldn't." Olivia pretended to check her watch, though the exhausted yawn that followed wasn't fake. "I'm sorry to cut this short, but I should really get going."

Cash helped her back onto Freckles, and on the ride back, every step of the horse under her seemed to aggravate Olivia's frustration. She should have stuck to her original plan. She should have gone straight home when Rachel didn't show up instead of talking to Cash as though they were friends. Because all tonight had accomplished was a growing ache in her chest. Their conversation about her life in Colorado had acted like a shovel, digging up a grave of memories that weren't buried deeply enough. If Olivia hadn't miscarried, she'd have a three-month-old right now. And while being a single mother wouldn't have been ideal, she *would* have made it work. Her love for that child had been instant. When she lost the baby, her feelings had bounced from mind-numbing grief to relief that the baby wouldn't be born into the mess she'd made. And that relief came with its own sense of guilt. How could she be okay with losing a child at all? But *okay* definitely wasn't the word she would use to describe how she'd felt about it then or now.

Before she'd met Josh, she used to dream about a man exactly like Cash for a husband—kind, Christian, hardworking, good sense of humor. She stole a glance at him riding next to her, drinking in the way he looked at home in a saddle. His strong jawline jutted out, a touch of concentration lining his forehead as he watched the fences along their path. Definitely not a chore to look at the man.

But the combination of it all only amounted to one thing: regret. Though she'd hoped her move would leave behind the guilt and shame she'd experienced in Colorado, it had hitched a ride shotgun and taken up permanent residence in her new life. And until Olivia figured out how to move beyond those chains—until she could forgive herself for the past—she had no business dreaming about the future.

Rachel came down the stairs as Cash finished his second cup of coffee. She was dressed for school, hair and makeup done. If only she didn't wear such dark stuff around her eyes. But he had to pick his battles.

And the one about to go down weighed in as more important.

To say he'd been furious last night when Rachel didn't show up would be an understatement. Cash had spent an extra hour rubbing down the horses after Olivia left, using the time to calm down and pray for wisdom and patience. After, he'd come inside to find Rachel in her room, listening to her iPod as though nothing had happened.

Jaw clenched tight, he'd walked away without saying anything, knowing he couldn't handle a conversation right then.

Thanks to a good night's rest, he felt as if they might be able to talk in a civilized manner this morning. Maybe Rachel had a good excuse. After all, she was a young girl grieving the deaths of her parents, not just his little sister driving him nuts.

Rachel's toast popped, and she spread peanut butter on it before dropping into the chair across from him.

Cash twisted his coffee cup back and forth, slowly releasing the air from his lungs. "We need to talk about last night."

"I know." Rachel's blond eyebrows scrunched together, her tone petulant.

Guess the night of sleep hadn't improved her mood.

Cash kept an even tone. "Where were you?"

"I forgot it was Thursday and that I was supposed to be here for tutoring."

Did he believe that? He didn't know. He only knew he was tired of fighting with the girl across from him. He missed his little sister. The one who looked up to him instead of glaring at him.

"Were you with Blake?"

Rachel took her sweet time before nodding. At least she still told him the truth about that.

"Rach, do you think I want to get on you about this stuff? Coach Grayson takes time out of her schedule to come help you. She doesn't gain anything out of it, and she doesn't get paid for it. It's offensive for you not to show up."

Rachel's perma-scowl softened and her chin lowered. "I know. I'm sorry."

Before Cash could even begin to hope, those green eyes flashed with defiance and she crossed her arms. "Coach Grayson only comes because she wants to see you. I did the two of you a favor by leaving you alone."

Cash barely kept from groaning. "That's not true and you know it." His little sister also knew just how to push his buttons. Resisting the temptation to argue further with her, Cash popped up from his chair and strode to the sink. His coffee cup clattered against the stainless steel while his body hummed with tension, craving the release physical labor offered. He stomped across the kitchen and out the door, boots kicking up dust as he crossed to the large garage next to the barn. If he was going to get so much guff over Olivia, he should at least be able to date the woman. But no, he got the worst of both worlds. No Olivia and a snarky sister to boot.

Watching the sunset last night, Cash had fought the temptation to let his mind wander into more-than-friends territory. Thankfully Olivia had cut the evening short. He might have promised himself not to date anyone while raising Rachel, but in truth, no one had tempted him until now.

Even Jack had noticed, ribbing him when they'd gone fishing on Saturday.

"So, are you going to ask the girl out or what? I'm beginning to think you're a perpetual bachelor."

The jab felt a little too close to the truth.

"Is this about Rachel?" Jack had been the only one who'd put up with Cash after his parents' deaths, the only one to continually pull him out of the black abyss he'd fallen into. His friend deserved an answer, though Cash didn't feel much like giving one.

"Isn't it always?"

"It doesn't have to be."

"Yes." Cash had released a deep breath as the truth of what he'd said ricocheted through him, confirming once again what he already knew. "It does."

What Jack didn't understand—what no one fully understood—was that Cash owed Rachel.

If he'd stuck to his original plans the day of his parents' accident, his mom would still be alive, possibly even his dad. Rachel would have the best mother in the world to guide her and Cash wouldn't be left struggling to give Rachel the life she deserved. The life he'd had.

So, yes, it *was* about Rachel. And it needed to be.

Which meant Cash had to ignore how amazing Olivia had looked throwing a pair of boots on those toned legs of hers. He shook his head, wishing Olivia's appeal would fly out of his mind with the motion.

Unfortunately, that didn't seem like a viable option. So Cash had come up with a different idea. In order to help him keep his promise, he needed to tell Olivia about it. Maybe if he was honest and up-front about everything, it would make sticking to his plan easier.

All of this for a teenage girl who cared about nothing but herself. One he loved more than his own life. Cash's parents had given him a great childhood, lots of attention and a house filled with love and laughter. Why couldn't he give Rachel the same? Days like this made him miss his parents so much that he physically ached.

He climbed into the dusty ranch Jeep and started it, then stared at the wheel, a plan beginning to form. Turning off the ignition, he jumped out and switched to his truck, pulling up to the front of the house just as Rachel came down the porch steps.

He motioned for her to open the passenger door. Surprisingly it stayed connected to the vehicle when she did. "What?" Anger drew a line through the light smattering of freckles on her forehead.

"Get in."

"What for?"

"I'm driving you to school."

Her mouth swung open far enough for Cash to see the empty spots where her wisdom teeth had come out last year.

"You're kidding."

"I wish I was. I don't have time to cart your butt around, but I don't have any other choice. Somehow, you have to figure out that your actions affect other people. You can have your Jeep back on Monday."

"No." Rachel whispered the word as her eyes squeezed shut.

Cash tried not to enjoy the look of panic and despair that filled her face. "You better get in or you're going to be late."

Chapter 6

Olivia finished correcting the last period's papers and stacked them in her box for Monday.

"Coach Grayson?" Rachel Maddox slunk into the French room.

"Hey, Rachel. What's up?"

Valerie Nettles stood in the hallway, and Olivia waved at the less dramatic girl while she waited for the one standing in front of her to speak.

"I—" Rachel stared at her shuffling flip-flops. "I just wanted to say sorry for not showing up last night. I forgot, but I know that's not an excuse."

Olivia barely resisted a smile at the forced apology. "It's okay. Are you going to be there next week? Because I really don't want to hang out with your brother any more than necessary."

Olivia had hoped for a smile from the teenager, maybe even a laugh. Instead, Rachel crossed her arms. "Yeah, I will." Her sulky demeanor softened a touch. "Thanks."

The quiet word surprised Olivia. "No problem. I'll see you at the game tonight?"

"We'll be there. See you later, Coach." Rachel caught up with Valerie and the two of them disappeared down the hall.

Olivia stood and stretched, glancing out her window toward the parking lot. A group of kids stood in a circle with two squad cars parked near them. Unease slithered down the back of her neck. She hurried down the hall and pushed out the door, using a hand to shade against the bright sun.

The students seemed calm. Most of them milled about talking to each other. Cheerleaders had signs ready for when the football team came out of the school to load the bus.

Olivia approached one of the squad cars and waited as the officer rolled down his window. It couldn't be too bad if he was still in his car.

"I'm one of the teachers here. Is something wrong?"

The gray-haired man pointed a thumb over his shoulder. "Just waiting for the bus. We escort the football team and the student cars that follow."

He *must* be joking. Olivia managed to say thank-you and back away before giving in to her laughter. A police escort to a football game? Only in Texas. These players were treated like rock stars. She turned to go back inside, running smack into someone.

"Sorry." She took a step back. "Didn't mean to bowl

you over. I—" Olivia's words stopped. The supermodel from church adjusted the belt over her frilly bright green shirt that cascaded down to long toothpick legs in skinny jeans and wedge sandals. She tossed fiery red hair and flashed bright white teeth.

"It's okay, sweetie, don't worry about a thing." Her voice had a syrupy quality that made Olivia resist a cringe. "I'm Tera Lawton, and I've been meaning to introduce myself to you. Seeing as how the whole town knows you've arrived and who you are. I'm the dance team coach. It's a part-time thing in the afternoons and evenings, so I'm not around during the school day."

Pity. Olivia chided herself for the bad attitude. "It's nice to meet you." She took a step to the right, wanting to get back to her classroom and away from the sugary-fake personality in front of her.

"Wait." Tera touched Olivia's arm. "I've seen you talking to Cash and thought you might want to know..." She leaned closer, as if the two of them were friends sharing secrets. "He's quite the heartbreaker. With you being new in town, I just thought I'd give you a warning so that you don't get hurt." Tera's lower lip slipped into a pout. "I mean, we wouldn't want our new French teacher to leave town with a broken heart, would we?"

Olivia didn't have words. At least, not ones she would voice. Janie had told her Cash had dated this woman. If so, Olivia didn't need to fear that he'd ever be interested in her. She and Tera were nothing alike in personality or looks.

The woman's eyes narrowed before she smoothed her features and flashed another fake smile. "Anyway, if anyone knows about the man, it's me. I thought you'd want to know his nature before you got more—" she tilted her head "—involved."

Olivia wanted to scream that she and Cash weren't dating, that they were only trying to help a struggling teenager, but Tera wiggled her fingers and took off across the parking lot, corralling the dance team into cars.

She walked back to her classroom, Tera's words sending a shiver of recognition down her spine. The girl was right. Probably not about the heartbreaker part, as Olivia couldn't see Cash being that way, but the bitter beauty queen had brought a truth into the light. Under the guise of helping Rachel, Olivia's heart could too easily slip and slide toward Cash.

And that wasn't something she could let happen. Not with her past hanging over her like a thundercloud. Olivia wanted to find the forgiveness and healing she knew God had already granted but that she couldn't seem to grasp.

She needed to feel new. So far, she was still waiting.

Which meant she needed to keep a tight leash on her growing attraction to Cash. Since she'd already started tutoring Rachel, she would follow through on that. But Cash's request to help him with his sister?

If it meant spending even more time with the man, Olivia just couldn't do it. She had to back away.

The Fredericksburg High School Billie Goats went for a two-point conversion and Cash cheered when they scored. For most of the first half, his gaze had bounced from his little sister—wearing a number eighty-two jersey and cheering for Blake—to the football game to Olivia and Janie sitting in the front row with Tucker.

Cash had allowed Rachel to ride to the game and back with the Nettles family since she didn't have a vehicle at her disposal and he wasn't mean enough to make her ride with him. She would have melted the seats in the truck with all of that anger. Trish had promised to get Rachel straight home after the game. Who knew, maybe some of Val's even-keeled nature would rub off on Rach tonight. Like it hadn't done for the past seventeen years.

At halftime, Cash headed from the visitors' section to the concessions stand. He talked to a few people on the way, and by the time he reached the line it almost hit the bleachers.

He resisted a groan when he recognized Tera's trademark red spirals in front of him in line.

Maybe if he took a step back and—

"Cash." Tera spotted him and practically purred. "You're just the person I wanted to see."

Shocking.

"I've been having all this trouble at my house." She threaded fingers through her hair in a move that looked practiced as a haze of overpowering perfume surrounded them. "My kitchen sink keeps leaking. I've been under it a bunch of times, but I can't get it working right. I wondered if you might be able to swing by some time and take a look."

Did Tera really think a line like that would work? Did she think anyone believed her lies? Hard to comprehend that the girl's honey-smothered southern drawl had once been attractive to him. Now it made his skin crawl. Cash extracted his arm from Tera's clawlike grip with a shake of his head. How did she get her nails into him so quickly? "Not going to happen, Lawton."

Tera's eyes narrowed, and Cash turned and scanned the crowd. One day she'd finally get that he wasn't interested. Would never be interested. The fact that she thought something could be possible between them still amazed him.

Olivia approached the line behind him, and Cash couldn't help his grin or the relief he felt in seeing an honest, friendly face. She looked cute in khaki shorts and a red Battlin' Billies T-shirt, ponytail swinging across her shoulders.

When she spotted him, Olivia froze a few steps away.

"Hey." Cash tugged on the brim of his cap.

"Hey, Cash. How are you?"

Not that great if he counted Olivia's formal tone or the way she looked everywhere but at him.

"I better go find Janie."

"Didn't you just get in line?"

She shifted from one foot to the other. "Yeah, but I think Janie needs me."

What was going on? Why was Olivia acting so strange?

Cash pointed past her shoulder. "Actually, Janie's right behind you."

"Hey, y'all." Janie hiked Tucker further up on her hip and approached the two of them. "Tuck's been fussing the whole game, and I think maybe he's getting his two-year molars. The boy's a hot mess." Janie flashed

Olivia an apologetic look. "Liv, I'm so sorry, but I think I better take him home."

Olivia rubbed a hand across Tucker's back. "It's not a problem. I don't mind leaving."

Cash glanced between the two girls, his gaze landing on Olivia. "I can drive you home if you want to stay."

She waved away his offer. "I'm fine going—"

"Cash." Janie perked up, interrupting Olivia. "That would be so great. I absolutely do not want Olivia to have to leave the game. If you guys see Jack, let him know we left. I'll send him a text for later but I don't want him wondering. Thanks!" Janie waved and took off for the parking lot almost at a run, Tucker bouncing on her hip, diaper bag swinging from her shoulder. The woman sure seemed in an all-fired hurry to leave, but then, if Tucker didn't feel well, Cash could understand that.

The concession line moved forward and Tera peeked around Cash.

"Looks like we're finally moving." Fake surprise dashed across Tera's face. "Olivia, it's so great to see you again."

When did the two of them meet?

Olivia greeted Tera and then didn't follow the line as it inched forward. "You know, I don't think I want anything anymore. I'll meet you at the bleachers."

"I'm good. I'll go with you."

By the time they made their way back to the visitors' section, the second half had started. Olivia sat as stiff as if she'd ridden bareback yesterday. She cheered; she talked to other people.

She just didn't talk to Cash.

When Tera climbed the bleachers, she glared at Olivia the whole way up.

Cash sighed. Now everything made more sense.

Olivia concentrated on the headlights cutting through the pitch-black night instead of the man across the truck cab from her.

Janie. Olivia couldn't believe her friend had bolted like that, leaving her with Cash. Now what was she supposed to do? She'd have to tell him that she couldn't help with Rachel any more than tutoring. But how would she explain that?

You see, Cash, I'm attracted to you and I don't want to be. I need time to work through my past, and I can't help your sister because I don't want to be around you more than necessary. Sound good?

She resisted a snort.

Instead of taking her home, Cash drove to the Dairy Queen drive-through. Olivia opened her mouth to protest, then changed her mind. While the need to escape remained, the desire to drown herself in a Blizzard won out.

"What would you like?"

"Heath Blizzard with chocolate ice cream."

Cash didn't raise an eyebrow. He ordered hers and a meal for himself plus a shake.

"I didn't have time to eat dinner before the game," he explained.

Then why had he gotten out of the concessions line with her? He must be starving.

They got the food from the window and Cash backed into a parking spot. He grabbed the bag. "Come on."

Cash hopped out of the truck and went around to the back, where he unlatched the tailgate and took a seat. Olivia had no choice but to follow. She pushed open her door, moving at a much slower pace. At the rear of the truck, she pulled herself up on the opposite side of the tailgate.

He offered her a fry, which she declined. Death by chocolate sounded much better.

Cash scooted back and twisted sideways across the truck bed, stretching his legs out. Wearing jeans, gray tennis shoes and a vintage Billies T-shirt that had to be from his own high school football days, the man still managed to look drop-dead you-know-what.

Annoying habit of his.

"Is that a grass-fed burger?"

Cash laughed, choking on his bite. "No, city girl. It's not." He took a sip of his shake. "Every so often I partake of a corn-and-grain–raised burger like the rest of the world."

Olivia's lips quirked up without her permission.

"I see you met Tera. I assume an apology is in order."

The grin fell off her face. How had Cash figured that out?

"If I know Tera, the meeting wasn't pleasant."

"Do you know Tera?" Olivia ate a bite of ice cream and cringed at the jealousy in her voice. Did she need any more proof that she should be backing away from Cash?

"Unfortunately, yes." His sigh echoed between

them. "We dated during high school and into college. When I moved away for school, Tera stayed here. I found out when I came back on break that she'd been cheating on me. When I confronted her about it, at first she denied it. But eventually she admitted it and we parted ways."

Olivia had been right. She and Tera were nothing alike. Sympathy prompted her to peel her clammy thighs from the tailgate, scoot back against the opposite side of the truck bed and stretch her legs parallel to Cash's. "I'm sorry."

"Trust me, it was for the best." He crumpled the hamburger paper and tossed it in the bag. "That wasn't the only thing Tera and I disagreed on. She never shared my desire to…wait."

Wait? As in wait for marriage? Olivia's heart broke a little bit hearing those words.

"My parents always talked about it, and I know that's part of why they had such a great marriage." He shrugged. "I just want to do things God's way."

"Me, too," Olivia whispered. She hadn't done things God's way in the past, but she wanted to now. If only she had never walked away from her beliefs, from God. If only she'd run from Josh instead of letting him in. But she knew better than anyone that *if onlys* could crush a spirit.

"If it was just the cheating and breakup between Tera and me, I'd be able to let things go. But it didn't end there. After college, I moved back to the ranch. Tera would try to gain my attention in town, but I didn't have any interest in her anymore. One day she called saying she was sick and needed someone to get her a few things from the store. I wondered why she'd called me, but then, she didn't have that many friends left in town. I was supposed to go to Austin for a cattle auction with my dad, but I decided to check on Tera instead. Unfortunately, I was far too loyal back then."

A thread of tension seeped into the conversation, and Olivia set her ice cream down on the metal truck bed.

"When I got over there, I found out she wasn't sick at all. She just wanted to convince me we should get back together." Cash's fingers dug into the back of his neck. "I was upset with her for lying. We fought and I left." His gaze lifted to meet hers, and the pain there stole Olivia's breath. "Because I went to check on Tera, my mom decided to go with my dad to the auction that day. On the drive back that night they were killed."

"I'm so sorry." Olivia didn't have words for that kind of regret.

Cash took a minute before continuing. "Now you know why I can't stand lying. It's the one thing I can't forgive. It hurts too many people, and it never ends well. Rachel knows it, and so far, I think she's always told me the truth." He shifted one ankle over the other, taking a drink of his shake.

"After losing them, I had so many questions. What if I'd gone? Would I have been driving? Would I have seen the truck and avoided the accident? At least if I'd gone, my mom would still be here to raise Rachel. But now Rachel's stuck with me. I need to give her a good life, the life she would have had if my parents were still alive." Cash's shoulders lifted. "It's sort of like a volleyball game. I don't want to take my eye off the ball—Rachel—for one second. I don't want to have any regrets or wonder if I could have done more. I promised after our parents died that I wouldn't date until Rachel was out of high school and on her way to college. I promised myself that Rachel would get my undivided attention."

Gracious. Olivia swiped under her eyes. She could understand that. She could get behind that kind of commitment.

"That's why I keep asking you for more. I hoped you might be able to help me understand Rachel. Or give me advice. I'm not even sure what I'm asking for in terms of her. I guess I just need…something. Some help. And she does, too."

Olivia had thought she needed to back away from Cash in order to stop her feelings from growing, but now that she knew he didn't plan to date, it made everything so much easier. She could help him with Rachel and take the time to sort through her past without the possibility of a relationship developing between them. Knowing he had a promise to keep made Olivia relax for the first time since she'd met Cash. As long as they'd both made the decision not to date, they could actually be friends. And with how much they saw each other, that sounded far better than her previous plan.

"I'm not sure how much help I'll be, or what advice I have to give, but I'll do everything I can to help her. And you. I'm officially on Team Rachel."

Her conscience threw up a red flare at the way Cash's answering smile made her stomach do a cartwheel, but she ignored the warning sign and the sensation. With both of them on the same page, she felt confident she would stick to her plan.

Unlike the last time.

Chapter 7

Olivia woke to a sense of foreboding.

Strange. Shouldn't she feel good about how the evening had ended with Cash? Their conversation last night might have come after a bit of turmoil and tension, but in the end, Olivia felt so much better about helping Rachel. She even felt peace about being friends with Cash.

They had come to an understanding, and Cash had given her another great reason to keep her heart from falling for him.

After their first conversation, she and Cash had spent an hour talking about how to help Rachel. The man definitely had his heart in the right place. Somehow he'd figure out what to do with the girl, if not by experience then by sheer determination.

Olivia had come home, put on *You've Got Mail*, which ran on a loop in her DVD player, and fallen asleep on the couch. Sometime during the night she'd shuffled from the sofa to her bed.

Now, she shrugged off her white down comforter along with the niggling apprehension and padded through the small living room that connected to her even smaller kitchen. The apartment had the basic appliances, including a dishwasher and a window air-conditioning unit that did a surprisingly good job of keeping her place cool.

Olivia fumbled with the coffee filter and grounds, gasping when it hit her.

The enormity of what she'd done made her stumble to the whitewashed table under the kitchen window and sink into a chair.

She'd said she agreed with Cash's decision about waiting for marriage…which she did.

But it sounded as though she'd made the same one… which she hadn't.

So now, added to her long list of sins, was a lie she hadn't even known she'd told. And now that she knew how Cash felt about lying, telling the truth would be all the more painful.

Tucker threw a tractor across the sandbox and then giggled. Olivia tried not to laugh with him, but the boy was incredibly cute.

"Let's not throw, Tucker."

He threw another toy and chortled again.

"Do you want to swing?"

The adorable monster picked up a cup and didn't

respond. Olivia grabbed his hand before he could toss it and helped him dig into the sand. It distracted him and he began to dig and dump, dig and dump. Olivia brushed her hands against her denim capris to remove the sand, then twisted her hair to one shoulder of her black tank top, wishing for a breeze to cool them off.

This morning, Janie had shown up at Olivia's door to go dress shopping for tonight. Jack had managed to keep the anniversary plan a surprise, and Janie had been smiling even wider than usual.

"Girl, I can't believe you didn't tell me. You're supposed to have my back."

"Like you had mine last night at the football game? How's Tucker's tooth, by the way?"

Janie had grinned, shoulders lifting in innocence. "Better overnight."

The woman needed to give up on her matchmaking ideas, especially since Cash and Olivia were both in agreement on not dating.

As for Olivia's lie of omission last night with Cash… even after processing all day, she didn't know what to do about that. Truthfully, she wasn't ready to talk to anyone about what had happened between her and Josh. The man had walked away from her when she told him she was pregnant, saying he didn't want a family— even though they had talked about a future together. And then while she'd been dealing with the miscarriage on her own, he'd started dating another teacher at the same school. All last year she'd had to work with both of them while her heart continued to bleed. That kind of hurt didn't mend easily, nor did the constant ache of wondering if her stress had caused her miscarriage.

But despite the fact that she didn't plan to discuss any of that with anyone anytime soon, the question remained…would Cash consider what she'd said last night—or hadn't said—a lie?

Tucker scooped another cupful of sand, and she ran a hand along his soft hair. Though being with him reminded her of the baby she'd lost, Olivia knew his sweet personality also brought healing, and she was all for that.

Tucker lifted the cupful of sand and tipped it to his mouth. He got half into his mouth and down his throat before Olivia smacked it away. Wheezing, Tucker tried to breathe through the particles blocking his airway.

Olivia grabbed him and flipped him so that he faced down. She dug into his mouth, pulling out sand as fast as she could. When she got most of it out, he continued to choke and wheeze. She flew into the house and ran the water in the kitchen sink. Would wetting the sand make it better or worse? She didn't have a clue. Tipping him forward again, she began the same process, this time with water.

Finally, he sputtered and caught his breath. Olivia set him on the counter next to the sink and helped him drink a few sips of water. It must have loosened the last of the sand from his airway, because he started splashing his bare feet in the sink.

Olivia's knees swayed. What if she hadn't been able to help him? What if Tucker—?

Bracing her hands against the counter on either side of Tucker as he played, Olivia took a few deep breaths and tried to calm her nerves. When her heart stopped pounding in her ears, she cleaned the sand off Tucker's hands and feet, dried them with a paper towel and then picked him up.

"Time for dinner." With shaky arms, Olivia put Tucker in the high chair and gave him a bowl of applesauce and a plastic spoon. He went to work on that while she warmed up his peas and noodles.

When she turned back, Tucker had applesauce in his eyebrows and spread across the tray. She switched the bowl out with the plate in her hand, and Tucker immediately sent peas flying across the kitchen.

So she could pretty much count herself as the worst babysitter *ever*.

The doorbell rang and Olivia checked to make sure Tucker was buckled into the high chair before going to answer.

Through the glass storm door, she could see Cash standing on the front step.

She swung the door open, answering his confused look. "Jack and Janie are gone for their anniversary dinner. I'm babysitting." A crash sounded in the kitchen. "Come on in."

Olivia arrived in time to see Tucker dump the last of his noodles over the side of the tray, like the dump truck he'd just been playing with in the sandbox.

Cash followed her into the kitchen and raised one eyebrow. "Who won the fight?"

"Tucker." Olivia surveyed the small turn-of-the-century kitchen with bright red cabinets that had been clean minutes before. "Definitely Tucker."

"Need some help?"

More than you know. "I need to give him a bath and clean up this mess."

"Which one do you want me to do?"

If Cash gave Tucker a bath, Olivia couldn't harm the poor kid any further.

"I'll take kitchen duty. Although, he's hardly eaten."

"No problem." Cash fed Tucker a big bowl of applesauce, a banana and a plate of noodles in a matter of minutes. Show-off. Then he pulled Tucker from the high chair and flew him into the bathroom while Olivia switched from sweeping up peas to wiping cupboards.

From the sound of the commotion and fun happening in the bathroom, the bathwater would be all over and not just in the tub. She smiled at the banter between Tucker and "Unc Cas." Cash sure knew his way around a kid. Maybe because he was so much older than Rachel. Olivia *would not* dwell on what an attractive quality that was in a man.

What was Cash doing here, anyway? Olivia hadn't even asked. She'd just put him straight to work.

She finished cleaning the kitchen and headed down the hall in time to catch Tucker's flight from bathtub to changing table.

Cash laid him down, and Olivia put on his lotion and diapered him. They managed to get the squirmy monkey into pajamas and into his crib. He sucked his thumb, staring up at them with curious eyes.

Olivia and Cash shared a grin before turning on Tucker's mobile and sending stars dancing across his darkened ceiling. They moved down the hall and into the living room.

Cash leaned against the back of the chocolate couch Janie referred to as pleather and braced his hands beside him, stretching his heather-brown T-shirt across muscular shoulders. Tonight, he wore jeans and boots—a slightly different casual look than last night. Same effect.

"Thanks for the help."

"You're welcome. I don't know how Jack and Janie keep up with that boy."

"Me either. He almost needed an ER visit tonight, and I was sitting right next to him." As Olivia told Cash the story, the reality of what could have happened made her body feel as limp as one of Tucker's cooked noodles.

Cash barely bent to look into her eyes. She loved that he had to do that. "You do know he would have done the same thing with Janie or Jack here. It wasn't your fault."

If only that statement could apply to the rest of her life. "I'm not sure about that, but I am glad he's okay."

"Me, too." Cash glanced at the front door. "I guess I better get going. Janie texted me this afternoon and asked if I could come by and look at her car tonight. Weird, huh? Especially with them being gone for their anniversary. Did they drive her car or Jack's?"

"Hers." Olivia bit her lip. She was going to have a talk with Janie about her matchmaking. Two nights in a row was a step too far, though the thought did make Olivia hold back a laugh. How could such a sweet bundle of energy like Janie have such a plotting nature? "She didn't mention anything to me."

Cash shrugged. "Maybe she meant to say tomorrow night."

Not even a chance. "You fix cars too?"

"I can usually pinpoint what's wrong, at least. Mechanical work is not Jack's strong suit."

Despite Janie's interference, Olivia was actually thankful for Cash's presence. He'd helped her with Tucker and made the end of the evening go much better than the first half. "Since you're here, do you want to hang out? I'm just waiting for Jack and Janie to get back at this point. They'll be gone late. We could watch a movie or something."

Cash paused before answering, and Olivia felt sure he'd head right back out the door. Just as she started to regret asking, he nodded. "Sure."

Her shoulders relaxed. "I'll make popcorn. You choose a movie."

Torture. Cash knew of no other word that could more perfectly describe watching a movie with Olivia. After putting Tucker down, she'd pulled her hair up into a ponytail, and her tanned shoulders and black tank top did little to help him concentrate on the TV.

He didn't even know what movie he'd picked. Some chick flick. Cash had guessed Olivia would like it, but her laughter told him it had comedy as well. He had watched a little, more enjoying the sound of her amusement than the movie itself.

His and Olivia's conversation last night about Rachel and not wanting to date had ended well. Until he'd gone home and realized that saying and doing were two different things. Olivia's personality, combined with an athletic body and striking blue eyes, wasn't easy to ignore.

But that's what Cash needed to do. He didn't have any choice but to keep her firmly in the friend category.

He'd thought telling Olivia about his promise would make things easier, but the conversation hadn't taken away that *something* in his gut that said he could be missing out on his future. Last night he'd even found out that Olivia believed the same things as him.

She had all of the qualities he wanted in a wife, and Cash couldn't pursue a relationship with her. He felt trapped in some kind of self-imposed prison. But he could be confident he was following God's will in regards to his promise about Rachel. At least he had that.

The movie ended, and Olivia leaned forward, digging in her purse by the foot of the couch. She took out a red egg-looking thing, twisted it open and slid it across her lips.

Something strawberry and sweet bombarded his senses. *Mercy.* The woman needed to stop smelling so good.

"What did you say?"

He *had not* said that out loud. "I said…that smells good. What is it?"

"Lip balm." She held it in front of him. "Want some?"

Yes. He did. But he wanted the application to come from her lips. It took everything in Cash not to lean forward and find out if her lips were as sweet as she smelled. How long had it been since he'd kissed someone? Years. But he knew absence had nothing to do with the desire to kiss this woman.

"I'm fine. Thanks." *Fine.* Right.

Cash needed to focus on something besides Olivia.

He could always think about his sister—like he should be doing anyway. Yep. That worked for dissolving his way-past-friendship thoughts.

He shoved off the couch and stood. "I'd better go. I'll see you at church tomorrow?"

Olivia nodded just as the front door opened and Jack and Janie spilled over the threshold. Janie had a look of amusement—and was that victory?—on her face and Jack had one of shock.

"Date night?" Jack switched to a grin, and Cash barely resisted rolling his eyes like Rach. Sure, he and Olivia had watched a movie together, and yes, he'd thought once or twice about holding her hand. After seeing her yawn, he'd even wondered if Olivia might fall asleep against his shoulder—but none of that had happened.

Although the situation did look a bit like a date. Cash could only imagine the months of ribbing that would come from this moment.

Jack's amusement increased, but he turned to Olivia instead of Cash. "When you said you wanted to hang out with your favorite little man, I thought you were talking about Tucker."

Pink raced up Olivia's cheeks, and she looked as if she wanted to climb under the couch. Funny. It wasn't like her not to have a witty retort for Jack.

The overwhelming urge to protect Olivia from Jack's teasing prompted Cash to say his goodbyes and move to the front door. Maybe tomorrow morning he'd head to church early. He'd sit in the sanctuary, listen to the music before the service and talk to God about this whole mess. Maybe God could help him remember that being friends with Olivia didn't give him a free pass to let his feelings grow. Because despite his and Olivia's conversation last night, Cash could use a reminder.

A scuffling noise sounded on the church roof, and Olivia glanced at Janie. Her friend shrugged in answer to Olivia's silent question, mouth twitching. Last night, after the embarrassing end to the evening with Cash, Olivia had talked to Janie about her matchmaking. She'd agreed to stop, but this morning the woman couldn't keep the amusement off her face. Had Olivia realized Jack would tease her just as much, she would have considered skipping church.

Good thing she hadn't. The sermon was on forgiveness today. Could there be a better day for her to pay attention? But as Pastor Rick read through the parable of the unmerciful servant, the scratching noise sounded from the roof again and again.

"Search your heart. Have you forgiven those who've sinned against you? Have you forgiven yourselves? Some of you find it easier to forgive others but forget that includes you."

Gracious. Olivia could answer both of those questions with one word: *no.*

How did God do that? How did he take a sermon meant for the whole church and make it speak directly to her? Olivia knew she needed to forgive Josh and herself. She just didn't know how to accomplish it.

At the end of the service, people filtered out, most still talking about the noises on the roof.

Olivia and Janie walked to the back of the church. Jack had gone out during the service to see if he could help figure out what was going on. Now he stood near a group of teenagers, along with Cash, a few other parents and a bunch of church staff members.

Janie pulled Jack aside. "What's going on?"

He glanced at the group before taking a few more steps away. "That noise during the service was a bunch of teenagers up on the roof."

Janie frowned. "How did they even get up there?"

"I don't know. I'm guessing there's a way up somewhere for maintenance, and they must have found it. Thankfully, no one got hurt."

"That's such a relief." Olivia scanned the group until she spotted Rachel. "Was Rachel one of the kids?"

"Yep."

Olivia's stomach rolled. Cash would be irate. He'd been mad about Rachel skipping out on tutoring—and that was small potatoes compared to this. When the circle of teenagers and staff started to break up, Olivia headed for Cash and pulled him to the side.

"Are you okay?"

"No." Worry lines covered his face. "What am I supposed to do with her?"

Olivia resisted reaching up to smooth away the stress marring his features. If only she could help.

"Can you send her home and give yourself some time to cool down?"

"What? I can't. I have to discipline her even though I'm running out of ideas in that department. She's already without a vehicle."

"You asked me for help with her, and here it is. Let her be for a bit. Take a break and calm down. She'll be even more worried about what you're going to do and

you'll have some time to think. Let's do something…
go for a hike, maybe. We'll see what we can come up
with together."

Cash's gaze landed on Rachel and his lips pulled
into a thin line.

"I can't." He stared past Olivia as though she didn't
even exist. "I just can't let it go like that." After shaking his head, Cash released a deep breath and went
over to Rachel. Seconds later, the two of them left the
church, leaving Olivia struggling for her own answers.

Wasn't she supposed to be helping him? Hadn't he
asked her for advice?

Though she attempted to shake off the dismissal, it
hurt far more than it should.

Janie came over carrying Tucker and he lunged into
Olivia's arms. She hugged the small, squirmy bundle as
though he could make all things new. But he couldn't
do that for her. Only God could. And after all of this
time and all of her prayers and efforts in that regard,
she still didn't feel as if she was moving forward.

If anything, today felt like a big step back.

Had she forgiven Josh? No.

Had she forgiven herself? No.

Was she a help at all to the struggling teenage girl
she'd pledged to support?

Another big fat no. Her team might be winning volleyball games, but Olivia felt nowhere near a victory.

Chapter 8

"Hey, Cocoa." Olivia bent to greet her friend, who lay sprawled across the Maddoxes' front porch. She scratched behind Cocoa's ears, grinning at the leg that started tapping against the wooden planks. The cuts on Cocoa's face seemed to be healing. Olivia could hardly see them anymore. And the one on the dog's shoulder? She wouldn't be checking that one.

She knocked. "Come in." Rachel's shout came through the inch the inside door stood open.

Olivia walked in and set her things on the table. Instead of Rachel doing homework and Cash warming up dinner, the teenager stood by the stove.

"Dinner should be ready in a few."

"Do you need help with anything?"

"No, thanks. Cash is working or something, so it's

just me and you. I'm making mac and cheese." Rachel motioned to the blue box on the counter. "Sorry it's not much."

"It's plenty for me. I love mac and cheese." Olivia leaned back against the counter, an opportunity for the evening blossoming in her mind. Without Cash here, maybe Olivia could get Rachel to open up about her life.

They never had time at volleyball for Olivia to crack through Rachel's barrier. Plus, they actually had to accomplish something at practice. Last night they'd lost their first match. The Billies had played hard, but the other team had played better. It was the kind of loss Olivia didn't get too upset about. Although she was glad they'd meet the same team again later in the season. It would be nice to redeem themselves with a win.

"So—" Olivia's question got cut off when a huge commotion sounded outside. Cocoa started barking like crazy, and the spoon Rachel had been stirring with clattered across the counter.

Rachel flew to the back of the house and disappeared. Olivia followed, going through the mudroom and out the back door.

Outside, Rachel stood a few yards from what Olivia assumed was a chicken coop, yelling at the crazed Cocoa. Her legs were in a wide stance, hair flowing down the back of her blue T-shirt like some Wild West woman. Cocoa rushed around the structure excitedly, rotating between growls and barks.

"Cocoa. No." Rachel commanded the dog with a strong voice, but Cocoa didn't listen. "She's going to get hurt. I'm going in."

"What?" *Into what?* "Rachel, what is going on?"

"There's something in there. Probably whatever tore Cocoa up the last time."

Olivia had to yell above the roar of dog and chickens. "You can't go in there. I'll go." She pushed past Rachel and ran to the coop, imagining her face would look something like Cocoa's in a few seconds. She wrenched the door open, then slammed it shut, hoping the noise would scare away whatever lurked inside. After yanking it wide open again, Olivia only made it a few yards back before a raccoon came flying out. Instead of running, it paused in front of her.

If ever there was a moment to faint, this was it. Beady black eyes stared her down, and Olivia's legs almost gave out, depositing her at eye level with the animal. Why hadn't she grabbed a stick or something to protect herself?

Had the raccoon just hissed?

Instead of acting large or intimidating or any other thing she'd ever heard about dealing with a wild animal, Olivia turned tail and ran in the other direction. She grabbed Rachel along the way and didn't stop until she reached the back of the house. Only then did she pause to turn back. She saw the back end of the raccoon as it disappeared into the tall grass.

"Cocoa." They both yelled at the dog when she took off after the raccoon. Thankfully, Cocoa came back. How could she not remember what had happened the last time?

Rachel grabbed Cocoa's collar and made her way into the house, leaving Olivia to follow at a much slower and shakier pace. When she passed through the mudroom, Cocoa whined at being confined to the space. Olivia gave her a sympathetic pat on the head, then made her way into the kitchen.

Rachel stood near the stove again. "I think I might have overcooked the noodles."

You think? "They'll be fine." Olivia helped herself to a glass from the cupboard and filled it with water from the sink. She drank the whole thing, then moved to the table and collapsed into one of the chairs. Her legs felt as if she'd just finished a three-day volleyball tournament in college.

Rachel, on the other hand, seemed completely calm. She got out the milk and butter, mixed the noodles with the cheese packet, and set the pot in the middle of the table. Two bowls followed.

"Fork or spoon?"

"Fork."

"I knew there was something strange about you."

Olivia choked on a laugh. Had ornery Rachel Maddox made a joke? She suddenly felt thankful for their facing-down-the-wild-animal experience outside. Maybe it would swing their relationship in a new direction. One where Olivia could actually help the girl.

They dished the food, and Olivia took a bite, trying to hide her distaste as a congealed glob of soft noodles filled her mouth. She looked up to find Rachel staring at her bowl, eyebrows pulled together and lips pursed.

The girl stirred her noodles with a spoon, then dropped it into the bowl with a clang. "That's disgusting."

"They're just a little overdone. It's not like you were standing over the stove watching them."

Rachel huffed. It seemed to be one of her favorite noises. "At least Cocoa didn't get hurt." She tucked a strand of buttercream hair behind her ear, her voice a whisper.

Olivia agreed with her. The girl had a heart. She just didn't want anyone to know it. "So...I assume you're never allowed to leave the ranch again?"

Rachel rolled her eyes, but her lips curved a bit. "Only for school and volleyball through this weekend. I hadn't even finished the last grounding when he took away my Jeep. He just tacked on another week."

Olivia didn't blame him. She had racked her brain all week trying to think of ways to help Rachel, but she kept coming up short. Cash already did so many things right. He ate dinner with Rachel most nights, went to all of her games, supported her in every way he knew how. Rachel just seemed to be some unsolvable mystery.

She looked down at the table. "I thought he was going to take away the homecoming dance. And I mean, crawling up on the church roof was not my best move, I'll admit that. But next weekend?" She looked up with such hope in those green eyes that Olivia's breath stuttered. "I really want to go. We got a limo and everything."

"Are you going with Blake?" Olivia would have to be in another country not to notice Blake and Rachel together around school, after practice, after the football games.

"Yeah."

"So where's your dress? Do I get to see it, or is it a surprise?"

At the last staff meeting, Olivia had been daydreaming and gotten roped into chaperoning the dance. But she didn't mind. Since she was one of the few single teachers without kids, she could hang out with a bunch of teenagers for one night. What was the difference? She did it all day.

Rachel fidgeted with her napkin, studying the daisy print much longer than she usually studied her schoolwork. "I don't have a dress yet." She shrugged as if it didn't matter, but of course it did. "Cash wouldn't let me drive, and now I'm not supposed to leave again. I don't know when I'll have time to look. Mrs. Nettles asked me if I wanted to go when she took Val, but—" Rachel got up and cleared their bowls of uneaten macaroni and cheese, depositing them in the sink. "But I don't always want to crash on them."

"Can I go with you?"

The bowls clinked and Rachel glanced up. "You'd want to?"

"Of course. Where could we go?"

"There's a mall down in Kerrville."

That was where Olivia had gone dress shopping with Janie. "Is that all the way to Mexico?"

No laugh. No smile. Man, the girl was tough to crack.

"It's about thirty minutes."

"Is that the best place to go?"

Rachel loaded the dishes in the dishwasher. "We could go to Austin, but that's over an hour away. My aunt and uncle live there. We could stay with them, but then you wouldn't want to go."

Wouldn't she? Why not? What did Olivia have holding her here that Rachel's sad look couldn't pull her away from?

Rachel opened the freezer and took out a carton of mint chocolate chip, then got out two white bowls and set the items on the table.

After retrieving the ice cream scoop, she heaped a generous amount into each bowl. "Dinner is served."

When a fork appeared next to her bowl, Olivia laughed. She got up to get her own spoon, thinking she had more in common with this teenage girl than she'd realized. Including a heart that needed some healing. After that sermon on Sunday, Olivia had decided to start praying more consistently about how to grant forgiveness. To herself and others.

She took a bite, pointing to the bowl with her spoon. "This is my kind of meal." The mint ice cream had shaved pieces of chocolate—Olivia's favorite—and she ate another spoonful before jumping back into the dress conversation. "I really don't mind going to Austin to shop. I think it would be fun. But how are we going to go this weekend if you're grounded?"

Rachel shrugged, the hurt back on her face.

"Check with your brother and see if he'll let you go with me. If he says yes, how about Saturday?"

When Rachel's lips lifted, Olivia resisted the urge to break into song. A Rachel smile earned her at least five points. Maybe ten.

If Cash searched Google for the word *exhausted*, his own haggard picture would pop up.

Over a dozen longhorns had escaped through a broken fence, it had taken most of the day to fix the water system *and* he'd been out working until ten o'clock and had missed seeing Olivia.

That last one shouldn't matter so much, but it did.

He entered the house through the back mudroom and took off his boots, then proceeded into the kitchen. The first floor of the house was quiet and barely lit, making him wonder at the whereabouts of his sister. Hopefully she hadn't sneaked out. He didn't have the energy for trouble tonight.

After downing a glass of water, he opened the fridge, leaning against the door as he rummaged for leftovers. He came up with a questionable-looking slice of pizza and flipped on the kitchen light to better examine it. No mold greeted him, so he took a bite. It couldn't kill him.

"Cash." Rachel's voice startled him.

She was sitting on the couch, earbuds in her hand as if she'd just plucked them out.

"Hey." Cash walked over to the chocolate recliner chair that partially faced the couch and dropped in. He set the piece of pizza on his jeans—now it probably *could* kill him—and pulled the footrest close. After propping up his feet, he let out a breath.

"Long day?"

"Never ending." He slapped a hand against his chest in mock surprise and looked over his shoulder. "Did my little sister just ask about my day? I must have walked into the wrong house."

Rachel snorted—the snotty kind, not the humorous kind. There went that sweet sibling moment.

She tossed her iPod onto the couch cushion and

shifted forward. "Cash, a raccoon got into the chicken coop. It almost attacked Coach Grayson."

Pizza lodged in his throat and Cash coughed a number of times before he could speak. "Please tell me you did not just say what I think you said."

"It didn't, really." Rachel rolled her eyes. "I mean, Coach Grayson kind of…faced it down. Have a sense of humor, brother."

He'd definitely stumbled into some strange parallel universe.

"We were trying to scare it out before it got to the chickens and before Cocoa got hurt. She was going wild." She paused, looking as if she blinked away tears. Cash leaned forward, worry knotting his gut. What else had happened?

"You're going to have to…check the coop. I couldn't bear to look—"

"I'll take care of it."

He'd forgotten what a soft, sensitive thing she could be. Not that he wanted to deal with anything like that either, but still. Lately Rachel had been all brick walls, guns blazing.

"Cash, is there any way I can go shopping this weekend? I need a dress for the homecoming dance and—"

Cash tuned her out, hurt rippling across his chest. Just once he thought Rachel might be thinking about someone besides herself. But she only wanted a way out of her grounding. For climbing on the church roof, of all things. Truth be told, when he'd driven home from church Sunday, he'd held back a laugh. How did the girl come up with these crazy shenanigans? If it hadn't been dangerous, he really would have laughed—

behind closed doors. But the fact that she could have been hurt?

Cash felt his own walls go up. Rachel was his responsibility, and somehow he would keep her safe. Even if he had to lock her up at home to do it.

Rachel finished her spiel. "So, can I go?"

"No." He stood, went to lock the front door, then turned off the kitchen lights. "No, you can't go."

"But I don't have any time next week. I have practice every night or a game, and then the dance is Saturday."

With each word, her pitch increased with panic.

"I'm going to bed, Rach."

He ignored her screech and went upstairs. After showering, he climbed into bed, only wanting one thing. He wanted to call Olivia, to hear about her day, to have her voice be the last thing he heard before he drifted off to sleep.

But that didn't sound like friendship to him. So he didn't let himself call. Seemed it was a denying kind of night around the Maddox house.

"I'm trying to understand why he'd say no." Olivia clapped with Janie when the football team ran out on the field. Tonight's home game had the stands packed, the crowd wild.

Janie shifted Tucker on her lap and dug through the diaper bag until she found a toy car. He clutched it in his chubby hand and then whirled it across Janie's black shirt and down her red capris. "That's strange. It doesn't sound like Cash to be so harsh."

"I know." Olivia released a breath, wishing her frustration would go with it. "I'm not even sure what he said. Rachel came into my classroom this morning looking like her shuttered self. She didn't say anything other than that he'd said no."

Olivia couldn't be more confused. The man had asked her for help with his little sister, and the two times she'd offered, he'd refused. Why had he asked her at all?

"Speaking of…" Janie tipped her head toward Cash as he entered their row. When he reached them, Janie stood up to give him a hug. Olivia only managed a curt wave.

Usually Cash sat in the alumni section, but tonight he moved down the row until he sat next to her. When he nudged her right shoulder with his left, Olivia ignored the move, keeping her eyes on the field. Cash leaned into her line of vision, forehead creased, Billies baseball cap hitched up. "What's going on? Rachel said you came out to the ranch last night."

Was the man joking?

"Um, yes, I did. Rachel and I met up with a raccoon, and then we ate ice cream for dinner and did some homework." *And then I got her to open up and you ruined it.*

"I heard about the chicken coop. Sorry about that, city girl."

"I have seen a chicken coop before. I'm from Colorado, not Manhattan."

Cash frowned and leaned back as though Olivia's words had physical power. The referee blew the whistle for the game to start and Olivia turned her attention back to the field. When Cash tucked a strand of hair behind her right ear, his touch made her jump a full volleyball off the bleachers. Was he trying to read her face or make her crazy?

"What's wrong with you? Everywhere I go some girl is mad at me. Rachel wouldn't even talk to me this morning."

"Are you surprised? You told her no for shopping this weekend."

"How did you know about that?"

"It was my idea."

"What?"

He looked so confused, it only made her more frustrated.

"I told her I would take her shopping. She doesn't have anyone else, buckaroo. Do you think she wants to tag along with her friends and their moms all the time? Or have to go shopping by herself for a homecoming dress? I got the girl to agree and smile. Genuinely smile. She seemed excited. We talked about going to the mall or even down to Austin to stay with your aunt and uncle for a night. And then you swooped in and killed the idea even though you asked me to help her!" Olivia borrowed a huff from Rachel.

A slow grin spread across Cash's face, reminding Olivia of hot fudge melting ice cream. She wanted to grab a dishcloth and wipe it away.

"You are amazing."

What?

Cash leaned closer. "I didn't know any of this. I was exhausted last night, and I didn't hear everything Rachel said. I thought she was just being Rach and trying to get out of a punishment."

Olivia started to relax, realizing her shoulders were almost touching her ears.

"And she is still trying to get out of a punishment, but if it's to hang out with you, that's different. You're better for her than a week of grounding."

Her cheeks heated enough to set the field grass on fire.

Cash's low voice continued near her ear. "So, yes, Olivia Grayson, you can take my sister shopping. You can pretty much do anything you want and I'd be fine with it."

The idea Olivia had right now did not fall into the friendship category, so she shifted away a few inches, unable to stop the smile that spread across her face and the warmth that went all the way down to her tennis shoes.

Janie leaned forward and faced them. "Hey, you two, I don't know if you noticed, but there's a football game going on." She grinned. "And we just scored a touchdown."

Chapter 9

Olivia plucked her iPod from the cup holder in the center console and passed it to Rachel. "Pick something out."

It took Rachel about ten miles to sort through Olivia's playlist and find something they could agree on—The Band Perry. Good thing Olivia liked country music or the state of Texas might very well drive her mad.

The teenager kicked off her flip-flops, tucking long legs beneath cutoff jean shorts. Her eyes closed as she crossed her arms over the *can you dig it* phrase on her bright blue T-shirt. The *O* was a small volleyball. Olivia would contemplate stealing the shirt if there was even a chance it would fit.

The sun shone down, she had a steaming cup of coffee in her cup holder and a half-grumpy teenager beside her. What more could she want?

For Cash to have hitched a ride along. Oops. Today had nothing to do with Cash. Even though his words from the game last night still reverberated in her head, Olivia wasn't going to dwell on them. Or him.

Today was all about befriending Rachel and getting the girl to open up.

This morning before they'd left, Olivia had second-guessed agreeing to stay with Cash and Rachel's aunt and uncle for a night. That would make it look...as if she and Cash were in a relationship. Of course they weren't, but everyone in the town of Fredericksburg probably already thought they were. And now who knew what Cash and Rachel's aunt and uncle would think?

Olivia shook off the thoughts. God could handle it. *Hello.* She hadn't even prayed about it. Taking the time while Rachel stared out her window and presumably woke up, Olivia talked to God about the day and the girl. After, she felt peace. And when Rachel turned to her with a smile, Olivia thought they just might get somewhere today.

About an hour later, they turned into the driveway of a yellow house. A petite woman with short white hair flew out the door, arms waving. Dressed in lime-green capris and a flowing white shirt, she pulled Rachel out of the car and hugged her for a long minute. Rachel made introductions, and the next thing Olivia knew, she was enfolded in the same hug by Rachel's aunt Libby.

The woman leaned back and studied Olivia with a smile creasing her eyes, the hazel color reminding Olivia of Cash's. Gorgeous looks must run in the family.

"Aren't you cute as a button? Tall, but that's perfect for my nephew."

Olivia ignored the comment and the way Rachel looked up from her phone and scowled.

"You look like Cash. You have the same eyes."

Libby winked. "His daddy and I didn't look a lot alike, but we did share at least one feature. Come on in, y'all. I've got some lunch set out and then a whole day of shopping planned."

Olivia and Rachel shared a grin and followed her inside, leaving their overnight bags by the door.

"Hey, Uncle Dean." Rachel shyly hugged her uncle, who also wrapped her in a long hug.

"We missed you this summer, kiddo."

Libby turned to Olivia. "Usually Rachel spends a month with us in the summer, but this year she didn't want to leave her friends." Libby pretended to wipe away tears. "I don't know why that girl doesn't love us anymore."

Rachel giggled.

"I guess we're getting too old, aren't we, Dean?"

"Hey, I'm a year younger than you. Don't be calling me old."

Libby's hands landed on her hips. "And he'll never let me forget it. How old are you, Olivia? If you don't mind me asking."

"Twenty-six. Soon to be twenty-seven."

"That's nice." Libby didn't say anything more, but Olivia could see her doing the math.

Too bad she couldn't answer Libby's unspoken thought out loud. *Yes, Cash is twenty-seven—older*

than me, not younger. And no, I don't see any loving,
teasing relationships like yours in my near future.

Libby poured glasses of sweet tea. "Let's eat some
lunch. Then we'll leave old Dean here to his afternoon
nap and get some girl time in."

An hour later, the three of them loaded into the car.
Libby had a map with the stores outlined and a descrip-
tion of each one. "Rachel, look this over and tell me
where you want to start."

Olivia smiled back when Libby's eyes crinkled in
the rearview mirror.

"Aunt Libby, these are boutique stores. They're way
out of my—"

"I don't want to hear it. I'm buying the dress."

"But I have mon—"

"Do you really want to fight with me?" Libby leveled a steel gaze at Rachel. "I know I come off all
Texan and sweet, but I grew up on that ranch, too, little girl. Let me spoil you a little. You know all of your
cousins moved out of the house and are long gone. At
least give me this."

"You can buy me a dress," Olivia piped up from the
backseat, and both Rachel and Libby laughed, easing
the tension.

"Are you going to prom, too, Olivia?"

"It's homecoming, Aunt Libby."

"Right, homecoming."

"I am a chaperone, but I'm joking about the dress.
I'll wear something I have."

Libby glanced in the rearview mirror. "We'll see
about that."

The first stop was a swanky bridal store with a curtained dressing room area and a chandelier lighting the space. Olivia felt thankful she'd at least stepped up her typical shorts/tank/flip-flops combination to a multicolored ruffled tank top, tailored jean shorts and strappy flats.

Rachel walked the rows, choosing what she wanted to try on, and Libby and Olivia carted stacks of dresses to the dressing room.

They settled in to wait while Rachel tried on dress after dress. Rachel's opinions came quickly.

"Too pink."

"Too short."

"Too long."

"Not enough cleavage."

That one earned a tongue clucking from Libby.

"Too much cleavage," Libby announced on the next one and sent Rachel back to change again.

Oh, my. Thank You, God, for sending Libby on this outing with us. Olivia wasn't sure she would have had the guts to tell Rachel anything was too short or had too much cleavage—even though it would have been true.

They put a bright orange dress on hold, then worked their way through three more stores in the area. By the fourth, Olivia needed a big chocolate bar, a coffee and a nap.

Libby approached Olivia with her arms full of dresses and tilted her head toward the dressing rooms.

"All right, Frenchie, you're up."

Olivia laughed. "No way. I'm exhausted just watching Rachel try on dresses."

Rachel came out of the dressing room in a blue number. "I don't like this dress, but I had to tell you not to mess with Aunt Libby, Coach Grayson. She won't take no for an answer."

Rachel glowed like a flower that had been fertilized with Miracle-Gro, and Olivia didn't want to do anything to take the happy off her face.

"Fine." She grumbled and took the pile of dresses, making Rachel and Libby laugh.

The first dress barely covered her derriere. Why did they make dresses so short these days? Or maybe it was that her legs were twice as long as the rest of the population. Olivia showed the second one to Rachel and Libby—a gold number that went to the floor. She received two *no*s and headed back in. She didn't like the third, but she showed them the flowing mint-green dress anyway.

"I like that one better, but it's still not great." Rachel's teenage tact made Olivia laugh. But she agreed with the girl. Rachel was in a different dress than the last time Olivia had been out—a black one this time.

"That looks great on you." It covered all the right places and swept down to the floor. "It's pretty."

"But it's black." Rachel's nose wrinkled.

They both retreated to their dressing rooms. Olivia pulled the last dress off the hanger. Short and sequined, the deep blue dress gave her hope. Not prom looking. Not old-lady looking.

No way would it look right on her. She tried it on, analyzing in the mirror. It showed off her legs but still looked modest enough for a teenage dance. Though sleeveless and quite simple, it had enough sparkle to be interesting.

Probably way out of her price range. Olivia dug th

tag out of her armpit and tried not to dance. *Clearance.*
Teacher-speak for *yes, you may buy.*

She flew out of the dressing room to a round of applause from Rachel and Libby. After they oohed and
aahed, Olivia changed back into her clothes and then
paid for her dress—refusing Libby's generous offer
to pay.

She set her package on the floor and sat next to
Libby on the viewing couch, tempted to rest her head
against the woman's shoulder.

"This is it!" Rachel squealed. Olivia had never heard
the girl put so much excitement into anything before—
even their near miss with a raccoon. Rachel flew out
of the dressing room and stood in front of the three-
way mirror, her eyes alight, a smile blooming across
her face.

Her happiness took Olivia's breath away, and that
wasn't considering the way Rachel looked in the dress.
She looked like a princess. It was long enough that
Cash wouldn't demand she stay home, had enough cov-
erage in the front that she looked modest and was the
prettiest shade of soft silver.

Libby swiped real tears. "I feel like you're getting
married and we found the perfect dress."

They all laughed.

"Wrap that baby up," Libby commanded the dress
attendant. "I need a highly sugared coffee."

Rachel headed back into the changing room while
Olivia imagined a salted caramel mocha drenched in
whipped cream flowing into her exhausted system. "I
think you and I are going to be besties."

Libby laughed. "That's good, since you're going to be my niece."

Olivia's head jerked back. "I'm not—you do know that Cash and I aren't—"

"I know my nephew has some crazy ideas about life. He thinks if he controls everything, he can give Rachel the same childhood he had. He can't make that happen." Libby sniffed again, fingertips checking for runaway mascara. "I'm an emotional mess. Just wait until your sixties, girl. Anyway, Warren and Sharon are gone and nothing is going to bring them back. Rachel's life isn't going to be the same as Cash's."

Libby's love for Rachel was obvious, and Rachel seemed so happy spending time with her aunt. Even her reaction to Dean earlier had been sweet.

"Why didn't you and Dean…?"

"Why didn't we raise Rachel?"

Olivia nodded.

"We talked about it. We prayed about it. But in the end, we all came to the same conclusion—Rachel was supposed to stay on the ranch. Even she agreed. So while I know she and Cash sometimes have trouble…"

Olivia snorted and Libby grinned.

"I think they're right where God wants them to be. Both of them. I also think that once my nephew figures out he can't control everything, he'll be knocking down your door. So be ready." Libby's mouth curved, reminding Olivia of Janie and one of her all-knowing grins.

Olivia didn't know how to respond to that, so she looked back toward the dressing room to check on Rachel. But instead of changing, Rachel stood a mere foot behind them, phone clenched in her fist. A scowl lined her face, replacing the pretty glow from only minutes earlier.

Had she heard their conversation?

By the way she gave Libby and Olivia the triple threat—crossed arms, rolled eyes *and* a huff—Olivia imagined she had.

Her stomach dropped down to her shopping bag on the floor. She'd had one plan today—shower attention on Rachel and get her to open up. Yet somehow she'd managed to make the teenager feel less than, or as if Olivia was here because of Cash instead of Rachel.

When Rachel stomped up to the counter, Libby stood, giving Olivia's arm a reassuring squeeze. "It will be okay."

If only Olivia believed her.

Val's jump serve careened off the other team's defensive specialist and into the stands, sending the team into wild celebration along with the rest of the gym. Olivia and Trish celebrated the win together, then gave their players high fives and hugs before heading over to shake the other coaches' hands.

Cash waved from the other side of the gym, and Olivia waved back. He didn't come over to talk to her, and she felt relieved. Rachel still seemed upset with Olivia from this past weekend. She'd hardly spoken on the drive home Sunday, leaving Olivia feeling awful about the way things had turned out. She'd just wanted to help the girl. Why did it have to be so hard? Now she understood how Cash felt.

When the gym cleared, Olivia packed up her clipboard and grabbed the bin of volleyballs to return to the storage room.

"Hey, Olivia, wait up." Gil Schmidt's voice made her stop and turn as he jogged over to her. "Great game."

"Thanks." She knew a permanent smile accompanied the word. Winning definitely ranked as one of her favorite pastimes.

"I hear we're both working the homecoming dance this weekend. That's what happens to the single teachers—we get the weekend duty."

She laughed, her mind going back to the dress she'd found. Could she really wear it? What would the other teachers be wearing? Maybe she should just save it for another time.

When are you ever going to need a dress like that, Liv?

For a friend's rehearsal dinner or wedding. That familiar ache lodged in her chest. Surely someone else would be getting married soon and Olivia would be carted back to Colorado to pretend that it didn't bother her to watch everyone else fall in love and walk down the aisle.

"So, what do you think?"

"What? Sorry, Gil. My mind was wandering."

"I wondered if you wanted to grab something to eat. I'm starving and thought maybe you didn't have time to eat before the game."

Her stomach growled in response to his question.

"Don't worry, I don't mean as a date. Anyone in this town can see you and Cash—"

"We're not dating." Her words sliced the air like a knife, but Gil just raised his hands and laughed.

"So, are you hungry?"

She was. And it would be nice to hang out with someone besides Cash for a change. Gil was easy to be around in a way that Cash wasn't. She wouldn't have to keep her feelings in check with the man in front of her. He looked cute in jeans and a green polo, making Olivia regret her hasty first impression of him.

Too bad he still didn't compare to the cowboy who'd recently stood across the gym from her as if a chasm stretched between them.

"Sure. Dinner sounds great. Just let me pack up my things."

Chapter 10

You can't go. Cash clamped his back teeth together to keep from saying the words. When had his little sister grown into this beauty in front of him?

She and Val had been upstairs for most of the afternoon, commandeering the bathroom with more makeup, hair products and strange curling and straightening contraptions than he'd ever seen. He'd actually felt thankful to have a million things to do out on the ranch.

But now the two of them came down the stairs, smiling and looking far too old for their age. Cash swallowed the unwanted emotions in his throat. Rachel would not be okay with a big show of sap.

"You better take the gun, Rach."

Rachel grinned at the implied compliment, looking

happier than she had all week. She'd come back from
her trip to Austin with a scowl etched in stone on her
face. Cash had expected her to come home happy. Or
not as ornery as usual. But Rachel never ceased to surprise him. She hadn't said much to him about the trip,
but he'd managed to learn that she had found a dress
and that Aunt Libby and Uncle Dean were well.

And that was it.

Maybe Olivia had done a better job of getting
through to her. Rachel needed a mentor in her life,
and if Olivia was willing to take on that role, nothing
would make Cash happier.

Except for the fact that it only made him more attracted to the woman. Hopefully it didn't show. After
the match on Wednesday, he'd forced himself to leave
without talking to her. As though he had something to
prove. He sort of did—to himself and the town. Surely
he could stay away from her for a few nights.

On Thursday, Olivia had come for tutoring, but
she'd left after helping Rachel. Cash had let that slide—
just like every other night when he got in from working and his fingers itched to pick up the phone and call
Olivia. Somehow he managed to resist.

He still had some self-control left in his life.

"We're headed over to Val's house. Her mom wants
to take pictures and the limo is picking us up from
here."

Pictures. He knew he'd forgotten something. "Have
Trish send me some." Cash moved to hug Rachel—
careful not to muss her hair or dress—surprised when
he accepted the gesture. "You look beautiful, sis. Just
like Mom."

She blinked quickly. "Thanks."

Cash chuckled when Val and Rachel climbed into the Wrangler, hiking their dresses up to make it in and showing the flip-flops on their feet. He'd seen a few bags go into the Jeep and imagined their other shoes were in there. Not that he knew for sure.

Rachel jumped out of the car and flew back up the porch steps, looking like the little girl he remembered from before their parents' deaths.

"I forgot something." Up the stairs she went, leaving Cash stunned at the memories. Rachel's face had been alight, her smile wide. He'd like to see it that way every day.

Back down the stairs she came with a tiny purse in her hand. "I can't wait to see Coach Grayson in her new dress." Rachel came and went like a breeze, stopping in front of him to pop up and peck a kiss on his cheek. He felt as if a bull had knocked him over.

"Thanks for letting me go shopping last weekend."

"No problem."

"Did you know Coach Grayson is dating Mr. Schmidt?"

What? The strangely timed statement stole all of Cash's words.

"A bunch of people saw them out together after the game on Wednesday." Rachel studied his face and continued talking as if her question hadn't leveled him to the ground. "I kind of thought you and she were…"

"We're not."

"Okay." She shrugged. "See you later."

Then she flew back out the door with her sparkling dress, shimmering makeup and a piece of Cash's jaw

* * *

Cash checked the clock for the thousandth time, but it was only five minutes later than the last time he'd checked: 7:55 p.m. The dance hadn't even started, and he was already agitated. Maybe he should go for a drive. He needed to keep his mind off what Rachel had said. Even if Olivia and Gil were dating, it was none of his business.

He picked up the phone and dialed Jack, surprised when his friend answered.

"Hey, aren't you at the dance tonight?"

"Nope. I'm on the couch supervising Tuck."

"How did you get out of chaperoning?"

"I paid attention in the staff meeting while Olivia was probably daydreaming about you. I had my excuses all lined up."

Cash imagined the middle part of that statement wasn't true. Wouldn't he know if Olivia was really dating Gil? Why wouldn't she have said something?

"So, what can I do for you?"

It took Cash a few seconds to register Jack's wry drawl. "Nothing."

"I'm glad we had this little chat."

Cash laughed and hung up.

Now what? It was 7:59. He strode over to the fridge and opened the door, scrounging for something. Nothing looked good. They were out of milk and bread. He could hit the grocery store. It would be dead on a Saturday night.

Grabbing his keys, he hopped in the truck, driving with the windows down and the country station cranked.

The H-E-B was as he'd expected. Cash grabbed a cart and rolled through the lanes, stocking up on frozen pizzas, pizza rolls, chips and any other man food he could find. In the cookie aisle he hit the jackpot with a couple packages of Double Stuf Oreos. He needed ice cream, too. The girls had demolished his mint chocolate chip stash.

By the time he got to the cash register, his cart looked as if a teenager had packed it. He went back and added a bunch of bananas and a bag of apples to even things out.

"Hello, Cash." Mrs. Brine greeted him at the checkout. The woman knew everything about every person in town—probably due to her job location and amazing sense of hearing. Whisper something across a room and Mrs. Brine would catch it.

"How are you tonight, Mrs. Brine?"

The woman blushed and clucked when he greeted her. "You'd best be saving those charms for someone younger. I hear you and Coach Grayson are on the outs."

Cash resisted the urge to growl. "We're not—" Forget it. It didn't matter what everyone thought. She finished ringing up his groceries, and he headed out to the truck. After throwing everything in the back, he jumped in and roared out of the lot.

What now? It was only a few minutes after nine. When the truck turned toward school like a horse with a mind of its own, Cash let it.

He parked at the back of the full lot, head falling to the steering wheel. What was wrong with him? He didn't need this. Didn't need to be checking up on Olivia like—

An ambulance siren blared and came closer, pulling into the lot and up to the front doors of the school. Cash hopped out, staying to the side as they rolled a stretcher in, knowing he needed to find his sister in order to calm the anxious blood roaring through his veins.

In the gym, Cash spotted Olivia and strode in her direction. He grabbed her arm and then winced when she jumped.

"Sorry. Didn't mean to shock you. Have you seen Rachel?"

Was that hurt on her face?

"Last I saw she was dancing with a group of her friends." Olivia scanned the crowd and pointed. "She's right there."

Cash found Rachel's light blond locks bouncing in time to the music. She laughed at something, her head tipped back with joy he hadn't seen in ages.

If she saw him, she'd lose that in an instant.

"Come on." He grabbed Olivia's hand, pulling her through the mass of students until they spilled out into the school entrance where the EMT helped a young girl onto a stretcher.

"Do you know what's going on out here?"

"I believe she had an allergic reaction to some of the food and she didn't have her EpiPen."

Cash stopped. Not only had he interrupted Olivia's evening, he'd acted like a bear. "Can you take a break?"

She looked at him as if he'd asked her to scoot the moon over a few inches. When Gil walked in their direction, Cash's shoulders tensed up into his neck.

"Hey, Gil." Olivia motioned to the outside doors. "I'm going to take a few minutes. I'll be back."

Gil waved. "Sounds good."

And that was that. The man kept walking toward the gym, not looking bothered in the least. Cash and Olivia walked outside while Cash tried to calm his skittish pulse.

Now what?

They walked to his truck and he pulled the tailgate down. It seemed to be their place. After a second of analyzing, Olivia turned backward and lifted herself up. And that's when Cash lost his ability to speak for the second time in one evening. How had he not noticed what Olivia was wearing?

Her dress showed off her gorgeous legs and muscular arms, the perfect blend of mouthwatering and modest. The deep blue shimmered when she shifted on the tailgate, attempting to pull her skirt down. She was dressed like that and Cash offered her a truck tailgate to sit on?

Smooth move, Maddox.

Olivia's hair was pulled into some kind of messy knot at the back of her neck. Little wisps broke free and played in the evening breeze, dancing around her face. She had dangly earrings on and heels on her feet that probably made her the same height as him. Cash resisted the urge to pull her back down and see if their lips matched up.

"You look gorgeous."

Her eyes widened. "Thank you."

"I think you should wear that dress out to the ranch for tutoring next week."

She laughed and he scooted to a sitting position on the tailgate next to her, trying for nonchalance. "So, what's new?"

Olivia looked over at him, amusement creasing the corners of her mouth.

"You pulled me out of a school dance to see what's new?"

Cash winced. He didn't even want to admit his real reason for being on school property to himself, let alone Olivia. His choices now seemed few.

Cut and run. Keep his mouth shut. Or lie.

And only two of those were possibilities.

Olivia wished she could read Cash's mind. He was acting crazy tonight.

"I'm sorry. I saw the ambulance and I freaked out."

Which still didn't explain why he'd been in the vicinity of the school in the first place. The man might be acting strange, but he still managed to turn heads. His simple white T-shirt molded over shoulder and arm muscles that made her feel a little crazy herself.

Resist, Liv. The man's not here for you. Then why was he here?

"Are you okay?"

"Yes." He let out a deep breath.

Olivia waited, letting the breeze cool her skin. The gym had been piping hot. She was ready to be done with all of those dramatic hormonal teenagers, kick off her heels and drop onto her couch.

"So, anything new?" Cash reminded her of a sprinkler, going over the same area again and again and getting the same results.

"Nothing that I can think of." She'd just seen the man on Thursday night. "Did I mention how great your aunt and uncle are?"

Cash smiled for the first time, and Olivia's heart plummeted. Gracious, he made her blood spin.

"You may have mentioned that, but I agree. They are pretty great."

"Yep." Silence again. Olivia shifted, wondering how she was going to climb down from the truck tailgate and keep her skirt from riding up.

"I should probably go ba—"

"Are you dating Gil?"

"What?"

"Nothing."

Olivia's eyelids shuttered. "Am I dating Gil Schmidt?" She opened her eyes to find Cash staring down at his hands. "No, I am not. But I did go to dinner with him after the game on Wednesday."

"How come?"

"Because he asked and I was hungry."

Cash's gaze switched to her, his face broadcasting feelings she didn't think she was supposed to see. "I'm sorry. I know it's none of my business. You know this town and I just heard—"

"Don't you know not to believe everything you hear?"

At Olivia's teasing, Cash's lips barely curved. "Yes, ma'am. I do. I mean, I don't believe it. I just—" He slid a hand under the twisted hair at the back of Olivia's neck, pulling her forward until his forehead rested against hers. If not for her shallow breathing, Olivia would imagine her heart had just plain stopped.

When Cash pulled back just enough for his gaze to memorize her lips, Olivia shivered. "Don't."

A wounded look crossed his face, his hand dropping to his lap like a stone sinking to the bottom of a lake. Olivia snagged his hand and squeezed, wanting to erase that hurt.

"Rachel was so upset last weekend, and I think it was because your aunt was talking to me about you. I think she does need your full attention. It wasn't jealousy, but I'm not sure how to describe it."

She waited until those mesmerizing eyes clung to hers. "Don't go back on your promise." *Like I went back on mine.*

He traced a thumb along her cheekbone. "Liv." Cash's voice came across so soft and sweet, she'd never be able to resist if he offered another kiss.

Olivia hopped down from the truck and away from Cash's touch, feeling as though she'd ripped a Band-Aid off tender, burned skin. She adjusted the skirt of her dress and glanced at the building. "I should get back inside."

He jumped down too, only this time, he kept a foot of space between them. Good thing, since Olivia's resistance reserves had all gone into that one moment.

"I'm sorry about that." Cash rubbed the back of his neck, causing Olivia's nape to tingle with remorse at the absence of his touch. "You're right. I might not like it, but I know you're right."

Cash closed the tailgate, leaving his hands on it while his head tipped forward. Then he raised his jaw, determination traveling down his straightened back.

He faced her. "I'll walk you back inside."

"You don't need to." Her words were wasted. No matter how many times Olivia tried to refuse him, she knew he'd do exactly what he said. He was as sturdy as an oak. Completely dependable. Not the type of man to be anything but straightforward. If he had kissed her tonight, he would have been full of remorse. And then he would have backed away from her—maybe completely. It was better this way—with a barrier between them, with Rachel between them. By walking away from this moment, not only was Olivia helping Cash keep the promise he'd made, she was getting exactly what she wanted—enough distance to keep her heart from falling.

The thought couldn't be more disappointing.

Chapter 11

Cash watched Olivia as she carried a pitcher of sweet tea across Jack's parents' backyard. She was wearing a bright yellow sundress, and his mouth felt as though he hadn't had a sip of water in weeks. Though it wasn't the clothes that presented a problem. Olivia in tennis shoes and athletic gear gave him the same symptoms.

When she stopped to chat with Mrs. Smith, he forced himself to turn away. It had been three weeks since that moment at the homecoming dance. He and Olivia had gone back to friendship, neither of them mentioning the current that had flowed between them that night—and if he admitted it, ever since.

"Hello? Did you hear anything I just said?" Jack punched Cash on the arm, making the lemonade in his hand slosh over the rim of the red plastic cup and drip to the freshly cut grass beneath his tennis shoes. "You didn't, did you? I try to discuss football with my best friend and he can't stop drooling over the volleyball coach."

"Hey." Cash returned Jack's arm punch, making his tea slosh, too. "Keep it down."

The Smiths' backyard overflowed with parents, students, fall sports teams and anyone else who'd finagled an invite to Jack and Janie's annual midseason party. They hosted it at Jack's parents' because the house and yard had way more room, but Janie and Jack did a majority of the preparation.

Jack shook the moisture from his hand. "I don't think there's a person here who doesn't know you have a thing for Olivia."

Cash groaned and his friend grinned.

"How many times do I have to tell you that it's not like that with us?"

"As many times as you look at her that way."

Cash adjusted the brim of his Billies baseball hat, thankful for the cover. This conversation was not what he needed right now. He didn't need any encouragement to think about Olivia.

"Hey, brother." His sister greeted him as she walked past with Val, giving him just the reminder he needed for why he had to resist the pull Olivia had on him. Rachel had improved so much over the last month, and Olivia had a lot to do with that. The girl talked more. She even smiled sometimes. And greeting him in public just now? She wouldn't have done that a few weeks ago. Rachel and Olivia had buddied up. When Olivia came out to the ranch on Thursdays, she and Rachel chatted the whole time they worked.

Cash watched his sister walk away with a mixture of joy and sadness in his gut. It seemed if he wanted the one to be happy, he couldn't have the other. He definitely did not want to mess with Rachel's improvement.

"Did you eat yet?" Jack asked.

"Nope. But I'm about to." The Smiths provided the meat, and everyone else chipped in with side dishes: plates of corn on the cob, homemade potato salad, green beans, pasta salad, spicy pinto beans, mashed potatoes and fried okra cascaded down the old picnic table like a wedding procession. Cash's mouth watered at the sight. The table's legs looked as though they might give out and sink into the green grass. And that didn't even include the separate table covered in pies, cobbler, brownies and cookies.

He and Jack went through the line, then carried their heaping plates to where Janie and Olivia sat in a circle of folding chairs.

Cash was surprised to see the two of them taking a break. He settled next to Olivia, realizing he'd missed her this week. She'd only skipped one Thursday to help Janie prep for the party, yet it felt like weeks since he'd talked to her.

"What's going on?"

She wiped her mouth with a napkin. "I'm exhausted. I didn't think there was much that could wear me out more than shopping with your sister for a day, but this takes the cake."

He answered her tired but beautiful smile with one of his own.

"What's going on with you?" she asked.

"I've just been roping and riding."

She laughed, then leaned closer. The movement caused her soft brown hair to swing in his direction. "How's the deal going with that grocery store in Austin?"

"Still haven't agreed on anything. They want me to come down so low that I'll barely make a profit."

A frown pulled on her lips. "I'll keep praying."

If his heart hitched a bit at her words, Cash ignored it. "Thanks."

"Olivia, I can't believe you didn't tell us," Janie interrupted, her voice full of accusation. "I had to find out from Facebook." She held up her phone, the Facebook app still open on the screen.

Olivia's eyes widened as she swallowed a bite of potato salad. "What?"

"Your birthday is next Saturday!"

"Oh, right." Olivia seemed relieved. Over what?

"We're definitely going out for Olivia's birthday, aren't we, boys?"

Jack and Cash agreed while Janie kept right on talking. "What should we do? I know—"

"Nothing. We don't need to do a thing."

"Now that's about the craziest thing I've ever heard. Don't y'all celebrate birthday week up in Colorado?"

"My wife seems to think the whole month of her birthday revolves around her."

Janie flashed her husband a scathing look. "I don't just think it. It does revolve around me."

They all laughed.

"Girl, you need to milk this thing."

Olivia stood. "I'm good, Janie. I promise."

Jack and Olivia went to throw their plates away, leaving Cash with Janie.

"We are so doing something for her."

Cash couldn't agree more. "Let me plan it."

The words must have surprised Janie as much as they surprised him, because she reeled back in her chair. Now that the idea had formed, Cash liked it.

"Trust me, Janie. I can handle this."

The lines on Janie's face softened. "Oh, Cash." She didn't have to say any more to communicate what she was thinking.

He stood and went to throw his plate away too. Cash might not be able to date Olivia or let his feelings progress beyond friendship, but he could plan something special for her birthday. He could care *about* her...just not *for* her. There was a difference.

He hoped.

At five o'clock on Saturday evening, Olivia answered the knock on her apartment door to find a breathless Janie on her step.

"Happy birthday!" Janie brushed past Olivia and into her apartment, a bag over her shoulder and some kind of makeup kit in her hand. "Are we ready to get ready?"

Olivia glanced down at her favorite jeans and her new shirt. "I am ready."

Janie winked. "No, you're not."

"Wait. Where are we going? I thought we were going out to dinner?"

"That's part of it." Janie disappeared into Olivia's

bedroom, then came back out, propping hands onto her slim hips. "What are you waiting for?"

To stop being confused.

Olivia followed Janie into her bedroom, only to find the blue dress she'd worn to homecoming pulled out of the back of her closet.

"What are you doing with that thing?"

"I'm about to wrestle it on your body. Cash said—" Janie pursed her lips. "Trust me. You need to wear this dress."

"But I'd look like an idiot going anywhere in this town dressed like that."

"Not…anywhere." Janie took the dress off the hanger while Olivia's mind raced.

"What are you wearing?"

Janie went over to Olivia's bed, grabbed the bag she'd been carrying and pulled out the dress she'd worn to her anniversary dinner. Flowing, strapless and soft pink, it easily compared in dressiness to Olivia's.

"I didn't think Bejas Grill had a dress code."

Janie laughed. "I can tell you we are definitely *not* going to Bejas Grill."

"Then where are we going?"

Janie tilted her head. "Sorry, girl. You won't get a thing out of me."

Olivia groaned. What choice did she have?

She put the dress on, wishing her heart would get excited about the evening. Her friends had planned a birthday night for her. Shouldn't she be happy about that? But she could only think about turning twenty-seven. This was definitely not where she'd expected to be at this point in her life. She'd always thought she would be married by this age. Maybe even expecting. Instead, thoughts of the past had plagued her all day like a coffee stain on her favorite white shirt. But tonight wasn't the time to process any of those. She'd been doing that for over a year and hadn't gotten much beyond anger and remorse. Surely she could take a night off.

Janie tugged Olivia into the bathroom. "Let's do our hair and makeup. It will be just like prom."

Janie's comment made Olivia laugh, and her tense body began to relax. What did she have to be upset about? Sure, she was about to spend the evening with a man who was becoming far more than a friend in her heart. But between their mutual commitment to Rachel and her inability to move beyond—or talk about—the past, their relationship would stay officially friend zoned.

According to Janie, birthdays were like free days. So Olivia would call in sick on all of her heartbreak and just enjoy herself for the evening.

A little fun couldn't hurt, could it?

"This is too much." Olivia sucked in a breath when they rounded the bend and the restaurant came into view. Cash did his best to keep his focus on the long drive instead of the stunning woman across the cab of the truck from him.

The Rose Hill Manor sign welcomed them, along with a two-story white building that boasted porches on both levels. Lights glowed from inside, illuminating the restaurant as dusk settled over the evening.

"Janie, I can't believe you did this." Olivia directed her comment to the backseat.

From the seat behind him, Janie nudged Cash on the back of the head before answering Olivia. "It's a French menu tonight."

Thankfully Janie didn't finish the rest of that sentence: *and I didn't come up with it, Cash did.*

He didn't want Olivia to know that he'd planned the evening, because he didn't want to do anything to ignite the kindling that smoldered between them. Tonight was about making Olivia's birthday special. It had nothing to do with him, and everything to do with her.

Cash parked, and they all got out and walked up to check in with the maître d'.

"I do have your reservations and they're setting up your table now. Would you care to wait on the veranda for a few minutes?"

"Sure." Cash stepped away.

Janie announced she needed to use the restroom and Olivia agreed. They linked arms, heads tipped together as they walked down the hall.

Jack and Cash moved outside, and his friend sank into one of the wrought-iron chairs that lined the porch veranda. "Why do women always go to the bathroom together? What do they do in there?"

Cash took the seat next to Jack. "I don't have a clue."

"I think there's a TV in there playing sports."

His mouth hitched up. "I doubt that."

Jack pulled on the top button of his shirt. "I thought Janie was going to make me wear a tie. I'm glad she stopped at the dress shirt."

Cash grinned and adjusted his dress pants—which

he only wore to weddings and funerals—wishing for a pair of jeans right about now. Had he been wrong to plan all of this? Was it too much?

"They're ready to seat us." Olivia and Janie spilled outside, but Cash only had eyes for Liv. His memory of that dress did not do it—or her—justice.

He winced. Planning this evening might not have been his wisest move. But what could he do about that now? Even if he could escape the night, he didn't want to. And that concerned him even more.

"That was beyond delicious. Honey-lacquered duck, chestnut soup and then *mignardises*." Olivia let out a contented sigh as they walked outside and down the front steps of the restaurant. She hadn't eaten like that since her trip to France. It only made her want to go back and eat in tiny cafés and drink coffee near the Seine. All with the man next to her.

Oops. Scratch that last thought. Her plans for avoiding the past tonight should probably also exclude any thoughts of an unattainable future.

Enjoying the evening would work much better that way.

"No one has any idea what you just said or what we just ate."

Olivia rewarded Jack's comment with a punch on the arm.

How could she have dreaded this night? She couldn't ask for a better group of friends. Her stomach hurt from all the laughter during the meal. Jack and Cash had been comical when the amuse-bouche had arrived at the table. As if the whole meal consisted of those few small bites. She'd explained that it was something the chef thought would complement the meal and a small taste of what was to come. From then on, the evening had just gotten sillier. She couldn't remember when she'd had more fun.

They loaded in the truck and Cash drove back to Jack and Janie's house.

"Let's go change. I'm ready for the second half of my birthday night. I mean, Olivia's birthday night."

Janie's comment made them all laugh.

"Wait. There's more?"

"It's not as fancy." Cash answered Olivia and then cleared his throat. "Right, Janie?" He glanced in the rearview mirror.

"Right, Cash."

Her dry tone made Olivia's lips curve. What was going on between Janie and Cash tonight? Could Janie be back to her matchmaking? Ever since the night Olivia had babysat Tucker and talked to Janie, her friend hadn't made any more attempts to push them together. At least, not that Olivia knew of.

When they got back to the Smiths', Olivia popped over to her apartment to change while the other three went to Jack and Janie's. She'd been told casual. Did that mean jeans or yoga pants? Cash had said something about outside, so Olivia opted for the jeans and shirt she'd been wearing earlier. Her hair and makeup looked silly with the casual outfit, but she just grinned at the bright-eyed girl in the mirror.

The sound of Tucker's screams greeted her on the sidewalk as she walked back to the Smiths'. After knocking on the glass door, she let herself in, finding everyone gathered in the small kitchen.

"He's been like this all night off and on." Jack's mom ran frustrated fingers through her hair. "I'd distract him and then all of a sudden he'd get upset again."

Janie held Tucker to her shoulder, soothing him while she comforted Jack's mom at the same time. "It sounds like an ear infection to me." She ran a hand over Tucker's forehead as his eyelids drooped. "He was like this when he had one before. Jack, can you get the ibuprofen?"

Jack rummaged through the cupboards, then slipped the dropper into Tucker's mouth. The tired boy took the dose without complaint.

"I'll rock him for a bit." Janie looked to Olivia. "Can you help me?"

"Sure." Olivia followed Janie into Tucker's room and took the stack of folded clothes off the rocking chair so Janie could sit.

"Thanks. Could you put those on the dresser? I didn't get them put away before we left."

Olivia did while Janie set the chair in motion.

"I'm sorry for ruining your birthday."

Olivia smoothed a hand across Tucker's dinosaur footie pajamas at the top of the pile, mouth curving up. "I am pretty upset with you."

Janie laughed, but Tucker didn't move from his cuddled position against her shoulder. He'd popped a thumb into his mouth, and with each slide of the chair, his eyelids drooped a little more.

"You and Cash go on and finish the rest of the night. There's no reason for the evening to end. I'll put Tucker to sleep, and the medicine will kick in. In the morning I'll call Dr. Hoke and get a prescription." Janie smiled over the top of Tucker's head. "Sometimes it pays to be a nurse."

"How long will it take for him to feel better?"

"Probably by Monday. But if not, I can always call in sick. I...haven't been feeling great, so I wouldn't mind a day off."

Janie had been sick? When had Olivia missed this?

"I didn't know you weren't feeling well. Why didn't you say anything?"

Even in the soft light coming through the blinds, Olivia could see Janie's smile grow. "We haven't told anyone yet."

Olivia let out a squeak that made Tucker shift. "You're pregnant?" she whispered, but her excitement still came through.

Janie nodded. "We haven't even told our parents yet, so mum's the word. I'm only a few weeks along."

"Your secret is safe with me." Olivia checked her gut, surprised to find only warmth there instead of regret. She couldn't be happier for Janie and Jack. They were exactly the kind of parents who should keep right on having kids and filling up a whole house.

"So, go. Shoo. Have fun."

"How's Cash even going to know what the next plan is? I mean, weren't you in charge?"

"I'll only say this. I don't know the plan." Janie laughed softly. "Think about tonight and take a guess. That's all I'm going to say."

That made absolutely no sense. If Janie hadn't planned the evening, then...?

Cash.

The thought made Olivia's limbs feel the consistency of yogurt.

"Why would he do that?" Her whisper came out strangled.

"Oh, Liv, don't you know?"

"Janie, I can't—" Olivia would not go into her own issues right now. "He doesn't want to date because he wants to give Rachel his undivided attention."

Janie's sigh filled the room. "I've always wondered about that."

"I respect his decision, and I'm trying to be supportive of that. Rachel even seems to be getting better. I don't think she wants us dating either." Not to mention all of Olivia's reasons for staying detached. She moaned. "What am I supposed to do now?"

Janie got up and put Tucker in the crib, then waited to make sure he stayed sleeping. She walked over, placing her hands on Olivia's arms.

"I wish I knew, honey. I wish I knew."

Chapter 12

Cash opened the passenger door for Olivia, then went around to his side and got in. Jack and Janie had insisted he and Olivia finish her birthday evening without them. Which meant Cash was headed out to spend the rest of the night alone with Olivia on something that closely resembled a date.

He winced at the word. The promise he'd made in regards to raising Rachel seemed to be working. She improved day by day, and Cash didn't want to do anything to mess with that.

The whole point of the evening was to celebrate Olivia's birthday and make the night special. He could still manage that, couldn't he? He'd just have to remember that the girl across the cab from him was off-limits. For more than just tonight.

Cash pulled the truck away from the curb and glanced over at Olivia. She studied his hands, and Cash looked down to see his knuckles turning white. He loosened his grip on the steering wheel and flexed his fingers, willing himself to relax.

"Do I get to know where we're going this time?"

The question made him grin. "Nope. Just sit there and look pretty."

She laughed, easing a bit of the tension that filled the truck. Cash drove to the edge of town and then turned off onto a long, narrow dirt road. He could practically feel Olivia's curiosity boiling.

"Cash Maddox, I am not going night fishing."

His lips twitched. "Not it."

"Or for a walk in a field in the middle of the night."

He laughed and Olivia whacked him on the arm. Good. Let them get back to friendship instead of the limbo of attraction they seemed to dance around.

They pulled through the trees, revealing row upon row of vehicles surrounding a huge white barn.

"What?" Olivia leaned forward, hands on the dash. "Is that a movie?"

"Yep."

"That's so great. Whose place is this?"

"Gabe and Marcy Rowl's. On Saturday nights in the summer, they play a movie on the side of their barn. It's quite the attraction, but not everyone gets an invite."

"Really?"

"Not really, city girl. Anyone can come as long as they pay."

He received another jab to the arm.

Cash paid out the window, found a spot, put the

truck in reverse and then backed in. He hopped out and met Olivia at the tailgate. Cash situated the mess of blankets and pillows he'd thrown in until it looked semicomfortable. They both climbed in and Olivia sat back, straight into Cash's shoulder.

"Oops. Sorry." She scooted over a few inches, then leaned back again. "It's about to start."

"Yeah, the stuff with Tuck put us a bit behind. I wish he felt better."

"Me, too."

Their voices turned to whispers as the music started, making everything feel even more intimate. Cash glanced around at all of the other cars, reminding himself that he and Olivia weren't alone. It just felt like it.

"Oh, my." Olivia's arms flapped. "Did you—? How did—?"

She looked as though she might hyperventilate.

"What?" Cash grabbed her arm, trying to calm her with a firm touch. "What's wrong?"

She turned to him with tear-filled eyes, making his chest ache. What could possibly be wrong?

"It's my movie. It's *You've Got Mail*."

He'd forgotten about that part. Amazing what a couple pounds of ribs could get a person. But the way Olivia was looking at him... "Stinking Janie."

Olivia bit her lip. "She didn't *exactly* tell me you planned the night. I sort of guessed."

She leaned close, looking as if she might press a kiss to his cheek. When she shifted back, Cash resisted the urge to haul her into his arms and never let go.

"Thank you. This is the sweetest thing anyone has

ever done for me. Cash Maddox, you are the most irresistible—"

"Stop," he growled. "Don't tempt me, woman." He
sat back against the truck, crossing his arms to keep
from reaching for Olivia. Continuing this night had
not been the best idea.

Halfway through the movie, Olivia shifted. Between
the smell of her shampoo and the few inches closer to
him she'd ended up…for pity's sake. He needed to get
a handle on his emotions.

She moved again, and he bit back his amusement.
"You comfortable?"

"I'm good." When she tipped her head back to smile
at him, Cash's attention focused on a tempting place
to land a kiss. Definitely *not* good.

His phone buzzed in his pocket but he ignored it,
stuck in the moment with Olivia. When it quit and
started again, Cash shifted so that he could dig it out.
Olivia moved to the side, and the connection between
them thankfully ebbed.

Unknown Number flashed on his phone. "I'm going
to take this in the cab," he whispered to Olivia, then accepted the call so that he wouldn't lose it. After climbing inside and shutting the door, he spoke.

"This is Cash."

"Cash." The voice that answered made his blood
chill. "This is Sheriff Winston."

When Cash got into the truck cab, Olivia shifted a
few inches away from where he'd been sitting. Janie-
land birthdays might not have rules, but Olivia's heart
felt too tender for that.

The man had made a promise, and Olivia wanted to help him keep that promise. And although her attraction to him seemed to grow every day—despite her demanding it not to—she still didn't feel the freedom to let her heart go. When tempted to give in to her feelings for Cash, Olivia only needed to remember the night when she had agreed with him about waiting for marriage and hadn't told him about Josh or the baby. It made fear trickle through her limbs to think of telling him now. Would he consider her part of that conversation a lie?

She tried not to think about the answer to that question.

Cash appeared beside the bed of the truck, but instead of climbing in, he motioned for her to come closer. "We have to go. Rachel's in jail."

His whisper froze Olivia in place. No. Impossible. "But she's been—"

"So much better. I know." At Cash's dejected sigh, she pushed all of the blankets and pillows to the front of the truck bed and then jumped down from the tailgate.

Cash met her at the passenger door. "Is she injured?"

"No. She's fine." When he opened her door, Olivia climbed inside, pulse slowing a bit. As long as Rachel was safe, they would handle whatever had happened.

Oh, Liv. She sounded as though she was part of this family. But she wasn't.

Cash got into the cab and pulled out without lights until they were far enough from the movie not to disturb the others.

It took him a few miles to speak. "She lied to me."

Olivia sucked in a breath. The quietly spoken words twisted like a knife in her own conscience.

"She told me she was spending the night at Val's. Instead, she went to a party with Blake and a bunch of other kids. Val wasn't even there. They never even had plans." Cash's hands clenched the wheel, then released. "They were drinking. She got into a car with a drunk driver. Renner." The way Cash said the boy's name sent chills down Olivia's spine. "I need to go pick her up. They're not holding her. They're letting the kids who weren't driving go home."

Olivia reached across the space and squeezed his arm, knowing no words would comfort Cash right now. Rachel could have been killed. All of the kids could have been killed.

When Cash pulled up in front of Olivia's apartment, they both spoke at the same time.

"Thanks—"

"I'm sorry—"

Olivia attempted a smile. "Thank you for tonight."

Cash tugged on his shirt collar. "I'm sorry your birthday night was ruined."

"It wasn't. It was perfect." Olivia paused, weighing her next words. "Do you...want me to go with you to get Rachel?"

"I'll handle it, but thank you for offering."

"Sure." Olivia hopped out of the truck, and Cash started to open his door. "Cash, you don't need to walk me up. Just go."

"No." His wooden tone made her cringe. He got out and slammed his door, meeting her in front of the headlights. "She needs to stew in there a bit. Isn't that what you told me after Rachel climbed on the church roof?"

Storm clouds of frustration and worry rolled across Cash's face, making Olivia's heartbeats slow with dread. How could she help?

They walked up the wooden steps, and after unlocking her apartment door, Olivia turned and slipped her arms around Cash's waist. Gone was the chemistry between them from earlier. Now she just wanted to comfort.

Cash hugged her back, but after a minute, he loosened his hold. "I better go."

Dejection weighed down his shoulders as he walked down the stairs. When the truck pulled away, Olivia started to pray.

She might be able to award herself a few points for enjoying the night and not letting the past torment her, but on thoughts of the future, her score would be a whopping negative twenty. Because what she felt right now about Rachel and Cash was nowhere near as removed as it needed to be.

Even the coffee mug steaming in Olivia's hand didn't make the morning better. Everyone at the Monday morning staff meeting seemed to be functioning in silent mode because of Saturday night's trouble.

Gil took the chair next to her, then leaned close. "How are you holding up?"

She wobbled her hand in answer, trying not to trigger new tears. She'd done enough of that yesterday and a bucketful of praying, too. God could handle this. He had a plan for Rachel, even if Olivia couldn't see it.

When the principal entered the room and strode to the front of the long table the teachers sat at, Olivia's back straightened. She loved Mrs. Dain. The woman ran a good school, but this morning Olivia felt as if she was about to be sentenced for a crime. Or at least a few students were.

Jack looked at her from across the table, a silent understanding passing between them. His star running back had been driving. How much worse would all of this be for Blake?

Mrs. Dain filled the staff in on some of the details. A trooper out on Route 16 had seen the car leave a party and pulled the teens over before they could cause harm to anyone else. Blake had been charged with a DUI, while the passengers had been questioned and released without charges.

"Each of the students involved will be suspended for a week of school. Passengers are not eligible to play sports for two weeks."

No. Olivia glanced down, pretending to find interest in the papers in front of her. Rachel wouldn't be allowed to play right up to the state tournament. They only had two more matches, one of which they needed to win in order to even make it to state. Now her star hitter and blocker—and a young girl she cared very much about—would miss those games. Olivia had two practices to find a replacement for Rachel.

"And the driver, Blake, is not eligible to play sports for the rest of the year."

That statement sucked the air out of the room.

Mrs. Dain finished up with a few more announcements and dismissed the staff. Olivia sat at the table, stunned. Her heart ached for Rachel. The girl had a chance for a college scholarship. They'd worked so hard on bringing her grades up, and for what? For her to possibly throw that chance away.

What must Cash be feeling and thinking? If Olivia was this upset, he'd be tormented. And blaming himself.

Jack slipped into the vacated chair next to Olivia. "How is he?"

"When he dropped me off...I've never seen him like that. Angry, brooding. Kind of a deadly storm."

"Figured."

"What are you going to do without Blake?"

Jack's shoulders hitched. "Play football. Is your team going to be okay without Rachel?"

Olivia released a slow breath. "We're going to have to be."

Olivia shifted both bags to her left hand and knocked on the Maddoxes' front door, hoping she was doing the right thing. It had been a long week, and she imagined that Cash and Rachel could use some support. Last night's match had been rough. The team had been off their game without Rachel, their emotions on edge. Megan, a sophomore, had played in Rachel's spot. She'd done an exceptional job for being thrown into the position, but she just didn't compare to Rachel. Though they'd made a team effort, it hadn't been enough for a win.

Next week's game would dictate whether the team made it to the state tournament or if the season was over. If they did win, Rachel would be eligible to play just in time.

Olivia knocked again.

Cash answered the door wearing a white UT T-shirt and faded jeans. Despite the awful situation with Rachel and the weathered lines pulling down the corners of his mouth, the man still made her pulse jump-rope.

"Hey. What are you doing here?"

Olivia stepped inside, set the food and schoolwork bag on the floor and walked into Cash's arms. A deep shudder ricocheted through his chest as his arms came around her. He reminded her of a balloon with a pinhole in it, the air slowly leaking out of him.

After a minute he stepped back and squeezed her arms. "Thanks. I needed that." He grabbed her stuff from the floor, putting both bags on the table. "What's all this?"

"Dinner." She pointed to the Chinese takeout. "And I got all of Rachel's schoolwork from her teachers."

"Thank you. You didn't need to do all of that."

"I wanted to. So, where's the prisoner?"

Cash's grin gained a bit of traction before it faded. "Up in her room."

"I see the house looks perfectly clean."

"The house, laundry, mucking out stalls and anything else I can think of."

Cash moved to the front of the couch and collapsed onto the cushions. Olivia followed, sitting next to him and facing his profile.

She waited, knowing he needed to talk—even if he didn't know it.

Finally, he turned his dejected face in her direction. "I don't know what to do with her. I thought she was getting better and opening up. Her grades were improving." He let out a shuddering breath, looking far older than his twenty-seven years. "And now this… I don't think she realizes how serious this is, how bad it could have been." Stress lines cut through his forehead. "And on top of that, she did the one thing I asked her not to do. She lied."

Olivia nibbled on her lip, trying to ignore her own sense of panic and concentrate on Rachel. "She is a teenager. They make mistakes and—"

"So?" Cash shook his head. "It doesn't matter how old she is. How am I supposed to trust her again?" His sigh shook the couch. "I'm not sure how to protect her. I'm thinking about sending her to live with Uncle Dean and Aunt Libby." He looked as though someone had snuffed out his faith, his hope.

"Have you talked to them about it? What did they say?"

"They said they'll support us just like they've always done. They want to take some time for all of us to pray about it. So that's what we're doing."

"Does Rachel know?"

Cash slowly shook his head.

The magnitude of the discussion filled the first floor of the house. If Olivia felt as if she was drowning, what must Cash feel like? Did he expect her to have answers? She'd come here to be a support, but she didn't know how to help with this. "I don't know what to say."

Cash's shoulders fell.

"But I can pray."

He managed a sad smile. "We'll take all the prayers we can get."

Chapter 13

The bell rang and students flew from Olivia's classroom as if she'd given them a pop quiz. Which she had. She stacked the papers thrown onto her desk, then slipped them into her bag to take home.

"Coach Grayson?"

Olivia looked up to see Rachel standing in her classroom doorway. She played with her hair and looked everywhere but at Olivia.

"Hey, come on in."

"I know you need to get to practice." Rachel walked into the room and took a seat across from Olivia.

"I have a few minutes. What's up?"

"I finished my work for the week, so I wanted to let you know that you don't have to come out to help me tonight."

Olivia had to remind herself that was a good thing. She hadn't seen Cash since last Thursday at the ranch, but he had texted her before the game last night to say he was praying for her. Bless that man. She'd needed it. The girls had needed it, too. But they'd rallied, winning in five games without their star player. Olivia already felt the anticipation of Rachel coming back and having her team all together again. Maybe the girls felt it too.

"I'm so glad you won last night." Rachel echoed Olivia's thoughts and then swiped under her eyes.

Was she crying?

Olivia grabbed the tissue box and moved to the chair next to Rachel, setting the box on her desk.

"When I think about how I almost ruined our chance to go to state…" Moisture spilled onto her cheeks, and Olivia reached across to squeeze her hand.

"But you didn't. We made it."

"I'm sorry." Rachel sniffed, taking a tissue to wipe her cheeks and blow her nose. "I'm sorry for drinking and making things hard on the team. I'm sorry I was such a jerk to you in the beginning."

"I forgive you, Rach. You're young, and now you've learned a lesson that could change the rest of your life. Take it and run. Don't let the past weigh you down."

Wise advice. Maybe Olivia should try following it herself.

Rachel hooked hair behind her ear with a trembling hand. "I just wish…"

When she didn't continue, Olivia prompted her. "Wish what?"

"It's stupid."

"I'm all about stupid. Bring it on."

Rachel laughed and glanced to the side. "Blake's been such a jerk since that night."

Olivia's breath stuttered along with her pulse. "Rachel, he's never...he wouldn't hurt you, would he?"

Rachel's head swung back and forth. "No. It's not like that. It's just that he's been in such a horrible mood since he was cut from the team. He's been ranting and raving about losing his chance for a scholarship and how the school's punishment was far too severe."

"The school has a zero-tolerance policy for drinking and driving. It's not like they singled him out."

"I know. Plus, he made the decision. No one forced him to drink and drive, just like no one forced the rest of us to get into the car."

Olivia felt a rush of pride at Rachel taking responsibility for her own decisions. The girl had changed in the few months since school had started—no matter what Cash thought. Was he still thinking of sending her to Austin? Olivia had tried to pray with an open mind over the last week, but deep in her heart, she didn't want Rachel to go. And it had nothing to do with volleyball and everything to do with two people she cared deeply about.

"I kind of want to break up with Blake."

Rachel's whispered confession almost shocked Olivia out of her seat, but she forced herself to remain calm and wipe any surprise from her features.

"Then why don't you?" Cash would throw a parade. But Olivia didn't want to let his opinion taint hers, so she prayed for wisdom and waited for Rachel to speak.

The girl watched her hands as they twisted on the

desk. "I don't know. I guess because I was with him and made the same choice."

"Not the same choice. You didn't drive. And even though you did get into the car, you've changed, Rachel—in a good way. Not just in the last two weeks, but in the last few months."

I hope these are Your words, Lord. Olivia surged ahead. "You don't have to stay in the same relationship and suffer because of one bad decision. You're in high school, not married to the boy."

That earned a laugh from Rachel.

"Take a break from him, or from anyone. High school's a great time to hang out with friends. You don't need a boyfriend to have fun."

"*Fun* is not the word I would use to describe Blake lately." Rachel stood. "You'd better get to practice."

Olivia stood and hugged her, and then Rachel walked to the door and paused. "Can I come back to practice on Monday?"

A smile lifted Olivia's lips. "If you don't, I'm sending the whole team to track you down and drag you in."

The crowd roared around Olivia as the football team ran onto the field Friday night. She stood with Gil and a few other teachers, the stands rumbling under her blue tennis shoes. Tonight's conference football game would impact the team's standing and chance for making the state tournament in December. Hopefully they could win without Blake like they did last week.

Where was Janie? Olivia slipped her hands into the back pockets of her jeans and scanned the crowd. She hadn't heard much from her friend this week, but Janie would never miss a game.

Olivia turned back to the field to find Jack motioning to her from his sideline perch. She scooted along the row and jogged down the bleachers.

Jack met her at the edge of the grass, his face crowded with worry lines. "I can't get a hold of Janie. The baby—" He glanced down, cleared his throat. "She started spotting a few days ago and..."

"No." Olivia whispered the word, pain filling every fiber of her body. "Why didn't she call me?"

"Janie's tougher than she lets on and when she's in pain—" Jack scraped a hand across his chin. "She doesn't want anyone around. I told her to call you. She said she would after..." His Adam's apple bobbed. "She took the day off and Tucker went to day care, but our day care called and left me a couple of messages saying that Janie never picked up Tucker. I didn't see the missed calls until a few minutes ago. I talked to my parents, and they're heading over to get Tuck, but I need someone to check on Janie while they're getting him. Her parents are driving back from San Antonio right now, so they can't, and—"

"I'll go check on her. Don't worry. I'm sure she's just sleeping." Olivia struggled to believe her own words.

Jack's stance relaxed, but he still scanned the stands as though Janie might appear at any moment. "Thanks. I really appreciate it."

"I'll text you when I get there, so check your phone."

Jack nodded.

"And go win a football game."

He barely managed a smile.

* * *

"Janie?" Olivia knocked for the second time on the Smiths' door, heart hammering.

I'm going to feel so horrible for waking her up if she's sleeping.

When no one answered, she opened the storm door and tried the knob. It turned under her hand, and she stepped inside, pausing on the cheerful welcome mat. A moan came from the couch, and Olivia hurried around the front, finding her friend curled up in a ball, robe on with pajamas poking out.

"Janie?"

At her whisper, Janie opened groggy eyes. Olivia shuddered with relief, dropping to her knees. "You scared us half to death. I'm sorry I woke you up. We couldn't get a hold of you."

The horror of her friend's suffering caused the past to rear up. Olivia's mouth tasted like metal, and her legs felt as though they were made of lead. She sank from her knees to a sitting position on the hardwood floor.

"Sorry." Janie mumbled the word, eyelids drooping. Perspiration beaded her forehead, and her skin looked as if she hadn't seen the sun in years.

Olivia touched her wrist, shocked by the heat and erratic pulse.

"How long have you felt like this?"

"Last night and today." Janie took a shaky breath. "Did Jack tell you?"

Olivia nodded, tears pooling. "I'm so sorry. I feel so awful—"

Janie moaned and gripped her abdomen, then vomited into a bucket she had by the side of the couch.

Hands trembling, Olivia pulled out her cell and dialed 9-1-1. She might be overthinking. It could be a common flu or something simple, but her gut didn't agree with that assessment.

She only knew her miscarriage had been nothing like this.

"What happened?" Jack flew into the waiting room, still in his red team polo and khakis, eyes wild with fear.

Olivia popped up. "I told you not to leave the game. The doctor said—"

"I don't care about a stupid football game!" Agitation came off Jack in waves.

"She's okay." Olivia rushed to reassure him, hoping she was right. "They said her miscarriage went septic and—"

"Septic? What does that mean?"

"It's an infection in the uterus. She was running a fever. They're putting her on antibiotics, and they rushed her in for surgery." Olivia paused, searching for the right words and swallowing over the sawdust in her mouth. "They need to make sure there's nothing left to cause the infection."

"You mean no part of the baby."

Jack's painful words, spoken so softly, shot straight into Olivia's soul. She wanted to find the nearest trash can and be sick.

"Did they say anything else about Janie?" Hope and fear mingled in Jack's expression.

"They just said what they needed to do, they didn't

say—" They didn't say if her friend's life was in danger, but from what Olivia had seen on that couch…

Jack crumpled into a chair.

"I'm sure she's going to be fine, Jack. She's in great hands and we got here in time. They said it was good we didn't wait any longer."

He groaned. "I should have made her go in this morning when she was throwing up, but she's so stubborn. She said it was normal, that she would be fine. How do you argue with a headstrong nurse?" He dropped his head into his hands.

"I wouldn't have known either." Jack's dejected state made her feel helpless.

"Mr. Smith?" The doctor Olivia had seen earlier stood in the doorway, dressed in blue scrubs, his surgery mask pulled down around his neck.

Olivia tried to read his gaze, but she couldn't decipher a thing. The man must be practiced in the art of dealing with family—with good or bad news.

Jack popped up from the chair and braced himself in front of the doctor. "Yes, that's me."

"The surgery went well, but we need to monitor your wife to make sure she fights this infection. She's in the recovery room. You can see her now if you want to, but she's still pretty groggy."

"I want to see her." Jack choked over the words and then followed the doctor out of the room, leaving Olivia to drop into a chair. The trembling started in her legs, then moved to the rest of her body. Janie could have died today, and she wasn't in the clear yet.

Olivia held her head in her hands and prayed, for minutes or hours, she didn't know. Someone grabbed her hands and pulled her up. Her eyes flew open in time to see Cash's dusty shirt before he crushed her against his chest.

She leaned into him, soaking in all of his strength and warmth, letting it fill all the hollow places while tears streamed down her face. She didn't know how long she cried, just that Cash held her, rubbing her back. Finally her body shuddered and she felt the semblance of control coming back. What an outburst. And the man holding her didn't even know why. He thought all of it had to do with Janie—and most of it did—but he didn't know that part of it had to do with reliving the worst time of her life.

"I'm sorry."

Cash pulled back enough to retrieve a bandanna from his pocket. "You have nothing to apologize for." He wiped her face, then held it against her nose. "Blow."

She laughed through the tears. "I'm not blowing my nose with you holding it." She took the bandanna and then did as he said, stuffing it into her jeans pocket to clean later.

The tender way he looked at her…she just about crumbled again.

"How's Janie?"

Olivia filled him in on what little she knew.

After listening, Cash pulled her over to the chairs. He sank into one, tugging her into the one next to him.

The sleeves to his blue-and-green plaid work shirt were rolled up halfway between his wrist and elbow, and he brushed a hand across his chest. "Sorry. I may have mussed you up. I was out on the ranch when I heard and I'm a stinky, dusty mess."

"I may have added some snot to your shirt, so we're even."

He smiled, but the dark smudges under his eyes and the stubble on his cheeks made him look worn. The man took his responsibility for Rachel and the ranch very seriously, and Olivia worried about him.

"You've been working too hard again, buckaroo."

The lines around Cash's eyes crinkled. "I can handle it. I'm tough."

True. Sometimes too tough.

"Are you okay now?" He motioned to her tear-stained face. "Is this just about Janie or something else?"

The whisper in the back of her mind told her if she kept the past buried, it wouldn't define her. But her soul told a different story. She needed to tell him. But the question she'd been asking herself for months weighed down on her chest, stealing her breath.

Would he think she'd lied to him? And if yes, would he ever forgive her? Based on the way he'd reacted to Tera's and Rachel's lies, Olivia didn't hold out much hope. But despite the fact that she knew not telling Cash now would be a blatant lie and only make things worse, she couldn't force the words out.

What if she told him about Josh and he walked away?

She couldn't handle that kind of hurt on top of today's horrible memories. Her conscience screamed, trying to drown out the fear. *Just tell him the truth. Rip off the Band-Aid.*

"I—" She swallowed. "Just Janie." The words slipped out before Olivia could stop them, and she gripped the arms of her chair to keep herself upright.

Janie's parents clattered into the room and Cash stood, greeting them with hugs. Olivia popped up too, but couldn't move, couldn't join them. As Cash shared the medical updates with Janie's parents, Olivia's heart unraveled at the lie she'd just told. Why hadn't she told him the truth? Why couldn't she move past this?

She knew all of the right answers, knew that God wiped everything clean, yet she couldn't forgive herself for making a foolish mistake. Especially since she'd known better. And now, added to it, she'd hidden it from Cash. She felt sick, just like she had when she'd first arrived at the hospital.

Olivia hadn't thought it possible for her to actually make this situation worse, but she'd managed to accomplish exactly that. Now, not only did the past hold her captive, the future did too. Because she'd just lied to a man who would never forgive her.

Jack returned to the waiting room and everyone launched questions at him at once. He waved his arms to silence them. "She's awake and her fever is coming down with the medication. The doctor says as long as her body continues to fight the infection, she'll be okay."

Cash pulled Olivia close, tucking her into his shoulder. She closed her eyes, guilt slithering through her even as relief over Janie flooded her body.

"What did she say?" Janie's mom asked, wiping tears.

Jack scrubbed hands over his face and looked at the

floor, obviously fighting emotion. Finally, he cleared his throat while everyone in the room wiped moisture from their eyes. "She cried. And then she asked me if we won the football game."

"You did." Janie's dad gripped Jack's shoulder. "We heard it on the drive over."

Janie's words gave Olivia a glimmer of hope that, with time, her friend would heal.

If only she still had that same verdict for herself.

Chapter 14

Olivia and her team strode into the Strahan Coliseum for the state volleyball tournament, its maroon-and-yellow seats stretching end to end. A handful of other volleyball teams was spread through the stands or warming up on the court.

The nerves the girls had subdued on the almost two-hour bus ride to San Marcos seemed to swell with the size of the place.

Olivia checked in with the host to find out which locker room would temporarily be theirs. She sent the girls to change, then scanned the stands. The team had left early enough to watch the game before theirs, so only one or two sets of parents were in the stands. Olivia imagined that would change in the next hour or so. She'd even heard the football team talk about caravanning down together.

Janie wasn't up to traveling yet. She'd only spent one night in the hospital, but the infection had definitely drained her. Although she claimed to be feeling much better, a veil of pain was still visible in her eyes. And as Olivia knew from experience, that hurt would far outlast the physical.

In a red Billies coaching polo that matched Olivia's, Trish beckoned from the stands where she'd staked out a few rows. Olivia went up to meet her, and when the girls came out of the locker room, she and Trish waved them up. They lounged in the yellow chairs, legs draped every which way like only teenagers could do. Rachel had her iPod on, earbuds in, but she watched the game like everyone else. After watching each team win one game, Olivia motioned for her team to follow.

"Let's head over to the warm-up gym."

They walked over and she had the girls circle up, thankful they had the space to themselves. "I'm going to teach you a calming technique. Stick your stomachs out like this." She pushed her own out as an example. "Pretend you're filling up your stomach with air. Then when it feels like you're going to burst, let it out. Do that a couple of times."

Olivia winked at Trish, who turned the other way to hide her amusement. The girls followed her directions, some laughing when they couldn't hold the air any longer, others taking everything seriously.

"Coach, what is this supposed to do?" Val paused, stomach out, words strained because of the position she was trying to hold.

"Nothing." Olivia smiled. "You guys look hilarious. You really shouldn't do everything your coach says."

Val's air came out in a whoosh and the other girls followed suit, everyone howling with complaints and laughter. Olivia's shoulders relaxed when the tension seeped away from her team. They grabbed balls and started warming up, laughing and talking like they would back at their home gym. Exactly what Olivia wanted. She'd seen plenty of teams lose because of nerves.

When they went back to the main gym for their first match, Cash, Libby and Dean waved down at her from the stands. Olivia waved back, then turned her attention to the game. She'd told her girls absolutely no thinking about boys today. Surely the rule applied to her also. And after what she'd said to Cash at the hospital, it was one she would gladly follow.

They'd won the first match and lost the second, but Olivia couldn't be more proud. The girls had played so hard in that second match. Now, the team they'd lost to was headed for the first-place game while the Billies played for third.

Hopefully her team could rally and regain their momentum. A third-place trophy for the case at school would be nice.

The girls rounded up, stretching in the warm-up gym again. The tournament ran matches two out of three instead of three out of five like the normal season, but the team was still tired. Olivia felt time run together as the team gathered and ran out onto the main court. Trish talked to her, but Olivia couldn't focus on anything but the next match.

They won the coin toss and Olivia had Val serve.

Her strong, consistent serve would set the tone for the game, much like Rachel's had done earlier.

Olivia didn't realize she was holding her breath until the opposing team's receive was already in the setter's hands. Three hitters approached the net, and the Billies' blockers moved to meet them. Unable to get a hand on the hit, the ball spun to the floor.

At the last second Mandy lunged and got an arm under the ball. It bounced off and back toward the far corner of the court. Since the setter couldn't get it, Bridget used a bump to get the ball as close to the hitter as possible.

While it was nowhere near a good set, Rachel stayed poised on the outside left as the ball came her direction. She timed her ascent perfectly and turned her shoulders, pulling the ball straight down the line and completely avoiding the blockers who'd been expecting a cross court hit.

The ball bounced near the line, and when the line judge's arms flew forward, Olivia's team let out a cheer.

Evenly matched, the two teams volleyed over and over again, making it look easy to receive each other's hits and serves. Seldom did a ball hit the court without someone getting a hand underneath it. They quickly flew through two games, coming up with a win for each.

When neither team pulled more than two points away from each other during the third game, Olivia thought her knees might give out. Instead of sitting, she stayed on the edge of the court, half wishing she could run out there and play with them but knowing they had the skills to do it themselves.

The ball ended up in the Billies' hands with one point needed to win. As Rachel tossed the ball up for her serve, Olivia pushed air in and out of her lungs and prayed.

Rachel's nerves must have kicked in, because the serve barely made it over the net. The other team easily received and bumped to their setter, who put up a quick middle hit. Billies blockers were in the wrong spot, leaving the back row to receive the strong hit.

Mandy rolled under the ball, her flat arm giving it an arc but pushing it too close to the net for an easy set. Sarah called out for a number-one play—a short set just above the net—and jumped up, setting the ball straight into Valerie's outstretched hand. The other team's blockers scrambled, but it was too late. The ball touched down, the smack vibrating through the momentarily quiet coliseum.

And then the screaming started. The girls pulled her onto the court, dragging Trish, too. Olivia tried to wrap her mind around the win as celebrating students and parents poured out of the stands and filled the court. Congratulations came from all sides.

Rachel stood in front of her, face filled with joy. "Thank you." She hugged Olivia and Olivia squeezed the girl in return. Rachel blinked back moisture before someone grabbed her from behind and hugged her. Olivia looked up to see Cash striding across the court toward her. Instead of waving or mouthing congratulations, he tore across the space and scooped her up in a massive hug. In that moment, all of the people faded away. Let the whole town think whatever they wanted. Olivia let herself enjoy the moment in Cash's arms, knowing it wouldn't last.

It was a good thing Libby hugged her next or she might have fallen over. "I'm so proud of you, Frenchie," Libby whispered in Olivia's ear. "Thanks for loving my niece and nephew. We'll see you at Thanksgiving."

It wasn't until after the crowds had thinned and she'd endured the long bus ride home that Olivia let herself dwell on Libby's comments. Her head sank into her soft pillow, but the words marched through her mind, keeping her awake.

Since Olivia didn't have a clue what Libby meant about Thanksgiving, she'd let that slide.

But the love thing?

Did she love Cash? Sure. She loved Rachel and Cash. But was she in love with Cash? Olivia didn't know. But…it was a possibility. And the fact that she could consider that question meant something had begun to change inside her. What if God had been answering her prayers about healing from the past, but she'd just been so wrapped up in her own guilt and inability to forgive that she hadn't noticed?

She'd thought at the hospital with Janie that she'd never move on, that her painful past would never heal, but now Olivia realized that wasn't true. She *had* begun to let go—even if it was just a little at a time. God had used Cash to answer a prayer for her. That place she'd thought might be broken forever…it had begun to mend under the steady attention of this man's friendship. Where there'd only been darkness, she now felt a warmth, a light shimmering. It felt like hope. The way Cash treated her made her feel of worth.

Olivia groaned, dropping an arm over her face. A small corner of her heart had begun to bloom again because of Cash, and she wanted to give him the same respect he gave her. Which meant she needed to tell him the truth. She'd kept it from him because...because she didn't want to lose that feeling, didn't want to lose him as a friend.

Not being honest with Cash at the hospital had been a mistake. But Olivia couldn't go down the path of self-loathing again. This time, she would claim God's forgiveness for this lie. And she would tell Cash the truth.

She climbed out of bed, dropping to her knees. A little girl again, she came to her Father for the grace He'd already offered. Undeserved grace and forgiveness waited for her. And this time she planned to figure out a way to take it.

Aunt Libby stifled a yawn as she poured two cups of decaf. Cash and Rachel were staying the night in Austin before heading home tomorrow in the hopes that Cash could figure out a plan for Rachel. Not knowing what to do left him feeling ragged at the end of each day.

Uncle Dean sat on the sofa in the living room, the TV on, his soft snores floating into the kitchen. Rachel had been exhausted from the tournament and had gone to bed.

Cash couldn't be more proud of how she'd played today. She'd seemed different since her night at the sheriff's office. Could they be getting somewhere with her? He didn't want to hope as he had so many times before. At least tonight he could talk to Libby about his concerns.

His aunt set a steaming blue mug in front of him along with the creamer. He added a bit and then stirred while she took a seat across from him.

The same eyes he'd inherited pinned him to the chair. "So, tell me what's on your mind."

"I don't know what to do with her, Lib. Every time she seems to improve, something pulls her back down. This last time, with the drinking, she could have been killed."

"I know, honey. Trust me, we pray over the girl all the time."

"She's doing better again, but I'm almost afraid to hope. I can't help wondering if she should come here and live with you."

"Why? What can we give her that you can't?"

"Maybe she'd be...safer." Emotion clogged his throat. "What if I mess up? What if she gets hurt? What if something happens to her like Mom and Dad?"

Libby wiped away tears that seemed to be constantly present. "Cash Maddox, you know you can't control something like that. No one gives and takes away life but God. Rachel would be no safer here than with you. And as for messing up, you're the complete opposite. You'd do anything for her. You go to all of her games, love her when she's a brat, ask Olivia to tutor her when she needs help with schoolwork." Libby snagged a napkin and blew her nose. "Dean and I have been praying about it like we said, but neither of us think Rachel's supposed to move here."

Cash didn't know if the settling in his shoulders was relief or pressure.

"If you really can't do it, you know we will. But what we see is different from what you see. Rachel's a normal teenager dealing with some horrible things life's thrown her way. She's not doing drugs. She goes to school and wins volleyball games." Libby slammed her palms against the table, causing Uncle Dean's snore to break into three jagged parts. "You're doing a great job. Stop punishing yourself."

He'd been praying for a clear answer, and it didn't get much more direct than that. Relief trickled down his spine. No matter how crazy Rachel drove him, no matter how much he worried about her, he didn't want to lose her.

"So, are you going to tell me what happened?"

Cash tilted his head. "With Rach? You know what happened."

"No, crazy. With the woman you look at like she can make your mom's lasagna, wrap it up in a bow and fly it over to you."

Cash considered pretending he didn't know who Libby was talking about. Why did everyone think it fair game to bring up this subject with him? "Nothing's happened. We're the same as we've always been. Friends."

Libby snorted and Dean's snore followed suit before settling back to a quieter version.

"I'm not sure who you watched more at the tournament today—your sister or Olivia."

He could admit to a few glances and one hug, but that was it. Nothing to blow out of proportion. And if he'd fought the feeling all day that he had two girls on that court instead of one, he certainly wouldn't be admitting it to Libby.

"I can't see anyone, you know that. Rachel needs all of my attention, now more than ever. I promised—"

"You promised what?"

"That I wouldn't date anyone or take my attention away from Rachel. You know that if I'd gone with Dad that day, Mom would still be alive. If I hadn't trusted Tera and gone over to check on her, then Rachel wouldn't be stuck with me—"

"That's a lot of *if*s." Libby squeezed his hand, coffee ignored. "I hear you that you made a promise, but let me tell you something. You *cannot* give Rachel the same childhood you had. She's never going to have the same life you did. You had your parents for longer than she did, and that is *not* your fault. Life isn't fair. You didn't cause that accident. Your mom isn't gone because of you. God obviously wanted you on this earth, and you're going to have to accept His plan." She waved a manicured hand, voice rising. "Do you control the universe? Give and take away life? Are you God?"

"Of course not."

"You're acting like it."

Cash opened his mouth to protest, but Libby bareled right on by.

"Have you even asked Rachel?"

"Asked her what?"

"What she thinks of you dating. You've been making this decision without her input, assuming you know what she needs. She'd probably pick Olivia over you."

Cash couldn't decide whether to laugh or be offended.

"You're lovesick, boy. Don't lose Olivia because you're trying to control everything."

Cash kneaded the back of his neck, not quite sure what to do with this barrage of information.

"Have you asked God about this promise of yours?" Libby's words cut to Cash's soul in a way nothing else had so far. "Is it something He asked you to do or did you come up with it all on your own?"

"I—" The words stopped as doubt held his tongue. He wanted to tell Libby that he'd only been following God's plan in regards to Rachel.

But for the first time in his life, he didn't know if it was the truth.

Chapter 15

"I need to stop for gas." Cash glanced across the cab of the truck. Rachel didn't give any response, but who knew if she heard anything with those things in her ears.

After attending church this morning with Dean and Libby, they'd started back to Fredericksburg. Rachel had pretty much been glued to her phone or iPod, earbuds in the whole time, leaving Cash to sort through his skittish thoughts.

Libby's words had haunted him through much of the night, and now he couldn't stop yawning due to the lack of sleep.

Could Libby be right? Had he made up the promise because of his own desire for control?

Cash didn't know. He didn't know much of anything right now.

He didn't recall ever asking God, and he'd definitely never asked Rachel. But hadn't God given him the idea to make the promise in the first place? Where else would he come up with something like that?

Cash clicked through the stations until he found some country, but nothing calmed his mind. He could ask Rachel. She was sitting right next to him. Too bad he didn't know what to say.

At the next gas station, he pulled off to fill up. When he stopped, Rachel hopped out. Minutes later, she came back with a blue Gatorade in one hand and a coffee in the other.

"Thought you'd want a coffee since you can't stop yawning."

"Thanks." Surprised, Cash accepted the cup. His sister certainly had a sweet side…when she wanted to show it.

Rachel buckled up while he got back on Highway 290. When she didn't put her earbuds back in immediately, Cash's mind took off at speeds his horse would know well. Should he ask her about what Libby had said?

"Rach."

She glanced at him, fingers pausing from doing something on her phone. "Yeah?"

"You did great yesterday. I'm really proud of you."

She smiled, then glanced out her window. "Thanks."

"And I'm proud of you for how you acted these last few weeks after the…"

"The incident?"

"Is that what we're calling it now?"

"I'd rather not call it anything, but it did happen."

True. "Can I ask you a question?"

"Sure." Rachel stretched the word out, probably wondering why he was acting so strange.

"Have you ever noticed that I don't date anyone?"

She propped her bare feet up on the dash. "I guess. I just assumed no one wanted to date you."

Cash's jaw came unhinged as he glanced at the girl. No humor showed on her face. "Are you joking?"

"Kind of." Her lips quirked up for a moment. "But you are my brother. That's weird."

He kept his focus on the white lines in front of him. "What would you think if I did date someone?"

"You mean Coach Grayson?"

Cash nodded.

"Why would I care? I like her better than you anyway."

Aunt Libby was right on one count. "You are on fire today."

Now his sister sported a full-fledged smile. "If anything, I've been wondering what's wrong with you. I thought maybe you didn't have the nerve to ask her out."

He'd just ignore that jab. "But I thought…Olivia said that when the two of you went to Austin to go dress shopping, you overheard Aunt Libby talking to her about me and that you looked upset. We thought you were upset about us. And then when you got back from that trip, you were so crabby." He swung an apologetic look in her direction. "You seemed unhappy."

Rachel sighed. "I was upset after that trip."

He knew it.

"But I wasn't upset about the two of you." Rachel

crossed her arms and glanced out her window. "I wa
upset because I kept getting texts from people who'c
seen Blake out with some other girl."

Despite the good news that she hadn't been upse
with him, Cash's heart plummeted. "Was he cheating?"

She shrugged. "I don't know. He said he wasn't, bu
I couldn't decide if I believed him."

Cash flexed white knuckles around the steering
wheel. And he hadn't liked the boy before...

"You don't have to freak out. Coach Grayson anc
I talked about Blake after the incident and I broke up
with him."

Huh. So really, Cash should be sending Rachel to
live with Olivia.

"So." When Cash continued, Rachel groaned. "I al
ways thought that if I didn't date...that you'd get all o
my attention and that maybe..."

"Maybe what?"

"That you'd have as great an upbringing as I had
That you'd feel loved and confident and—"

"And not screw up?" Rachel gave a cynical laugh
"How's that working for you, brother?" She continued
before Cash could say anything, feet dropping to the
floor mat as she turned slightly toward him. "Let me
tell you this. Whether you date anyone or not—that is
if you can find someone who'd say yes—doesn't matte
to me. If anything, you're better with Coach Grayson
around. She kind of...mellows you out."

Huh. "So you wouldn't feel cheated?"

"No, all right already? I know you do everything for
me, and now I find out you've given up everything for
me? I don't want that kind of pressure. Would you?"

No. He wouldn't.

Rachel popped her earbuds in, signaling the end f the conversation, but it only felt like the beginning r Cash.

He might have figured out what Rachel thought bout his dating, but now he needed to figure out what od thought. And that felt like a whole different battle.

Olivia entered the short-term parking lot at the Aus- n airport. Thursday-night traffic hadn't amounted to uch, so she'd gotten there faster than planned. Now he had tomorrow off and the whole weekend with er sister.

Cash had been so busy that Olivia hadn't seen him almost two weeks, except for a glimpse at church. welve days to be exact. And while she should feel re- eved about having the time to figure out what to say him and how to say it, the space only increased the umming tension she felt. After Lucy left, Olivia would ack Cash down and follow through on her plan to tell im about Josh and her miscarriage.

For now, she'd relax into this weekend with her sis- r. Three nights of distraction, of not thinking about 'ash or the mess she'd created. She'd been walking round saying a verse from Psalm 103: "As far as the ast is from the west, so far has He removed our trans- ressions from us." If only it felt that way. She'd taped very verse on forgiveness she could find to her bath- oom mirror. Lucy would probably think she'd gone razy. Olivia would tape one on her forehead if it would st sink through her hard skull. Somehow, she and

God were going to figure out this forgiveness thing together. Even if she broke again trying.

Olivia parked, going inside to meet Lucy instead of driving through passenger pickup like they'd talked about. Ten minutes later, she spotted her sister through the upstairs glass. Halfway down the escalator, Lucy started waving and squealing. She waited impatiently for the people on the escalator to clear into the baggage claim area, then flew at Olivia.

The enthusiastic hug almost knocked Olivia over and they garnered plenty of attention with their dramatics. Olivia held on to her sister, surprised to find tears forming. She'd missed this crazy woman.

Lucy's ash-blond hair hung down her back in loose curls, and she stood a half foot shorter than Olivia. No one would recognize they were sisters except for the blue of their eyes. Even their fashion sense differed. While Olivia opted for simple—jeans, ballet flats and a striped shirt—Lucy looked like a fashionable gypsy. Inches of bangle bracelets lined one wrist and her flowing bright orange shirt was accented with a beaded turquoise necklace. Skinny jeans and heeled brown ankle boots completed the look.

Lucy linked her arm with Olivia's, propelling her toward the guitar-themed baggage claim as live music floated down into the open space.

"Why didn't you just pack a carry-on?"

Her sister laughed. "You'll see in a minute." When the bright orange-and-pink striped bag came down the conveyor belt, it took two of them to lug the monstrosity off the carousel.

"Is this thing hand painted?"

Lucy beamed. "How else am I supposed to recognize it?"

"What did you pack? You're only going to be here three nights."

"I know you told me the weather would be nice, but you just never know. So I needed two outfits for every day, depending on whether it would be warm or cool. And all of that might have fit in a carry-on..." Lucy paused and Olivia imagined a drumroll. "Until I started on coordinating shoes."

Olivia chuckled, basking in the essence of Lucy. Her sister had been headstrong and adventurous even as a baby. Lucy followed the rules—she just tried to make the experience as fun as possible.

They walked toward short-term parking, Lucy pulling the suitcase that earned more than a few curious looks. After loading up, Olivia drove to Curra's Grill. They snagged a table on the patio and munched on chips and salsa while Lucy told Olivia stories from her last year of college.

"So, what's your plan when you're finished with school?" Olivia shifted back from the table when their food arrived. The server checked Lucy out, but she continued talking, oblivious to the young man's attention or the way his spiked hair and plentiful ear piercings seemed to perk up with interest. "I'm still trying to decide. I'd love to work at a dance school, but teaching a few classes won't pay the bills. I know I need to put my business degree to work, but—" Lucy shrugged. "I also don't want to sit behind a desk all day."

"I can't really see that happening."

"I know, right?" Lucy grinned.

"What about the dance place you're already teaching at part-time?"

She took a bite of her enchiladas. "I asked. They don't have any more hours for me, and they don't need any help in the office."

"I guess we'll have to pray about it."

No worry marred Lucy's smooth complexion. "Exactly. God can handle it."

Oh, to be young and innocent and *trusting* again. Olivia shook off the guilt before it could sink claws into her skin. Enough! She was working on it.

After they finished, the server cleared their plates and asked if they wanted dessert, his eyes never straying from Lucy. Maybe a few jumping jacks would gain the man's attention. Lucy ordered for them, and when he walked away, Olivia laughed. "Sis, you've got an admirer."

Lucy tucked a wedge of curls behind her ear and leaned forward. "I hadn't noticed. But I did notice you failed to bring up one topic of conversation."

Why had Olivia ever said anything to Lucy about Cash?

"Out with it. What's the latest with the cowboy? When do I get to meet him?"

"You don't."

"Why?" A line cut through Lucy's forehead.

"Because...I just don't have any plans for you to meet him."

Lucy waited while the server deposited their dessert on the table along with their check. After a generous spoonful of chocolate mocha cake, she turned her attention back to Olivia. "How am I going to decide what to call him if I don't even get to meet him?"

"You could call him Cash, since that is his name." Olivia took a bite, wishing this conversation would disappear as fast as the piece of cake between them. Not even chocolate made this better.

Lucy waved her spoon back and forth. "No way. *Way* too boring."

Olivia laughed.

"So really, tell me the latest."

What could she say? "Same old with us. We're not dating or anything, Lulu. We're just friends determined to help his little sister."

Lucy raised an eyebrow.

"I mean it. He's never even kissed me." But there had been a few moments that Olivia wondered if he might, and one almost kiss the night of the dance. Still, Olivia wasn't going to let her thoughts travel down that path. Nothing good could come from Cash breaking his promise to Rachel.

Lucy leaned forward. "Tell me this. Did you ever feel anything like this for Josh?"

Her sister only knew that Olivia and Josh had broken up, not the details of what had shattered her heart before and after that breakup. But Olivia sensed she couldn't as easily hide this truth from her sister—or herself.

She filled her lungs, letting the air out slowly. "No. Not even close."

"Liv, what are you going to do?"

Olivia didn't have an answer, so she tossed her sister's words back to her. "God can handle it."

Apparently her sister couldn't argue with that.

* * *

"This is crazy." The next evening, Olivia scanned her head-to-toe black clothing in the full-length mirror in her room. She had her hair pulled back into a ponytail and old tennis shoes on her feet. How had a Saturday evening girls' night turned into this?

"It's not that crazy. Besides, I look pretty good." Lucy rolled the top of her borrowed yoga pants over three times until they didn't drag on the ground. The long-sleeved black T-shirt she'd commandeered from Olivia's closet also dwarfed her frame, and Janie and Lucy dissolved into giggles. Again.

"You know, Janie, when I invited you to have dinner with us tonight, I thought you might be a *mature* influence in my sister's life."

Janie collapsed onto the bed. "I'm sorry." Her smile betrayed her words. "I just thought, why not? I've lived here all of my life except for college and I've never done it."

"Because it doesn't make any sense." Olivia tried to keep her amusement from showing on her face. Someone needed to be the voice of reason in this room.

During dinner, Olivia and Janie had made the mistake of telling Lucy about the town tradition of posing for nighttime photos with the honorary school mascot. And Lucy's idea had been born.

"That's exactly why we should do it. We need to experience life, and this is one thing none of us have done. *Why not* is the real question."

Janie looked at Lucy with awe. "I'm guessing you probably never got into trouble."

"She didn't. She can finagle her way out of anything."

Lucy preened, looking hilarious in Olivia's clothes. How did her sister not have a black top and bottom in that overstuffed bag of hers? Hiking out to take pictures with a billy goat in the dark of night was not at all the way Olivia had expected to spend a Saturday evening with her sister. Although, really, why was she surprised?

And the unnecessary black clothes? Lucy's idea, of course.

Lucy put one arm over her head and leaned to the side.

"What are you doing?"

She switched arms and leaned in the other direction, giving Olivia a look that said her actions should be obvious. "I'm stretching."

Janie snickered, and despite her attempt not to, Olivia laughed. After Lucy did a few leg stretches, Janie popped up from the bed. "Let's go so I can get changed."

The three of them walked over to the Smiths' house. Janie went to change, and Olivia introduced her sister to Jack, who sat on the couch watching TV.

He twisted over the back of the couch to shake Lucy's hand, eyebrows raised. "You ladies committing some crime tonight?"

They shook their heads. According to Janie, the Colborns enjoyed their goat's legendary status and didn't mind teenagers traipsing out to their farm to take pictures with it.

Olivia wondered how they felt about teachers doing the same.

When Janie flew back into the room wearing black sweats and a black T-shirt, Jack chuckled and turned back to the TV, raising one hand over his head. "I don't want to know."

Janie looped her arms around Jack's neck from behind and kissed him on the cheek. "Love you, honey."

"Yeah, yeah. Love you, too."

They pushed the door open, Jack's voice following them into the night. "Don't call me when you get arrested. I'll be sleeping."

They giggled all the way to Janie's car.

Chapter 16

Her students must have been making up stories, because Olivia didn't imagine the Colborns' goat had *ever* let anyone take a picture with it. Not only did they not have a photo with the three of them and the goat, Lucy had almost lost the tip of a finger.

Then, in their mad rush to get back to the car, the three of them had slipped and fallen in the mud from last night's rain. It had squished through Olivia's fingers and under her shoes like pudding. Though it smelled nothing like chocolate.

After doing her best to clean her hands with one of Tucker's wet wipes, Olivia brushed tears of laughter from her cheeks. *Thank You, God, for these two girls. What would I do without them?*

They parked on the street by Janie's house and

walked to Olivia's apartment, mud dropping off them with each step. Olivia felt like a walking piece of plaster—the more the mud dried, the harder it became to move. She considered borrowing Mrs. Faust's garden hose to spray them off outside.

Lucy stopped at the bottom of the stairs and Olivia and Janie crashed into her.

"Why are you stopping?"

Her sister stepped to the side and Olivia found herself face-to-face with Cash, sitting two steps from the bottom.

The man's amused grin made Olivia want to crawl up the stairs and into her apartment.

Olivia made introductions, and Lucy's smile grew to one of victory. How did her little sister always get what she wanted?

Lucy faced Cash. "It's a pleasure to meet you, rancher-cowboy-man. Now, if you'll excuse me, I feel I may be in need of a shower."

Cash laughed and moved down the stairs so that Lucy could go up, but his eyes never left Olivia. Warmth echoed through her despite the cooling temperatures.

"McCowboy!" Lucy paused with one hand on the apartment doorknob, throwing a victory fist in the air. "I knew I'd think of something."

When she walked inside and Cash turned to Olivia for answers, she just raised her hands. "Don't even ask."

Janie cleared her throat behind Olivia. "I'm sure Jack is wondering where I am." She took off down the driveway, leaving a muddy trail behind her.

"Do you have a second? I wanted to talk to you about something. Although—" Cash grinned "—maybe this isn't the best time."

Her heart thudded against her ribs. She needed to talk to him, too. "Sure." Olivia dropped down to the step, causing a cloud of dust to radiate from her clothes, and Cash sat next to her. Not only did he look amazing in a charcoal button-down shirt, jeans and boots, he smelled so good she wanted to lean closer and breathe him in. He didn't have a hat on tonight, leaving his golden-green eyes visible. They seemed so serious. What was going on? Was he sending Rachel to Austin?

"Lucy's in the shower or I'd go..."

Cash removed a piece of mud from behind her ear, causing Olivia's skin to prickle. "From what you've told me about your sister, this situation somehow makes sense. And you don't need to shower." He took in every inch of her face. "You're cute even covered in mud."

What? Cash normally did not make that kind of comment. He was always so...careful. And Olivia felt thankful for that. She needed that barrier between them, especially now, when she planned to be honest with him. How much harder would that be if they were more than friends?

"And...manure?"

At Cash's question, she glanced at her formerly blue, now mud-bathed tennis shoes, torn between embarrassment and laughter. "There might be a bit of that involved."

Cash laughed. "Now we're even, since you've seen me the same way."

* * *

Olivia pulled her ponytail to the shoulder away from Cash, giving him full access to her profile and neck. Even smelling like the ranch and dusted in mud, she made his pulse take off at a sprint.

"So, what's up?"

Over the last two weeks, Cash had been meeting with Pastor Rick. He'd realized a number of things during their counseling sessions, and each time he learned something new, he wanted to share it with one person… Olivia. But between the ranch and the meetings, Cash had barely fit in time for meals. Every day he got up before the sun and went to bed long after it set.

"I had something good happen with Rachel."

Olivia glanced up with interest from the muddy fingernails she'd been scraping. The fact that the woman next to him obviously loved his sister only made her more attractive. More irresistible.

"Are you going to tell me what you girls were doing, by the way?"

"Maybe later." She smiled. "Tell me what happened with Rachel."

Cash told her about the trip to Austin and the conversation on the car ride home. "So Libby and Dean don't feel like she should move to Austin, and she wasn't upset about us."

"I'm so glad to hear we didn't make things worse. I assume that means Rachel's staying?"

"Yep."

At his answer, her lips tipped up with pure joy. "That is really good news."

He couldn't help memorizing her face. It felt like months since he'd seen her. "I've missed you."

By the way Olivia's mouth formed an O, Cash imagined she hadn't been expecting that kind of statement from him. He'd never allowed himself to say it before, but now, after talking to Pastor Rick, he felt the freedom. It felt good. Except for the way Olivia's nose scrunched up and she studied the stairs under them instead of him. That part didn't feel very hopeful.

Was she embarrassed? Or just trying to help him keep his promise about Rachel? He was about to find out.

"After I realized that my promise wasn't helping Rachel, I needed to figure out if I'd made the whole thing up or if God wanted me to make a promise like that."

He had Olivia's attention now. "What did you figure out?"

"I met with Pastor Rick. I didn't want to throw away years of commitment because—" *Because I wanted you.* "Anyway, we prayed about it, and then I decided to fast about it, too. God brought me to a number of verses about control, and I finally accepted that I did come up with it on my own." Cash couldn't believe how much lighter he felt since then.

He stretched his legs out in front of him. "I thought that if I controlled everything with Rachel, if I tried hard enough, if I gave her every ounce of my attention, that she would have a better life. Pastor Rick challenged me to give that control back to God instead of trusting in myself and my ability to parent. I'm not saying it's going to be easy, but I'm trying."

Olivia's eyes widened, and she took a deep breath.

"That…is really great news." Her hand brushed across his shoulders. "I think this back could use a break from all of that stress. I'm so glad to hear you're not going to attempt everything on your own anymore."

"Me, too."

Concern etched into Olivia's forehead, but it quickly turned to excitement as she shifted toward him. "If you worked through that, did you…talk about anything else? Did you talk to Pastor Rick about your parents' deaths…or Tera?"

"No. We didn't talk about anything else. What about Tera?"

"Do you think…I mean—" Olivia's ponytail flew across her shoulders as her head shook back and forth. "I'll admit she's not my favorite person, and I'm no expert on forgiveness, but do you think you'll ever move past what happened?"

"I forgave Tera a while ago." His shoulders slipped up. "But there's a difference between forgiving and forgetting. She taught me a lesson that day. Lying has consequences. Nothing will change the fact that Tera's lie was my mom's death sentence. She'd already lied to me once by cheating, and I should never have trusted her again. Now, once my trust is broken, I'm done. Life's much simpler that way."

Olivia's hand pressed against her neck and she shifted forward again.

"Even with Rach…" Cash shook his head. "I'm still struggling over the lie she told me about that party. I don't know if I'll ever trust her again the way I used to. But she is my sister." He rubbed hands down his jeans and gave a short laugh. "So I guess I'm stuck with her even if I can't trust her."

Olivia looked a little green in the face. Had she encountered something tonight that would make her faint? Just what had the girls been doing?

She popped up from the step, and he resisted tugging her back down. Now what? Cash wanted to say something about them, but he couldn't find the words. After all of this time, he had the freedom, just not the guts like Rachel had said.

"Lucy's probably out of the shower by now. So I guess I better..." Olivia tilted her head toward the apartment. "But I'm glad to hear your good news."

Cash's heart dropped under the stairs. Was he really going to let her walk away? He stood and watched her jog up the stairs.

"Liv, wait." He followed, catching her at the top of the landing. "What are you doing for Thanksgiving? Can you come to the ranch? Libby and Dean will be there." *And me.*

She nibbled on her lower lip, and Cash fisted his hands to keep from hauling her into his arms.

"Sure. Thanks."

She walked into the apartment, and it took Cash minutes to make his feet work. He was walking away from the woman he wanted. Again. And this time he didn't even have an excuse.

Olivia towel dried her freshly showered hair and walked into the living room, expecting to find her sister sprawled out on the couch. Instead, she found Lucy in the bedroom spread across the double bed at a di-

agonal angle, sleeping soundly. Olivia tiptoed back out
into the living room, knowing she wouldn't be able to
sleep right now. Her body felt jittery. Unsettled. She
wished she didn't know why.

Hearing Cash's news tonight had rocked her delicately balanced world. With Cash not believing in
his promise not to date anymore, Olivia had feared
he might say something about them…and then what
would she say?

Over the last two weeks, Olivia had felt as though
she was moving forward with letting go, with forgiveness. She'd expected to see Cash and tell him everything. Faith that Cash would be understanding, that
God would meet her in that moment and give her
strength had even begun to grow. But she hadn't imagined this kind of news. It changed everything. Because
with the chance for something more between her and
Cash, she had even more to lose.

For a moment tonight, she'd been so excited thinking maybe he'd processed his trust issues with Pastor Rick, hoping it would pave the way for what she
needed to tell him.

But no. The lie she'd woven between them still
haunted her, and after hearing what Cash had said
about trust, how could she ever tell him now?

Thankfully he'd left tonight without saying more.

Olivia tossed her towel onto the back of the cream
slipcovered couch, then went into the kitchen and made
a package of ramen noodles in the microwave. She
toyed with the sleeves of her white cotton T-shirt while
she waited for the beep, nervous energy thrumming
through her. After grabbing a spoon, she took the bowl

from the microwave and sat on the couch, tucking her legs beneath her. She wore her third and last clean pair of yoga pants. Good thing she had enough—not that she'd ever done yoga—to keep herself and her sister supplied.

She turned on *You've Got Mail*, but it didn't have the typical calming effect. Olivia finished the ramen and set the empty bowl on the coffee table. After a bit, she shifted to a reclining position, but instead of watching the movie, she studied the ceiling. She jumped up and went back to the kitchen, searching the cupboard next to the refrigerator. Finding a package of Dove Promises, she took two, then changed her mind and grabbed a third. Traipsing through a pasture definitely earned her an extra chocolate.

Olivia unwrapped the blue foil and popped one in her mouth, almost choking when she read the promise on the inside.

Hold on to love.

What kind of promise was that? She balled the wrapper and threw it in the trash can, then unwrapped the second. Not going to read that one. They were like strange chocolate fortune cookies that made no sense. She bought them for the chocolate but for some reason could never resist checking the message.

Not tonight.

After finishing the third, she threw the other wrappers in the trash, surprised when her phone beeped. At this time of night it would normally be Lucy. But since her sister was asleep in the other room… Olivia grabbed her phone off the kitchen table and checked the text.

It was from Cash.

Are you up?

A wry smile curved her lips as she texted back.

Yes.

What had Rachel done now? Olivia almost dreaded the next text.

Open your door.

Olivia dropped the phone onto the table with a clatter. Had he left a note? A package? She yanked open the door, startled to see him there. "Cash? What's wrong?"

He grabbed her hand and tugged her onto the landing, pulling the door shut behind her.

"Is Lucy up?"

She'd barely shaken her head when Cash's hands stilled the movement, his lips descending on hers with a need and desire she understood well.

Oh, my. How long had she wanted this with this man? Pretty much since she'd laid eyes on him in her classroom. But then she hadn't had all of the friendship and history pulling her in, making him irresistible. Olivia let herself fall into the kiss, into the softness of his lips and the way his warm hand slid under her still damp hair, urging her closer.

Cash gentled the kiss, but he didn't stop. Olivia didn't want him to stop. Ever. If she was only going to kiss the man once, she might as well enjoy every moment.

His lips left hers to press soft kisses against her closed eyelids. "Liv." The warmth of her name whispered along the corners of her mouth. "You taste like chocolate."

He lowered his forehead to hers, and Olivia left her eyes closed. Maybe if she didn't look, the moment would never end.

"Hey." Cash's hoarse voice broadcast a smile. "I have a question to ask you."

Olivia opened her eyes, seeing all the words he hadn't said written across his face.

"Will you go on a date with me?"

She wanted to say yes so badly. She wanted to pull him back down until his lips met hers again, ignore the tears fighting for release, and pretend she hadn't lied, that her painful past didn't stand between them like a bodyguard.

Her fingers skimmed up his arms, his warm skin begging her to tug him closer, to let him make all of her mistakes disappear, if only for a minute. His mint breath hovered over her lips, and she held back a groan at him being so close, offering her everything she wanted but couldn't have.

"I—I can't."

Cash's fingers froze at the back of her neck, his Adam's apple bobbing.

"I need some time. I need to pray about…some things."

His hand fell like a rock, taking her heart with it. Cash tried to wipe the hurt from his face, but Olivia knew it would stay in her mind like a photo she couldn't delete. A fitting reminder of the pain she'd caused.

As Cash drove away, Olivia finally knew the answer to the question she'd asked herself after the volleyball tournament. Was she in love with Cash Maddox?

Yes. So much that her heart ached at the knowledge, and her breath stuttered with panic at the thought that she'd just let him walk away without telling him everything.

She leaned back against her apartment door, sliding down until she crashed on the landing. She wanted Cash forever, wanted to handle everything life threw their way—including Rachel—together.

It should be the best news, realizing she loved Cash, but instead it felt like a crushing blow. Because the only way to keep him—telling him the truth—was the one thing that guaranteed she would lose him.

Chapter 17

What was wrong with him?

Cash threw the bag of dog food for Cocoa into the back of the truck along with the rest of the supplies he'd picked up, then slammed the tailgate shut. He strode to the driver's side door and hopped in, feeling a bit like Rachel when he almost took the door off the hinges.

When a woman said she needed to pray about something, a man said "Yes, ma'am," walked away and let her. But with each passing day that he didn't know what held Olivia back, Cash's impatience grew. She'd come to Thanksgiving at the ranch, and they acted like friends, but they rarely saw each other outside of Olivia tutoring Rachel.

The worst part? Cash missed his best friend. And he didn't know how to get her back. Had he been wrong all this time? Had he imagined her having feelings be-yond friendship for him? He hadn't imagined that kiss. There had to be some truth in that moment.

He groaned thinking about it—about how he'd like a repeat performance. If only his brooding would quit when he turned in to the ranch drive, but if the last few weeks were any indication, it had built a house right next to his and planned to stay.

He didn't like this side of himself. Olivia had been his biggest support with Rachel and his commitment not to date. He should do the same for her, but his pa-tience seemed to be running out. Especially now that he had the freedom to ask her for a relationship. Yet that option had been tabled, and Cash didn't know how much longer he could go without asking what held her back.

He needed to talk to her. Tonight at the champi-onship football game in San Antonio, he'd track her down. Surely she could share with him what worried her—and most importantly, what held her heart. That question concerned him the most, because he'd thought the answer would be him. Cash would never push her into a relationship, but he had to ask. Maybe he could pray about it, too. They were friends, and every time he did see her, she seemed sad. And that might be his least favorite thing about this whole situation.

The Alamodome filled with cheers as the Billies ran off the field at halftime. Janie had left Tucker at home with her parents so she could enjoy the game, but she seemed too filled with energy and nerves to actually sit still. In the first half, she'd popped out of her seat more times than Olivia could count.

"Relax. Jack can handle it and we're seven points ahead." Olivia tugged on her friend's hand, but Janie didn't sit even as the people in the stands around them filtered out to get snacks during the break. "Besides, it's just a football game."

That got her attention. Janie swung in Olivia's direction. "You definitely can't call yourself a Texan with that kind of attitude."

"I'm joking. I'm just as nervous for Jack as you are." *Maybe not quite.*

Janie wrung her hands. "I'm going to pop down by the locker room and see if I can catch him on the way back out."

Olivia watched her friend scoot down the row and then stood herself, stretching arms over her head. She needed a break from sitting, and she could use a soda. Scanning the crowd behind her, she relaxed after finding no sign of Cash. She knew he was here, but she didn't know what to say to him. Olivia had been on her knees since their kiss, praying for some answers, some way out of this mess she'd made. If God forgave her for the past, why couldn't she move on? Why couldn't she tell Cash the truth?

She still didn't know the answer to that first question. But the second answer came easily. The fear that Cash wouldn't forgive her for lying kept her paralyzed.

At the top of the stairs, Olivia made her way to the concessions line. After a wait, she purchased a Diet Coke. When she turned from the counter, the face she saw made her stomach jump with a mixture of dread and excitement. Cash stood across the crowd, wearing the same vintage gray Billies T-shirt he'd worn the night they'd first talked about his promise not to date—the night she'd kept her past from him without realizing what she'd done.

He slowly made his way through the people until he stood in front of her, nudging one of her red-and-white Asics with his gray tennis shoe.

"New shoes?" He raised an eyebrow with the question.

"Had to replace the pair ruined by the goat."

Since she'd told them the story at Thanksgiving, Cash laughed.

Olivia had also hoped that a new pair of tennis shoes would lift her spirits in the way jewelry or flowers did for most girls. It hadn't worked.

His eyes traveled up her jeans and red Billies hoodie, landing on her face with a smile. Despite the stress of seeing him, her lips tipped up in response to his. No denying it. She'd missed this man. She'd fallen head-over-flip-flops in love with him, and he didn't have a clue because she didn't know how to tell him that or anything else she needed to tell him.

He tilted his head. "You want to walk around a bit during halftime?"

A walk in a public place couldn't make anything worse than Olivia already had. She accepted and they moved forward.

"Rachel's talking about going to Colorado for college."

Olivia glanced at Cash, but the typical worry didn't cover his face.

"To my dad?"

"Yep."

Olivia felt a real smile for the first time in weeks. "That's great news. My dad would be so good for her. He's such a great coach. Not that I'm biased."

Cash nudged her shoulder with his. "I'm a little biased myself toward his daughter."

You shouldn't be. They greeted a few parents from school before the crowd thinned as people returned to their seats. Olivia turned her attention back to Cash as they continued walking. "How do you feel about Rachel going out of state?"

"I'm all about letting go."

"Really?"

Cash laughed. "Nope. But I'm working on it."

At least the man was honest. Unlike her.

"So listen, I was hoping we could talk. I know you need time, and I want to give you that, but I'm also—" Cash stopped walking and Olivia paused with him. "I'm struggling with patience. I know you were patient with me, and I want to be the same for you."

Who knew she could hurt in so many places at once?

"Anyway, if it's something you can tell me, then maybe I can pray about it too."

Olivia's heart sank to the floor. How could she tell him here? In the middle of a football game? But she did need to talk to him. Even if she lost him in the process, it would be better than this. "We should talk." The words almost choked her. "After the game?"

"Sure. Ride back with me?"

The hour drive back to Fredericksburg would be the perfect opportunity for Olivia to bare her soul, tell

Cash the truth…and possibly lose him forever. "That works."

Cash glanced around the now-empty concessions area before taking one step toward her, then another. Olivia retreated until her back hit the wall, air whooshing out of her.

He stood close enough that with a slight lean, his lips could touch hers. One arm snaked around her to press against the wall, and his other hand came up, thumb slipping across the traitorous area that now held back a whimper.

"You know what, Liv Grayson? You are hard *not* to kiss." He paused. Swallowed. Pushed off the wall and took a step back. "But I'll wait until you're ready. You're worth waiting for."

Those words… *You're worth waiting for.* Hope burst from a dormant ember to a roaring fire inside of her. Maybe they had a chance. Didn't she know his heart? She had to believe he'd meet her confession with grace.

Olivia fisted her hands in the front of his T-shirt, tugging him forward until they were only a moment apart. She rose slightly until her lips were parallel with his and drowned herself in his eyes, wishing she could say the words out loud.

Love me. Don't give up on me.

And then, because her heart felt too achingly full to say all of that, because she might only have today, she whispered two little words.

"Kiss me."

Cash pulled her behind a wall that blocked them from any remaining parents or students, and then he did exactly that.

* * *

Pandemonium erupted as the kick went through the goalposts, pulling the Billies further ahead and clinching the win. State champions. Cash cheered and whistled, laughing as the team doused Jack with ice. He'd have liked to get in on that part.

Jack looked up into the stands until he found Janie and waved. She looked like a blubbering mess from Cash's vantage point twenty rows up. She kept alternating between cheering, crying, and hugging Olivia. Cash would have liked to get in on that last part, too. And hopefully he would. Maybe tonight, if that kiss was any indication. He felt so giddy that he got Olivia to himself for the ride home that if Jack knew his thoughts right now, his friend would never stop making fun of him. *Ever.*

Cash went down onto the field with the rest of the crowd and spent about an hour celebrating, congratulating Jack and the rest of the players. It brought Cash right back to high school. They'd gone to state, but they hadn't won. Now Jack had the championship ring he deserved for so many years of hard work.

Rachel waved from where she stood with a group of her friends—including Blake Renner. Concern rolled through Cash's gut. The fact that Renner had come to support the team even though he wasn't eligible to play showed some maturity. But it didn't stop Cash from giving thanks that Blake stood across the circle from Rachel instead of next to her.

His goodwill had limits.

He spotted Olivia and made his way through the throng of people in her direction. "You ready?"

Olivia held his gaze for a long minute before nodding. "I am." A light filled her eyes that hadn't been there in a while. She hugged Janie and said goodbye.

"Actually—" she grinned at him "—I need to use the restroom and then I'm ready to go."

They walked up the stairs and Cash reached for her hand. Her fingers threaded through his, and when she glanced up with those big blue eyes, his heart tumbled.

This woman definitely turned him into the biggest sap on the planet.

Olivia grabbed her purse from the back of the bathroom door and slipped it on her shoulder, taking a deep breath that didn't do anything to calm her. Her hands had a slight tremor, but despite the trepidation holding her captive, she knew what she had to do. Olivia didn't want to live with the past or this lie holding her down anymore.

Tonight, she would tell Cash. And she prayed that somehow he would meet her with grace and forgiveness.

She started to turn the lock, pausing when a voice from outside the stall made her wince.

Tera. Ugh.

Olivia jerked her hand back. It wasn't that Olivia couldn't handle the woman. Just that right now, she didn't want to deal with anything but the conversation she needed to have with Cash.

"Hey, sweetie. How are you? How are things with that boyfriend of yours?"

Great. Tera had started a new conversation. If Olivia left the stall now, she'd hardly be able to escape.

It would look as if she'd been eavesdropping. Which she was doing, but not on purpose.

Olivia got the hand sanitizer from her purse and squirted it on her palm.

"How did you know? We actually just got back together."

The voice that answered Tera made Olivia's world spin to a stop. She would recognize Rachel's voice anywhere. And that comment…Olivia must have misheard. Rachel had gotten back together with Blake? When? Why? She hadn't said a thing to Olivia about it. Every time the girl took two steps forward she seemed to take one giant leap back. That boy was not good news. And Cash would not be happy about this.

"That's so great!" Tera bubbled, and Olivia barely resisted running out of the stall and muzzling her. "You're being safe, right?"

Olivia reeled back. Tera *had not* just said that. Rachel would never—

"I think…" Rachel's voice lowered, and Olivia strained to hear. "I think we might, you know, for the first time."

Gripping her purse strap between white knuckles, Olivia resisted the urge to turn around and be sick.

"I know you kids are going to do what you're going to do, so I always tell my girls to be safe."

Safe. Olivia wanted to scream. There wasn't one thing safe about it. How could Tera go around spreading lies and influencing girls like this?

Their voices stopped, and after waiting a few seconds to make sure she no longer heard them, Olivia scrambled from the stall. She only spared the sink a

glance, knowing she couldn't risk even one momen
of not finding Rachel. Especially if this *event* were t
happen tonight.

In the hallway, Cash stood from where he'd bee
leaning against the wall waiting for her.

"Have you seen your sister?"

He pointed to the left. "She went that way."

"I have to talk to her. I'm sorry. I'll be back."

Olivia took off at a jog and spotted Rachel jus
ahead. "Rach, wait up."

Rachel did, and Olivia caught up to her before sh
had time to process what she was going to say. Sh
tugged the girl around the corner to the stairs en
trance leading into the stadium. Not exactly private
but hardly any people still milled about this late afte
the game.

Now what?

"Rachel." Olivia swallowed a few times and tried t
still her shaking hands. Her voice dropped to a whisper
"Were you just in the bathroom talking about Blake?

Rachel's eyes flew wide open, and a hand covere
her mouth. She shook her head, then stopped. "Yes
Are you going to yell at me?"

"No." Emotions tightened her throat. "Oh, Rachel
Why?"

She crossed her arms and shrugged. "He loves me
We talked about the past few months and he apolo
gized. Before this we'd been dating for a year and I'v
been making him wait all this time. I just—I love him
and he says that if I love him and trust him, that…"

She didn't have to finish the words. "That's not love
Rach. Asking you for something like that isn't love."

Rachel's eyes narrowed. "What if I don't want to ait? What if I don't think it matters anymore?"

Olivia struggled for air, feeling as though someone eld her head underwater. She had a choice. She could ll Rachel about her own past and hope it helped…or e could keep it to herself.

If it could help at all, if it could save Rachel from aking the same mistake…Olivia had to tell her. She ifted, then held back a gasp at what she saw in her eripheral vision. Cash had followed her. Since Ra- el stood tucked behind the wall at the entrance to e stairs, she couldn't see him. But from her position the corner…Olivia could.

He stood a few yards away behind a closed con- essions cart. By his shuttered eyes and the way he oked as if he'd been kicked by a horse, Olivia knew e'd heard the first half of her conversation with Ra- el. Which meant if she told Rachel everything, Cash ould hear at the same time.

The tears Olivia had been fighting all day begged or release. Before, she'd held out hope that if she con- essed her lie to Cash, if she told him everything, that aybe, just maybe, he'd be able to forgive her for not lling the truth.

But now? If he heard her tell Rachel?

He'd never forgive her.

She could wait and tell him, but Olivia couldn't let achel suffer like that. Not when she knew the pain at would come from Rachel making the decision she lanned to make.

Olivia took a small step forward so that the wall locked the visual of Cash from her mind, but it didn't

erase the truth that he still stood, listening to ever
word she said.

"There was another teacher at my old school in De
ver. At first I didn't plan to be more than friends wit
him because we didn't share the same beliefs, but wit
persistence, he wore me down. Eventually, we starte
dating. I had always wanted to wait until marriage, b
with time, that felt less and less important."

Rachel crossed her arms, but she nodded.

"I was tired of waiting for some perfect man tha
didn't exist. I walked away from God, from His plar
thinking I knew better." Olivia wiped her cheeks. '
didn't think it mattered anymore."

Teenage voices sounded behind her, and Olivi
waited for them to pass by before continuing.

"I thought I was being smart. Safe." The word cam
out as a hiss. "But that stuff doesn't work all the time
And it does nothing to protect the rest of you."

This time, she had Rachel's full attention. The girl'
arms fell to her sides. "What happened?"

"I got pregnant. When I told him, that's when
found out his true nature. He said he wasn't in the ma
ket for a family. He walked away as if I meant nothin
to him. It was beyond awful. I was so stressed out, fu
of regret. Two weeks later, I miscarried."

Rachel's eyes widened, filled with a sheen of mois
ture, and her hand slipped up to cover her mouth.

"Losing the baby just added to my shame. I won
dered if my stress caused the miscarriage. And…" Ol
ivia's voice shook along with her body. "I still had t
work at the same school with him. While I was suffer
ing from the decisions I'd made and trying to functio

after the miscarriage, he moved on and started dating another teacher at our school. So all last year I had to deal with that." She shuddered and dug a tissue from her purse. "Every moment I want to go back. Every moment I wish someone would have pulled me aside and told me that something that seemed like nothing would become everything. That's the world's lie, Rachel Maddox. It matters."

It matters. Olivia stumbled under the weight of that truth. That's why she'd had such a hard time letting go of her past. It mattered, whether she was twenty-five or seventeen.

"God cares about you. Everything you do matters. And this—this is big. Way bigger than you know right now." Olivia grabbed Rachel's arms. "Don't do it. Don't make the same mistake I did. So many people love you. Cash loves you. Your aunt and uncle love you. I love you."

Tears streamed down Rachel's cheeks, and Olivia pulled the girl into a hug, thankful when she accepted the gesture. Rachel sniffled. "Thank you for telling me." That whisper held a lot of pain. Olivia imagined this one conversation wouldn't be enough, but they would have more. She'd make sure of it.

Rachel moved back, wiping under her eyes and coming away with black mascara. An eye roll followed. "I must look horrible."

Olivia smiled, thinking this felt like home territory with Rachel. "A little like that raccoon we saw."

That earned a grin from the teenager in front of her. Olivia wiped her own tears with the tips of her fingers.

"I'm sure I'm no better. Thanks a lot for making me cry in a public place."

Rachel laughed. "I need to go find Val. I think I'm going to stay there tonight." Olivia had done everything she could. Now she would pray, pray, pray. "I promise I'll really go to Val's." Rachel stared at her hands. "I won't see Blake tonight."

Olivia's shoulders sagged in relief. "I'm here if you need anything."

"Thanks. And I won't tell anyone what you told me. I'm not that way."

"I know. I trust you." *And the one person I care about just found out in the worst possible way.*

Chapter 18

Cash sank behind the closed concessions cart as his sister took off in the opposite direction.

The conversation he'd just heard made him want to keep sliding down until he hit the floor and then curl up in the fetal position. His baby sister. How could she even be thinking such a thing? Hadn't he talked to her so many times? Didn't his prayers work at all?

At least he could be thankful Olivia had talked to Rachel. His sister would never have listened to him like that. But then, he didn't have a story to tell that would have an impact the way Olivia's did. One Cash had never heard before. At first, he hadn't believed it was true, but then, as the details went on...

He buried his head in his hands. How could Olivia have kept something like that from him? What else hadn't she told him? Did he even know her at all? It wasn't that he didn't have grace over her past. If anything, the guy sounded like a jerk. But even when she knew how much he craved the truth, even when she knew how much it mattered to him, she had lied.

"Cash?"

He looked up. Olivia stood in front of him, looking as tormented as he felt. Must have been hard on her, actually telling the truth.

"I'm so sorry." Her hands twisted, then slipped into the pockets of her red sweatshirt. "I didn't want you to find out like that."

He stood and crossed his arms, fingers digging into his biceps until the knuckles went white and the skin underneath turned red. "How did you want me to find out? Were you ever planning to tell me?"

Her mouth opened and shut. Moisture filled her eyes and spilled down her cheeks, but she didn't wipe it away. "You—" Her voice wobbled along with her head. "You wouldn't believe me if I told you."

The sight of this woman in tears... While she'd taken his heart and trampled it, he could barely tamp down the urge that begged him to sweep across the space and comfort *her*.

He felt beaten. Betrayed. That last word was the one he needed to remember. Because he knew better than to let someone betray him twice.

"I asked you at the hospital and you said you were only upset about Janie. All of this time and you never said a thing. You even implied... We talked about what we wanted that night after the football game." Disbelief filled his lungs with cement. "You never gave any indication. Not once."

Olivia's whimper bounced off him as a deep breath shuddered from his chest. "I thought you were nothing like Tera, but I guess that's not true." Something cold took over his body, his words. "No wonder you were so curious what I thought about her. Neither of you seem to realize lying affects the lives of those around you. Neither of you cares about anything but yourselves."

That spark of *something* flashed in Olivia's eyes. She took a step forward, and he half expected a finger to poke into his chest. "I am *nothing* like Tera."

An hour ago he would have believed that, but right now he could barely think past the pain throbbing in his head. "Looks the same from where I'm standing."

Olivia took a step back from Cash and his hurtful words, feeling as though she'd been pummeled. Yes, she'd kept her past from him. She'd lied. She regretted it with everything in her. If she could go back—story of her life—she'd tell him earlier, before she'd ever let the lie pass through her lips, and erase the last few minutes of pain for both of them. But she couldn't. And nothing she said right now would make any difference. She could have said she'd planned to tell him tonight, but he would never believe her now.

Olivia had known this conversation wouldn't go well. She'd thought Cash would be hurt, wounded, but she hadn't expected him to lash out like this. And comparing her to Tera, saying she didn't care about anyone but herself...he obviously didn't know her at all.

All of this time she hadn't wanted her past to de-

fine her. Olivia had wanted to find a way to move forward and forgive herself. But now, she was right back
where she'd started.

Would she never be more than the sum of her mistakes?

She took a step back, knowing she needed to escape. Again. "I'll find my own ride home." Hopefully
Janie hadn't left yet. And Olivia still needed to track
down the lovely Tera Lawton and have a few words
with the woman.

When Cash didn't protest, didn't ask her to stay and
work things out, didn't take back his pain-inducing
words, Olivia turned and walked away. She thought
she'd understood a broken heart before, but it didn't
compare to this. Last time, she'd been broken into a
thousand pieces. But now? More like a million.

So much for that new beginning.

"If you could redo one thing, what would it be?" Olivia closed the devotional after reading the last question. The morning light shone across Olivia's apartment
table, her coffee and Rachel's Coke between them. "I
guess you already know my answer to that question."

Rachel glanced to the side. "Yeah."

"What about you?"

Olivia had learned a few things about the girl in
front of her over their last few meetings. She would
talk about serious things, but she took her time.

So while Rachel studied her fingernails, Olivia
waited. Since that night at the football game, she'd
seen Rachel a number of times and they'd continued to
talk about her future decisions. So far, Rachel had been

very receptive, and Olivia prayed daily for a hedge of protection around the teenager.

But while Olivia had seen Rachel, she hadn't seen Cash.

He'd made himself scarce since the night of the football championship, and Olivia didn't blame him. She'd lied. She took full responsibility for that. And after the way Cash had responded, she didn't have any hope that they'd be able to work through this.

Somehow, she needed to adjust to the fact that their chance for something more was over...but it hurt. It felt a bit like her bones after the day she'd gone horseback riding with Cash. Only instead of healing, this pain stayed lodged right around her heart.

At least one good thing had come from that horrible night. Ever since she'd opened up to Rachel, Olivia had begun to feel the freedom she'd been longing for all of this time. She'd thought burying her past would liberate her from the guilt, but the opposite turned out to be true.

Too bad she'd figured that out too late.

"I guess—" Rachel's words pulled Olivia back to the present. "The day my parents died, I got into a fight with my mom right before they left." Rachel looked away, but when her gaze collided with Olivia's, the visible pain felt like a knife to her soul. "I wish our last words had been good."

Olivia wiped a few tears from her cheeks. She'd been so emotional lately, as if crying could purge the pain from her body.

"Do you think she hated me? Do you think she forgave me for being such a brat?"

For the love. Olivia needed a whole box of tissues for this conversation. How could Rachel have lived with that kind of hurt all of this time? Olivia prayed silently, wanting to choose her words wisely. "I may not have known your mom, but I know this. She loved you with a mother's love. It's like God's love. It's unstoppable. We can't do anything so bad that He won't love us anymore, and I know your mom would have felt the same way. That's the beauty of grace."

We can't do anything so bad that He won't love us anymore.

Olivia's eyes momentarily fell shut. There it was. The reminder, the absolution she needed. The deliverance from her mistakes came too late for her and Cash, but hopefully not for Rachel.

"That's what I thought." Rachel tucked a lock of hair behind her ear. "But I just—it's good to hear it."

For me, too.

"You know, sometimes I think I learn more from this Bible study than you do."

Rachel laughed, and Olivia got up and retrieved the tissue box. Unlike herself, the teenager remained composed.

"I suppose you've got to get going." Rachel stood.

"I probably should." Though heading back to Colorado for Christmas didn't fill Olivia with the same joy it had only weeks ago. "Sorry I don't have much time."

"No problem. I'll see you when you get back?"

"Of course." Olivia hugged Rachel, then waved goodbye as the girl headed down the apartment stairs. She went back inside, grabbed her already packed suitcase and tugged it down the stairs. After rolling over to Janie's, she knocked on the front door.

The inside door stood open, and when Tucker peeked through the glass storm door, Olivia left her suitcase on the step and let herself in. She scooped him up, kissing his sweet, baby powder-scented hair.

"Quit eating my son!" Janie came out of the kitchen smiling. "I'll be ready in a sec." She headed down the hall and Olivia tossed Tucker up in the air, ignoring the familiar longing in her chest when he giggled. She'd secretly begun to dream of this kind of life with Cash…but now she needed to move beyond that. Nothing would fill the chasm between them created by her lie and his response. How long would it take this hurt to ebb away? She couldn't fathom an answer that didn't discourage her.

When Janie reappeared, ready to go, the girls left Tucker with Jack, then headed for the Austin airport.

"Thanks for driving me all this way. You know that I could have left my car at the airport."

"It's not a problem. Besides, I think I might stay in Austin and shop for a bit." Janie glanced at Olivia with pink-tinged cheeks. "They have a certain store that I like and the doctor said it's okay to try again."

Despite the awfulness of the past weeks, joy rushed through Olivia at seeing her friend filled with hope again. "Have you seen the way your husband looks at you? I don't think you need any of that."

Janie preened. "I am rather wonderful."

"And humble."

"Exactly." Janie's face went from amused to serious in seconds. "Any news with Cash?"

"No. He doesn't want to see me." She'd told Janie everything. Right down to the last detail. Again, she'd been greeted with grace. Tears. Hugs. Bless Janie, Olivia could have moved anywhere in the country, but God had definitely known she needed this woman in her life.

"You have got to talk to him. Apologize. Tell him why you lied. The two of you are the most stubborn people I've ever met. Both of you think you can control everything, neither of you—"

"He doesn't want to hear it!"

"Did you call him? Did you show up on his doorstep and camp out until he agreed to talk to you?"

Nope. Olivia hadn't done that and Janie knew it.

"This is what I'm talking about. You have to forgive yourself for the past *and* for lying to Cash. You had reasons. They might not have been perfect, but what's done is done. Time to forgive, girl."

"I have." *I think.* "I'm trying." And that was the truth. For the first time, Olivia felt the guilt over her past slipping away. She'd even begun to forgive Josh— though he'd probably never express remorse—choosing to praise God for rescuing her from that situation.

"Including Cash?"

Olivia crossed her arms.

"He didn't handle that moment well, but he was upset. Add him to your list of people to forgive. Maybe then you'd actually be able to go to him and talk to him about all of this."

Olivia wanted to be done with this conversation, but Janie's small car offered little escape. Probably calculated by the woman next to her.

"You're wearing some prideful britches to think that you know better than the God of the universe. His son already died for that forgiveness. For you and for that jerk ex-boyfriend of yours, for Cash, for me. It's done. The price has already been paid. Bless your heart, Liv, but you're like a homeless person who won't take handouts."

Goose bumps erupted across Olivia's skin. How did Janie pack that kind of punch with such sweetness?

"I think there's two kinds of guilt. The sinning kind, when God is telling you what you're doing isn't right, and then the kind where you dwell on mistakes so much that you're not worshipping God. One can be used for good. The other? You need to let go of."

Olivia sighed. "When did you get so smart?"

Janie winked. "I've always been brilliant."

Despite the serious subject, a laugh slipped out. Only Janie could throw all her words on the table in that manner and still come across as loving.

Janie joined in with her own laughter. "I'm sorry that all came flying out like that, but I had to say it. Trust me, I understand mourning for the baby you lost and the decisions you made." She sniffed. "That pain's not just going to go away. But the anger can. And forgiveness can change those wounds from bleeding and throbbing to an ache that heals over time."

As usual, Olivia imagined Janie wouldn't back down until she got what she wanted. But her friend didn't understand that Cash would never forgive Olivia. Since her plans didn't include talking to him, Olivia settled for a truth she could agree to. "I'll think about it."

"You think about it, and I'll do some praying." Janie's victory grin flashed. "That should soften that stubborn heart of yours a little quicker."

Chapter 19

The ranch Jeep bumped in from the pasture, jarring Cash's stressed body. This morning he'd received a phone call from the grocery store in Austin that hadn't improved his already horrible mood. They'd partnered with another ranch, not him. Cash had been kicking around his disappointment ever since. Supplying the store wouldn't have been easy, but the extra income would have been nice. Especially with Rachel headed off to college at the end of summer. Still, it would have meant a larger herd, more ranch hands and even longer hours. Not that many more hours existed in a day.

Cash left the Jeep running by the garage, hopped out and opened the door, then drove inside. The ranch truck and Jeep needed an oil change, and Cash had volunteered. Frank and the other men had looked relieved.

Between the store and what had happened with Olivia, Cash's mood had morphed from crabby to downright unbearable. No one wanted to be around him. When the ranch hands saw him coming, everyone scattered. Despite time to process, Cash still couldn't wrap his mind around the fact that Olivia had lied to him. He shouldn't be thinking about her at all, but his pigheaded brain didn't listen to logic anymore.

He pulled on the brake, turned off the ignition and jumped out just as his sister came in. "What's up?"

"Just came to find you."

Did the girl have good or bad news for him? Rachel hadn't been around much over Christmas break. Of course she spent Christmas at the ranch with Cash and Dean and Libby, but other than that, she'd been off traipsing with her friends most of the days. Cash could only pray and hope she wasn't doing what he'd overheard her talking to Olivia about. He'd confronted her the next day, and they'd talked, but short of locking her up, he didn't know how to protect her.

That probably wasn't helping his mood.

"So…how long are we going to have to deal with stompy, crabby Cash around here?"

He opened the hood. "As long as it takes."

"To do what? Get over Coach Grayson?"

Cash's hand stilled on the oil cap.

"Doesn't she come back tomorrow? What happened between you two anyway?"

Cash hadn't said anything to Rachel about what had happened between him and Olivia the night of the football game. Olivia must not have either if his sister still didn't know. Of course, it only took a little observation to decipher that he and Olivia hadn't seen each other since that night. He really did not want to discuss this with his little sister. Huh. That's probably what she felt like talking to him about boys.

"Did you want to discuss Blake again?" Cash finished removing the oil cap and winced at his own callousness.

Rachel crossed her arms. "I already told you I'm not going to do anything stupid. Unlike you, I've been talking to Coach Grayson. She's been helping me. You need to let this go. I'm working through it."

He tossed the cap onto the workbench with more force than necessary. He didn't like it when Rachel was right.

His sister slid backward onto the workbench, legs dangling in a carefree swing. "You should just give up everything you could have with Coach and hole up like you did after Mom and Dad died." Rachel's smooth voice brimmed with sarcastic sweetness she could patent. "Because your life was so much better when you lived that way."

Cash grabbed the socket wrench and oil pan, dropped to the ground, and slid under the Jeep.

"You should run and hide." She upped the volume of her voice. "Because you know what? People can hurt you." Her face appeared at the side of the Jeep where she bent down. "People disappoint. They make bad decisions. They drink with their friends, choose stupid boyfriends." Her voice whispered under the Jeep engine, ripe with pain and wobbling with emotion. "They can even die and leave you."

He sucked in a breath but continued working.

"So if you push away everyone you love, that would be safest." Rachel clapped her hands together slowly. "Bravo, brother. You managed to isolate yourself. No hurt there."

The oil gushed out into the pan as Rachel's words stabbed him.

Everyone you love.

Cash dropped an arm over his face.

He loved Olivia.

One mistake wouldn't change how he felt about her. Nothing could stop him from missing her, from needing her every second of the day.

"I don't get it anyway. Shouldn't you be upset with Ms. Lawton, not Coach?"

What? Cash pushed out from under the Jeep and faced his sister as she stood. "What did Tera do?"

Rachel's fingers landed on her throat. "Coach didn't tell you?" Her words were a strangled whisper.

Cash shook his head. When Rachel took a step back, he growled, "What happened?"

"She…" Rachel bit her lip.

"Rach, tell me."

She stalled, but eventually the story about what Tera had said in the bathroom spilled out of her. Cash balled his fists, tension radiating up his arms and into his shoulders. "Is that everything that happened?"

"Everything I was there for. But one of my friends said they saw Coach Grayson talking to Ms. Lawton that night as they were leaving the stadium. I guess it was a pretty big commotion. She said something to Ms. Lawton about never talking to me again. Told her to stay away from me or something like that." Rachel shrugged as though she didn't care, but her lips slid up. "Coach Grayson's tough. I like that about her."

He did too.

Rachel took a step back.

"Wait."

She paused, head tilted.

"I'm sorry I've been so ornery, and that I'm not better at helping you through the stuff with Blake." He grabbed a rag, wiping his grease-covered hands. "I wish I could be more like Mom and Dad, that I could have given you the life you would have had with them." It didn't exactly fit the current conversation, but he needed to say it. He'd been thinking it for years. Cash took a steadying breath. "I'm sorry I'm not them. That I'm an idiot who doesn't know what I'm doing half the time."

"I never expected you to be Mom or Dad. And you're not an idiot." Her lips curved. "Those are words I never thought I would say." Amusement flashed across her face before she scowled and poked him on the chest. "You need to let go of feeling responsible for everything. You don't have to make up anything to me. Believe it or not, big brother, I think you've done a pretty good job." She slid the toe of her shoe across the dusty cement. "I mean, I know I'm not the easiest kid." Her green eyes met his, shimmering with just a hint of moisture. "But I thought we were doing okay."

Something unknotted in him. They were doing okay. They'd had a couple of close calls, but each time *someone* had protected his sister, and it hadn't been him.

"Besides, in a few more months I'll be off to college and out of your hair."

"Would you believe I'm not quite ready for you to be out of my hair?"

She smiled. "Maybe." Her arms crossed. "Don't think the change in subject means you're off the hook about Coach."

The way she sounded like the older sibling made him tamp down a smile. But not one part of him had forgotten about Olivia.

"If there's anything I've learned in the last few weeks, it's that God's in charge of our lives. He sent Coach Grayson to fight for me." Her eyes narrowed. "He sent her for you, too. Now this is a case where you're treading awfully close to idiot. You'd better figure it out before you lose her altogether."

He definitely didn't like it when his sister was right.

"Are we good here?" Rachel waved a hand between them, eyebrow quirked. "Did we solve all of your issues?"

His mouth hitched. "Don't you have somewhere to be?"

She laughed. "Always." Her Converse shoes kicked up dust as she took off, giving a wave over her shoulder on her way out of the garage.

The knowledge that he couldn't make up their parents' deaths to Rachel—that she didn't expect him to—filled him with relief. But at the thought of Olivia, tension tightened his muscles again.

He'd assumed a lie made Olivia just like Tera. But that couldn't be further from the truth. He owed her an apology. And a thank-you. She must have confronted Tera *after* he'd been a jerk.

The way he'd responded to Olivia the night of the

football championship came rushing back, ripping into his soul. She might have lied about her past, but when it came to protecting Rachel, she'd been willing to give up her secret. She would have known even while she told Rachel the story that he would be upset, yet she'd done it to save his sister.

He'd thought he'd worked through his control issues...but it turned out he still needed some work. Especially in the area of trust.

Cash had a choice to make. He could either cling to control and live life alone like Rachel said, or he could trust God instead of himself. Trust that God had placed Olivia in his life because she was exactly who he needed, exactly who Rachel needed. Trust that he did know her heart.

Olivia had most likely been too scared or wounded to tell him about her past when she had the opportunity. And now he'd only added to that pain. All because he couldn't trust, because he didn't want to get hurt again, just like his mouthy, wise little sister said.

Maybe when the snarky girl went off to college, she should get a counseling degree.

Olivia's return to Texas filled her with excitement and trepidation. Once again, she'd worked through her past, telling her parents and sister the truth about what happened with Josh. Each time she did, Olivia felt her freedom increase. She'd taken a walk through the Garden of the Gods by her parents' house and had a big conversation with God...and when she left that place, she knew she'd turned over another new leaf. She'd be fighting for forgiveness from now on. Every time guilt or shame tried to slip into her mind, she would send it right back out again.

Janie had been right…though Olivia hadn't relished telling her on the drive back from the airport. Her friend had also been happy to know that Olivia had a ranch field trip planned for this afternoon. She needed to talk to a certain cowboy and apologize for not telling him the truth. Though Cash's response had wounded her, Olivia knew his words had been spoken from a place of hurt…and that they weren't true. She planned to use this new superpower she had and *forgive* him. Even if Cash couldn't move past her lie, Olivia knew one thing: she would forgive herself this time. She wouldn't live her life like that anymore.

Olivia pulled up to the ranch house and stopped in front. She tore up the stairs before she lost her nerve and knocked on the front door. Colorado had been spitting cold when she left, but despite the much warmer Texas weather and the fact that Olivia wore jeans with her favorite waffle-knit blue cardigan sweater, she still shivered. She scuffed the sole of one brown ballet flat across the Maddox porch as she waited for someone to answer.

Rachel opened the door, greeting Olivia with a hug that went a long way toward calming her jumpy heart.

She followed the teenager inside. "Is your brother home?"

"No. He's out on the ranch somewhere."

Olivia didn't want to wait and give herself the opportunity to back out of her plan. She had to talk to him. Now. "Any chance I could borrow a Jeep? And you could point me in the right direction?"

Rachel rolled her eyes, but the smile that accompanied the look told Olivia her true feelings. A set of keys slid along the kitchen counter. "You can take mine."

Olivia grabbed them. "Thanks, Rach!" She rushed out the front door and over to Rachel's Wrangler, yanking open the driver's door. Stick shift. Why hadn't she ever learned how to drive one of these things?

"Give me the keys." Rachel stood behind her, palm out. "I'll give you a ride."

Olivia gave her the keys and a hug, eliciting a laugh.

"Coach, I didn't know you were such a sap."

She flew around the Jeep and into the passenger seat. "Only over your brother."

Rachel groaned, but as the Jeep dipped and bumped over the rough terrain, the girl's lips curved again.

Finally, they spotted the old ranch truck. Rachel pulled up and Olivia hopped out. "Thanks!"

"You're welcome. Don't let him go all stubborn on you. He's got some issues. You might have to use Cocoa to corral him into a good decision."

Olivia laughed and waved, then scanned the field as Rachel took off back toward the house. She could see two men on horses, two standing, and beyond them, the herd. But with their distance from the truck, Olivia couldn't pick out Cash. Did Rachel have to drive off so fast? Olivia suddenly felt very alone.

She shook off the fear and strode toward the ranch truck. Cash had once thought her worth waiting for, and now she needed to prove he was worth fighting for. At the open tailgate, Olivia pulled herself up, then stood in the bed of the truck, using her hand to shade the sun. Still no way to recognize the man she wanted for her future husband.

She cupped hands around her mouth, ignored her racing heartbeat and yelled at the highest volume she could muster, "Cash Maddox!"

Four cowboy hats turned toward her. Olivia's stomach seemed to bounce along the metal truck bed when one man and horse pulled away from the group and came in her direction. Cash's green-and-gray plaid shirtsleeves were rolled up, and his tanned arms flexed when he pulled the horse to a stop by the bed of the truck.

When he started to dismount, Olivia held up a hand. "Stay there. I have something to say."

Cash responded with a slow head nod. Oh, man. What had she planned to say? All the words disappeared, leaving her chest fluttering.

After one steadying breath, she jumped in. "I shouldn't have lied to you. At first I didn't mean to, but then…" Tears? Seriously? She'd planned to be so strong during this speech. Olivia ignored the moisture slipping down her cheeks. "Then I lied because I was afraid. And it hurt so much to talk about it. I didn't want anyone to know. I thought if I kept everything hidden, that I could start over in Texas without all of that pain. Turns out, that's not how it works. The guilt and shame just followed me. I've finally figured out how to move on. I've finally forgiven myself."

Cash shifted on his horse but didn't speak.

"And I'm so sorry for not telling you the truth. I really hope you can forgive me, because—" Olivia paused, wishing for armor in case a rejection followed her words. She might be David facing Goliath, but she could do this. It was real this time. God approved. Only instead of five stones, she had three words. "I love you."

Cash slid down from the horse and put one boot on the bumper, pulling himself up into the truck bed with her. He paused a foot away, looking larger than life. Close, but still not quite attainable. "Are you done?"

Olivia pressed her lips together and nodded.

"Will you forgive me for what I said, for how I responded that night?"

Hope rose up. "I already have."

One stride brought him to her. He buried fingers in her hair, studying her face with such raw emotion that chills erupted across her skin. "I love you, too." In the next moment, his lips met hers, filled with a stunning mix of need and apology. She melted at the message, feeling the last vestiges of hurt release. The kiss wrapped her in forgiveness, in grace, in the future. When cheers and whistles sounded from the ranch hands, Cash's lips left hers to share a smile. He lifted his hat and waved it over his head in response to the guys, his gaze never leaving hers.

He thumbed the moisture from her cheeks. "I'm sorry for not letting anything go, for not trusting you. Even though you hid it, I know your real heart. And you are *nothing* like Tera."

The air rushed from her lungs. "It's about time you figured that out."

His lips traced across her damp cheeks and found her mouth again, distracting them from conversation for a minute. He broke the kiss to the sound of a few more whistles and someone calling out, "'Bout time!"

Olivia laughed and winced. "I'm sorry if I embarrassed you in front of the guys."

Humor danced in his eyes. "You can embarrass me anytime you want. Weren't you supposed to fly back tomorrow?"

She squinted at him. "Yeah. My flight was canceled over break and I had to reschedule. Why?"

"I planned to ask Janie to stay home so that I could pick you up at the airport. I had a few things to say to you." The slow curve of his lips made her legs turn to liquid. He tucked a piece of hair behind her ear, mischievous smile growing. "But now you said *I love you* first."

Olivia groaned. "That's going to be our thing, isn't it? That I said it first?"

"Yep." Cash scooped her up in a hug that made her feet fly off the truck bed. "You're going to have to live with that forever."

Forever. Olivia's arms wrapped around his neck. "Deal."

Epilogue

Olivia grabbed her bag of papers to grade and headed for the school parking lot. The March sun shone down, and despite the fact that she planned to catch up on grading during spring break, she couldn't help the smile on her face...especially when she noticed Cash leaning against his boat attached to his truck in the school parking lot.

She approached, using a hand to shade against the sun. "Going somewhere?"

Cash's arms were crisscrossed against his black Henley shirt, his grin growing with each step she took. "Just hoping to take a beautiful girl fishing."

"Don't you have to work?"

"I'm taking the day off."

"Spending the day with you I'm sure about. But fishing?" Her nose wrinkled, shoulders lifting. "I might have to be convinced."

With a slow grin, Cash reached out, fisting the sides of the sweatshirt she wore open over a white V-neck T-shirt, tugging her forward until her flip-flops met his tennis shoes and his lips found hers.

She would crash into this man any day.

When he broke the kiss and stepped back, Olivia swayed, then righted her balance. "Okay." Her lips curved. "I'm in."

Cash opened the passenger door to his truck. "Your chariot awaits."

Olivia put her things into the backseat. The drive to the lake was peaceful, beautiful and filled with one of her favorite things—the man next to her. Soon, Cash backed the boat into the water and they flew across the lake. Olivia gathered her windblown hair and held it in a twist at the back of her neck until he slowed and put the anchor down.

He grabbed the fishing poles and handed her one. It took the man less than a minute to get his line baited and cork floating on the surface of the water.

Olivia slipped out of her sweatshirt, nibbling on her lip as she tried to bait the hook.

"Need some help, city girl? I'll do it for you." Cash's amused tone wasn't helping anything.

"No. I'll do it myself." Slimy thing.

"You could use one of the lures in the tackle box. Check it out and see if that would be easier to use as bait instead of the worm."

"I can do it."

"Could you grab the red lure out of the tackle box,

hen? I'm thinking about switching. The fish aren't
biting on the worms."

Olivia borrowed a Rachel-sized huff and tossed the
worm back into the can. Couldn't the man get the lure
himself? She wiped her dirty hand on her jeans and
reached for the tackle box, noticing a cooler in the boat.
Had Cash packed a picnic? The day was getting better.
And if that cooler contained chocolate, then the fishing might be worth it.

Four drawers opened on either side as Olivia pulled
the tackle box open. Lures of every color, shape and
size competed for space. But the small black velvet
jewelry box? That was a new addition.

Cash made his way down to her end of the boat and
took the seat across from her. "Open it."

She picked it up and slowly flipped back the lid.
Nestled inside was a platinum diamond ring that glim-
mered in the sunshine.

Olivia glanced up to see Cash leaning forward.

"It was my mom's. And I really want it to be yours."

She opened her mouth to answer, but Cash tugged
her forward until only inches separated them. "Now
just hold on. I'm not done asking."

His hands slid along her arms, settling at her wrists.
Could he feel her fluttering pulse? "Liv Grayson,
thank you for being the first to say *I love you*—" Ol-
via squeaked in protest and Cash's chest shook with
quiet laughter before he continued. "For being my sister's confidante and mentor, and the love of my life.
Will you marry me?"

"Are you done ask—" A firm kiss stopped her sassy
reply.

"Answer the question, woman."

"Yes." Definitely yes.

Cash slipped the ring on her finger, and she sucke[d] in a breath as she studied the new addition.

It fit.

"How did you get it sized already?"

"I didn't. I thought we could do it after. But I shoul[d] have known we wouldn't need to. You're perfect fo[r] me. Why wouldn't the ring fit?"

Cash lifted her hand, kissing the back of the ring an[d] her finger. "I wish my parents could be here to mee[t] you. But I know they know. They always prayed fo[r] my future wife, even when I was young and though[t] marriage and girls were gross. Although now I have [a] slightly different opinion about marriage."

Olivia laughed, fighting a surge of emotions at th[e] same time. "You know, I think those prayers lived o[n] even when they didn't, because it definitely took som[e] prayer to get the two of us together."

"I've never thought of it that way, but I'm sure you'r[e] right. Which, if I understand marriage correctly, i[s] something I need to plan to say a lot over the next.. fifty years or so."

"Sounds good to me."

He laughed, tucking a strand of wind-loosened hai[r] behind her ear. "I'm thinking we elope. France?"

"I'd marry you in a barn with Cocoa as the rin[g] bearer."

"Now that sounds like a good idea. Although get[-] ting married in the back of a truck seems more fitting with our relationship."

Olivia laughed. "I can picture it now. What did I art?"

"Us." His lips met hers as his hands threaded rough her hair, that simple soap smell he sported lling her senses. Images of the future flashed through r mind—children running through the ranch house, unt Rachel teaching them the art of stubborn, Janie d Jack as surrogate aunt and uncle, lots of hard work, ve and laughter.

Olivia sighed when the kiss ended. "You are seri-sly brilliant, buckaroo."

"Why?" Cash narrowed his eyes, though the laugh nes at the corners crinkled. "Because I asked you to arry me?"

"Well, that, too. But also because you proposed hile fishing. Which I now like infinitely better than did ten minutes ago."

Cash's laugh echoed off the water. "I might have to gree with you." His arms tightened around her. "Be-use you are definitely the best thing I've ever caught hile fishing."

* * * * *

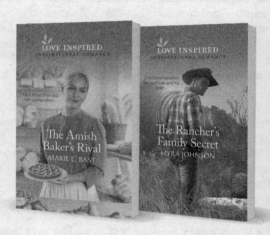

car will be perfect for your needs," Ruby assured Aaron,
ching down to scratch the poodle's head.

"That froufrou dog? No way, ma'am. Not gonna happen."

"Excuse me?" She'd expected him to hesitate but not
nright reject her idea.

"Look, Ruby, if you like Oscar so much, then keep him
yourself. I need a man's dog by my side, not some…
e…"

"Poodle?" Ruby suggested, her eyebrows disappearing
eath her long ginger bangs.

"Right. Lead me to where you keep the German
oherds, and I'll pick one out myself."

"Hmm," Ruby said, rubbing her chin as if considering his
uest, although she really wasn't. "No."

"No?"

"No," she repeated firmly. "First off, we don't currently
e a German shepherd as part of our program."

"I'd even take a pit bull." He was beginning to sound
perate.

"Look, Aaron. Either you're going to have to learn to
t me or you may as well just leave now before we start.
s isn't going to work unless you're ready to listen to me
do whatever I tell you to do."

LIEXP0621

His eyebrows furrowed. "I understand chain of comma
ma'am. There were many times as a marine when I di
exactly agree with my superiors, but I understood wh
was important to follow orders."

"Okay. Let's go with that."

"For me," Aaron continued, "following orders is bla
and-white. My marines' lives under my command o
depended on it. But as you can see, I'm having diffic
making that transition in this situation. We're not talk
people's lives here."

"I disagree. We're very much talking lives—*yours*.
may not yet have a clear vision of what you'll be able to
with Oscar, but a service dog can make all the difference

"Yes, but you just insisted the best dog for me i
poodle. I'm sorry, but if you knew anything about me at
you'd know the last dog in the world I'd choose woul
a poodle."

"And yet I still believe I'm right," said Ruby with a
smile. Somehow, she had to convince this man she kr
what she was doing. "I carefully studied your file before
arrived, Aaron, and specially selected Oscar for you to w
with. I'm the expert here. So how are we going to get c
this hurdle?"

"I have orders to make this work. How will it look
give up before I even start the process?" He shook his he
"No. Don't answer that. It will look as if I wasn't abl
complete my mission. That's never going to happen.
always pull through, no matter what."

Don't miss
The Marine's Mission *by Deb Kastner,*
available July 2021 wherever
Love Inspired books and ebooks are sold.

LoveInspired.com

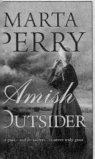
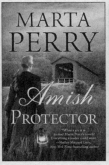

Love Harlequin romance?

DISCOVER.

Be the first to find out about promotions, news and exclusive content!

Facebook.com/HarlequinBooks

Twitter.com/HarlequinBooks

Instagram.com/HarlequinBooks

Pinterest.com/HarlequinBooks

You Tube YouTube.com/HarlequinBooks

ReaderService.com

EXPLORE.

Sign up for the Harlequin e-newsletter and download a free book from any series at **TryHarlequin.com**

CONNECT.

Join our Harlequin community to share your thoughts and connect with other romance readers!
Facebook.com/groups/HarlequinConnectio

HSOCIA

HARLEQUIN

Heartfelt or thrilling, passionate or uplifting—Harlequin is more than just happily-ever-after.

With twelve different series to choose from and ew books available every month, you are sure to find stories that will move you, uplift you, inspire and delight you.